# MEFIBOSET
## CRIPPLED PRINCE

## KATHERYN MADDOX HADDAD

*Mefiboset: Crippled Prince*

# DEDICATED TO THE HANDICAPPED
throughout the world who have become
## OVERCOMERS &
## CHAMPIONS

# ACKNOWLEDGMENT
I would like to express my appreciation to fellow author
and my medical advisor regarding causes of paralysis in
the lower extremities
and their maintenance

Braxton DeGarmo, MD
retired ER doctor
who now writing suspense & thrillers

# COMMENTARY IN NARRATIVE FORM

# TABLE OF CONTENTS

# HAVE FUN LISTENING TO THE CAMELS
**http://bit.ly/ListenCamels**

# MAP 1:  MAJOR CITIES & FORESTS IN IN 1000 BC

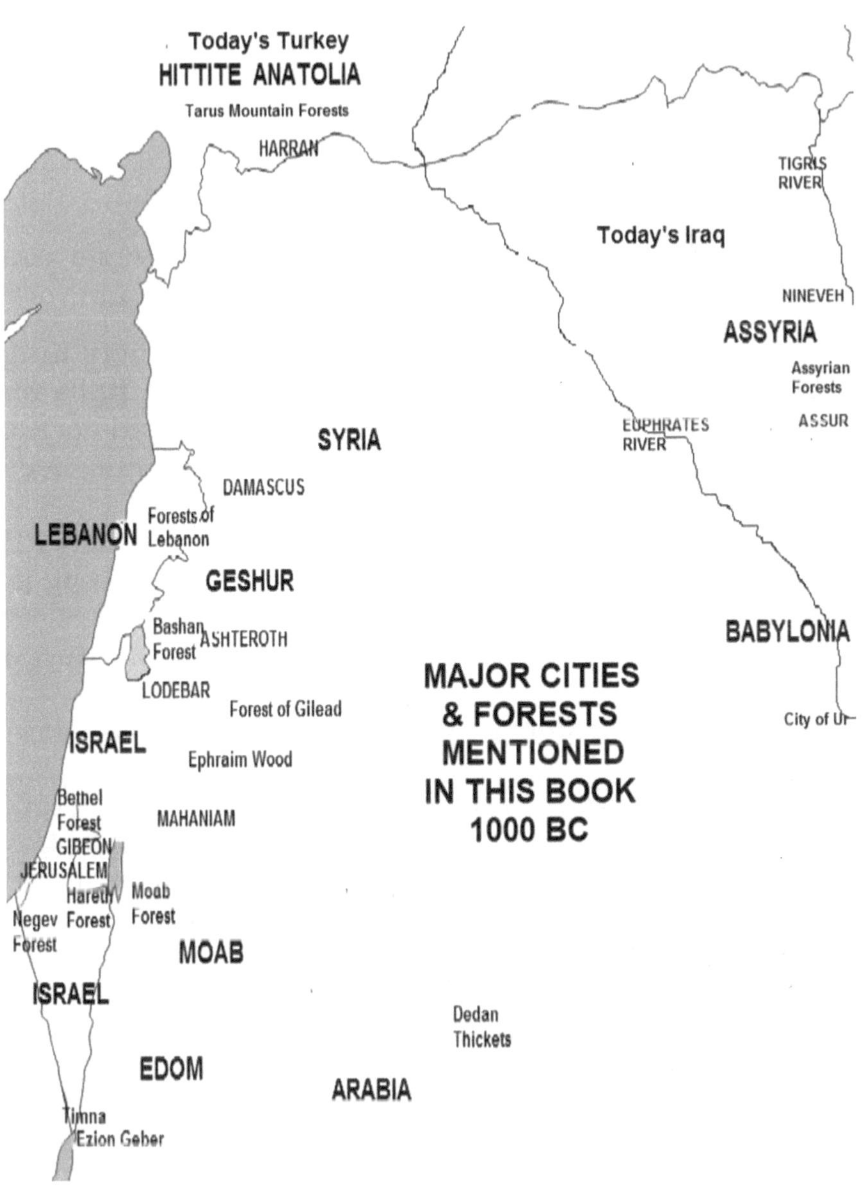

# 1 ~ RETREAT

"**A**ll dead! They're all dead! Escape while you can!"

The youngest and now the only legitimate son of King Saul rushes through the opened palace gates. He pulls on the reins and jumps off his chariot. Blood is spattered across his face, his limbs, his uniform. The prince stands, legs apart, his eyes wild while he warns his family.

"Hurry!" His husky voice echoes around the courtyard and up the walls of each of the three floors surrounding it. "Mother. Where are you?"

"Both Saul and Jonathan?" The now widowed queen screams.

"And all my brothers. Their army is after me now. Hurry!"

"Mefiboset, where are you?" Nurse Fadia screams from a third-story balcony where the heirs' apartments are.

"I right here," five-year-old Sett giggles. "Come 'n find me," he sings.

Petite Arabian Fadia rushes into her charge's room and hears another giggle. *Be calm,* she tells herself, *or he will never come out.* "Oh, my, I must give up. You win," she says playfully, hoping little Sett does not sense the trembling in her voice.

She hears another giggle behind her, turns, and sees Sett standing in full view, wagging his head back and forth, his little white teeth showing his delight.

With all the strength she can muster, she grabs up the husky and tall-for-his-age boy and stumbles out of his apartment to the three flights of stairs.

Starting down the steps, her entire body trembles. She tries to will her knees to not buckle and her tears to not come. Sett pushes at her chest. "I don't wanna go down there," he objects, as he continues to twist in her arms. "I wanna stay here and play."

Fadia's dark hair falls in front of her eyes, and she clings to the boy, hoping this time he does not get his way. Less and less, she can see the next step below her.

Two more chariots rush in from the battle. King Saul's illegitimate sons and Sett's other uncles.

Sett continues to wiggle and fight his nurse to free himself of her grasp. "Lemme down. Lemme down. I wanna play."

She clings hard. "Oh, Jehovah God. Give me strength."

"Mother, where are you?" Prince Isboset calls out.

The queen shouts, "I'm over here."

The boy screams in the nurse's ear. The sound mingles with the shouts of others in the terrified royal household scrambling to the family chariots now pulled into the courtyard below.

Another scream from Sett. Fadia's heart pounds and her weakening arms strain.

She hears the husky voices in the courtyard of the king's illegitimate sons as they rush toward the steps to get to their mother.

"Help me," Fadia calls out to the one closest to her. "Help me!"

Mefiboset, the boy's namesake half-uncle, climbs two steps at a time toward them.

"Help me!"

"I don't wanna go. I wanna play. Lemme go."

"Help me!"

"Mother, where are you?"

"Are all the chariots out?"

"Hurry, everyone."

"Help me!"

"I'm coming."

 "I don't wanna go."

"Help me!"

"They'll be here any moment."

 "I'm coming."

"I wanna play."

"Help me!"

Before the uncle and nurse can reach each other, the boy breaks free of his nurse's weakened arms and tumbles feet first.

"No!" Fadia screams, tears rushing down her face, her eyes wide. "Noooo!"

The uncle, still bloodied from battle, lunges toward the boy, arms stretched in front of him.

It is not enough.

Little Sett lands two steps below the nurse, his feet hitting the sharp outer edge, his arms flailing. He screams and tumbles toward his uncle. He bounces onto his back and is swept up into awaiting strong arms that have arrived too late.

Uncle Mefiboset hugs the screaming boy to him, pivots, and heads back down toward the courtyard.

Servants scramble to hitch awaiting chariots to horses. Guards rush up to the four palace watchtowers with bows and arrows and shout down for more ammunition.

"Mother, there you are," the prince calls out.

"Is the boy okay?" the queen screams. "Where is Fadia?"

They look up and see the young lady, barely out of her teens, slumped halfway down the lowest flight of stairs, face in her lap, hands over her head, screaming.

"Hurry, Fadia. We've got to go now."

The queen mother rushes up the steps, puts her arm around the nurse, and coaxes her down to an awaiting chariot. "We can't wait any longer. You must come now."

Ziba, steward of the house, appears. He shouts to the royal family.

"My sons and I will stay behind to take care of things. Go. Go!"

With the royal family now all accounted for, five chariots rush out of King Saul's palace and head east down the steep, winding, treacherous road toward Jericho and the Jordan River.

The horses snort and pant, pulling their cargo down the hill that is Gibeon, over rocks and bumps on the road. The passengers hang on to the sides of the chariots to keep from falling out.

Fadia sits in the bottom of her chariot, screaming Sett in her lap. She sucks in a deep breath, puts her head down onto his, and forces out a song between sobs. She prays he can hear it despite the screaming and yelling and hoof pounding, and wheels bouncing on the road.

Round and round on the precarious curves, wheels skimming drop-offs on one side, cliffs on the other. Hurry to Jericho, the Jordan, the stronghold, safety. Hurry. Live.

They see Jericho ahead. The men guide their horses around the city, sometimes their chariots only one wheel. Don't look back. Strain. Rush. Charge ahead.

Still the shouting and screaming and snorting and scraping and bouncing and escaping.

"Hurry! They're right behind us. Hurry!"

The royal family arrives at the Jordan River. It is low. They do not let up. The horses and their cargo plunge down the embankment, into the knee-deep water and push against its resistance until they are on the other shore. Back up the other side, they head farther east.

Now in the foothills. Higher. Still struggling to stay alive.

The men snap their whips above the horses' heads. The horses push on, straining, eyes wide, mouths agape, white sweat forming on their bodies.

On higher and higher. Keep running. Running from death. Running from doom. Running from what once was.

They see it ahead of them—Mahanaim. The royal stronghold. They do not try to slow the horses. They know they have been spotted from the watchtowers, and the gates swung wide for them.

They rush inside the fortress and toward the palace within it, which Saul had built as a duplicate of his palace back in Gibeon. Once inside, the experienced drivers slow their horses gradually, taking them in circles around the coral-and-black tiled courtyard until they can come to a halt.

By the time the royal family members begin to tumble out of their chariots, the gates have been closed and barred, and stronghold soldiers have rushed up to the parapet along the top of the wall.

Queen Mother Ahinoam hurries over to the chariot where her injured grandson lies, still screaming. Nurse Fadia looks up, trembling, tears streaking her dusty face.

"My lady. My lady" is all she can say.

The queen mother calls over to Prince Isboset, now her only son, "Come take Mefiboset up to his room. Quickly."

Princess Merab, Saul's daughter, rushes over to Barzillai, her father-in-law. "They're right behind us,. and little Sett has been injured, and...oh, help us!" She has her five young sons in tow.

"Grandfather. Grandfather," her sons call out.

"Not now," she screeches at them, tears taking hold.

Barzillai, overseer of the stronghold and self-made physician to the soldiers on duty, calls for his assistant. They follow the grandmother, son, and grandson up the steps.

Little Sett is laid on a bed in his father's spacious apartment and Barzillai moves into place.

"Where is he hurt?" he calls out with his deep voice over the boy's continued screaming.

"His legs," still-bloodied Prince Isboset shouts back, holding onto the boy to keep him from squirming.

For the first time, they see it. Sett's little feet are turned out sideways and a bone is protruding from each ankle.

"Lemme up!" Sett shouts. "Daddy. Daddy. Lemme up. Hurt, Daddy. Hurt. Help me, Daddy. Daddy...."

The boy goes silent. The adults look at each other in horror.

"No!" Queen Ahinoam shouts, her bow-shaped mouth twisted. "Not him too." Her screams fall into an abyss of shrill muttering. "Not our Sett. Please, not our little Sett."

"He's not dead, Your Majesty," Barzillai says with his bass voice, touching the woman's arm. "Your little prince is asleep."

She wipes her tears with her handkerchief and tucks it back in the scarlet belt around her gold tunic. She lets her green robe slide off her shoulders.

We must do something about those feet while we can," Barzillai continues.

From his kneeling position by the bed, Barzillai motions to his assistant standing by. The assistant sees the boy's feet and knows what to do. He walks around to the other side of the bed, hangs on to the boy with sure grasp, looks up at Barzillai, and nods. Barzillai pushes the bones back through the skin, and the servant wraps the legs as tight as he dares.

That done, the two men signal each other once again, the servant's hands once more grasping the boy's torso. Barzillai forces one of the feet to the front position. The boy groans but does not open his eyes. He does the same with the other foot. Then he and the servant each wrap a foot in strong linen.

Barzillai stands and wipes his brow. Prince Isboset stands by his mother, who is leaning her head against his strong shoulder.

"I will go down and tell the others we have everything under control," Barzillai says. He makes his way back down into the courtyard. "Prince Mefiboset will be fine," he says in a low tone. Standing before him are the boy's uncle and namesake, another uncle, and the queen mother's rival, Rizpah, the delicate redheaded mistress.

He looks around the courtyard. "Where is the nurse?" he asks. An uncle signals with his eyes toward one of the chariots.

Fadia slumps still on the floor of the chariot, bent over into a ball, and trembling.

"Come," Barzillai says, touching the young lady's shoulder.

"He stopped crying," she whimpers, raising her head. "I killed him."

"Come out of the chariot now," Barzillai assures. "The boy is going to be just fine."

He holds out both hands, she unrolls, takes them, and climbs out of the chariot.

"Why don't you go up and see him? He will need you when he wakes."

Fadia makes her way up the steps to the apartment of his now-dead father, Crown-Prince Jonathan. She pauses in the doorway. As she does, she hears the men down in the courtyard.

"Now what? With Father dead, who will be king? His only, but youngest son, or his oldest grandson?"

"Be quiet," she hears a woman's voice say. "Do you want them to hear you?"

From within the child's room, Queen Ahinoam looks over at the nurse and forces a smile.

"I'm so sorry, my lady. It's all my fault."

"Shhh, child," Aninoam says, briefly forgetting the loss of her husband and three of her sons.

"Come, Mother," Isboset finally says. "We need to make some decisions." He gently helps her up and walks beside her as they ascend the steps into a new world.

Ahinoim's daughter, Prince Isboset, Saul's mistress, and her two sons have gone to their apartments. The large courtyard is now empty and silent. The horses have been unhitched and put in their stalls on one side and the chariots on the other side.

The two turn now and walk to another set of steps, the imposing steps leading from the ground to the open second-floor throne room, and begin their ascent. Soldiers stand by and open the doors into the grandest room in the kingdom, and close them as the two enter.

Holding on to each other, they look before them at the empty throne. They look at the smaller thrones on each side—one for crown prince Jonathan, and one for the queen mother.

Ahinoam walks forward one small step at a time, her delicate frame still being supported by Isboset, who is head and shoulders taller than her. When they arrive at Saul's throne, she kneels before it, bows her head, and silently weeps.

When she finally looks up, she sees her youngest son, thirty-seven years old and as big as his father, sitting on the throne. Gone are his tears.

"Mother. What do you think?" Isboset asks, grinning.

She looks away from her son over to a blank wall.

"Where are they now?" she whimpers. "Are the vultures on them yet? Do you think you could go back and find their bodies?"

"It is too dangerous, Mother," her son replies, angry at the change of subject. "It is Philistine territory now. Everyone knows Father is gone. Jonathan, too and my other brothers. Our army is gone, and the enemy has taken over."

"Yes, I suppose you're right," Ahinoam says so low he can just make out her words.

"Mother, we need to make some decisions before the kingdom falls apart. I must take my place as king immediately."

He sits with his hands on both ivory-inlaid arms, feet apart, and looking around the room, his head held high as though surveying his kingdom.

She looks back at him and now realizes what he has

done.

"Son, let's not think about that right now," her pleading voice louder. "Let us mourn your father and your brothers. Come now. Come down from there. I need you."

The son obeys and lets her guide him to a bench along a side wall. They sit in silence. After a long while, the main door is opened, and they realize it is growing dark. A servant enters with a torch to set on the wall for them.

"The evening meal will be ready shortly. Is that your pleasure, Your Majesty?" the servant asks.

"Where is she?" Ahinoam asks the servant.

The servant understands. "Rizpah and both her sons are in her apartment."

By this, Ahinoam knows her husband's mistress is not far away, the apartment for the king and his two women being behind the throne room.

"Well, I suppose they deserve to eat too. But why? Why do her sons get to live, while all but one of mine have to die?"

No one answers. She rises from the bench and slowly steps back down the grand staircase to the dining hall.

She and Isboset seat themselves at the front table where the royal family normally sits. Her daughter, Merab, and her five sons sit with them.

There are four empty chairs at the table. Chairs of the king and his sons who will never return.

Mistress Rizpah and her two sons sit away from them in a front corner.

After eating the little they can, they each walk slowly to their apartments. Queen Ahinoam does not go directly to hers. She walks to the apartment of her grandson.

Fadia is sitting on little Sett's bed with his head is in her lap. He is whimpering, and she is brushing the hair off his forehead. She hears the queen enter, stands, curtsies, and returns to her place next to Prince Mefiboset.

"The physician brought me some tea to give him for pain whenever he wakes up," the nurse says, her voice low and scratchy.

"Take extra good care of him, Fadia. You may just have the next king in your lap." She turns and closes the door behind her.

Sleep does not come that night to the household of King Saul, the king that used to be.

The royal family imitates what they believe to be sleep, but no longer are sure. The royal family imitates a rest they do not feel. The family imitates a reality they struggle to find, then wish away.

Morning comes. The servants stir and go to the apartments of the royal family and the family of the other woman. One by one, loved ones King Saul has left behind go to the dining hall, make a pretense of eating, then go to the courtyard to find a bench and resume their mourning.

Prince Isboset goes to his normal bench, but instead of sitting, he stands on it.

"Attention, everyone," he announces. "As your new king, I will be holding an audience in the throne room later today for any problems the people here in Mahanaim have."

Heads jerk up.

"What?"

"What is he saying?"

Ahinoam stands. She purses her lips, glares, and calls over to her son.

"Get down from there, Isboset. No one said you were king. The oldest son is always the king. You are the youngest son. You know that."

"But Mother, the oldest son of the oldest son is unfit to rule. He is too young and too lame. Whoever heard of a crippled king?"

"As for him being too young, I will rule until he is old enough to take over. As for him being too lame, give it time. His feet will heal, and he will walk as erect and proud as any king ever did."

"No, Mother. You are wrong. With too much delay, the kingdom will fall apart."

"We shall wait as long as it takes. Say no more."

They hear feet on the steps leading from the children's apartments on the third floor. Everyone looks up and sees a servant carrying little Sett down, the nurse behind them.

The conversation comes to a halt as the child is set on a mat on the tiled pavement. His nurse sits beside him. "Fadee, my legs hurt," he whimpers.

"Then we shall get your mind off your legs. Did I ever tell you about a crippled prince? He lived a very long time ago. He was the grandson of Prince Abraham, just like you are the grandson of King Saul. One day, this big man wrestled an angel and injured his thigh. His leg never healed.

"Then, guess what? God gave him a new name—Isra-El. Do you know what that means? It means Prince of God. As soon as he became crippled, he became the crippled prince."

Sett giggles. "Like me?"

"Yes. Kind of like you."

Sett giggles again and brings smiles to the rest of the family listening in.

"But being crippled did not hold him back, for crippled Prince Isra-El had twelve sons, and all of us descend from one of those sons. Do you know which son of crippled Prince Isra-El you descend from?"

Sett tips his head and shrugs his shoulders.

"Benjamin."

Setts giggles, then his eyes change as he remembers his pain. He tries to be brave. Fighting back returning tears, he looks up at his nurse.

"Did crippled Prince Isra-El ever become a king?" he asks.

# 2 ~ THE IMPOSSIBLE

"It has been six months since the accident," Isboset announces. "He still cannot walk. What are we waiting for?"

Isboset, big and tall like his father, three brothers, grandfather, and every other male in the family, paces.

"Stop that right now," Queen Mother Ahinoam rebuts. "He is the oldest son of the oldest son, and time will not change that fact." Today she is wearing a white tunic with a blue and green robe.

"But, Mother..."

"You are thirty-eight years old now and should be ashamed of the way you are acting." Ahinoam, taller than many other women, but still delicate in facial features and mannerisms, shakes her finger at her son.

There is a knock on the outside gate, and those within hearing distance in the courtyard look to see who the gatekeeper will be letting in.

"Oh, yes, come in, Barzillai. We have been expecting you," the queen mother says. "Come sit. One of the maids will bring you new wine to refresh you."

"I don't want any new wine, Your Majesty. I just want the boy to heal. Oh, madam, I am so sorry."

The skinny man, scarcely taller than his queen, takes out a handkerchief and wipes his bulbous nose.

"You did the best you could. I was there. Remember?" she responds. "I have not seen a physician treat broken bones any better than you did."

"But my knowledge is so limited. Oh, I can treat the soldiers here at the fortress, but they are bigger and tougher. I did something wrong with little Sett. I just do not know what."

Barzillai sits with hands on his knees and looking down at the marble-tiled pavement.

"Well, perhaps exercising his feet will help him heal," she says.

"That may be the problem. Maybe we exercised them too soon."

"Now, what?"

Barzillai stands and paces, his hands behind him. "I have been reading about a physician in India who believes you can see the strings that go through the body that can cause pain. He calls them nerves. He says they come out of the bone that goes down the middle of your back."

"How could that cause Sett to be unable to walk?"

"He says the body strings can be damaged just like muscles can be. If cutting muscles makes someone unable to move, maybe cutting nerves could make someone unable to feel pain and able to walk. I don't know. He lived a long time ago. I just don't know."

Red-headed Mefiboset, Saul's youngest son by his mistress, Rizpah. walks out to the courtyard and notices the two older people in conversation. He does not approach them.

"Come on over, Mefiboset," the queen says. She has long ago decided being polite to the other woman's sons is the only way she is going to deal with the awkward living arrangement.

"We were just discussing your little brother's condition. You seem to be closer to him than anyone except his father." She pauses and dwells a moment on her lost Jonathan.

"Do you think there are strings of some kind inside people's bodies that makes them feel things, especially pain?”

“I don’t know,” he says, squatting on the tiled pavement in front of them. “Maybe.”

She turns to her Barzillai. “Do you think you could give him something to make him sleep, then cut one of his ankles open to see if you see any such strings?”

“Even if I did, what would I do with them? That Indian physician did not say.”

“Maybe if you see two loose ends, you can tie them back together somehow.”

“I don’t know,” Barzillai says.

“Would it hurt to try?” Mefiboset asks.

“I don’t suppose so. He would just have another incision to deal with, but I could give him tea or even opium for the pain.”

“Then, let’s do it,” the queen responds. “We shall do it tomorrow.”

“Well,” Mefiboset says, “if the little guy is going to go through more pain tomorrow, he should have some fun today while he has a chance.” With that, the youngest uncle of the injured king-to-be jumps up, tips his head to the queen mother, and bounds up the steps to the child’s room.

“Peek-a-boo,” he says from around the corner of his open door. “I see you.”

Sett giggles. “Oh, Uncle Mee. You are funny.”

The older man jumps into the room, acting like a frog with strong legs. Realizing what he has just done, he immediately gets on all fours and squirms without using his legs on his belly. “Guess what I am?” he says.

“A fish. You’re a fish.”

“Would you like to be a fish with me? C'mon. Let’s be fishes together.”

Nurse Fadia smiles and moves out of the way so the much-stronger man can lift the boy and put him on his belly.

“Oh, my! You are growing so much. Pretty soon, you will be as heavy as your, as your, uh, uncle.”

“Yeah. I’m pretty heavy all right,” Sett, now six years

old, says.

The two squirm and wiggle around the room on their bellies until the older one gets bored.

"Wanna sing a song?"

"Yup," Sett replies, leaning over on one arm and looking up.

Now in a sitting position, both of his feet still bound, he grins.

"Ummm. Let's sing our hero song," Uncle Mefiboset says.

*There is a hero big and tall.*
*He's the strongest of them all.*
*He will never make you sad*
*Cause Jonathan's my dad.*

The two sing their song over and over, sitting on the floor and rejoicing as they always had before.

Now they stop. It is quiet. "Do you think I will ever see my dad again?" the boy asks, looking up at his uncle with large dark eyes.

"Oh, my, lad. Yes. He will make sure of that. Right now, he has gone far away. But someday, when you are grown up and old, you will be able to see him again."

"Well, I'm glad he named me after you, 'cause you're so much fun."

"And we'll keep on having fun, won't we?" Mefiboset says, poking the boy in his tummy and making him giggle.

The next day, Fadia feeds him in his room and encourages him to play hard and wear himself out.

Barzillai arrives. He and the queen go into the boy's room. She is wearing a brown tunic and red robe and no jewelry.

"This nice man is going to make you kind of sleepy," Ahinoam says, taking Sett's little hand in her own. "Then maybe you can dream you're playing. Okay? Now, he is going to help you up onto this table."

"I want Mee to do it," he says. "I want Mee."

Mefiboset is summed, immediately arrives, and effortlessly lifts the big boy onto the table.

"Let's sing our song now," his uncle says. "There is a hero big and tall...."

Barzillai places a drop of opium on the boy's tongue. Two hours later, the stronghold's physician stands and takes a deep breath.

"I don't know if those strings I found were nerves or not. I tied them together the best I could. Now we wait."

More months ago by.

"Mother, it has been a year since Father and Jonathan died."

Today the queen is wearing a blue tunic with a green and white robe. She has donned a gold bracelet. "Don't forget your other brothers, Malchishua and Abinadab. They suffered and died too, you know."

"Don't change the subject, Mother. We can wait no longer. I must become king. The kingdom is falling apart." Isboset stands in front of his mother, forcing her to look up when speaking to him.

"Who said the kingdom is falling apart?" Ahinoam says, looking down at the embroidery work in her lap.

"Everyone."

"And who might everyone be?"

"Well, everyone."

"That's what I thought. Barzillai has sent for a doctor from Egypt. He will be here any day now. He has guaranteed Barzillai that he can fix Sett's feet so he will be able to walk."

"And I suppose you paid him out of the royal treasury. Funds are getting low. We're not collecting as many taxes now that Judah has seceded from the kingdom, thanks to this delay. And for what? For nothing."

Isboset raises his big arms and lifts his dark eyes toward the sky above the open courtyard. "You're killing us, Mother."

"What did you say?"

Isboset looks down at his mother and takes a step back. "I didn't mean it that way," he says with a softer voice.

"Go to your apartments," she orders. "Now."

"I'm not a child, Mother."

"You're acting like one. Now leave. The physician from Egypt will be here this afternoon, and I do not want you around when he comes."

Two hours later, the expected knock comes on the stronghold gate. The gatekeeper lets the two physicians in. They walk forward to the queen and bow.

"Your Majesty, may I present to you Im-Hotep, by far the most respected physician in all of Egypt, and I might add, all the world."

Im-Hotep is of average height and thin. He wears a short white tunic tucked under a red belt. His thigh-length white *shendyt* wrapped around his hips is joined at his waist. He toys with a large leather pouch with its strap slung over his shoulder. His black hair is thick and wiry. He bows low before the queen.

"Thank you for coming," Ahinoam responds. "Please have a seat. I would like to know what you think about this critical situation."

Servants approach with individual wooden seats for the men.

"I have not seen the boy yet, of course, Your Majesty. But I believe the problem is not in the strings that some call nerves. I believe the problem could be from the spine, the long bone that goes down the middle of one's back." He pauses.

"I have had patients with their spine crushed. And, even though there was no direct injury to their legs, they became paralyzed and could no longer walk. Might I ask if he was dropped on his back?"

The queen turns to a maid serving cool water to the guests. "Would you kindly fetch Fadia for me, and stay with the boy until she returns?"

Momentarily they watch Fadia approach. Although

she had rushed down the steps, as soon as she had seen the men, she slows, moves her hands behind her, and lowers her head.

"Come here, child. No one is going to hurt you or blame you. We have been through this before. The boy had just grown too big for you to lift. You are not to blame. But, now, this man from Egypt has a question or two for you. Answer them, and you may return to your work."

"Yes, my lady," Fadia says.

"Young lady," Im-Hotep begins, "was the boy dropped on his back?"

"No, sir. He was dropped on his feet, then bounced over onto his back."

"He bounced. Hmmm. I see. Thank you very much."

He turns to the queen. "May I see him now?"

She rises. "Certainly."

The men follow her up the steps and to Sett's room. He is playing on a mat, both legs bandaged up to the knee.

"Hey, there, big boy," the physician says. "Would you like to go for a ride and be up on this table over here?"

Sett looks up at the strange man with the thick black hair with suspicion. He looks over at his grandmother and at Barzillai. "I want Mee. I want Mee to lift me up."

Ahinoam motions to Fadia, who leaves the room. Shortly they hear a deep sing-song voice.

"Where is my big Sett? Where is he hiding? Oh, I know."

With that, Uncle Mefiboset enters the room with a bound, crouching and jumping. He notices the visitors but keeps his eyes on Sett. He lifts the boy onto the table, pokes Sett in the belly, and waits for the boy to giggle.

"Now, let's see what these big men want with us. They'd better be nice, or we'll beat up on 'em, huh?" he says, stepping aside.

The Egyptian doctor steps forward, smiles, and begins humming a song. He gently rolls the boy onto his front and feels around his spine.

"Does this hurt? Do you feel that? How about now?"

A few moments later, he motions for Mefiboset to return the boy to the floor, and puts out his hand as an indication to the queen that he will follow her out of the room. They descend to the courtyard and reseat themselves on their respective benches.

"Well, I believe he injured his spine fairly low. We can always treat an open wound caused by a spine injury, but not the spine itself. I am very sorry, Your Majesty. But there is nothing I can do for him."

A month later, Barzillai returns alone to the palace. "I have had this thought in the back of my mind, Your Majesty, but have hesitated to bring it up because it would cause the boy much additional pain."

Ahinoam sets her embroidery work in her lap, stares at the tiled pavement, over at the watchtower in one corner of the stronghold, then over to Barzillai. Tears form in her eyes. She sighs. "If it will bring back the use of his feet," she says in a whisper, "I guess we should try it. Would the pain be temporary?"

"It would last as long as it did when he originally broke his ankles, and maybe longer."

The woman presses her lips together, looks at a spider crawling along the pavement, then back up to her friend. "What are you proposing?"

"We break them again. There is a new method over in Arabia for fixing broken bones. They lay sticks of wood on both sides of the broken bone, then wrap them with bandages stiffened with ground seashells and egg whites."

Tears return to her eyes. The queen sighs. "Oh, how can I put him through that again? How can I?"

She raises her hand to her forehead and stands. She walks to the statue of her husband in the middle of the courtyard, looks up at it with swollen eyes, hugs herself, walks away from it, and returns to Barzillai.

"Is there no other way?"

"I have run out of ideas, my lady."

"My innocent little boy. Can you ever forgive me?" she says, looking up in the direction of his room.

She sighs and looks back over at Barzillai. "Okay. But make sure you give him plenty of tea to put him asleep and plenty of opium. You will not leave his side until he tells you he has no more pain. Is that clear?"

"Yes, Your Majesty. I am so sorry, Your Majesty. Shall I do it tomorrow?"

"No, I want time to send for his aunts—Mecal and Merab. They need to be here too. It's been a year since Mera went back home. Mecal is with her new husband. We shall do it one month from today." She sighs, and her thoughts drift to things she does not want to think on.

The next month arrives all too soon. Everyone in the family has been told. They gather in the courtyard early. There is petite red-headed Rizpah, the mistress, with her two big red-headed untitled sons, Mefiboset and Armoni. There is Sett's aunt, Princess Merab, with her five big sons sitting near her. There are Sett's aunt, Princess Mecal, and her brother, Prince Isboset, both without children.

Their benches are in a long row facing the bedrooms and balconies. They all know which door belongs to their little Sett.

No one speaks.

The women sit with their hands folded in their laps. The men sit the same way sometimes or lean over with their hands clasped between their knees sometimes.

A knock on the outside gate.

They know.

The doorman lets Barzillai and an assistant in. He pauses to acknowledge the awaiting relatives. Queen Mother Ahinoam rises and leads the way up the steps. Behind these three is Uncle Mefiboset, who has received a special request to attend.

Slowly up the high steps to the little boy who does not realize what he is about to face. Higher up the steps. One hand span at a time. They arrive at the landing and walk along the balcony to his room. They enter.

No one smiles. Little Sett, playing on the floor, looks at the somber faces and puckers up his mouth. "I didn't do anything bad," the now seven-year-old boy says. "I didn't do anything bad. Don't hurt me."

Mefiboset breaks ranks and rushes to the boy, whisking him up onto the table the boy dreads. In a flash, Sett's uncle holds his fingers on the outside edges of his mouth, stretching it as far as he can, and above his eyelids. He sticks out his tongue. "Lardle! Lardle! Lardle," he says, crossing his eyes.

The boy giggles.

"Let's play a game," the uncle says, wagging his head back and forth.

Sett smiles. "I like games."

"It's a make-believe game. Let's pretend that we are fighting a raging battle to save good people from bad people. And guess what? In that battle is you," he pokes Sett in the belly, "and me," he pokes himself in the belly, "and Jonathan, your very brave father. Okay?"

"I don't 'member my father very well anymore," Sett says with a frown and a pucker.

"Well, he remembers you. Now, we are all three together, and we are being very, very brave. Can you be brave? Show me how brave you are."

Sett bares his teeth, raises his fists in the air, and growls in his little-boy voice.

"Very good, Sett. You are, indeed, very brave. Now, some rocks are beginning to fall on us, and they hurt, but we are being brave anyway."

"Ruh, Ruh, Ruh," Sett says in his growling voice.

"That's right. Now a big rock is going to fall on you, and you are going to hurt. But your brave father is going to come over after a while and lift the painful rock off of you."

Sett no longer smiles. He looks up at his uncle with watery eyes. "Uncle Mee, am I going to hurt right now?"

Mefiboset draws the boy close to him, so he does not

see the unmanly tears. "Yes, son. You are going to hurt right now."

Barzillai steps forward and gives Sett a small cup of tea.

"Drink this tea. It is very good."

While Sett is drinking, Mefiboset breaks away, rushes down to the courtyard, and sits next to his mother. Rizpah takes his hand.

In silence, they wait.

The air is still. They hear a lone wolf off in the distance. They dare not look at each other.

Then comes the scream.

The scream they knew had to come. The scream that is almost otherworldly. The scream that comes from deep in the soul.

Tears rush to the eyes of the women. The men bite their lip and grit their teeth.

Now the other scream.

The women lay their heads over on the shoulder of the person next to them and whimper. The men put their arms around them and squeeze, trying to squeeze away the terrible sounds of the air above them, in them, and a part of them.

One of the men stands and paces then reseats himself.

A servant walks toward them, then changes his mind and retreats.

Some shake, their tears now taking control.

An hour later, Barzillai's assistant comes down to the courtyard.

"It is done," he says, then leaves.

They sit in silence a while longer. Finally, Aunt Mecal stands. "Well," she whispers to the rest of the family, "I need to go see him."

One at a time, the family members go to little Sett's room, the room of the next king of Israel. He does not know they are there. He sleeps the sleep of opium.

A month goes by. The special stiffened bandages are

never taken off the boy.

"My feet hurt," he says.

"That means they are healing," he is always told.

Two months. When the stiff bandages become dirty or begin to unravel, another layer of seashell stiffened bandages is wrapped around his feet and ankles.

Three months.

The day comes when complete healing is to be pronounced. Once again, the family is assembled. This time, they are in a celebrating mood. This is the day their little Sett will be whole again and become Israel's boy king.

Barzillai arrives. He smiles and shakes hands with everyone present. He walks up to Queen Mother Ahinoam and bows. "Your Majesty. Shall we?"

She stands, smiles broadly, and leads the procession once again up the long steps to the boy's room. The family sits in the courtyard as they had before and waits, but this time with smiles.

A happy silence. An anticipating silence. Waiting for the good news.

"No!"

Everyone looks up in the direction of the child's room.

"No!"

"It cannot be!"

Nurse Fadia walks out to the balcony and goes halfway down the steps. She grows limp. Uncle Mefiboset rushes up the steps and arrives just in time to catch her. She whispers to him.

He looks down at the family.

"His feet have shrunk and have no life left in them. His feet are completely dead."

Isboset stands and smiles. "Well, I guess that means I am now the king."

# 3 ~ HAIL TO THE KING

*T*he royal procession arrives once again at the family palace on a hill that is Gibeon beyond the Jordan River and north of Jerusalem. It has been three years. Three years since the death of their beloved husband and father and his three sons. Three years since they had run for their lives.

They ride through the main gate into the palace complex. Two guards are on duty at the gate. One guard is on duty at each of the four watchtowers with barracks below. The barracks are nearly empty. The guards are Steward Ziba's sons.

Now they are home again, and everything is different. The only surviving son of Saul, Isboset, is now king. Oldest son of the oldest son, Sett, is doomed to lifeless feet the rest of his existence on earth. Nothing will ever be the same again.

To the left of the vast courtyard are the stables, cordoned off with an inside wall and ten marble columns, and to the right is the carriage house, also cordoned off with an inside wall and ten columns.

"Ah, yes. Home. Nothing like it," Isboset says, strutting.

In the middle of the courtyard—large enough to drive five chariots and their horses in a circle within it—is a large reflecting pool. Sometimes there are fish in it. Marble benches are scattered around the courtyard for the comfort of the royal family.

The pavement is covered with marble tiles in blue and red geometric patterns. Walls depict battles of Warrior King Saul against Moab, Ammon, Edom, Zobah, Philistia, and Amalek.

"Welcome home! Welcome home!"

It is Ziba, servant of the palace since he was seven years old. Now steward of the palace at age fifty.

No more emptying the sand in the pails of the royal toilet rooms. No more bowing and scraping and humiliation. Now steward, and for the past three years in complete control of all things involving the palace.

"Isboset, now King Isboset. How grand, Your Majesty," Ziba says, bowing his head but not any of the rest of his body. "Come. I have arranged for you to have your father's apartment."

"Uh, Ziba," Queen Mother Ahinoam interjects, "he does not really want apartments next to us old women— Rizpah and I. He will keep his apartment on the top floor. I have given him the apartments of two of his brothers also. He will have more room up there."

"Uh, yes, Your Majesty," Ziba says.

"And who have we here?" Ziba asks without smiling, as tall red-headed Mefiboset walks in with a child on his back. Nurse Fadia follows.

"I am Prince Sett, and this is my horse, Uncle Mefiboset."

"How delightful," Ziba says with a sneer while turning away.

"Look at all the children here," Sett says. "I will have lots of friends to play with."

"Young sir," Ziba responds, turning back to the family embarrassment, "these are my children. I have many of them."

"Yuppie," Sett replies. "How many do you have?"

"I have fifteen children from age thirty down to age one. However, they all have their jobs to do in the household, and it would not be seemly for a prince to be playing with the servants."

"But..."

Isboset motions for Ziba to step aside with him. "From henceforward, he is never to be seen. He will stay in his apartment at all times. That means he will eat, sleep, and play in his apartment. Is that clear?"

"Yes, Your Majesty," Ziba says. "These were exactly my own thoughts."

As Uncle Mefiboset walks toward the steps leading to the third-floor apartments, his half-brother, Isboset, stands on a bench and claps his hands. "Attention, everyone. I would like to have a banquet next week to celebrate my coming to the throne."

The main structure that catches everyone's attention as they enter the palace complex is the grand stairway at the far end of the courtyard six man-lengths wide leading up to the second floor. At the top are folding doors which, when pulled back, reveal King Saul's throne room. King Isboset walks up the grand steps to claim his throne.

"Yuppie," Sett says. "A party."

"Oh, we are going to have our own party," Uncle Mefiboset says. "And it will be a lot better than theirs. Isn't that right, my prince?"

On each side of the grand stairway are double doors to the dining hall and public reception room. On the other side of those doors are steps leading up to the walled-in parts of the second floor not occupied by the throne room, and on up to the third floor. Balconies lead to outside doors into royal apartments on the second and third floors. The king and his wife and mistress have apartments on the second floor. The princes and princesses have apartments on the third floor.

"Yup," the boy says as his namesake uncle heads up the side steps, still being followed by Nurse Fadia.

Once inside Sett's spacious apartment, they stop in the middle of the room and grow quiet.

"This is where my father lived, isn't it?" eight-year-old Sett asks.

"Yes," Mefiboset says almost in a whisper. "It is your father's apartment."

They look around at the bed Jonathan had slept in, the hooks on the wall where he had hung his clothes, more hooks where he had hung his armor, his shoes in one corner, a few scrolls in a basket, a table and chair for writing. Colorful rugs scattered around the multi-colored marble tiled floor.

"It's almost like his room at the stronghold," Mefiboset says.

"Let me down over by his shoes," Sett says.

Sitting among them, he chooses a sandal and slides it onto one of his useless feet.

"He sure had big feet, my father did," he says with a grin. "Do you think my feet will ever be that big?"

"I don't know. Would you like me to cut his sandals down for you?"

"No, I can't wear sandals. Not enough protection. I can't feel my feet, so wouldn't know if I bumped something. I will just look at them. Fadia always told me, 'we have to adjust.'"

"Well, it certainly is dusty in this apartment," Fadia says. "It is going to take some doing to get it cleaned up for you."

"Excuse me, Your Highness." It is a child's voice. "I have been sent to see if you are hungry."

Sett grins, and his eyes sparkle.

"Hi. Come in. What is your name?"

"My name is Akiva, but I'm not supposed to play with you."

Though the same age as Sett, Akiva is not as tall as Sett and is thin. He is wearing a plain brown tunic and is barefoot.

"That's okay," Sett replies. "We can do other things. We can talk."

"Well, they didn't tell me I couldn't talk to you, so I suppose it's okay. I'm one of his slaves."

"You mean, one of Isboset's servants," Uncle Mefiboset says.

"No. Ziba has his own slaves. There are twenty of us."

"Where did Ziba get the money buy you?" Uncle Mefiboset asks.

"I do not know, but we were all bought over the past three years."

"Is that so?" Mefiboset replies, pulling on his red beard.

"Oh, he had the money, all right. He always has money." He turns to the boy. "Are you hungry?"

"I will tell you if I am hungry," Sett says with a glint in his eye, "if you will let me teach you a song."

"Well, I guess singing is like talking, so okay."

*There is a hero big and tall.*
*He's the strongest of them all.*
*He will never make you sad*
*Cause Jonathan's my dad.*

Akiva does not smile. "I never knew my father."

"Oh. Then you can sing a song you like and teach it to me."

"Okay, here is my favorite."

*God made the world, and God made the tree.*
*Look out the window, and you can see.*

"I like that song. Okay, for my dinner, I would like ummmm."

"Oh, you don't get your choice. I was just sent to ask if you were hungry. I will bring your meal to you in a little while. I have to wait until no one is watching. My master says he and I—and of course your family—are the only ones in the palace who know you are here, and he will reward me if I keep our secret."

With that, Akiva leaves.

Three days later, on his regular visit, Sett has a surprise for Akiva.

"How do you like my new crutches? My nurse always says, 'We have to adjust,' so helped me design them, and my uncle had them made for me. See? They have three legs at the bottom of each one so they can stand on their own without being held up. So now, all I have to do is swing my feet between them while they take the steps for me, and I can be as tall as you."

"You'll have to have a pair made for me," Akiva says, "so we can race each other."

"My nurse is teaching me some tricks with the crutches. Maybe I'll teach them to you too."

From then on, the boys race across Sett's spacious ten-man-lengths wide apartment every day. They swear secrecy, so they do not get caught actually playing.

Weeks go by, then months. Finally, a year.

"Today is my birthday," Akiva announces to Sett one day. "I am ten years old."

"Me too," Sett says.

"Then how come you are so much bigger than me? You're as tall as your grownup nurse."

"My whole family is really, really tall. Some people call us giants, and sometimes I feel like one.

"Well, for my birthday, I am going to tell you a story," Akiva announces. "It is really a riddle."

"Oh, goody. I love riddles. So, tell me your story. Come, sit on the cushion across from me."

"Well, once upon a time, there was a big palace. Some of the servants were nice, but not all of them. Some of them were mean."

"I have to go down and do your laundry, Sett. I'll be back after a while," Fadia says.

"Okay, Fadia." He turns back to Akiva. "What makes people mean?"

"Don't interrupt. This is my story. Now, the oldest mean man in the palace had lived there most of his life. His father sold him to be a slave when he was about our age because his father was drunk all the time and did not work very much."

Sett looks out a window, then wags his head back and forth as he listens.

"But the boy was smart. At first, he carried out the stinky sand pails in the toilets—the worst job in the whole palace. But, he wanted a better job. So one day, he told his master, the king, that one of the other servants had spilled the stinky sand pails all over one of the halls. So the king made them trade jobs, and the boy got to help pile hay in the stables instead. But he wanted an even better job. So one day, he told the king one of the horse trainers was beating the horses. So the king made them trade jobs, and he got to be a horse trainer."

"Wow. He was really loyal to the king, wasn't he?" Sett says.

"Oh, no. He was only loyal to himself. Most of what he told his master, the king, were lies so he could get a better job."

"What did he do next?"

"He decided to take over being the master of all the slaves."

"But that's impossible," Sett replies.

"Not to this man who lies all the time."

"But the only way to get rid of his master, the king, would be to kill him."

"Exactly."

Silence.

"Well, tell me the rest of the story," Sett says with a grin. "This is exciting."

"That's all there is. The story isn't finished."

"It looks like it is going to have to be solved by you and me," the prince replies.

"I want to find the answer to the riddle of who will kill

the king, but I do not know how." Akiva is not smiling.

"We can become spies. That would be fun."

"Maybe I could be a spy," Akiva says, "but you can't."

"Who said so? I already am a spy."

"You are not."

"Am too."

"Not."

"I'll prove it. My nurse is not back yet. Follow me."

Sett crawls over to his father's table, pulls himself up onto his knees, and pushes the table aside. He pushes on the wall behind the table, and some of it opens up like a door.

"Wowww," Akiva says, eyes wide. "Where does it go?"

"I'll show you. But I can't show all of it to you because my nurse will be coming back soon."

Sett grabs a lit lamp off the table and crawls into the hidden passageway with Akiva behind him.

"Do you always have lit lamps in the daytime?"

"I have a shadowy room. I want the lamps to be lit. That's one of the advantages of being a prince. And you don't have to crawl with me. The ceiling is high enough to stand."

They crawl on together. They come to some narrow steps, sit on them, and bounce their way down to the second floor. They hear voices. It is the king's apartment.

"I can hear everything he says," Sett says.

"Won't you get caught?"

"No. My father made this passageway, and he was smarter than everyone. Now we've gotta go back."

They arrive at Sett's apartment just as Nurse Fadia returns.

"Well, I gotta be going," Akiva says. He winks at Sett and is gone.

Over the next few months, Akiva watches from the courtyard when Fadia arrives to do the daily laundry and slips up to Sett's apartment. They explore more and more of the palace through the secret passage.

"We still haven't been able to solve the riddle of the

mean man wanting to kill the king of the palace," Akiva says one day.

"I'll start spying at night after my nurse goes to sleep," Sett announces.

Three weeks later, when Akiva arrives, Sett is beaming.

"Did you figure out the answer to the riddle of the mean man?"

"Yes, and it is bad. I heard Ziba talking to two of his oldest sons. They were actually talking about killing the king. Your story is real, isn't it?"

"What should we do?" Akiva asks.

"We've got to warn the king. He's my uncle," Sett says. "But you'll have to be the one to do it."

"They don't let me near his door," Akiva says. "What can I do?"

"Well, you could etch a note of warning on a tile the cooks put his bread on."

"Okay, I'll try that. They let me in the kitchen to pick up your food."

Four days later, Akiva has news for Sett.

"Well, I etched the warning to him and made sure it was at his place in the dining hall."

"Then, we shall wait. If he leaves the palace, we know we have been successful. If he stays, we need to keep trying."

The next day Akiva returns to Sett's apartment.

"I don't think he has left. Did you see anything out your window?"

"No, he hasn't left. I heard him in his apartment last night.

"What else can we try?" Akiva asks.

"Do you know which saddle he uses when he goes riding each day?" Sett asks.

"I can find out. So, I should try to slip a message into his saddle. Right?"

"Yes. And do it as soon as you can. He is still in danger. I know he is."

The boys wait and hope. By the second day, they realize their failure when the king is still in the palace.

"I am getting really worried. I guess I can write on a small piece of papyrus and slip it into his apartment from the secret passageway," Sett says. "Don't know if there is a way to do it, but I will try."

The following day Sett reports his success to Akiva when he comes by with his next meal.

"I found a crack in the wall and slipped a note to him. Let's just hope a maid who can't read doesn't find it first and throw it away."

Failure once again. The king is still in the palace, and no extra guards have been put in place.

"The king's killers aren't going to wait much longer," Sett tells Akiva. "I have to tell a grown-up."

"Can she be trusted?"

"My nurse? Not her. No one would pay any attention to her. I hardly do anymore myself."

"You're not thinking of..."

"I'm going to tell my Uncle Mefiboset. He is the king's half-brother. And, even if they don't like each other, surely Uncle Mefiboset will warn him. Can you tell him I need to see him?"

"Oh, I couldn't do that. I am not allowed to talk to any of the royal family members. You'll just have to wait until he decides on his own to come see you."

Akiva leaves, and Fadia returns with his laundry done.

"Uh, Fadia, do we have any red cloth?"

"I suppose we do. What do you want to do with it?"

"Make a flag."

"You're not allowed to hang anything out your window. You know that."

"Actually, I didn't mean a flag. I mean, I might want you to make a robe for me from it."

"Why? They won't let you go anywhere."

"I want it anyway. So, can you give me the red cloth?"

Fadia goes to a basket in a corner and pulls out a piece

of red cotton. Later in the day, when she goes down to do Sett's daily laundry, he hangs the red cloth from his window.

"You are going to get caught," Sett's uncle says, entering the apartment without knocking. He heads straight for the window and pulls in the red signal.

"Now, what is so important?"

"Someone in the palace wants to kill the king."

"You certainly are desperate to see me if that's the only story you can come up with. Okay, so I haven't been to see you lately. I'll stay now, and you can ride on my back."

"No, Uncle Mee. It's true. I heard him talking to two of the servants about it."

"How did you hear that?"

"Uh, well, I just did."

The two play a while, and Mefiboset leaves.

Later that afternoon, they hear it. Up and down the corridors, along the balconies, and down in the courtyard. King Isboset has been stabbed in his bed.

"The king is dead!"

Little Prince Mefiboset is next.

# 4 ~ UNFORGETTABLE

Queen Mother Ahinoam arrives at her grandson's spacious apartment on the third floor. She is wearing a red tunic with elaborate embroidered white robe. Sett is lying on his bed.

"Oh, my sweet boy, you are crying. We are all crying. We will miss our King Isboset."

"It's not just that, Grandmother. I tried to warn him, but didn't know how."

"How could you have known? Well, no matter. It is a terrible thing, and my heart is breaking over my last son. The servants who did this have escaped and are probably going down to see David. David will probably become king next. That's what everyone says, and I believe it."

"What will happen to us, Grandmother?"

"That is what I came to talk to you about. If David is made king, he may try to kill you."

"Why me?"

"Because you are the only legitimate descendant of King Saul still alive. You must escape."

"But what about you and Mefiboset and the others?"

"We women are not a threat to his throne. He will probably take us into his harem. And Mefiboset and Armoni are not legal heirs, so they are not a threat to him. He will just probably take us all to his fortress."

"Why can't I go with you?"

"I already told you. You are the direct descendant of

King Saul and of his oldest son. You are the oldest son of the oldest son. You must escape."

She hears the door open and turns in that direction.

"Oh, here is Mefiboset now. Did you get everything arranged?" she asks her rival's son.

"Yes, Your Majesty. I have lined up three donkeys— one for the boy...."

"I'm not a boy anymore. I'm as tall as Fadia."

"Okay. One for our young man here, one for his nurse...."

"She's not my nurse anymore. She is my tutor."

"Quit interrupting your uncle," Ahinoam urges.

"I have one donkey for Sett, one for Fadia, and one to carry supplies. The supplies include a tent, one change of clothes for each of them, and food and water for them and the animals. The food should last a few days."

"Fadia, come here," Ahinoam says, looking over toward a bench where the servant is mending.

"Didn't you say you were originally from Arabia?"

"Yes, Your Majesty. I am from Madain Saleh."

"And how long have you been with us?"

"I came with my widowed mother when she indentured herself to you. I was ten years old at the time. I am now twenty-six."

"And you have cared for Sett since he was born. Am I correct?"

"Yes, my lady."

"Would you know how to return to your people on your own?"

"Yes, my lady. I would just cross to the eastern side of the Jordan River and follow it down toward the Red Sea. It is somewhere along that highway. I do not know exactly where, but could ask around."

"That is sufficient," Ahinoam says. "So, it is settled. You will leave tomorrow at dawn. I do not think David knows about the assassination yet, and that will give us a little time."

She looks over at her grandson.

"Yes, we know it is confusing for you. You will be leaving your family behind. Don't worry, dear. We will know where you are. Perhaps we can send for you someday."

Sett tries to control his tears. "I don't want to go without you, Grandmother. And without Uncle Mefiboset. And without my whole family. Go with me, Grandmother."

"Be strong, Mefiboset. You could still be king someday. It is not too early for you to learn to be strong. Now, do you think you can do that?"

He wipes away a tear. "I will try, Grandmother."

Ahinoam smiles at her grandson.

"Remember, Sett," Fadia says, "We must adjust."

"We are going to have one last night together. It is going to be the most special night of your life, one you will never forget," Ahinoam says.

Sett smiles.

"To start with, you are going to eat with the rest of us in the dining hall, and you are going to sit in the king's seat. For one evening, you will be our king."

Sett's brows raise, his eyes grow wide, and his head juts forward. He says nothing.

"I have never seen you speechless before," Uncle Mefiboset says.

"I don't know what to say. Me the king? Me?"

"Yes, for one evening, you will be king of the palace. And after that, you will be king in our hearts."

Sett smiles and hugs his grandmother.

"Thank you, Your Majesty," he says.

"You are welcome, Your Majesty," she replies with a proud smile.

"Now I have arranged for the royal tunic and robe to be shortened so you can wear them tonight. And the crown too. We'll fix it somehow so it does not slip down past your ears."

Everyone leaves, including the nurse, and Sett is left alone.

Bitter sweetness.

He takes hold of his three-footed crutches and works his way around his apartment, swinging his useless feet as they do the stepping for him.

He suddenly remembers his new freedom. *I can go anywhere I want.* Sett opens his door, and his crutches walk him out to the corridor he had not been in for two years. A guard is on each side of the door. They salute their king.

"Uh, which way is it to the stairs?" he asks. "I seem to have forgotten."

"This way, Your Majesty," one of the guards says. "If you will allow me, you can climb onto my back, and I will take you down myself."

Sett grins.

"It will be my pleasure," the guard adds.

Sett hands his crutches to the other guard, and the three go out to the balcony and descend toward the courtyard below.

"Hey, look, everyone!" Uncle Mefiboset says from below. "Our king."

All the people in the courtyard—royalty and servants alike—look up and applaud. When he reaches the bottom step and takes up his crutches, everyone bows low.

No one moves.

Sett looks around, his brow furrowed over his dark eyes. He hears, "Ahem" and notices his uncle peeking and mouthing the words he is supposed to say.

"Oh, yes," Sett says in his most manly voice. "You may rise." Everyone returns to a standing position.

Sett looks over at his uncle. "Uh, I believe I would like to go to the stables and perhaps take a ride into town, into Gibeon."

Mefiboset smiles and indicates for the new king to go ahead of him.

Sett expertly swings his legs, trying to keep his drooping feet together, and moves his three-footed crutches, the left one, then the right one, then left, then right, just like substitute feet.

As Mefiboset follows the new king, he motions to some of the guards who have been doubled at each interior and exterior entrance. Mules are saddled, and Sett it swung up onto his by his uncle, who is larger even than the soldiers in the royal guard.

Four soldiers ride ahead, two by two. Four soldiers ride behind. And one soldier rides on each side of Sett and Mefiboset.

Slowly they make their way down and through the town surrounding the palace. People step aside and bow. They are not sure what is happening other than the fact that the king they are used to seeing is not the one on the king's mule.

One boy does not bow. He is close to Sett's age, or perhaps a little older. He glares at the king and raises his fist at him until someone next to him forces him down onto his knees.

The entourage continues through the city until it is at the bottom of the Gibeon hill. They ride out into the country a little way.

"Trees are fun," Sett tells his uncle.

"I guess they are," comes the reply.

"Without trees, nobody could climb them or swing from them or have fun under them. Besides, what would everything look like without bunches of trees?"

"I cannot imagine," Mefiboset says. "A desert, I guess."

"Well, that will never happen here. Our land will always be full of all kinds of trees for people to play in."

"Shall we return to the palace now, Your Majesty?" Mefiboset says.

They turn and go back the way they had come.

"My people do not look very happy," Sett says.

"Your grandfather tried to exterminate all the Gibeonites a long time ago. They never forgot it."

"Well, I can see why. Did you know the servants around the palace call Grandfather Mad Saul? I'll bet you didn't know I knew that, but I do. I know a lot of things you don't think I do. You'd be surprised."

"Yes, Your Majesty. I am sure I would be."

They arrive back at the palace, and Sett is returned to the third floor to dress for the royal banquet.

Two hours later, Sett is wearing a royal tunic in red, a royal robe in purple, and a crown that is heavy and awkward on his head.

"Do I have to wear the crown?" he asks his grandmother, who has joined him in his apartment. She is wearing a gold tunic and red robe with yellow fringe. She has on a gold necklace, earrings, armband, and rings. On her head is her queen's crown.

"No, of course not. I will have it placed on a pillow, and someone will follow you with it. Now, there is something else you need to do before we eat. Come with me."

A guard takes Sett onto his back and follows the Queen Mother to the second floor, then stops.

"Sett, I am going to take you into the king's apartment, the one my beloved Saul lived in. There is a door from it that leads to a very special room. I want you to go through that door with me."

"Yes, Grandmother."

"You will not need your crutches. Two of the guards will be on each side of you and will lift you by your elbows so you can make a dignified entrance into your throne room."

"Throne room, Grandmother? You're going to let me sit on the king's throne?"

She smiles and puts her hand under the boy king's chin. "I'm not only going to let you, but I am going to insist upon it. I will walk out first and sit on my queen's throne. Then you will come out and sit next to me on the king's throne."

"Yes, my lady."

Ahinoam leans over and kisses her king on the cheek. "Shall we?"

Trumpets blare on the other side of the door. The procession begins, and when Sett is escorted out, he sees a grand stairway six man-length wide leading all the way down from the second-floor throne room to the courtyard. The family and guests are assembled there waiting for him.

As soon as he sees them, they all bow deeply and wait for a signal from the trumpets that they may rise. He looks over at his throne. It is made of copper-colored alabaster and is the largest chair he has ever seen. Next to it is the smaller green-colored alabaster queen's throne on one side and a crown prince's throne on the other side.

Once the king is settled on his throne, he is given the gold scepter with ruby and pearl tip.

The horns blast, and his audience rises. They call out to Sett in unison.

"Hail to the king. Hail to King Mefiboset. Long live the king."

"Hail to the king. Hail to King Mefiboset. Long live the king."

"Hail to the king. Hail to King Mefiboset. Long live the king."

Sett tries not to grin. He does, anyway.

He looks over at his grandmother, and she winks. He does not realize she is imagining her Jonathan sitting on that throne. *Sett looks so much like his father.*

As the crowd below calls out their declaration of fealty, Sett leans on his chair arm closest to the queen.

"I always wondered where these big steps led to," he tells her. "There were always doors at the top of them. I never knew."

"Now you do, my child. Now you do."

She gives the signal, and the horns blare again.

"Is your scepter out? Hold it out a little way," she coaxes.

One by one, people below in the courtyard ascend the grand stairs, approach their king, bow, touch the tip of his scepter, then return to the courtyard.

When the ceremony is completed, Sett looks over at his grandmother.

"Whew. I didn't know being a king was such hard work. Am I going to be allowed to eat?"

"And that is what is next. We will leave out the back door into the king's apartment, the way we came in, and a soldier will take you down a back way to the banquet hall. Everything is ready for us."

Sett and his grandmother enter the banquet hall, and everyone rises. He looks up at his grandmother, and she smiles. "Take your seat in your grandfather's chair. Remember, you are the king now."

Sett is seated, and everyone else sits. As the food is brought out, he puts his hands on the arms of the king's large chair made of alabaster like the throne. He looks around at the tall ceiling with colorful tiles all the way up to the pinnacle, and the marvelous flickers of light coming down from the large golden olive oil lamps suspended from the ceiling everywhere.

Most of all, he looks out at everyone who has come to honor him as their king. "Grandmother, I am so happy."

The evening goes by like a fantasy. One that Sett never dared to dream. But now a reality. At least for one day, a reality. King for a day. A taste of what might have been.

That night Sett does not sleep. Or perhaps he does. He plays over and over in his head what had happened over the past few hours, what it had been like to be king. *I never, ever want to forget.*

Now it is daylight. Now reality returns. Uncle Mefiboset shakes Sett. "Okay, Your Majesty. It's time to rise and get ready to leave."

Sett stirs and raises the covers over his head.

"For your safety, you must go."

He puts the covers back down and swings his legs around. He wipes unmanly tears from his eyes.

"I don't want to leave you and Grandmother and everyone else."

"I know," Mefiboset says, sitting next to his nephew and putting a big, bulky arm over his shoulder. "But we must protect your life until we know how much of a threat David feels you are to him."

"Is he going to be king of everything now?"

"Yes, I am sure that is what will happen. Now, you must get ready to go. The donkeys are already loaded. We waited until the last moment for you."

"Where is Grandmother?"

"She is downstairs in the courtyard waiting for you."

Sett looks over at the royal clothes he had worn the day before. He knows he cannot take them with him. He dresses in a plain tunic and robe, and Mefiboset offers him his back one last time.

Down in the courtyard, Sett and his grandmother share the same bench.

"I will miss you, my child, my king. But we will be together again someday."

"Promise?"

"Promise. Now Fadia is out there waiting for you. Obey her, even though you are as tall as her. You are only eleven years old. Your body may be grown, but you must give your mind a chance to catch up."

Sett grins.

"Besides, you are not nearly through growing. Your grandfather was ten hand spans tall. Your father was too. You will probably reach that same height. Your mother was a tall woman."

"I never knew my mother."

"She was a beautiful and gentlewoman. It broke your father's heart when she died giving birth to you. But he took comfort having you to help fill the void. Now, it is time."

Mefiboset hands his nephew his crutches.

Sett kisses his grandmother and makes his way toward the outer gate.

"Hurry, Sett," Fadia says. "We must leave while we can. Once again, we must adjust."

Uncle Mefiboset helps him up on his donkey. "This is the last time you will be helped. The donkey is low enough you should be able to climb on and off okay. You have strong arms.

"This is also the last time you will be guarded. Keep an alert eye on your surroundings. Do what Fadia tells you, even if you are bigger."

The three donkeys go out the east gate toward the Jordan River. They do not hurry.

"May Jehovah be your guardian!" Mefiboset calls out.

Within a day, Sett and his nurse are on the other side of the Jordan. They turn south to follow it toward the Red Sea.

Slowly they travel. One day. Two days. Three days. Four.

"I see a caravan up ahead," Fadia says. "Perhaps they can tell us how much farther we need to go."

Fadia, Sett, and their supply donkey approach the leader of the caravan. He sees them and pulls on the reins of his Arabian palomino. He is heavily tanned, has leathery skin and a hoarse voice.

"May I be of service to you? What are you doing out here in the desert traveling alone?"

"Oh, we're not alone," Fadia says. "Well, not exactly."

"Where are you headed?"

"Just south of here a little way. To my home town, Madain Saleh. I have family there. They are probably traveling north to meet us. They are probably almost here now."

"Is it food that you need?"

"Uh, yes. That is what we need."

The caravan leader turns and looks down the procession.

"See that man with the camel wearing that blue-and-red striped robe? Go see him. He will fix you up."

"Thank you very much," Fadia says, already headed in the direction of the camel and man with the striped robe.

When they arrive, Fadia calls up to the man. "Sir, someone said you have extra food. We need some. We have money and can pay you."

The man in the striped robe smiles and prods his camel to kneel and let him off. He walks around Sett and Fadia, eyeing them and humming.

"Where are you headed?" he asks.

"To my home. It is not very far from here, and some people in my family are probably nearly here to meet us right now."

He puts his hand up to his chin and pulls on his beard.

"Hmmm. I see. Well, I can sell you extra food, but you will have to accompany us to the next oasis. The food is packed very tightly behind my camel's saddle. I think there is an oasis not far from here. Is that satisfactory with you?"

"Of course," Fadia replies, her voice low.

The man in the striped robe remounts his camel and resumes heading toward the oasis. Fadia, Sett, and their supply donkey travel beside him.

As promised, they arrive at an oasis about the time the sun turns red for the evening.

"Wait here," the man in the striped robe says.

He walks forward, and they can tell he is speaking to the caravan leader. A bag of money is shoved at the caravan leader.

The man in the striped robe walks back to Fadia and Sett. He has in his hand a long heavy chain. He wraps one end around Fadia's waist and locks it, then wraps the other end around Sett.

"He drove a hard bargain, but I decided your youth was in your favor."

Fadia and Sett stare at the man in horror.

"You are now my slaves."

# 5 ~ INTO THE UNKNOWN

As they ride in the wrong direction to an unknown destination, Fadia moves her donkey close to Sett.

"Once again, Sett, we must adjust. So, no matter what, do not let them know you can't walk," she whispers.

"But I can walk," he replies.

"You know what I mean. If they find out you cannot walk, they will kill you and leave you out in the desert for the vultures. Also, keep doing what you have been doing: Don't talk. Let me do the talking. I know how Arabians think. After all, I am Arabian."

"You are?"

Night arrives.

"Uh, sir," Fadia says, "we have a tent in our supplies. Would you mind if we slept in it?"

"Just don't get your chains tangled up and choke yourselves," the man in the striped robe says. He looks over at Sett. "Well, get down, boy, and help your mother set up the tent."

"Uh, he isn't feeling well," Fadia says. "Of course, it is just temporary. I will set up the tent and help him off the donkey. He should be fine in a few days."

A week passes. The caravan has picked up a few new travelers and lost a few. Still, it trudges across the desert.

"The oases are as big as villages in some places but just large enough for an inn in other places," Sett says. "Why do you think there are more trees in some places than others?”

"Maybe the wood was needed for ships. Or to panel walls. Or make furniture.”

"Where do trees come from?”

"They come from seeds.”

"Well, why don't they plant tree seeds when they cut trees down instead of letting the land become desert? I don't like deserts.”

"You ask too many questions, Sett.”

"Hey, quit talking down there,” the man in the striped robe calls down from his camel.

Another week. On they travel eastward.

"We're out of food,” Fadia whispers to Sett. "We don't dare complain.”

"That's easy for you because you're so small,” Sett whispers.

"We're the same size,” she snaps back.

"But I'm a man, and men need more food than women.”

"You're only eleven. You may be big for your age, but you are still eleven. And don't forget it.”

Their owner on the camel glares down at them, and Fadia bursts out in a song.

"All that singing can be saved for later, you two. So shut up.”

Week three. Still traveling. Still slowly making their way east to an unknown place and unknown future.

The man in the striped robe gives them food. "Can't let you get skinny.”

The wind continues to pick up. Sett and Fadia pull up their robes to cover their heads and protect their eyes. It is quieter than usual in the caravan.

Miniature cyclones pop up around them. Everyone watches and hopes they do not grow and the sand engulf them.

More wind. The sky turns blue-brown, then solid brown.

Blowing. Whistling. Howling.

The caravan leader pulls out and gallops back along the parade of travelers.

"Down, everyone. Down!"

Fadia jumps off her donkey. Sett slides off his and down to the ground. They urge their three donkeys down. Two oblige while the third stays standing, but with his eyes closed. They huddle together, heads down, and wait to be buried.

On it comes. The unrelenting wind and sand. It hits bare skin they had forgotten to cover, and stings. It engulfs their world like a dragon running over them.

Eyes closed. Lips pressed under. Head ducked.

They wait. Everyone waits. Beyond human control, they wait.

Fadia prays to her goddess of protection, Al-Uzza, of Madain Saleh. Sett prays to his one God, Jehovah, of Israel that his father and grandmother had told him about.

The wind is less noisy, and Sett dares look up. "Fadia, I think it's gone."

Fadia stands and looks around, as does everyone else. *I've got to get him off the ground before anyone notices.*

She sees the crutches hidden in the folds of the tent still on the donkey. She gets them to Sett, then stands between him and the man in the striped robe, so he does not see how Sett gets on his donkey.

Week five.

"How are your feet?" Fadia asks after they crawl out of their tent one morning. "Are you checking them for cuts and scrapes?"

"Yes, ma'am."

"How about hot spots? Do any parts feel hot down deep at the bone when you touch them?"

"No. No hot spots."

"Did you pick up any thorns or anything like that yesterday?"

"Oh, I forgot to check for that."

"You know you need to be vigilant. Without feeling in your feet, you have to rely on what you see and what you feel with your hands. You know that."

"Yes, I know. But sometimes I get tired of checking all the time."

"Here is some oil. Put it on your feet before you put your boots on."

"It's a good thing my feet can't feel anything. Otherwise, they would get too hot."

"Well, you will never be able to wear sandals. Too dangerous for you."

"I know. I know."

They are both quiet while Sett does his early morning foot check. He looks over at his nurse.

"Thanks for making me do this. I think I'd skip it a lot if you weren't prodding me."

"That's what I'm for," Fadia says.

Week six.

"We are almost there, young lady," their new owner says. "But, of course, you do not know where 'there' is. We are approaching the great city of Ur—surrounded by rivers and canals, and crowned by the Indian Sea."

"Oh, this is the land of our ancestor, Abraham," Sett says, forgetting Fadia's warning.

"You can talk, after all, boy. Well, a lot of people's ancestors came from here. It is a very old city. It has been here one or maybe two thousand years. No one knows for sure. We just know it is old."

Fadia watches, trying to hide her panic. *What are they going to do to Sett as soon as they learn he is crippled?*

Toward the end of the day, they notice seagulls flying overhead. The air is cooler. Some of the animals in the caravan raise their heads to sniff the new air.

Just before sunset, they see a tower. They know they have arrived. Sett is told it is called a ziggurat.

The order is given for everyone to camp for the night. Sett does not sleep. Or if he does, he dreams he does not.

*Where am I?*

Morning comes. There is more talk than usual. And laughter. And chatter. It does not take long to break camp. No need for more supplies. They have arrived.

As they draw nearer the city, the tower grows larger. Now they see a wide bridge over a river surrounding the city. On the other side of the bridge is a wide gate with watchtowers on both sides.

Sett looks both ways, trying to estimate the size of the city. He cannot see the end of it either way. It seems to be almost round.

As they pass through the gate, they realize the wall is as thick as three or four city streets. On their right are shops in a bazaar. Over to their left, they see a harbor.

At this point, people in the caravan separate. The man in the striped robe calls down to Sett and Fadia.

"The slave market is right ahead. Now is your chance to show off."

"But I thought we were your slaves," Sett blurts out before Fadia can stop him.

"Yes and no. I bought you so I can resell you. It's my business. Now, put on your best smiles and show off your muscles and anything else that will tantalize buyers to pay me more than it cost me to buy you. Okay, here we are."

As the man in the striped robe urges his camel to kneel, Sett and Fadia realize they will have to go up steps to a platform. A crowd is already gathering.

"Hurry," Fadia whispers. "Get up on there before anyone notices your crutches. Then I'll stand by you to hold you up and put your crutches behind me. You can lean on me up there."

"Well, look at that, would you?" the man in the striped robe says, grinning. "I've never seen slaves so anxious to get sold."

The auction begins with a woman and baby. The auctioneer makes her turn in a circle, then throw the baby to him so people can see more of her.

"My baby!" she screams.

"Ten copper coins," someone calls out.

"Twenty."

"One hundred copper coins."

"A silver coin."

"Sold to the man with the silver coin."

"I don't want the baby. Throw it in the river."

The mother screams, her new owner chains her hands behind her, and she disappears down the street in the direction of the high tower.

"Now, here is a young man who is tall and robust, and look at the muscles on those arms. I'll bet he could handle the heaviest sword made with one hand, and the longest spear in the other. Hold your arms out, young man."

Sett extends his arms and Fadia strains. She can hold him up no longer. Sett slumps to the floor of the platform.

"Get up, you scoundrel," the man in the striped robe shouts from the street below. "Get up!"

The auctioneer stares down at Sett, then grins.

"It seems our friend here is trying to pass on a worthless piece of flesh. Get him out of here, and do it now! Why didn't I bring my dagger? Someone else will have to eliminate him."

Sett remembers his lessons back in the palace. He looks at Fadia and waits for her signal. She nods her head while handing him his hidden crutches. With strong arms, he propels his legs and useless feet above his head. Fadia steps aside.

"I said, get him out of.... What?"

Sett tips his head up and looks around at his audience. He grins broadly and walks upside down on his crutches around the platform.

Fadia, too, grins, claps her hands, and looks around at the gathered crowd. Others catch on and join in the applause. Now everyone in the audience is clapping and laughing.

Others in the surrounding market hear the

commotion and wander over in hopes of joining in the fun.

"Look at that!"

"It's a miracle."

"He's walking upside down."

"That's the best show I have ever seen."

"Hey, I'll give you one silver coin for him."

"I'll give you five."

"I'll bump you up to ten."

The crowd grows. Sett strains to keep up his strength and his performance.

"I'll give you thirty silver coins."

"Seventy."

"One hundred. One hundred silver coins." The voice is booming, and everyone recognizes it.

Garash, owner of the gold mine and married to the beautiful Eshida of local nobility, walks forward and hands the money to the auctioneer who, in turn, hands part of it to the man in the striped robe.

"You can jump down now," Garash growls at Sett. "My chariot is over there. I assume you can walk upright too."

"Yes, sir. But the woman with me..."

"I don't care if she is your wife, your mother, or your sister. I don't want her. She isn't worth a second look. Forget her."

Sett looks back at Fadia. "But she's my nur... She's my trainer. She shows me how to do my tricks. And, he forms a broad grin, "she keeps my feet from looking funny."

Garash pauses and looks back at Fadia. "What else can you do besides keep this young man's feet from looking funny?"

"I can make incense. My people are famous for it."

"I'll throw her in free," the man in the striped robe says. "After all, you made me a rich man today."

Garash pulls the large blue shawl with gold fringe up from his elbow and puts it back on his shoulder. He is careful not to brush it against his carefully-curled long beard.

"Okay, you can come. But, if my wife does not like you, you get fed to the sharks down at the sea. Is that clear?"

Fadia does not smile, nor does she look at Sett. "Yes, sir."

"Now, you two are going to walk behind me. You cannot escape, so do not try. My chariot is over there." He stares at Sett. "And do not expect any special treatment. You will not ride in the chariot. You will walk behind it or whatever it is you do to get from one place to the other."

"What about our three mules?"

"Bring them with you. But, you are not allowed to ride them. Is that clear?"

As Sett and his nurse make their way into a future confounded with the unknown and unexpected, Fadia whispers, "Once again, Sett, we must adjust."

The big man climbs into his four-wheeled gilded chariot with a high front and hitched to two horses. Without looking back, he heads closer to the ziggurat tower that is three times higher than King Saul's palace and twice as long and wide. There is a wall around the tower, and some other large buildings which Sett assumes are palaces or temples.

They turn right at the wall and proceed past it until they come to some larger houses. Their new master stops in front of the one with a gold-plated gate and statues of lions on both sides. He pounds on the double gate, and is let in by a man whom Sett assumes is another slave. The walls are a full man length thick.

"Get these two new ones settled in. Then I want them put to work in the kitchen area. He can grind wheat for now, and she can cook."

Sett and Fadia stare at the opulence that is more than that of King Saul. They enter an outer courtyard with blue lapis lazuli and white crystal tiles covering the pavement. To their left are stables and chariots separated from view by a wall and red columns. To their right is a receiving room and banquet hall with more red columns down the middle of it. The ceiling is so high, Sett and Fadia can hardly see it.

"What have we here?" A thin woman walks into the main courtyard just as her husband hands the reins of the chariot and horses to yet another slave. She is wearing a green tunic and long red fringed shawl, and gold jewelry around her neck, arms, hands, and fingers.

"Well, dear, you have your entertainment for tomorrow night's banquet. Now you won't have to worry about the party being dull."

"Which one? Her or him?"

"Him. Do your trick for my wife," he tells Sett. Sett complies.

"Is that all he can do? If so, I don't want him."

"Are you never happy, Eshida?"

"We shall see, dear. If the guests are happy, I shall be happy. And what about her? I don't need any more cooks."

"She's a special cook. She can make incense. Tomorrow, one of the maids can take her to the city to pick out what she needs. If Ur doesn't have it, we'll send for it in India. Just whatever she needs. Then your house will be the envy of the neighborhood as the scents waft through the air."

"You're not fooling me," she says. "Our air does not need wafting."

"Well, she is also the boy's trainer. We shall see what other tricks he can do tomorrow at the banquet. Now, I'm hungry."

The next day is busy for everyone and is full of strange new customs and names and clothing and ways of doing things.

Fadia is able to find what she needs at the bazaar and prepares the incense to be burned at the banquet. Sett is given a bright red loincloth to wear since it will show when he is upside down, and a short blue tunic tied at the waist, so it does not fall over his head and blind him. He requests and is given a long piece of green linen that he wraps around both feet, so people do not see their deformity.

He practices his tricks and tries new ones. *Will it be enough?*

Early evening comes, and guests arrive. Sett is kept in a small room with other slaves in the back of the house.

Then it is time for his performance. He makes his way across the inner family courtyard—similar to the outer one, but smaller and with gold plating on the walls, then on to the outer courtyard for receiving guests. As he approaches the banquet hall, he rises up onto his crutches and enters.

"And here he is now," Garash calls out. "Just look at him perform the impossible."

Applause. Laughter. Delight.

Sett hears a harp in the background as he makes his way between the low tables and around the red columns going across the middle of the large hall. He continues until he has passed by every table. Then he starts back the way he had come.

"Is that all he can do?" someone calls out.

"He's getting a little boring."

*Oh, no. What if I am fed to the sharks?*

Although he had not practiced it for long, Sett shifts his weight onto just one crutch and holds the other crutch up so it is parallel to his raised legs.

Renewed applause. Renewed laughter. Renewed delight.

*The sharks go hungry tomorrow,* Sett tells himself.

Then the silence again. Silence except for the harp.

*Quick. Think of something.*

He makes his way over to the harp, lowers himself, and whispers, "Can you follow me?"

The harpist nods.

The grandson of King Saul, now far away from home, sits on a table nearest the harpist and raises his arms toward the multi-colored tiled ceiling so high he can hardly see it.

*There is a hero big and tall.*
*He's the strongest of them all.*
*He will never make you sad*

*Cause Jonathan's my dad.*

"He sings! He's a singer and a trick walker both," someone calls out.

"Garash, where did you get this boy?"

"Can I borrow him next week when my wife's family comes for a visit?"

"Can he sing while standing on his head?"

"Can he perform for our patron god, Nanna, or his daughter, Innana,, over at the temple?"

"Hold on, everyone," Garash says, raising his hands. "For now, he is exclusively for my wife and I. If I ever decide to share him, it will be with the god Nanna.

"By the way," Esheda announces, "my daughter, Thura, just may be the next high priestess for Nanna. After all, she is royalty on my side of the family. So, yes, I believe he will end up singing over at the temple, and in my daughter's palace.

"Oh, and do you smell that amazing aroma?" The guests raise their heads and look at the many large gold lamps hanging from the ceiling and lighting the hall with five wicks in each of them. "That incense was made by his companion. This day, we have indeed been blessed by the god of the great city of Ur."

# 6 ~ THE TREES

"**I**n the three years I have been here, I have never heard my ancestor mentioned. I had always thought he was rich and powerful in Ur."

Sett is sitting at the wheel grinding barley into flour for the day's supply of bread.

"Who was your ancestor?" Utul asks, turning his own grinding wheel.

"Terah. He had a son, Abraham, who emigrated to a land about three months ride from here. His descendants became known as Hebrews. That's what I am."

"You're right. We never heard of him."

It is a clear day, but the air is dusty from the ever-present sand blowing in and around the city. Sett is grateful for the many trees planted along the streets of the city for beauty and breaking the effects of the hot wind.

"I think my ancestor, Abraham, was mad when he left. He didn't like the city's gods. Maybe the priests were after him for blasphemy and were trying to kill him."

"And maybe they destroyed all documents with his name on them."

"He must have really made them mad. Ha, ha. Do you think we have enough flour ground up yet?"

"No," Utul replies. "They're having company tonight."

"Oh, I forgot." Sett is quiet for a moment. "Do you know what else I forgot? My Hebrew holy book says the first humans in the world lived in a grand garden where the Tigris and Euphrates Rivers meet. Don't they meet south of here, just before emptying into the sea?"

"What do you have to do after this?" Utul asks, only half-listening to his friend.

"Master Garash wants me to get the gold plating replaced on my performance crutches. It's starting to fall off.

"Are you still doing those tricks with your crutches for their company?"

"Ha! Not only that, but they are hiring me out now. As though the owner of the biggest gold mine anywhere needs the money. Have you ever been to where the rivers meet?"

"Yeah, once. Why? Do you want to see it?"

"Do you think you could get us a ride?"

"Don't they still have the three donkeys you brought with you? Why don't you ask the master if you can use a couple of them some afternoon?"

Four days later, Sett has obtained permission to use the three donkeys he and Fadia had arrived with. It is now mid-afternoon.

"Thank you for including me in your little excursion," Fadia says. "You may not have known it, but, after listening to you and remembering what your family used to believe in, I have decided to reject the goddess I used to worship and only believe in your Jehovah as the creator of heaven and earth."

Sett grins. "You have? Why did you never tell me?"

"I thought you knew. So, if God put the first people on earth near here, I would like to see it."

The three leave out the northeast gate of the city, next to the fortress. They cross the bridge and follow the river south. They work their way past the ancient city of Eridu.

They are careful to stay out of the frequent marshes between them and the Tigris River which they can see to the west.

Utul talks about the weather, donkeys, crops and whatever he can think of. Sett and Fadia are quiet.

*We are about to walk on holy ground,* Sett tells himself.

*We are about to enter the Garden of God.*

"Well, there it is," Utul finally announces. "This is where the Tigris and Euphrates meet."

Sett looks everywhere in front and behind him. He looks to both sides. He strains to find it. He juts his head a little forward as though it will help him see better. His eyes squint. His brow furrows. His upper lip curls. His heartbeat increases.

Still he looks and searches and stares. His breathing becomes short. His intake of breath becomes stronger as though his lungs are starving.

"But...."

Still the searching.

"You must be wrong, Utul. That's not the Tigris. That's another river. Someone must have changed its name from something else."

"Oh, no!" Fadia cries out. She slides off her donkey and walks, taking small steps at first. Then faster. Then running. Running in circles her eyes fixed on the clouds above, her arms wide apart.

"No! No!"

She stops and goes over to Sett, still on his donkey. She says nothing.

Sett slides off his donkey, supports himself with his crutches and lets Fadia, now a foot shorter than him, hug him around the neck.

Both in tears, they turn and make their way side by side to the point where the waters of the Tigris and Euphrates meet. They stare.

It is gone.

All gone.

Nothing left of the Garden of God.

"Why?" Sett asks in a whisper. "What happened?"

Silence a little longer.

Sett makes his way along the river bank. *Let me see. I wonder where the flowers were. And the fruit trees for their meals. And the Tree of Life. And...*

"Where are the trees?" he calls over to Utul. "There are no trees."

"I don't know," Utul replies, still on his donkey. "There haven't been any trees here since I was born. I don't remember anyone ever saying there were trees here."

"But there used to be. Who cut down the trees? And why didn't they replace them?"

Sett makes his way a little farther, pauses, and works his way down his three-footed crutches to sit in the empty place that had been the delight of God, the home of Adam and Eve.

He puts his hand on the sand and slides it around as though, in the process, he can make the former glory reappear.

*Did they actually walk here? Did they actually smell the flowers and eat the fruit and sit in the shade of the trees here?*

He puts his head down on the sand as though embracing it. He closes his eyes and imagines walking and talking with Adam and Eve on this very spot, talking and laughing and sharing.

When he opens his eyes, Utul is standing over him.

"Are you all right?" Utul asks.

Sett does not speak. He takes hold of his crutches and with strong, muscular arms, lifts himself back to a standing position. He wipes his eyes with the edge of his sleeve and turns toward his donkey.

"If they needed those holy trees so bad, why didn't they at least plant more trees here? Why let the Garden become desert?

"I do not know," Utul says, walking beside him.

A scream.

Sett jerks his head around. "What was that? Where is Fadia?"

He sees Fadia on the floor of the desert. Utul rushes to her, squats, and puts her head in his lap.

"Fadia, what happened?" Sett calls out, making his

way to her.

"A snake got her," Utul replies.

Sett whistles and all three donkeys wander over to him.

"Fadia, do you think you can get up there if Utul and I help?"

"I think so," she whispers.

She lets go of her ankle where the snake had bitten her and the two men take hold of an arm. Utul grabs the reins of the closest donkey to bring it closer. Util lifts her torso while Sett swings her legs up onto the animal.

Sett gets up onto his own ride and draws it close enough to his former nurse that he can reach over and give her enough support she does not fall off.

He takes one last look at the deserted and desecrated Garden of Eden, and turns his attention back to the living.

They head north, both men watching Fadia closely as she weeps and groans in pain.

As she grows weaker, Utul rides to the other side of her and provides additional support.

Sett sings. With his translucent baritone voice, he sings. No longer the boyish bell-clear voice of three years earlier when he first began entertaining his master and mistress. Now the voice of a young man.

> *God of Eden, please do hear me.*
> *Come aid your wounded child.*
> *So she can continually*
> *Give love that's undefiled.*

"We have just passed Eridu," Utul tells the petite woman struggling to stay alive.

"Stay strong, Fadia," Sett says. "Remember how you always told me, 'We must adjust'?"

They ride along in silence, choosing to go slowly so as to slow down the poison in her system, rather than rush and cause her more pain and distress.

"I remember when I injured my feet. I'll bet you didn't know that. But I do. I did not understand what was going on. You were just trying to save me."

*God of heaven and earth, keep my nurse alive.*

"Then all the pain that followed as the doctors tried to heal my feet. But you stayed by me and even let me cry. You didn't try to force me to be brave. And that in itself made me brave."

*Jehovah, I cannot lose her.*

"You blamed yourself for my injuries. I never understood the guilt you must have borne for me all these years."

*Lord of all, heal her.*

"Now I think I know. I let you come out here into the desert where that serpent found you, just like it found Eve so long ago. But this time, you are going to outwit the serpent. Aren't you, Fadia?"

Sett looks over at her. Her head is bobbing and her eyes are closed.

*Please God, let her only be asleep.*

At last, they arrive back at Ur and their master's house. They shout and the gatekeeper lets them in.

"Mistress!" Utul shouts. "It's Fadia. A snake got her!"

He slides off his donkey. Utul and the gatekeeper ease Fadia off hers. Just as they lower her to the ground, Esheda enters the outer courtyard.

"Hurry, bring her back here."

She directs them to the inner courtyard and a side room used for traveling guests. "Go get my daughter Thura," she says to the gatekeeper. "Hurry!"

"They should have made her priestess of Nanna. She has healing powers. They knew that."

Sett and Utul do not reply. Sett pushes the hair out of his Fadia's eyes. "Shhh, my little one," he says, reminiscent of the days when she had soothed him.

"Just because she is only half nobility," Esheda laments, "they chose her cousin instead. They will be sorry someday. Oh, there you are Thura. Fadia has been bitten by a serpent."

Sett moves aside. Thura kneels, stares a moment, then spits on the wound. "My saliva will heal her," she pronounces. "She will be up and mixing her incense by tomorrow."

"Thank you, daughter," Mistress Esheda says. Now, everyone, back to work."

Sett looks up at his mistress but does not speak. She understands.

"Well, okay. But we are having company again tonight and you will be expected to entertain."

"Yes, mistress," he says.

Now they are left alone. Sett hums. He hums the songs she had comforted him with all those many years while he was growing up and had so many problems to overcome.

"My little one," he sometimes whispers, his big bulky fourteen-year-old frame now dwarfing hers.

Unmanly tears come to his eyes. "How can I survive this complicated world without you, Faddy. You were more than my nurse. You were the mother I never knew. If it hadn't been for you and Uncle Mee...."

Someone opens the door and he sees it is dark out in the courtyard.

"Would you like something to eat?" one of the maids asks.

Sett looks at her with swollen eyes and shakes his head. She closes the door back and he resumes his vigil.

"Remember, Faddy, when you helped me design my crutches? You were brilliant. Everyone else wanted me to balance myself on one stick. You said there should be three sticks at the bottom so it could stand on its own like three feet. You were always so smart. You always thought of everything, my Faddy."

He hums again.

And prays.

"Shhh, my little one," he says whenever she groans.

Then all is quiet.

At dawn, his nurse, Fadia, dies.

Someone opens the door and sees him with his head on her lap.

Within the hour, there is a brief funeral held by the other slaves. The mistress provides a linen cloth to wrap her in. Sett is given help putting her on her donkey for the last time. He takes the reins, leading her out of the city on his own donkey, and across the bridge they had crossed together the day before.

Slowly he rides down the same road leading to the holy spot they had walked together only hours earlier.

He passes Eridu. On he goes as the Tigris and Euphrates Rivers draw closer to each other.

Once again he arrives where the two rivers join. He slides off his donkey, works his way over to Fadia, and slides her gently to the ground.

He has brought a shovel. It seems hopeless, but he must try, just as everything else in the world sometimes seems hopeless.

He sits and shovels a place in the sand and the spot is quickly filled with more sand. He digs deeper so he can get to the dry clay below the sand. With muscled arms used to supporting his entire bulky weight, he shovels deeper and deeper down into what was once the Garden of Eden for the sake of another victim of a serpent.

He remembers back to two other deaths that had occurred when he was almost too young to understand.

*Father, I wish I could have buried you. Grandfather too. I no longer remember what either of you looked like. I just remember you looked like giants next to other people. If only I could have buried you.*

Just as the sun reaches the pinnacle of the sky, Sett has the grave dug. He sits in the sand next to his nurse and kisses her on the cheek through the linen strips she had been wrapped in that morning. He scoots her over to the opening and, as gently as he can, lowers her into her grave.

He covers his nurse and hums one of the lullabies she had used to sing to him.

He surveys the surrounding barrenness, then lifts his eyes to the clouds beginning to turn pink.

"Can you ever bring joy back to your garden, God? Can Fadia's presence bring that joy back? And your trees? Your precious trees that once gave life? Will you ever plant them here again?"

Sett crosses the bridge into the grand city of Ur just before the gates are closed for the night.

When he arrives back at his master's home, he approaches Garash.

"Sir, she taught me a little about making incense. I will try to do her job and mine both."

"We shall see. In the meantime, my guests will begin coming any time now. Put on your costume. And did you get your performing crutches regilded? I hope so. Now go and ready yourself. Be quick."

Just as Sett finishes changing into his colorful costume and repairing the crutch that is losing its gold plating, a servant knocks on his door.

"They are here. They are wanting to laugh. Hurry."

Sett makes his way out of the room he shares with other slaves, into the inner family courtyard, then to the outer courtyard, and into the banquet room.

The guests applaud and laugh.

Sett laughs with them. Inside, he weeps.

# 7 ~ THE JEWELER

"**H**ey, Sett! What are you doing in the bazaar today?"

"Mind your own business," he calls back to the potter. "I'm on a mission."

"Well, come here and tell me what your mission is. I won't tell anyone."

"You will spread it all over town. I have known you five years and you can't fool me."

"Aw, c'm on. I'll share part of my lunch with you."

Sett works his way over to the potter's booth. "It had better be good."

"Would a peach satisfy you?"

Sett smiles, grabs the peach, leans against the counter and takes a slurpy bite.

"So, what's the big secret?"

"Well, tomorrow is my master's wife's birthday."

"And?"

"And he sent me to pick out some gold jewelry for her."

"You are in the wrong part of town for that, friend. Turn right at this corner, and go closer to the temple complex of Nanna."

"I've never been inside," Sett says, taking another bite of his peach.

"You haven't even climbed up the temple tower whenever the Euphrates flooded?"

"No. I never wanted to. I just climbed on top of my

master's house. There's nothing in that tower anyway but dirt."

"True. But it is a magnificent monument don't you agree? Up there it can be seen by the whole city—the magnificent temple to Nanna at the top."

Sett throws his peach pit down on the ground, kicks it with his crutch, grins goodbye to his friend, and turns at the corner as instructed.

As he draws closer to the shops nearest the palace of the priestess, he notices the shops are better built with a better quality of bricks. Some have even been painted.

He passes a shop that sells perfume. Another shop sells pearls imported from India. Then he sees ahead something that stops his heart.

She has long black hair down to her waist, straight but thick eyebrows, full lips, a delicate straight nose, and a smile only for Sett.

He grins and speeds up his progress to her booth.

"Perfect," he says, drawing closer.

"Perfect what?" she asks.

He arrives and looks into her eyes. "You."

She giggles.

"What?"

"I mean your jewelry. It's gold, isn't it?"

"Well, yes."

"Then I have found perfection. Do you make all this jewelry yourself?"

"Not quite. I am apprenticing. Would you like me to show you the ones I made myself?"

"Show me anything, and I will follow."

"Follow? I'm not going anywhere, silly. I'm always here every day."

"Did I say follow? I meant swallow. I just ate a peach. Do you have anything that looks like a peach?"

The young lady giggles again.

"What is your name, by the way? My name is Sett. It's short for Mefiboset. When someone calls me to dinner using my full name, by the time I get there, everyone has already eaten and there's no food left for me. So, I just tell people to call me Sett."

"You are crazy. Well, if you must know," she replies, "my name is Kissara."

"Hmmm. I had an ancestress who lived here and her name was almost the same as yours—Sara. That must be a good omen."

"Okay, this one." She holds up a chain with a round pendant hanging from it. "This one looks like a peach or an apple or a big toe, or...oh, excuse me. I didn't mean to..."

"That's all right," Sett replies. "Neither one of my big toes work. Besides, your necklace looks a lot better than either of my big toes, and I like the way you blush."

"I am not blushing."

"Yes, you are." He reaches up and touches her creamy cheek. "Right there," he moves his hand over to the other cheek, "and right there."

"Are you going to buy something or not?" she says, wrinkling her forehead and glaring at him.

"You're not scaring me," he replies. "I do not take kindly to threats. I refuse to buy anything until I have seen everything you have made."

"They're not all here. Some are still with my mother at home."

Sett quickly files away in his mind that she is a free woman and still living with her parents.

"Then I shall return tomorrow and....uh, oh. Can't come back tomorrow. I've got to buy something today. So, do you have any earrings or finger rings to match your peach necklace?"

"Who are they for? Perhaps I can help you."

"They are for Esheda, wife of Garash."

"Oh. That's who I buy my gold from, or at least my mother does. Let me see. I think Eshcda would rather have this necklace."

She holds up one with several strands, and round

pendants hanging side by side from them all.

"Oh, an entire peach tree," Sett responds. "So, how much is it?"

"With the matching earrings, it will be 500 pieces of silver."

"Hmmm… He gave me 400 pieces of silver. Would you take that?"

"Of course." She holds out a delicate hand, and Sett gives her his entire money pouch.

"I have an alabaster box to put it in. Would you like that too?"

"Yes, but you have wiped out my supply of money."

"Since her birthday is tomorrow, you can come back in two days and pay me for the alabaster box."

"You trust me that much?"

"I trust everyone who likes peaches and has ugly toes," she says.

The necklace and earrings carefully placed in a linen-lined alabaster box, she hands it to him, and he leaves.

"How old are you?" she calls to him.

"Sixteen."

"I'm fourteen."

As Sett passes the pottery shop, he hears the sound of his friend's voice.

"What are you grinning so big for?" he asks Sett.

"Oh, nothing," and keeps going.

That night, Sett decides he is in love. *But she is a free woman and has her health and… Stop that. You have surmounted other things harder than this.*

The day after Esheda's birthday, he approaches her. "Mistress, I have an idea that you may like. I could make extra incense to sell. Of course I would have to go into town more often to buy the ingredients. I could give you all the profit, of course keeping back only that which would be necessary to buy the ingredients."

"What a splendid idea, Sett. Garash does not give me enough household money to have any left over for extras.

When would you like to start?"

"Right now, if you like. I have finished my grinding work for the day."

"Fine. Follow me."

Sett follows her into the counting room where gold and other coins are stored, pours what he will need in a pouch, and smiles.

"Thank you, Sett. We are now in the incense business."

Sett happily makes his way to the potter's shop, turns right, and heads to the gold jewelry shop and his very own Kissara.

"You're back," she says.

"You never did show me everything you made."

"It's not all here. I told you, part of it is still at home."

"Then I shall keep returning every day until I have seen it all."

"But, if I make more every evening at home, you will never see it all."

Sett winks. "Good arrangement, my peach, don't you think?"

Every day thereafter except the Sabbath, Sett returns to Kissara's shop to see what she has for sale.

"Why do you skip one day a week?" she asks one day, twisting a strand of hair around her finger.

"Because I am Hebrew and our God tells us to rest on that day. I can't rest from everything that day, but I do the best I can, and that includes my walks to town."

"I never heard of your God. I thought everyone in Ur was a follower of Nanna. After all, Nanna owns Ur."

"Well, Jehovah God owns the whole world. He made everything in the world, even that gold you make jewelry from."

"That's impossible. One god cannot do everything."

"That is what makes Jehovah God so special: He can and did make everything."

"But that wouldn't leave anything for the other gods to

do."

"That's okay because they don't exist anyway. And you know what else?"

"What?"

"He loves you."

"The gods don't love anyone. Well, they may love their priests, but that's all."

"Jehovah God not only loves you, but he knows your name and everything about you."

"You're so silly. That's impossible."

"You already said that. Well, I've got to buy some spices. See you tomorrow."

One day three months later on one of Sett's visits, Kissara is quiet.

"What's wrong, my peach?"

"I'm too embarrassed to say."

"C'mon. You can tell me."

"That's the problem. It's, well, it's about you."

"Oh. You want to know how my feet got this way. I wasn't born like this, you know."

"Well, yes and no. I have been wondering about your feet. I didn't know you weren't born this way."

"My nurse was running with me one day and dropped me."

"You had a nurse? I thought you were a slave."

"I am now, but I haven't always been."

"Oh, were you in an army that lost a battle with our army, so ended up being our slave?"

"No. We were going down into Arabia to my nurse's home city, and were kidnapped."

"How terrible. You said twice you had a nurse. Where was your mother? Oh, I am prying. I'm sorry."

"That's okay, Kissara. Tomorrow, why don't I try to come a little early so I can tell you about myself?"

"I haven't embarrassed you?"

Sett reaches over and taps the end of her dainty, straight nose. "Not at all, little one."

He turns to leave.

"Oh, and what made you so big? You said you are only sixteen."

"I'll cover that tomorrow too."

That night on his bed, Sett prays once more about his Kissara. "Jehovah, will I lose her tomorrow? Don't let me lose her. I love her."

He does not sleep. Eventually morning comes. Sett does his flour grinding job, puts together spices of his special formula for a new kind of incense, then picks up the pouch of coins always set out for him to replenish his supplies at the bazaar.

When Sett returns to Kissara's shop, she has a customer. He leaves and picks up some spices. When he returns, the customer is gone, but Kissara is crying.

"My little one. What's wrong?" he asks, tapping the end of her nose.

"I thought you had left for good."

"Oh, that will never happen. I will never leave you. I promise. Now, would you like me to tell you about myself out here at your counter, or back where you are?"

She raises the counter so Sett can scoot in, and shows him a seat.

"I am about to tell you some things that may be hard for you to believe. So, before I tell you, will you promise to believe anyway? Promise?"

"What is it? What could be too hard to believe?"

"Kissara, I am a prince."

Her lips parts and she giggles. "You a prince? Hu, hu, ha." She notices he is not smiling. "You are serious, aren't you?"

"Yes, and it is not easy to be a prince. My grandfather was Saul, great Warrior King of all Israel, King of all the Hebrews. My father was his oldest born and was supposed to take over as king next, but he was killed in the same battle his father was. So, that left me. I am the firstborn son of the firstborn son. So, I became the crown prince, the heir apparent to the throne."

He pauses.

"You're a king?" She twists a strand of her dark hair around her finger.

"Well, I was for a day. But no more. While I have been gone, a man named David probably took over as king. That's why my nurse and I were running both times. The first time it was because my father and grandfather were killed and the family thought the Philistines would try to kill me next. That's when she dropped me and my feet died. I was five then."

"You have been, uh, that way for many years?" she asks.

"The second time we ran was after my uncle—who became king instead of me—was killed. My family thought King David would try to kill me, so we tried to escape to Arabia. By then I was eleven. And that's how we ended being kidnapped and brought here instead. It has been five years."

Silence.

"You do believe me, don't you?"

Kissara looks at the floor, then the wall, then back at Sett. "So that's why you always talked with educated words. You really were educated."

"Yes. My education ended when I was eleven, but my nurse taught me things in private after we came here."

"That doesn't explain why you are so big and tall."

"My grandfather was not only a full head taller than everyone else, his shoulders were higher than anyone else's head. When even a tall man stood next to him, he only came up to his arm pit."

"So, your grandfather was kind of a giant, then your father was gigantic too, and you inherited it."

"That's about right."

"And you're a king."

"Not anymore. Just a prince."

She giggles at the floor. "Just a prince, he says."

"I may not even be that anymore. Well, I have to be

going. Tomorrow will be your turn. I don't know anything about you."

Heading to his master's house, Sett does not notice when his potter friend calls out to him as he passes. *It went better than I thought it would. But will she feel the same way tomorrow after she has thought about it? And after she has told her parents?*

The next day after his chores are done, he heads out the gate.

"Wait a moment, young man."

He hears the voice of his master. *Oh, no. He has extra work for me today.*

"I understand you have been helping my wife with a little side business." Garash is not smiling.

"Uh, yes sir. Is that displeasing to you?"

"No. But you need to make more incense. She cannot keep up with the orders."

"Yes, sir. I am going to the bazaar right now."

"Good. Be on your way then. And don't bother grinding barley flour anymore."

"Thank you, sir."

Sett rushes down the street, turning right at the potter's shop, and finally arrives at the jewelry shop. The shutter is closed.

*She is refusing to see me anymore. Her parents have made her move her shop. I'll never find her now.*

"Whew! I am really running late this morning."

He smiles when he hears her lyrical voice and swivels around. He waits while she opens the shutter, raises the counter up, and lets him in.

"Before any customers come, I will tell you about me, though it is boring compared to you. It is only my mother and I. My father died a year ago. My mother and I have tried to keep his business going. She has always made all the jewelry. Now I take care of the shop instead of my father, and help make some of the jewelry. And that's it. No princess, no queen, no assassinations, no kidnappings. Just my mother and me doing the best we can."

"Kissara, my peach," Sett replies with a serious expression, "tomorrow, if I come early right at daybreak, will you take me to meet your mother? I would like to meet her, and I think it is only fair that she meet me. After all, if I am going to make you my wife someday…"

He pauses. It is out in the open. He watches her eyes. He watches to see if she begins wrapping a strand of her hair around her finger. He watches to see if she closes her eyes or frowns or runs away.

"Oh, my Setty. My dear, dear Setty."

Kissara wraps her arms around his waist and lays her head on his chest.

"Do you think your mother will say yes?" Sett asks. "After all, I am a slave."

She looks up at him. "It is not illegal here. We will work out something. We will figure out a way to buy your freedom."

"And my God. Can you believe in my God above all the others who aren't gods at all? People in Ur will not like it."

"Yes, your God will be my God. No matter what."

More weeks go by. Months.

One day, while Sett is in town purchasing his daily supply of incense spices, he hears a low, growly voice.

"Kind sir," the growly voice asks the spice dealer, "you used to have a man here who sold gold jewelry. Is he still in Ur?"

"Excuse me," Sett says. "I am on my way there now. You can go with me. Excuse the crutches. I promise to not slow you down."

"My, you are a big one, boy. I fear you will have to slow down for me."

"Looks like we are about even then. Just turn right, and her shop is up this street."

"Her shop? I am looking for a man."

"He died last year. His wife and daughter are running it now. They have kept the business going and still make fine quality gold jewelry."

They arrive at the shop, and introductions are made.

"Young lady, my name is Machir. I am from Lodebar in the land of Galilee, the northern part of Israel. I am here to…"

"Me too!" Sett says with a wide grin.

"You too, what, young man?"

"I'm from Israel too."

"He was the king," Kissara adds.

"What?" Machir squints his eyes, pulls on his beard, and runs his hand through his hair.

"What did you say, young lady?"

"He was the king," she repeats, not seeing Sett shake his head at her.

Machir steps back and looks up at Sett, who he estimates to be a full head taller than him, despite his fifty-two years. He looks over at the grinning young lady, then back at Sett. He takes hold of the shop counter, and his knuckles turn white.

"Quick, Kissara," Sett say, "hand that stool over the counter."

In a moment, Machir is sitting on the stool in front of the gold jewelry shop. Sett kneels in front of him.

"You," Machir begins, then pauses, "you look just like him."

"Like who?"

"Your father, Crown Prince Jonathan. And your grandfather, King Saul too. Such handsome men they were."

Kissara watches, then giggles. "You were right, after all, Setty."

"Where have you been?" Machir asks. "Everyone thought you were dead."

"That's what they were supposed to think," Sett explains everything. "But I no longer want to go back. Well, I miss my grandmother. And I miss Uncle Mefiboset. And all the others. How are they, anyway?"

"David took over as king, conquered Jebus—they call

it Jerusalem now—and built a palace there. It's above the fortress high up on Mount Zion, where he can see anyone coming from any direction."

"And my family?"

"He took the queen mother—your grandmother—and Saul's mistress Rizpah, and her two sons—your uncles—and moved them into his palace where he can keep an eye on them. Also, your Aunt Mecal, his first wife, is there, and another of your aunts and her sons."

"Everyone is there but me," Sett says.

"You need to go back."

Sett stares at Kissara. "No!"

His objections grow louder. "I won't go. I promised Kissara I would never leave her. No!"

# 8 ~ EMPTY RETURN

At Garash's house, negotiations take place. Machir offers to buy the young man back. Both Garash and Esheda object.

"I will meet your price, whatever it is."

"A thousand pieces of silver," Garash says, knowing Machir cannot meet his demands.

"Fine. I spent many years in Nippur, north of here. Give me a week to go there and come back, and I will have your money for you."

Sett is in his room, shared with the other male slaves, awaiting the outcome and praying. After an hour, his door opens, and Garash walks in.

"It is settled," he says.

"Good. I can stay here with you."

"I am afraid not. I demanded a thousand pieces of silver for you, and he will be bringing the money to me in a week."

"But Kissara. What about Kissara?" He fights back unwanted tears. "I was going to marry her when I got old enough."

"More than one young man has lost a woman in a business deal. You will survive." With that, Garash walks out of the room, closing the door and leaving Sett in the dark.

He opens the door again and sticks his head in. "By the way, why are you worth a thousand pieces of silver?"

Sett does not answer, so his master closes the door

again.

The following week is bittersweet. Sett makes up extra batches of incense and writes down some recipes for his mistress. The rest of the time he is with Kissara at her shop sometimes and at her home sometimes.

"I never understood why my daughter would want to marry a crippled man, but after meeting you, I understand. You are intelligent, reliable, strong, and talented. Well, and very handsome, I might add. You have my blessings, though I guess now it may never happen."

"Your blessing will keep me going until I can return," he says.

On the last day, Machir returns to the house of Garash and counts out the thousand pieces of silver.

"But why is he worth so much?" Garash asks once again.

"Go with us to the city gate. Once we are out on the other side, I will tell you."

On that last day, the three walk through the city, leading Machir's three large mules. They stop by the gold jewelry shop. Machir purchases a large supply which he carefully wraps and stores on the pack mule. The two men walk on ahead to give Sett a chance to say goodbye to Kissara and rejoin them.

"My mother blessed our marriage."

"I will come back for you, my peach," Sett promises

At the city gate, Garash stops and watches Machir and Sett mount their fine mules, cross the bridge over the Euphrates River and leave the city of Ur. Now on the other side, Machir turns and calls out to Sett's former master.

"Because he was the King of Israel!"

Now they are on the road toward home. They are quiet for a long time.

"Am I your slave now?" Sett asks.

"No, I bought your freedom."

They ride on through the marsh country between the two rivers, careful to stay on the raised road. Finally, they cross the Tigris River.

"Machir."

"Hmmm?"

"Is the palace still there?"

"As far as I know."

"Is my grandmother there?"

"No. Remember, I told you David took what remaining relatives you have and put them in his palace where he can keep an eye on them."

"Why do I have to go back if you bought my freedom?"

"Your family needs you."

"But you said David is caring for them."

"Someone needs to watch out for your grandfather's estate."

"I suppose so. But it's been five years. Wouldn't King David have claimed it as his?"

"Maybe. Probably. But you need to find out. You are the only one left in your family who is not locked up anywhere."

A week goes by. Two. Every night they camp at an oasis. Sometimes there is no oasis, and they camp in the barrenness and hope they are not caught out in the open unprotected during a storm.

Every night Sett brings up the barrenness.

"You're really obsessed with trees, Sett. Why do you even care?"

"I don't know why I care. Well, I love riding through trees. And sitting under them. There are a lot around Gibeon. Mefiboset says there were even more forests there when he was a boy."

Week three. Week four.

Every morning as soon as the sun is bright, Sett examines his feet for scrapes or bruises or spots that feel hot to his fingers. He presses hard on anything swelled to see if he feels pain way down in his bones. He puts oil on them.

"I'm going to have to get new boots soon."

"I'm sure there is a good cobbler in Gibeon," Machir

says. "Of course, you'll have to explain to him how they need to be made."

"Yes. It isn't hard, but he will have to put in extra protective layers for me."

Six long, hard weeks between worlds pass.

"You're almost home, Mefiboset," Machir says. "It has been a long, hard trip. I wasn't sure I should try to bring you along, but now I know it was the right thing to do.

"I have grown to respect you, despite your young age," he continues. "You have never complained. Well, you complained about leaving Kissara, and I completely understand. But, other than that..."

"Were you ever in love?" Sett asks Machir.

"Oh, yes. I am married to the most beautiful woman in the world. Her name is Aviva. No man could ever ask for a more devoted wife."

"Does she believe in the one real God, Jehovah?"

"She does now. I met her at a library in Nippur, not very far north of Ur where you were. My family lived there for a while. She was her father's only child, he let her be educated, and she liked libraries. Sometimes I think she is smarter than me."

"Kissara is smart. And she doesn't believe in Nanna anymore—the so-called god of Ur. She promised me she would not work on the Sabbath, just like Jehovah said. Even if I am not there, she will do this."

"I hope things work out for you, and you can go back and get her someday."

"Maybe she can live with me in my grandfather's palace."

"Maybe so," Machir says. "Do you know what that is up ahead of us? Does it look familiar to you?"

"It's a river, but I do not seem to recall it."

"It's the Jordan River, Son. You are almost home."

"You called me son. I barely remember my father."

"My wife and I never had any children. Does it bother you that I called you son?"

"No, it's okay. You've been a little like a father to me, I guess. Is your home near the river?"

"Yes, but farther north. I live in Lodebar, which is actually on the Yarmuk River, a branch of the Jordan. Lodebar is near where four roads meet each other and just south of a large lake called Galilee. Some call it the Sea of Galilee because it is so large."

"I never heard of that lake."

"That's because it is so far north of Gibeon. Okay, just let your mule guide himself across the river. He'll know what to do."

The water sprays up around Sett's legs. He cannot feel it on his feet, but it is cool and refreshing around his knees. He holds out his hands and dips them in the water, then splashes a little on his face.

The mules climb up the other bank of the river. Sett looks around. "Have I been here before? It looks a little familiar."

"I'm sure you have. Jericho is just ahead. We will stop there for the night. We can wash and get all the sand out of our hair, then eat a decent meal. There is still some daylight left. We'll stop at the market and see if we can buy a couple of good tunics and robes for us."

It is now the next day. The sun has just come up. The old man and the young man have just left the inn and are headed toward the west gate.

"The highway forks here," Machir says. "Shall we take the one that heads southwest and ends up at Jerusalem or the other one that goes northwest and ends up at Gibeon? Which one shall we take?"

Sett grins. "Such a question, sir! I want to go home. I want to go to Gibeon."

"Either way, it's a hard climb from Jericho up to either city."

At noon, they arrive on the outskirts of the longed for city of Gibeon. Sett looks up to the top of the hill where his grandfather's palace is.

"Do you remember it now?"

"It's been five years, but, yes, I remember it. I wonder if I will have to run for my life while living there ever again. I was five the first time. Eleven the second time. That's six years apart. I'm now seventeen. I sure hope it doesn't happen again."

The two men with their three mules work their way up the main street of Gibeon and arrive at the front gate of the palace.

"It looks like it has been maintained," Machir says.

He dismounts and pounds on the gate. They hear voices on the other side. Someone opens it with a broad grin.

"I was wondering when...."

The gatekeeper's smile disappears.

"Who is it?" The voice is low and nasal. A man about the age of Machir joins the gatekeeper. He is shorter than Machir, has a pointed nose, and is thin. His black eyes dart from the gatekeeper to the older and younger men standing before him. The thin man stares up at Sett, then down at his feet.

"It couldn't be," he snarls, his mouth dropping open. "No. It couldn't be."

"Yes, it's me. So good to see you again, Ziba." Sett wears a large grin. It fades. "Ziba. Don't you remember me?"

Ziba whispers something to the gatekeeper who disappears into the blue-and-red tiled courtyard. He looks back at Sett.

"Of course. Of course, dear boy. I almost didn't recognize you. You have grown to be so, well, big. Come in. Come in."

He turns and motions for a stable hand to come take over the mules.

"These are magnificent animals you have. Do they belong to you?"

"Oh, I would like to introduce to you my friend, Machir. He, well, it is a long story. He is just my friend. The animals belong to him."

"Welcome to the palace of Saul, greatest king in the history of Israel," Ziba says with a guarded smile. "Oh, and here is my son, Lechy. You may not remember him. Lechy is two years older than you, Sett."

Sett looks down at Lechy, who is about as tall as his father, but with a round face and bulbous nose. His head is held so high, he looks down at people he meets.

Sett smiles at Lechy, but the smile is not returned. He slides down off his mount and stands with his crutches until the mules have been led away to the stalls to the left of the courtyard between the black marble columns.

Ziba whispers something to Lechy, who then leaves out the front gate.

Sett looks around. He stares at the broad steps straight ahead, the width of six man-lengths, leading up to the second floor, but blocked by a series of folding doors. He remembers back to his last evening on the other side of those doors when he had sat on his grandfather's alabaster throne, grandmother Ahinoam by his side. Everyone in the courtyard had bowed down to him and said, "Hail to the king."

"I was king for a day, wasn't I?"

"Yes, you were, sir," Ziba replies. "You were king for a day. Then you disappeared. I thought you were dead. Oh, what am I thinking? Here you are standing in the courtyard, and I have not shown you a place to sit so we can visit."

"Oh, I'm not here for a visit, Ziba. I'm home," Sett says as they are led to marble benches. He and Machir seat themselves, and Sett continues to stand.

"When the stable hand is through taking my belongings off the mules," Sett says, "he can have them sent up to my apartment. I think I will take the one my grandfather had, the one on the other side of the throne room."

Ziba sits, looks up toward the cordoned off throne room, over to the front gate, then back at Sett. His hands are in his lap, then beside him on the bench. He twists his mouth and licks his lips.

Machir remains silent. He watches Ziba. His eyes never leave the man. At last, he catches Ziba's eye,, and they stare at each other.

Sett notices. *Would you look at that? There's a standoff here. What's going on?* Sett is not sure whether to smile at the antics of two old men or get out of the way of the arrows their eyes are shooting at each other.

A servant enters with a bowl of fruit and a tray of cheese. A second servant follows him with three goblets and a pitcher.

Ziba breaks his eye contact with Machir. "Here they are. Help yourself, boy. Oh, my. I have just called you a boy, Mefiboset. It was just yesterday that you were a boy. Well, you are still a boy to me. You will always be a boy." He pulls on his black beard and chuckles into it.

They hear a rattle at the gate. Ziba stands and hobbles in that direction as the gatekeeper opens it.

"Oh, there you are, Lechy. I see you found Yassib. Come in, both of you. Yassib, there is someone I would like you to meet. Follow me."

Yassib has an oval face and curly hair. His hands are folded together at his waist, even as he walks.

"Sett," he says, calling out. "I would like you to come meet Yassib. He is a neighbor. Actually, his family owns the property right next to Saul's property.

"Yassib, I would like you to meet the grandson of King Saul. Being a native Gibeonite, I am sure you remember stories of Saul's dealings with your people. How have you been since your family died, by the way?"

Sett rises and offers a hand to his neighbor. Yassib presses his lips together, glares at Sett, turns away, and walks back toward the outer gate.

"What's wrong with him?" Sett asks Ziba.

"Oh, something that happened between your grandfather and his grandfather and father years ago. He never got over it. Well, no matter. I'm sure he will soften and take to you in time. Why don't you follow my servant up to your grandfather's apartment?"

"You mean my apartment," Sett replies.

"And where would you like me to put—what was your friend's name?"

"My name is Machir, sir. Machir," he growls, standing.

"My apartment goes into two other apartments that belonged to his wife and mistress. I would like Machir to have one of those," Sett announces.

"Well, if you are sure that is what you want to do," Ziba replies. "Uh, Lechy, I guess they are going to be taking King Saul's apartments. You know, the ones on the second floor. Those."

"Yes, father," Lechy replies. "I understand." With that, he turns and catches up with Yassib. They leave out the front gate together.

Sett begins the procession, slowly manipulating one step after another. Machir patiently follows him.

The servants with their belongings stay behind the two, and progress up the stairs, taking one slow step at a time. They look down into the courtyard where Ziba stands watching, wagging his head back and forth with a smirk and a shrug of his shoulders.

They enter the spacious apartment of King Saul with its coral and black tiles on the ceiling and floor, and frescoes of Saul's victories on each wall. Columns supporting the floor above are black marble. Sett excuses the servants.

"Sir, there are a few things we need to take out so they are not in your way."

With that, the two servants take some average-size clothes off hooks on the wall, relatively small shoes on the floor, and several miscellaneous items and scrolls off a large table.

"Whose are they?" Sett asks.

"Oh, they were left here a long time ago by your grandfather. Everything is the just the way they were the day he left to fight that fateful battle with your father. A sad day it was for Israel. A sad day."

The two servants leave, but do not close the door. Machir walks over to close it, but as he does, he hears Ziba. "Have you made the arrangements?"

"Yes, sir." It is Lechy.

"I don't like any of this," Machir says upon closing the door.

"Why? What's wrong? You wanted to bring me home, and that is what you have done."

"I pride myself on being able to size people up within moments of meeting them. That Ziba is not to be trusted. Nor his son, nor any of the servants, nor that Yassib, the neighbor. I have never been wrong."

"Come on, Machir. They are just a little strange. But Ziba has served this household for the past, well, since my father was born."

"It is obvious he has taken over everything while you were gone. And I mean everything. Those clothes they took away were not the clothes of a giant like your grandfather. They were too small, even for you."

"You're wrong. Ziba would not do anything like that."

"I hope you are right. For your sake, I hope you are right."

Sett and Machir remain in the apartments the rest of the afternoon. They are brought their dinner by the servants and decide to just stay put the rest of the night. They excuse the servants.

"I am going to stay in here with you," Machir says. "Something is not right."

"Just think. I am going to sleep tonight in the bed of my grandfather," Sett says as he pulls back the covers, then pulls his feet around and under them. "Good-night, Machir."

Sleep comes. He dreams of his Kissara.

"What's that?"

Sett is awakened by heavy pounding on his floor and shouting. "So, you thought you could get away with it, did you?" The voice is Machir's.

Sett reaches over for the lamp, which has not quite gone out and quickly pours more oil in it. With the brighter light, he sees Machir with his knee in the back of a servant. Machir's foot is on the servant's hand with a knife in it.

"What's going on down there?" It is Ziba's voice from the third floor above them—the children's floor. He runs down the steps to the balcony until he reaches the open door into Sett's apartment.

"Your plot did not work," Machir says, twisting the servant's hand until he drops the knife, and forcing him to stand.

"You! I should have known I could not trust you," Ziba shrieks at the servant. "Lechy, tie him up downstairs. I will turn him in to the authorities first thing in the morning.

"I am truly sorry, Master Mefiboset," he says while staring at Machir. "I will set a guard at your door tonight."

"No, you will not. I will stand guard. Good-night, sir," Machir says to Ziba. He slams the door closed and slides an iron bar across it. He pulls a bench over by the locked door and sits on it.

"This house has never been very good to you, has it?" he says to Sett.

"I guess not. I just don't understand it. I trust Ziba with my life."

"Then you had better untrust him," Machir growls. He folds his bulky arms, leans his head back and closes his eyes.

Morning comes. Machir snorts and wakes himself. His head is slumped down toward his lap. He jerks it up and opens his eyes.

There is a knock on the door. It is Ziba. "Breakfast is downstairs in the dining hall. My sons and I will meet you there."

"He has more than that one son?" Machir grumbles. "In that case, I'll bet the man with the knife was one of them

"Oh, yes. He has fifteen," Sett replies, smiling.

They dress and break their fast with Ziba and his

sons. All the while, Machir grumbles to Sett. "You eat with the servants?"

They go out to the courtyard and sit by the reflecting pool.

"I thought you would like to ride around the property today," Ziba says. "Here is my...a small chariot already hitched up for you. Lechy will drive it for you."

"Yes, I'd like to do that, but I think I'd like to try driving it myself if you have a seat in it."

Ziba smiles. "That can easily be arranged."

"Oh, I love these trees," Sett tells Machir as they make their way down a back trail through the property.

A Gibeonite arrow whizzes by.

# 9 ~ ANOTHER ESCAPE

"I am truly sorry," Ziba says, watching Machir bring his and Sett's belongings down from the apartment. "Somehow, David's spies have made it into my household..."

"Your what?" Machir interrupts.

"Uh, Saul's household. I do not know how they found out Mefiboset is still alive, but it is obvious they have."

"This is only a temporary retreat," Machir says, his eyes glaring at Ziba. "Be assured, Mefiboset will return someday. Never forget it."

Sett rests on a bench in the courtyard as Machir's three mules are prepared.

"Ziba, if you can get word to them, would you tell my grandmother and Uncle Mefiboset I am still alive and will try to figure out a way to see them?"

"Of course I will, my boy."

As Sett and Machir head down through the main street of Gibeon and onto the highway, Machir speaks. "Don't bet on it."

"On what?"

"It will never happen. Your grandmother and uncle will never be told."

They ride a while in silence.

"Machir."

"Yes, lad."

"Why does everyone hate my family so much?" Sett asks, easing up on the reins so his mule can go at his own pace.

"That's just the way things are among the leaders of kingdoms. Kings fight each other to gain control of what they want, and their families suffer for it. It isn't your fault."

"Machir."

"Hmmm?"

"I don't remember much about my father, but I do remember he told me many times David was his friend. So, that means David is my friend too, not my enemy. Do you think that's right?"

"Could be. Could be. Now, let's stop talking and concentrate on this steep, winding road down to the Jordan Valley. Watch out for robbers. They're everywhere along this stretch."

Once more, they are in Jericho. They stop at an inn for the night.

Sett sleeps very little. When he does, he dreams he is with his father, Jonathan, again. They are walking under the trees on their land, laughing and talking and happy.

"I had him back again for a little while last night," Sett says the next morning.

"Who did you have back?" Machir asks.

"My father. During the night in my dreams, we were together again."

"Dreams can be bad or good. This one was good for you."

They leave Jericho through the north gate.

"We will cross to the other side of the Jordan when we get closer to my home. The road is a little better on the west side," Machir explains.

They work their way north until they can see the Jabbok River branch off from the Jordan and flow east. That night they sleep in their black goat-hair tent.

"We will be home in time for our evening meal," Machir tells Sett as they eat their cheese and figs to break their fast.

"What is Lodebar like?"

"It is a busy town. It is up in a valley where the Yarmuk

River branches off from the Jordan and flows east. There are several important crossroads nearby. One goes straight west to the Great Sea, one goes north around the west side of the Sea of Galilee, one goes north around the east side of the Sea of Galilee near Gadara, and one crosses the Jordan River. I chose to build my house there because the meeting of these trade routes is a perfect spot to sell the gold jewelry to traders."

"So this is where we are going to sell Kissara's jewelry that she actually touched with her own hands."

"Yes, you're going to touch what she did. I have a booth at the crossroads. You will go there every day, sit in the booth, and use your charms to sell the jewelry. I know you will do well."

"I thought you said I was not your slave."

"You're not. I plan to pay you a commission from everything you sell. You can do whatever you like with the money."

"I shall save it up so I can go Ur, and bring back Kissara to be my wife, and also bring her mother."

"That will be fine. Where will you live?"

"I don't know. I'd like to take her to my palace, but..."

"Well, you do not have to decide now."

"Machir."

"Hmmm?"

"Are there trees where you live?"

"It's very hilly with a lot of volcanic rock, but close to the Yarmuk River, there are. If you go as far as Ashteroth, there are forests everywhere you look.

"Where is Ashteroth?"

"A long day's ride northeast. It's in the kingdom of Gersha. And, about the same distance to the southeast of Lodebar is the Ephraim Wood to the southwest."

"Then I shall go visit both places someday."

"You are obsessed with trees. Sometimes you are strange, Sett, my boy."

"I'm afraid if I don't see and enjoy them now, they will

be gone by the time I am old."

"Well, that's a long time away. Okay, here is where those highways meet. We cross the Jordan now and will be home soon."

Just as the sun dips below the horizon behind them, Machir stops at a country house. "Lodebar itself is just over that hill up ahead," he says dismounting.

Machir knocks on his copper gate, and a servant answers it.

"Hello, master. Welcome back."

"Do I hear a familiar voice?"

A petite woman with curly hair and wearing a blue tunic with white embroidery down the front arrives from an inner courtyard. She rushes to Machir, and they embrace.

"Welcome home," Anlil says with a lyrical voice. "You were gone a little longer than I expected. I had begun to worry about you."

Machir's house reminds Sett of Garash's back in Ur, but on a smaller scale. The tiles covering the courtyard are green, and the columns supporting the second floor around the courtyard are red.

Having dismounted, Sett works his way toward the two. Anlil looks over at him.

"And who is this fine young man?" she asks.

"This is my new friend, Mefiboset. Everyone calls him Sett. I met him in Ur and brought him back because Israel is his home."

"Welcome home," she says. "Will you be with us for a while?"

"Yes," Machir says before Sett can reply. "I have hired him to go down to the crossroads every day and bring in customers."

"You understand gold jewelry?" she asks with a smile.

"Yes, ma'am."

"Well, come, let us eat. Then you can tell me all about your journey."

"Anlil," Machir says as they walk toward the dining

hall, "This young man is King Saul's grandson. We are going to keep him safe here until he can return to his home."

"Oh," Anlil stops and looks back at Sett, who is right behind them. "Now, I understand. We will do whatever we can to make you comfortable and safe while you are here."

"You can have the large guest room we have on the main floor, so you do not have to climb stairs," Machir explains.

The next day, Machir takes Sett back to the Jordan, where his roadside booth is. His is one of several, all well built, painted various colors, and decorated on the inside to best show off their particular product.

"We have dye traders and glass traders from over on the Great Sea coast; amber traders from up by the Nordic Sea; incense traders of frankincense and myrrh from Arabia; spice traders of cinnamon, cassia, cardamom, ginger, pepper and turmeric from India; copper traders from Persia and Egypt; tin merchants from Britannia—you name it. And of course, a gold-jewelry trader from Babylon—me."

"I had no idea," Sett says, smiling broadly. "I thought I was going to be sitting in a little run-down booth out in the middle of nowhere with no one to talk to besides an occasional traveler."

"We are like a bazaar with no town attached to it. You can hitch your mule here," Machir says as he unlocks a back door into the booth.

Once inside, he removes the shutter. Sett enters. "Here is your stool. I keep my stock of jewelry in this locked chest under the counter. Just put out two or three pieces. Be careful when you put your head down to bring out a new piece, that your customer doesn't grab what is already out and run while you are looking elsewhere."

"What about prices?"

"I have a list etched on this clay tablet. Go by that. If anyone wants a large supply, send them to my home. If they want a different kind of design, send them to my home. If they object to your price but are still interested, send them to my home. And that's about it."

"I think I am going to like this."

"Don't let them talk you into believing they are poor and need a necklace for their beloved wife who is dying. Don't believe any of their stories. They are full of them. Bargain with them over the price a little, but just enough to let them think they chiseled you. Got it?"

"Got it."

"Now, I am going to leave you. Good luck."

Sett is now alone. He looks around, pulls out a few pieces of Kissara's gold jewelry, and caresses it while imagining her at her own booth far to the east. His display pieces set out, he watches across the road as another booth is opened up for the day.

He hears a gurgling, low growl, then a high- pitched squeak which moves into a blithering honk, and smiles to himself. *Here come the camels.*

The day goes by quickly. When a few prospective customers pass by without even looking his way, Sett calls out in his clear baritone voice, "Gold for your sweetheart. Gold for your elegant robes. Gold to show off your fine animals." For variety, sometimes he sings his commercial.

*Come be bold.*
*Buy some gold*
*From finest mold.*

Each day Sett goes home with a small pouch of coins which he counts out to Machir. Machir, in turn, gives a little back to Sett as his share.

"I wrote a message to my Kissara yesterday telling her where I was. Today I found a trader headed to Ur who said he would deliver it for me."

"That is one of the benefits of working at an international trade crossroads like this," Machir replies.

Four weeks later, Sett is at his booth and hears more commotion than usual. He leans his head out of his booth.

"What's going on?" he asks the man in the glass booth across the road from him.

"The king and queen are coming."

"King and queen of what?"

"Gesher. It's just north of here along the Sea of Galilee and all the way east into the mountains!" the other merchant calls out. "I've never met a king or queen. Have you? I don't know how to act around them. I heard they're always short-tempered."

Sett grins.

The noise grows louder. Sett hears the tramping of feet, and, leaning out, he sees columns of soldiers marching from the south. They are five across. In front and beside them are mounted soldiers. After ten columns of infantry, there is another mounted soldier, then a litter with a mounted soldier on each side. He sees the soldier in front of the litter turn back toward the one beside the litter, then call out, "Halt."

The procession stops, and the soldiers stand in place. The soldier on Sett's side of the road is older and dressed grander than the others. He dismounts and holds on to the reins. The curtains of the litter open, a lady steps out, turns, then helps a grand lady out. The man is head and shoulders taller than most of the soldiers, and the woman is tall and graceful in her own right. Though neither wears a crown, Sett knows.

"May I interest Your Majesty in the finest gold jewelry from ancient Ur, the land of the Garden of God?" he calls out, holding up one of the necklaces.

The lady smiles and leads the gentleman behind her. She is wearing a scarlet robe and long gold tunic. Her veil matches her robe and is attached by a garland of amber stones.

As they draw near, Sett quickly unlocks the chest at his side and takes out the finest pieces he has. He lays them on a royal blue cloth on the counter.

"My lady," he resumes as she reaches his booth, "this

necklace was made especially for you to adorn your finest tunic and bring out the gold of your heart.”

By now, some of the other traders have moved in closer to watch the show.

“Oh, darling, I have been looking for something like this,” she says, looking up at the richly-dressed man.

“Do you have matching earrings?” she asks, turning back to Sett.

“Indeed, I do. I also have an upper-arm bracelet, ankle bracelet, and two rings in this ensemble.”

He extends his large hand, palm up, and the queen sets her hand in his. He slips one of the rings onto her delicate finger.

“Perfect,” he says, his eyes gleaming.

Sett then turns to the king. “And for you, Your Majesty, I have a gold pendant so large and heavy, only a man of your stature could wear it to advantage. The chain itself weighs more than ten silver chains.”

He holds it up. “You will see it has the finest pearl of India embedded in it.”

The king looks but says nothing. Sett hurries on. “Also, for you, sire, I can have a matching gold-handled dagger made.”

“You can?” the king replies.

“Of course, I would have to send back to Babylon where this jewelry originates. But I believe I could have it in your hands within a year.”

For the first time, the king smiles. “I am King Talmai, son of Ammihur.”

“Your Majesty,” Sett says, dipping his head until it is even with his hands on the counter. He waits.

“You may rise,” the king says. “You are a curious one. You are almost as tall as me, but you are not of my kingdom—the Rephaim. I have only heard of one other man outside my kingdom nearly as tall as me. Met him one time. He was king of Israel a dozen or so years ago.”

Sett does not reply. The king watches him. He looks

over at the jewelry his wife is admiring and back at Sett. The young man still does not reply. The eyes of the two men lock.

Nothing is said.

"Darling, what is it?" the queen finally asks, realizing what is going on.

"Nura, I believe we have just met the King of Israel."

Sett presses his lips together. His heartbeat increases.

King Talmai lowers his voice and leans in. "Are you in hiding?" he whispers. "I heard there is another king in Israel now. If you are in hiding, your secret is safe with me. Do you reside near here? It's okay, son. I won't tell."

"Yes, Your Majesty," Sett replies almost in a whisper. I am King Saul's grandson. My father was to be King Jonathan, but they were killed in the same battle. I live with Machir, the gold dealer, just outside of Lodebar."

King Talmai slaps his hand onto the counter and roars, "Then you and Machir will have to come visit us some time. We live up in the mountains at Ashtaroth. It's a big city with a big palace. Can't miss it," he laughs.

"I would be honored, sire."

"Now, we want everything you showed my wife and also this gold pendant that—how did you describe it?—is worthy only of a man of my stature. And when you are ready to come visit, send a message so we will be sure to be home and not gone off to war somewhere." He winks.

"Yes, Your Majesty," Sett replies. "And let me put your jewelry in something appropriate."

He reaches over and pulls out a shallow alabaster box, two hand spans square. Inside is royal blue fabric with cotton underneath.

Carefully, he lays the purchases in it and replaces the lid. By now, the royal ones have headed back to the litter, and a lady in waiting is there to collect the box.

The king and queen stop before arriving at the litter and realize everyone at the international market has bowed their head to the ground. The king clears his throat and announced, "You may rise."

With that, he remounts his horse, his queen and her lady in waiting disappear in the litter, and the marching of soldiers resumes.

Anxious to get back to Machir, Sett closes the shutters to the shop. He exits out the back door and locks it.

*I can't wait to tell him what happened today.*

With that, Sett turns and collapses.

# 10 ~ RUMORS

"**H**elp," Sett cries out. "Help me, someone!"

Still chattering fast and loud about the royal visit moments earlier, the other traders do not hear Sett's distress call bchind his booth.

"Help me!" hc crics again. Still, no one hears.

He looks over at his broken crutch.

He thinks of supporting himself with his strong arms while he climbs up to his knees, but decides that, even if he got that far, he could not support his bulky weight on just one crutch. *That one would break next.*

Twisting around, so he is on his front, he puts out an elbow, scoots himself up a couple of hand-spans, then puts out his other elbow. His elbows bleed from the rocky ground. He must keep going. One elbow, then the other and the other

He stops and cries out once again. "Help. Help me, someone," but still, no one hears.

Once again, scooting his body along the ground, dragging his useless feet behind him. Putting an elbow forward, scooting, another elbow, scooting.

"Sett, what happened?"

It is the glass trader from across the road.

"Thank God," Sett says, twisting his body around so he is on his back and can see his friend.

"What can I do?" the friend asks.

"First, bring my mule up close."

That done, Sett asks, "Do you have a low stool you can

bring over?"

The glass trader hurries to his booth and brings back a bench along with another friend.

"If each of you will put an arm under my arms and lift me a little, I think I can get on the bench."

With effort, the two men accomplish their task.

"No, this is not going to work," Sett says. "You can't lift me high enough to get me the rest of the way onto my mule. Let me think."

"Hey, I've got a horse and cart with straw in it to cushion my glass supply. Why don't we get you into my cart, and I'll take you home? Your mule can follow. Didn't you say you live in Lodebar?"

"Well, I live this side of the city, so you wouldn't have to take me all the way in. Thank you, friend. I will reward you for this."

"You have already rewarded me. That was quite a show you put on with the king and queen. Now, let's get you on my cart and home."

An hour later, Sett is at Machir's home and is being taken inside by two servants carrying him in a sitting position.

"Oh, no," Anlil says, entering the outer courtyard just as the servants set him on a bench. "What happened? You've got blood all over your arms. And look at your feet. The leather is torn in both of them. Are your feet bleeding?"

She kneels, not caring that blood is getting on her green tunic with the yellow embroidering on it. "Your ankle-to-toe straps are gone. No wonder your feet are drooping like that."

She unties the straps holding the high tops of the boots on and slips them off Sett's useless feet. She watches his eyes for signs of pain, then remembers he has no feeling in them.

"One of them is bleeding," she announces.

Sett looks over at his friends from the market. "Can you help me to bed? No matter how careful I am, sometimes they do get wounded. My feet do not heal well."

Machir has appeared from his office. Sett looks over at him. "Sir, I am so sorry. I cannot go back to work until my foot heals. If I do not keep it propped up, it will never heal. The scrape will just get larger and eat away at my foot."

"Take all the time you need, Sett. I have had a good rest since you have been here taking my place. Now, let us get you to bed."

Anlil goes to her kitchen area, grabs some olive oil and honey, and follows the two merchants from the market as they transport Sett to his room. Her maid follows her.

Machir follows the two merchants who had brought Sett home. "Thank you," he says, handing them each a brass coin. They both turn down the coin, then leave.

"You poor dear," Anlil says. "Let me wash your feet, then I'll put this treatment on them. It won't hurt to put it on both feet and not just the scraped one. Then we'll...."

She looks up at Sett and sees that he is asleep.

She applies her ointment to Sett's elbows and knees, wrapping them both to keep them protected. She puts his worn-through leather boots under his bed and applies honey and olive oil to his feet.

"Fix some tea for pain," she says to the maid next to her.

"But, ma'am, he cannot feel pain."

"Oh, I forgot again. Well, would you sit in here with him in case he wakes up and needs something?"

Anlil goes to the inner courtyard and joins her husband. "That boy has had so much bad luck in his life," she laments, picking up the embroidery she had been working on.

Machir looks over at his wife and shakes his head. "First, he is no longer a boy. He is nineteen years old. Second, do not ever talk about bad luck in his presence. He is one of the most positive people I have ever met. Let us not be the ones who change him."

"Sir, there is a messenger at the front gate who will

not leave his message with anyone but you or Mefiboset."

Machir rises and follows the gatekeeper.

"Are you Machir, the gold trader or Mefiboset?" the messenger asks. "I was instructed to give it to no one but one of you."

"I am Machir," he says, taking the small scroll and handing the messenger a brass coin.

The messenger leaves and Machir returns to the inner courtyard, reading it.

"It has King Talmai's seal on it. It is an invitation to Mefiboset, King of Israel, to visit with him in his palace next month. What is going on? How does the king know Sett? This could be a trap."

"He is safe for now. We shall let him sleep as long as he needs," Anlil says. "Maybe, when he wakes up, he can tell us if he knows anything about the message."

"I'll run into the city and hire some extra guards for tonight."

Morning comes without incident, but Sett still has not awakened. It is noon before he does.

"I am glad to see you feel a little better," Machir says, entering his room. "Sett, I have disturbing news. Yesterday, a message arrived for you from the King of Gesher."

Now sitting up in bed and leaning against the wall, Sett grins broadly.

"How did he find out about you?" Machir says, not smiling. "Your presence here is supposed to be a secret."

"Well, sit down, and I will tell you."

An hour later, it is Machir's turn to grin. "Young man, you constantly amaze me. You were born to be king, you know that?"

This time, Sett does not smile.

"Oh, I am sorry."

"No, I'm not worried about that. I'm worried about my feet and my boots. While my feet are healing, I need to get some new boots made. Do you know a cobbler? They need to be made in a certain way, and I do not know if that can be done in time to accept the king's invitation."

"You just stay here and rest. I shall send a servant into the city to bring back a cobbler."

Two days later, the cobbler arrives. He is short and ample around the waist. He has on a plain tunic and robe.

"I am sorry for the delay," he explains. "My donkey was sick, and I had to finally borrow someone else's. What can I do for you?"

He looks down at Sett's feet and puts his hand up under his chin. "Oh, my. I have heard of something like this. I don't think I can help you. It would be too complicated. I can make you a special pair of sandals, but not boots."

"No, I cannot wear sandals. I will explain to you how to make my boots. To start, just cut and shave a board to the size of my feet. It must be exactly the same dimensions in every way.

"Then put thick bolls of cotton over the board, and wrap leather around it to keep the cotton in.

"With that done, push my feet up so that they do not droop, and make my boots so that they only fit if my ankles and toes are in the right place.

"Finally, make straps I can wrap around my ankles, bring under the toes of my boots, then back up to my ankles. They will keep my feet propped up. They are healthier and heal better when they do not droop."

The cobbler stares at Sett's feet. He pulls on his unkempt beard. "I suppose I could put a lot of tacks in them to hold the leather to the wood."

"No. I cannot feel my feet, and if a tack came loose and created a blister or sore, it could be disastrous for me. Do you have some good glue? Do you think you can do that?"

"All I can say is, I will try. I will dedicate all this and next week to getting them made for you. Did you say you needed to wear them for a special occasion?"

"Well, yes, but the occasion is going to be a secret," Sett says with a wink.

As promised, Sett's boots arrive as scheduled.

"Too bad my feet didn't get fixed as fast as my boots," he says. "I just hope they are healed in time. I cannot possibly go see the king or anyone else if my feet are not healed. If they are not, it could be a disaster."

Two more weeks pass. Sett's feet have finally healed.

"I am ready to go. Lead the way," Sett tells the armed escort sent by the king to take him through the Mountains of Bashan to the palace.

The two work their way up the Yarmuk River northeast. They come to a fork in the river and decide to spend the night there with darkness falling sooner, now that it is winter.

They dismount, and while the escort sets up a leather tent for them, Sett works his way to the side of the road facing due west.

"Wow! Would you look at that?" he tells his escort. "That lake is the largest I have ever seen. Do you know its name?"

"Yes. It is called the Sea of Galilee."

Sett sees a log and sits on it. He gazes out over the lake, then on the other side of it to the west. "The plain down there looks pretty barren except for the river. Up here, we must be in a forest," he says, leaning back and letting the even breeze waft through his thick, black hair. "Don't you love how the branches whistle when the wind blows?"

"Never noticed. But, if you like trees, you will love Ashtaroth where the palace is. In the morning, we take the east branch of the Yarmuk until that one branches off, and we'll take the middle branch the rest of the way to the palace. It is high in the mountains and surrounded by forests."

"I can't wait."

As promised, Sett's escort delivers him to the palace gates before sundown. On each side of the large gates are giant thrones made of cedar which, his escort explains, is an invitation for the goddess Ashteroth, to sit on her throne in this place.

The escort orders the guards to let them in, and the

guards obey.

"This is where I leave you," the escort says. Sett works his way to the middle of a courtyard large enough to hold four of King Saul's courtyards.

To Sett's delight, the tiles have been artistically placed so that he feels as though he is walking on a forest. The columns supporting the upper floors around the periphery are large cedar tree trunks with just enough of the upper branches left on they seem to grow through the upper floors

Large pots of smaller evergreen trees are placed around the courtyard. In the middle of the courtyard is a large reflecting pool and a statue of Ashteroth rising up in the middle of it. The water is ice, it being late winter.

A servant approaches him.

"You are the grandson and heir apparent of King Saul, I presume. Follow me, Your Majesty. Your apartment is on the fourth floor."

The servant heads toward the steps, then realizes there is a tapping sound behind him. He turns.

"Oh, I did not realize. Does the king know?"

"I doubt it. He could not see my legs when we met. I should have warned you. Forgive me."

"No matter. There are two guest apartments on the first floor. You can have one of them."

After Sett settles in his apartment, he puts on his winter robe and returns to the courtyard to sit on one of the benches.

"You can't catch me," he hears a pretty brown-haired girl call out as she races around the pool, a younger child after her.

Sett watches and laughs. After a while, the girl stops running, notices Sett, and walks over to him.

"Hi. My name is Tamar. I am visiting with my grandparents. They are King and Queen of Gesher, and I am eight years old. What's your name?"

Sett reaches out and pats the little girl on the head. "Well, my name is Mefiboset, and I am nineteen years old, exactly eleven years older than you."

"Are King Talmai and Queen Nura your grandparents too?"

"I'm afraid not. My grandfather died a long time ago in a battle, and my grandmother is in someone else's palace right now."

"Whose palace is it?" Tamar asks.

"Well...."

"Excuse me, sir, but the evening meal is ready, and the king would like you to join him. Princess Tamar, you may join your grandmother in her dining hall."

Tamar looks over at Sett, then at the tiled pavement. She kicks a loose piece of tile. "Oh, all right," she replies.

Sett watches as the girl skips across the courtyard, then rises to follow the servant to the king's dining hall.

The hall's high ceiling is covered with tiles of every color as though imitating the forest in spring. The walls are frescoes of the king's triumphs. Large lamps are suspended from the ceiling throughout with large flames to both light and heat the room, aided by torches on the walls. In the middle of the hall is a statue of King Talmai.

"Welcome," King Talmai calls out. His voice echoes around the large room.

"I regret there aren't many of us tonight. I prefer this hall to be full of people, but it is winter and most of them prefer to stay home and not be caught out if a snowstorm hits."

Sett makes his way to the king's head table. A servant pulls back a chair for him next to the king.

"Did you find your accommodations satisfactory?" the king asks. "I am sorry I did not know about your injury. How long will it be before you can walk again?"

"Well, that is not something I plan on, Your Majesty. My feet were permanently injured when I was a child."

"Oh. Back when your grandfather was king?"

"About that time, yes."

"Well, you seem to have adjusted well. You are big and

strong like me. Now, let us eat and keep you big and strong."

The first course of their meal is brought in.

"Sire, I am curious about something. If you will indulge me, why is your city named after a goddess, Ashteroth?" Sett asks.

"Because she keeps our city growing and strong. She blesses our harvests and gives us many children."

"But, how do you know she exists? Do you have any proof?"

"People just know."

"I worship Jehovah who made heaven and earth and all that is in it," Seth says.

"So, you chose your god and I chose mine," the king replies, reaching for a dried fig.

"But I can prove Jehovah God exists. He made promises to our ancestors that came true decades later. Can you do that with Ashtaroth?"

"Young man, we all know she exists. Otherwise, why would gardens grow? Why don't I take you to see her temple tomorrow? It is grand."

"Yes, sire," Sett replies. "I stayed away from the temple to Nanna in Ur. But I was younger then."

The next day, a chariot waits outside the front gate. There is an attached bench on each side and behind the driver.

The chariot heads down off the peak on which the palace is located, across a lazy valley, and up a smaller peak. At the top is a round building surrounded by pillars. The roof is a dome. It is not as large as Sett had expected.

They stop in front and walk up the broad steps. The king talks as Sett manipulates his three-legged crutches up.

Once at the top, they are greeted by the high priest. He escorts them inside. The only thing in the magnificent building is a statue of a lady.

"There are rooms on both sides for the priests and guests," the high priest explains. "You can hardly see it from here, but on the other side of the great goddess is an altar of sacrifice. We sacrifice mostly cattle and mountain goats to her. After a sacrifice is cooked, we take the meat to one of the rooms to eat in her honor."

"But she is only a statue," Sett says. A magnificent statue, but still a statue. God cannot be confined to cold stone."

The priest squints at Sett, then looks over at the king. The king shrugs his shoulders at the priest and grins. "Your thinking is very limited, young man," the priest finally replies. "Are you Jewish?"

"Yes, I am."

"You Jews have no true concept of the many gods in the world."

"I guess we don't. I guess we don't want any God except the only God."

"Well, anyway, you have seen our city's deity," the king says, hurrying Sett back out of the temple. "You have to admit she has done well in being our guardian."

Back in the chariot, "By the way, she is honored by the trees," the king says. "I heard you love trees. Even down in the plains, there are groves of trees in honor of Ashtaroth and not allowed to be cut. That should please you."

Sett does not reply.

The rest of the week is spent visiting various parts of the city, enjoying the views from the city down into the valleys below, and eating good Gesher food.

Sett and the king talk about many things, including the politics of running a kingdom.

"Let me see, Sunita is ruler of India right now," King Talmai says.

"Ashur-Rabi is ruler of Assyria, and Eulmash-Shakin-Shumi is ruler of Babylon," Sett retorts. "At least they were when I was there. What about Arabia? Do we know who is ruling Arabia?"

"I think they're fighting over that right now, Sett. So many are nomads, they can't get together. But I know Menkheperre is the king—er uh pharaoh—of Egypt."

They walk through the woods, they watch the birds, they eat.

"I have a confession to make," the king says, sitting on a bench near the reflecting pool.

"It's about our daughter. Her name is Maacah. About twelve years ago, she married young King David. Tamar, who you visited with briefly while she was here, is our daughter's daughter, but she is also King David's daughter."

Sett stares at the king a moment. "Well, that's fine," he says.

"I was careful not to tell Tamar who you were. So I believe your secret is still safe."

"I have never doubted you, Your Majesty. Well, if you will excuse me, I need to go to my apartment to pack up for my trip back to Lodebar. I am sure I will enjoy your forests going home as much as I did coming here."

"I have arranged for you to have extra armed escorts returning to your home. We monarchs cannot be too careful, can we?" he says.

# 11 ~ REUNION

"Sir," the gatekeeper says to Machir a month later, "there is a messenger here from Gibeon."

"Who is the messenger? Did he identify himself?"

"He said he was sent by the steward of the palace, Ziba, and he is to leave the message only with Mefiboset."

Machir presses his lips together and glares at the gatekeeper. "Ziba pretends to be just a servant, but he can afford twenty slaves of his own, and supports his fifteen sons well in a palace that does not belong to him. He is nothing but trouble."

He raises his hand to the gatekeeper as though to wave off the messenger on the other side of the gate. "Just take the message from him and send him on his way. I will make sure Sett gets it."

As the small scroll is handed to Machir, he turns and calls out. "Sett, there is a letter here for you."

Sett comes out of his room. "Who would be writing me?"

"My big question is how anyone knows you are here."

Sett takes the scroll, sits on a courtyard bench in the springtime sun, and reads aloud.

Mefiboset. I trust you are well and that your feet are not any worse than they were when last I saw you.

You will be happy to know that I have kept King Saul's estate in good running order. Although it does not produce much, I get enough out of the attached farmland that I can at least keep the palace from going to ruins.

I am very sorry to be the bearer of bad news. The spies of King David have infiltrated again. Somehow, they found out where you are and that you even made a recent trip to visit the King and Queen of Gesher.

I assure you that I did not tell anyone. It was my secret. But, after listening to his spies, King David sent for me and forced me to tell him if King Saul had any descendants he did not know about.

Mefiboset, I did not want to tell him, but he forced me to. I would have kept your secret, but my household and I were threatened. what else could I have done?

"Not likely," Machir interrupts. "He is a snake."

Therefore, you may be receiving a visit shortly by the soldiers of King David. They will force you to go to Jerusalem with them. I fear for your life. Therefore, my advice to you is to go as far away from Lodebar as possible. Hide yourself and do it quickly before they arrive. Go so far away, no one will ever be able to find you.

All fifteen of my sons send you their greetings, especially Lechy.

"That's terrible. I am lucky to have Ziba watch out for me."

"Lucky to have that snake? You are too trusting, Sett. Have you always been this way? Only a fool would… Well, I didn't mean that you arc a fool; you are just young."

"So, what should I do?"

"I don't know. Let's think this through. If David knows, how do you think he found out?"

Machir stunds und paccs. He puts his hand up to his chin. "I'll bet that snake told him in hopes David would have you killed, and he could get title to the palace by default."

"I heard David wrote a beautiful dirge in honor of my father and King Saul. He can't be all bad."

A loud banging at the outer gate. "Open up in the name of David, King of Israel!" The banging again.

Machir's gatekeeper looks at him, then rushes to open the gate.

Eleven soldiers in sky blue uniforms march in. "We have orders to take Mefiboset back with us to King David in Jerusalem." He looks around the courtyard and walks up to Sett.

"Are you Mefiboset, grandson of King Saul, son of Crown Prince Jonathan and heir-apparent to their throne?"

"Well, yes and no," Sett says, glancing momentarily over at Machir.

"Come with us."

"Wait. You cannot just rush in here and expect him to drop everything and go with you," Machir objects.

"Sir, that is exactly what we expect."

"Just wait a moment!" he shouts, now standing between Sett and the officer. "He has done nothing to challenge King David's crown."

"Gentlemen," They hear a delicate voice. "I know you must be tired and hungry." It is Anlil wearing her red tunic with gold fringe at the neck, sleeves, and hem.

"I have goblets of the finest new wine being poured for you even as we speak. That will be followed shortly with plates piled high with cheese, dried figs and dates, nut, barley bread, and yogurt for dipping.

The unit leader shifts and looks back at his men.

"Please, gentlemen, just take off your helmets and set them in the corner where our gatekeeper is. He will guard them for you. Your weapons will be safe there also.

"After you have eaten and refreshed yourself, you can escort Mefiboset to the king."

The unit leader looks over at Machir, who smiles and shrugs his shoulders. He turns back to Anlil and takes off his helmet. "We would be most grateful, madam."

While the men indulge, Machir and Sett disappear to the young man's room.

"Let me pack a bag for you, son," he says, trying to hide quivering lips. "Now, let me see, you need your oil and salves for your feet. And the mirror I gave you so you can see the backside of your feet better. And here is your extra tunic and robe. You will need those. And, oh, son, I will miss you."

Machir puts both hands on Sett's young broad shoulders. "I do not know why I think this—may be because I distrust Ziba so much. But, since he claimed David is your enemy, my instincts tell me David wants instead to be your friend. I have good instincts."

The men embrace and pound each other on the back. Machir's arm is over Sett's shoulder when they come out of his room.

Out in the courtyard, they see the soldiers scattered around eating and enjoying themselves.

"They have decided to spend the night, Machir," Anlil says. "They said the outer courtyard will be fine for them. Then everyone can leave tomorrow morning when they are fresh."

Machir looks at his wife, smiles, and shakes his head. He walks over to her and whispers, "You are little, but always full of big surprises."

Sett overhears and grins with them.

The following morning Sett and the soldiers leave. Sett's mule is in the middle, with five soldiers riding on each side. Their unit leader rides in the front sometimes and in the back sometimes.

*I wonder what it will be like?*

Down out of the mountains of Gesher in the Bashan, they spend their first night.

*My father loved David.*

They cross the Yarmuk River, then turn west, cross the Jordan River, and spend another night.

*It seems I remember my father telling me it would be David, not him, who would be king after his father. Does David remember any of that?*

They work their way south along the Jordan River and spend their third night near the foothills of Mount Ebal.

*Does David love me like he did my father?*

Late on the fourth day, they arrive at the edge of Jerusalem. They pitch their leather military tents, and their unit leader sends a message to King David that they have arrived with their charge.

The following morning a new unit of ten arrives at the camp and takes charge of Sett. By their uniforms, Sett can tell they are part of the palace guard.

"We have orders to take Mefiboset up Mount Zion to the palace of King David."

They give Sett time to check his feet, clean up, put on his best tunic and robe, and comb his thick black hair.

They arrive at Jerusalem and enter through the north gate. They work their way up through the residential area, then past the fortress. They arrive at a retaining wall and go around the other side of it to the entrance to the newly-built palace of David, King of Israel.

The gates are opened wide, the procession enters, and everyone dismounts, including Sett, who has lowered his crutches before arranging himself on them, careful not to let his feet touch the ground.

The pavement in the large courtyard is tiled with white and blue. Openings have been left periodically for the planting of trees and flowering shrubs. The columns on both sides supporting the upper floors have been painted to look like clouds. Pots of planted flowers have been placed between the columns.

A servant dressed in a sky blue tunic approaches the young man. "Are you Mefiboset, grandson of King Saul, son of Crown Prince Jonathan and heir apparent to their throne?"

Sett holds his head up. "Yes, sir," he replies, his voice unsteady. "I guess I am."

"Follow me."

The servant leads Sett to an inner and more intimate courtyard. It is a duplicate of the outer courtyard except for broad and high steps at the far end. The servant pauses

"Can you manage these steps?"

"Yes, sir."

Slowly they make their way up the steps, so

reminiscent of the steps to his grandfather's throne room, the throne room where he, Sett, had ruled as king for a day so long ago when he was but eleven years old. Now he is twenty. Nine years have passed. *Will I live another year?*

Once at the top of the steps, they go down a long corridor to double doors. The guards, wearing their sky blue uniforms, open both doors and the servant leaves.

Sett passes through the doors and realizes there are several men and women in the room. The elaborate room is embellished with ivory, marble, and gold. A multi-colored carpet leads from the door to the far end where he sees a man wearing a crown and sitting on a throne. Sett takes a deep breath and waits for instructions. There are none. The king stares at him.

The doors behind Sett close. Sett moves forward a little way, eases down his crutches and falls prostrate on the floor before his king and his father's best friend. His arms are outstretched. His legs too. His forehead touches the floor.

He waits. *Will the sword come down on my neck now?* Still, he waits.

"Leave!" the voice from the throne roars. "All of you leave! Now!"

Sett hears feet of people he assumes to be attendants, officers, and members of David's family. The doors open. Soon the footsteps fade, and the doors are closed again.

Sett knows he is now alone with the king. Still, he remains prostrate. Then he hears footsteps heading from the throne to him.

Closer, the footsteps come. *Is there a sword? Will I be beheaded? Father, where ever you are, help me. You loved him once.*

He feels the king's breath on him. Sett clenches his teeth. His breathing now is almost impossible. He tries not to tremble in his last moments of life.

The king's hands touch Sett's shoulders and pull them up. Sett uses his strong arms to twist around and look up. The king kneels on the floor in front of him. Sett twists into a sitting position and looks into the eyes of his king, the eyes that are weeping.

"Oh, Jonathan, Jonathan. How I have missed you."

David lays Sett's head over on his shoulder and runs his hand through Sett's thick hair. With his other hand, he pats Sett's cheek. He kisses his forehead.

Sett feels the warm tears on his face and reaches around to return the king's embrace.

"Oh, Jonathan, Jonathan," David repeats. "No man ever had a friend like you. Oh, Jonathan, my Jonathan."

David now rocks Sett, still kneeling beside him. They silently rock and sway and weep and wish they could turn back time when Sett's father was still alive.

Finally, David puts his hands on Sett's shoulders and draws him back. Amidst his tears, he smiles.

"You look just like him. You look just like your father. Oh, why did it take me so long to find you?"

"I am twenty years old now," Sett says, not knowing what else to say.

David grins broadly. "And a fine twenty-year-old you are," he says.

"Are you... Uh... Well, are you going to kill me?"

David laughs aloud and shakes his head back and forth. "Of course not! Why would I kill you? You have brought light back into my life. You have brought Jonathan back to me."

He looks over at the crutches, then back to Sett. "Let me help you up."

"I can do it myself."

"Okay, big man. I shall let you do it yourself," David says, standing and handing Sett his crutches.

Once Sett is up again, David stands back and looks him over. "Even with those things you carry with you, you are taller than me. You came from a family of giants, so why wouldn't you be gigantic too? Oh, you look so like Jonathan."

He turns and puts a hand on Sett's shoulder.

"Come with me."

They walk toward the throne. David takes the two steps up to it and turns. "Come, my boy. Sit next to me."

"Oh, no, Your Majesty. I could never do that."

"If it weren't for the stubbornness of your old grandfather, you might have been the one sitting here. Come, sit next to me a moment and rest. We won't tell anyone."

Sett makes his way up the two steps and over to the lesser throne.

"Now, sit. I command you," David says with laughter in his voice.

The king rests his elbow on the arm of his throne and leans toward Sett.

"So, tell me what you have been doing all these years, other than running from me? C'mon. You can tell me."

Sett forms a slight smile. "Well, I met a woman."

"A woman! Of course! Every man needs a good woman. So, where is she? Are you going to marry her?"

"She is back in Ur. It's one of the places I lived while I was, well, running from you."

"Then we shall have to send for her. What is her name?"

"Kissara."

"A beautiful name, indeed."

"Your Majesty..."

"You don't have to call me that unless we're in public. By the way, what do your friends call you? They surely don't call you Mefiboset. That takes too long."

"They call me Sett."

"Then, Sett, you shall be."

"Sire, I heard you like to sing. I made up a song a long time ago. It is about my father. Would you like to hear it?"

"Would I? Would I? Of course, I would. Sing away, Sett."

*There is a hero big and tall.*
*He's the strongest of them all.*

*He will never make you sad
Cause Jonathan's my dad.*

David slaps the arm of his throne. That's a marvelous song. I shall learn it and sing it with you.

"Well, he wasn't your dad," Sett says, daring to tease with the King of Israel.

"I'll think of something to sing there—maybe *Jonathan's never bad*. How's that? So, how old were you when you composed your song?"

"I think I was six then. I used to sing it to my uncle. My father named me after him. He was actually my father's half-brother, so my half-uncle. But I loved him anyway."

"You were named after another Mefiboset?"

"You didn't know? I thought he was here at your palace with my grandmothers and my aunts and uncles."

David becomes serious. "Hmmm. You are right. I forgot about them. They are in a completely different wing of my palace. I never see the political pris... Well, I never see Saul's family."

Sett brightens up. "Oh, sire, could I see them? Well, if it is okay with you. I miss my grandmother and everyone else. I haven't seen my family since I was eleven years old."

"When you ended up in Ur?"

"Yes, then. Would it be possible to meet them?"

David, still serious, becomes quiet. "Well, perhaps it could be arranged someday."

He brightens and slaps his hand on his throne arm. "Well, from now on, you will live in my palace and eat with me."

"What about my family's palace in Gibeon? What has happened to it?"

"Who did you say is taking care of it?" David asks.

"Ziba. He came to serve with his father when he was a boy, and my grandfather was still alive. He is still there."

David looks at Sett. "Are those the best clothes you have? Where has the money from the produce farmed on your palace land been going?"

Sett squints at David.

"You don't know what I'm talking about, do you? That is your money. From now on, Ziba will pay you what is yours by right of inheritance as the firstborn of the firstborn."

"Then, can I go back to my family's palace?"

"It has been fifteen years since I lost Jonathan. I do not want to lose you again," David replies. "Stay here in my palace and eat at my table. Jonathan and I were closer than brothers. From now on, you will be considered part of my family."

They hear a knock on the wide doors into the throne room.

David takes a deep breath. "Well, I guess it's back to taking care of kingdom business. I guess you're going to have to...well, you know."

"Yes, Your Majesty," Sett says, rising from his lesser throne and working his way down the two steps. He turns, bows from the waist, and makes his way backward toward the door.

"Well, you don't have to go that far," David calls out to him. "Just go to the back of the room and open the doors so everyone can come back in. I will have someone show you to your apartment. You will live on the third floor where my children are if you think you can manipulate the steps."

"Sire, I do not deserve that. Just let me sleep in one of the rooms off the courtyard for your servants. It will be easier for me."

"As you wish."

As he leaves the courtyard, Sett notices people staring at him, and some even glaring. No one introduces himself to him.

*That's okay. I will make them like me. Maybe I can do my crutch trick for them. Well, maybe not. I was pretty young when I did that. I'll think of something.*

Sett does not see David the rest of the day. He makes his way back down to the courtyard, not sure what to do next.

Someone approaches about Sett's age. "My name is Elza, and I will be your personal servant. Come with me. I am making a room available for you. I think you will be very comfortable in it."

Sett enters and looks around. He sees that it is actually two adjoining rooms with a passageway between them. Tiles on the floor and ceiling are green and white. On the walls are frescoes of a city. In one corner, he sees a note by the artist. It is the city of Bethlehem. Right away, Sett likes it. He has a bed and some baskets for storage in one room. In the other, he has a table, a bench, more baskets for storage, and cushions on the floor to sit on.

That evening, Sett notices people headed to what he believes to be the dining hall. He checks with Elza and is told he is right. But by the time he finds out, everyone has disappeared into the dining hall.

"If the king expects you to eat at his table, then that is what you must do," Elza explains to Sett.

"But everyone is already there, and they have begun eating by now."

"No, they haven't. Knowing the king, he is waiting for you. He is fiercely loyal to his friends. You are his friend, aren't you?"

"He and my father were best friends a long time ago."

"Then go. Everyone is waiting for you. Go!" With that, Elza walks away.

Still, in the now-empty inner courtyard used mostly by family and close friends, Sett turns toward the dining hall. One crutch-step at a time. Clop. Clop. Pause. Clop. Clop. Pause. Clop. Clop. Pause.

He arrives at the door, and a servant lets him in. He looks around. Every eye watches him. No one smiles. A few whisper, but keep their eyes on him.

Clop. Clop. Pause. Clop. Clop. Pause. Clop. Clop. Pause.

"Come, my friend." It is the now-familiar voice of

David. The king rises to motion where he is, and everyone in the room follows protocol and rises with him.

Clop. Clop. Pause. Clop. Clop. Pause. Clop. Clop.

"Right up here by me and my wives," David calls out, waving. "Everyone! This is the son of the best friend I ever had: He is Mefiboset, son of Jonathan, and grandson of my predecessor, King Saul."

A collective gasp consumes the dining hall.

# 12 ~ OUTCAST

"**I**s the king crazy?" someone whispers.

"He is out of his mind."

"Before we know it, David and all of us will be out, and Saul's dynasty back in."

"Don't pay any attention to them," David says, leaning over to Sett, who he has seated in the place of Abigail, his second wife.

"Are you an archer like you father?" David asks.

"I guess I knew he was an archer, but never took it up myself. I don't know why unless I seemed to always be on the run. Well, not exactly that..."

David grins. "Don't worry about that. We have finally met, and we are friends for life, just as your father and I were. Oh, it is so good to have you back. I hope you don't mind me calling you Jonathan sometimes. So, anyway, you must take up archery. With strong arm muscles like you have, you could be a champion in no time."

"I'd like that, Your Majesty," Sett replies.

"Have you run into Ziba or his son, Lechy, yet?" David asks just before taking a bite of lamb. "Are they ever mad!"

"At me?"

"Well, at both of us. I told them they had to start giving you all the proceeds from the sale of whatever they farm on your grandfather's land. Now Lechy is over here telling me how they need that money to do this thing or another thing. I know their tricks. They get ample pay for their work as servants. When they get out of line, I just put them back in their place. They know that, if they push me too hard, they will be out of a job."

The dinner progresses, but not as usual. The normal chatter that goes on among the wives and children, the brothers and sisters, the military captains, and priests at the other tables does not bounce off the cedar paneled walls of the dining hall as usual. Instead, there is an undercurrent of angry looks and whisperings.

"Oh, my wife, Egglah, wants to meet you," David says. "Egglah, this is Sett. Sett, this is Egglah."

"Your Highness," Sett replies, dipping his head.

Egglah has a round face, full lips, and frizzy hair. She is wearing a white tunic with multicolored embroidery down the front, and a red robe. "I understand you like to sing," she says.

"Yes, I do."

"I come from a family of singers. I am Levite, and my ancestor is Kohath. They sing at the tabernacle services. I have a young son who sings with them—Ithream. Ithream said he would like to meet you."

The dinner progresses, and only David and Egglah, wife number six, speak to Sett.

"Meet me tomorrow late morning after I finish judging whatever needs to be judged," David says at the end of their first meal together. "Where will you be so I can send a servant after you?"

"I suppose I will be somewhere in the family courtyard, or my rooms, Your Majesty."

"That's fine. See you then."

The following day late in the morning, a servant goes to Sett's room, knocks, and enters. Sett is reclining on his bed.

"You are being summoned by His Majesty," the servant says. "He is really taken with you. What did you do?" he asks with a wink.

"It wasn't me. It was my father. They were best friends,

and he says I look just like my father, so it's like having Jonathan back. At least, that's what he keeps telling me." Sett twists around to the side of the bed, combs his thick hair and newly-trimmed beard, and grabs his crutches.

As they make their way across the courtyard, people glare at him. They go down a well-appointed wide corridor with high ceiling. When they reach a room at the end of the corridor, the servant lets Sett in and leaves.

"Out here," David says. "I love it out here on the balcony overlooking Kidron Valley. The little mountain on the other side is called the Mountain of the Olive Trees. What do you think of that, Jonathan?"

"I like it. I like trees. They provide shade and shelter, and their leaves sing to me."

"I'd like you to join me. I have composed several songs. Since you sang yours to me, I shall sing to you one of mine. It is about a special tree. Join in with me once you catch on to the tune.

*Blessed is the man whose delight is in the law of the LORD;*
*and in his law does he meditate day and night.*
*He shall be like a tree planted by the rivers of water,*
*That brings forth his fruit in his season;*
*His leaf also shall not wither;*
*And whatsoever he does shall prosper.*

"That is beautiful, sire. I wish I could compose songs like that."

David grows silent. "This is the one I especially wanted you to hear. It is about your father and grandfather.

*Saul and Jonathan were lovely and pleasant in their lives,*
*and in their death, they were not divided:*
*They were swifter than eagles,*
*They were stronger than lions.*

*How are the mighty fallen in the midst of the battle!*

*O, Jonathan, you have been slain.*

*I am distressed for you, my brother Jonathan:*
*Very pleasant have you been unto me:*
*Your love to me was wonderful,*
*Passing the love of women.*

*How are the mighty fallen.*

Tears return. Tears of David for the dearest friend he ever had. Tears of Mefiboset for the dearest father he never had the chance to truly know.

"You really did love my father, didn't you, sire."

"Not a day goes by, I do not think of him. You have no idea how comforting your presence has been to me. Do you mind very much if I call you Jonathan sometimes? It is so comforting as I grow older."

"I understand, sire."

They hear a knock on the door, and a servant enters. "Your Majesty, you have an appointment with your treasurer."

"Thank you. I will be right there," David responds.

He looks at Sett, puts his hands up to Sett's shoulders, and brings him close. He kisses him on each cheek and affectionately pounds his back. With nothing more said, he leaves.

A week later, a servant who Sett has never seen before knocks on his door. The servant is dressed in fine clothes, is as tall as Sett, and ample around the middle. But, when he speaks, his voice is high pitched. He has no beard.

"Are you Mefiboset?" the strange man asks.

Sett stands in his doorway, three-footed crutches in place. "Yes."

"King David has requested that I take you to the back wing of his palace where he keeps special guests. He thought you would like to visit some of them."

"I do not know anyone else in his palace."

"He ordered me to take you there anyway. It is an order I must carry out."

Sett stares at the man, then out to the courtyard, then at his feet, then back up at the man. Without saying more, he closes his door behind him and follows the strange man.

They go through a door Sett had thought was just a storeroom, but which is actually a corridor. The corridor is long, and the servant does not look back to see if Sett is keeping up.

At the far end of the corridor is a double door with a guard on each side. The guards open the doors, and Sett makes his way to the other side.

The servant turns and points to another closed door. "In there," is all he says before disappearing in the other direction.

Sett opens the door and stares.

"Oh, Sett. You are still alive."

"Grandmother?" he says.

An aged, stooped woman walks toward him, arms outstretched, both laughing and crying.

Sett shifts his elbows onto his crutches and envelops the woman in his arms as she lays her head on his chest. He lays one hand on her gray hair, bends over and kisses it.

Ahinoam looks up into his eyes and pulls him down toward her. She kisses him on both cheeks, his eyes, the tip of his nose. "Remember when I used to kiss you like this when you were a little boy?" she whispers.

"Yes, Grandmother, I remember."

She draws back far enough to see him better. "Now you are all grown up, and you look so much like your father. Your grandfather too. Seeing you again is like seeing them again."

"So I have been told," he says.

"Oh, what is wrong with me?" she says, pulling back from Sett. "Everyone is here."

Sett looks past his grandmother, trying to recall the past.

"You surely remember your old namesake red-headed uncle," the senior Mefiboset says, walking forward. He grabs Sett's hand and forearm, then bear hugs him. He draws back, leaving his hands on Sett's shoulders.

"I never thought I'd see the day that you would be taller than me, but you are very much taller than me. How did you manage that? Ha, ha."

He turns to the others in the room. "Come on, everyone. We have our little Sett back. You remember your other uncle, Armoni. And, of course, my mother, Rizpah, who still has her red hair, more than her sons do."

"Of course," Sett says, grinning and stretching his memory.

Each of the others step forward and give Sett a kiss on each cheek.

"What about me? Doesn't your old aunt count? I'm Merab, the aunt who was so busy raising five babies by myself, I hardly saw you." She walks forward and embraces her brother's son.

"I'm so glad to see you again. I guess I did neglect coming to see you when you were young. I'll never forget the day your grandmother called us all together when you were about six years old, and…"

She catches the eye of her mother and clears her throat. "Here are your cousins—all grown men now like you. Well, they are a little older than you, so you didn't get to see them much. But I hope now you will get to know each other better."

Sett looks back over at his grandmother.

"I don't understand. Why are you here and not out with everyone else in the palace?"

"Most kings kill off everyone in the family of their predecessor. David did not do that. Instead, he brought us here. We are his permanent guests. We will remain safe as long as we stay here under his roof."

"So, you have been here since my escape when I was eleven."

"Yes, Nine years. I thought you knew that."

"Well, maybe I did. I'm not sure. I do remember coming to Gibeon and asking Ziba to tell you where I was."

"Watch out for Ziba," former Queen Ahinoam warns. "His first job at the palace as a boy was carrying out manure. He worked his way up by lying about anyone whose job he wanted. Saul believed his stories and promoted him, but I never did. The man has been a liar all his life."

"I met his son, Lechy."

"Yes, I've heard about him. As treacherous as his father. But now, let us talk about pleasant things. What have you been doing?"

The next two hours are spent sharing stories of adventures and misadventures of the family since their separation.

The same tall man with the high-pitched voice enters the reception room. "It is time to go."

Everyone stiffens and stares. "Go where?" someone whispers.

"Was this the last meeting before our execution?" Uncle Mefiboset asks.

"No, nothing like that. You will go back to your rooms. The boy Mefiboset will be allowed back into David's palace." He motions for Sett to leave first. As he works his way toward the door, Sett looks over at his grandmother. "I will go over to Gibeon and check on things there."

He is hurried through the door before Ahinoam is allowed to respond. He does not see her smile of approval.

The next day, Sett approaches his personal servant, Elza.

"Uh, sir. Am I allowed to leave the palace?"

"Of course. You may come and go as you please."

"I came here with my own personal mule. Do you think it is still here?"

"I am sure it is. The king admires a fine, strong mule and orders that they all be given the greatest care."

"In that case, would someone prepare my mule for me?

I would like to take a ride up to Gibeon."

The servant stares a moment. "I'm sure that can be arranged. I will let you know as soon as it is ready for you. Will you require a platform of any kind to kneel on for mounting your mule?"

"I have managed without one, but it would be appreciated."

Sett sits on one of the benches between two blue-and-white columns in the outer courtyard and waits. His mule is located and brought out to him, along with a small stool. Sett expertly pulls his big frame and knees up onto the stool by manipulating his three-footed crutches. With strong arms, he lifts himself up onto the animal

Sett guides his mule out the north gate of the palace, down past the fortress, then through the rest of young Jerusalem. He turns toward what was once his home. He arrives just as the sun is ready to go down.

He knocks on the gate of his grandfather's palace. A servant he does not recognize answers it.

"Yes? May I help you?"

In his most authoritative voice, Sett announces who he is: "I am master and owner of the palace."

The confused servant looks up at Sett, still on his mule, then back into the courtyard.

"Who is it?"

The voice is not familiar to Sett.

"Master, this man says he is the master. Shall I have him chained?"

The man steps to the gate. He is a foot shorter than Sett, has a round face and bulbous nose. He holds his head up so high, he has to look down in order to see straight ahead of him.

"Oh," he says upon seeing Sett. "We were not expecting you."

Sett leads his mule into the blue and red tiled courtyard and looks around. Some of the pillars are small hairline cracks here and there. It has been two years since he has been in his palace, and then only for a few hours.

"Where is your father?" he asks.

"He has turned half of one of the storerooms into his office, and is checking how much money has been brought in this month so you can be given your share." Lechy's eyes dart around the courtyard as he speaks.

"Lead me to him."

"He is very busy."

"I need to see him."

Lechy walks toward the room where his father is and knocks on the door. Ziba calls out, "How many times have I told you not to disturb me when I am in here?"

"Father, it is Mefiboset."

"What does he want?" Ziba calls out through the closed door.

"That is fine," Sett says. "He is busy. I will see how he is doing another day."

Sett dismounts. He makes his way over to the side steps leading to King Saul's apartment on the second floor.

"Uh, sir," Lechy says. "You may wish to go through the throne room and inspect it also while you are here."

"That is fine."

As Sett makes his way up the grand staircase leading from the courtyard, he notices Lechy rushing up through the side stairs. *So, ole Ziba is still living in there.*

He moves through the throne room, remembering his one day of glory as king on the alabaster throne when he was eleven years old, pauses briefly, then exits through the back door into Saul's apartment. Just as he steps through, he hears the door leading to the outside steps slam shut and smiles to himself.

Sett looks around at the coral and black tiles on the floor and ceiling, the black marble columns supporting the floors above, and the frescoes of his grandfather's battle victories on the wall. Finally, he heads back down to the courtyard. As he arrives, he notices someone else there.

"Do we have guests?" he asks Lechy.

"Sir, you may remember meeting Yassib. He owns the land adjoining ours. We have been neighbors and friends all our life. Yassib is Gibeonite and now a Priest of Dagon.

"Our religion is dying out. We cannot let that happen," Yassib says. "I plan to do everything in my power to bring Dagon back to his former glory."

The young priest, who Sett judges to be about his same age, has an oval face and curly brown hair. He wears a tunic of blue and robe of white, both trimmed with gold fringe. On his head is a cone-shaped turban that matches his tunic.

"Yassib came over to borrow some scrolls from our...from Saul's library. No one reads them anyway."

"I read every book at my disposal," Yassib says, smiling, and holding his hands in a pose of prayer.

"I hope my grandfather's library will be pleasing to you. Perhaps you will find the Hebrew scriptures to your liking."

"Perhaps," Yassib says, not smiling.

Lechy and Yassib disappear to a back room. Sett hears one of them shouting, but cannot tell which man or what he is shouting about.

Moments later, they come out of the room. Yassib has two scrolls under his arm.

"Did you say you are King Saul's direct descendant?" Yassib asks.

"Yes, I am."

"He got himself killed, didn't he?"

Without waiting for a reply, Yassib leaves.

"He is bitter," Lechy explains, once they are alone again. "He has suffered much because of Saul. His family was killed. I don't blame him."

He looks at Sett, but Sett does not respond in kind.

"I'm thinking of moving back in."

# 13 ~ BETROTHAL

"**B**ut do you know for sure she still lives in Ur?"

Uncle Mefiboset asks Sett on a visit to the wing for political prisoners.

"I sent her a letter a couple years ago when I returned to Israel with Machir and ended up in Lodebar so she would know where I was. She never wrote back."

"That should tell you something. She has either lost interest in you, or she has moved away."

"Kissara loved me. And she would have no reason to leave a city where she and her mother were able to live decently."

"What if she was kidnapped like you were? What if she caught a disease and died?"

"What you say makes me even more worried than ever. I must go find her. Do not try to talk me out of going."

"You must certainly love her," Uncle Mefiboset says, leaning back against the wall and smiling.

"I do, Uncle, I do, although I do not understand it. She cannot lift anything heavy, she is slow, you cannot hear her in a crowd, and she giggles."

"That is part of the charm of women, my boy. Their delicacy brings out the protective nature in men, and their gentleness brings out the warmth that men do not otherwise know they have. Women are good for us."

Sett looks down at the floor, out the window, and over to his uncle. He presses his lips together in a slight smile and nods his head.

"So, which route are you taking?"

"There is more than one?" Sett asks.

"Yes, the southern route through Arabia and the northern route through Harran."

"Oh. Well, what do you think?"

"The northern route is most used. It goes up through Damascus in Syria, then to Harran in Anatolia, and over to Nineveh in Assyria. From there, you travel along the Euphrates River down to Ur in Babylonia. Some is desert, some is forested, some is marshes. But at least it is not all desert like the southern route."

"Then, that is what I shall do."

"What form of transportation are you going to use?"

"Just my mule as always."

"Have you thought of a camel for such a long trip? Or even an Arabian horse? We don't ride horses; they're not as strong and hearty as mules. But Arabian horses have been bred for the desert."

"I don't know much about camels or horses. I will stick with my trusty mule."

Sett rises. "Well, I had better make the arrangements. I'd like to be gone in the next couple days. Would you bring out my grandmother? I would like to say goodbye to her."

Two days later, Sett has found a caravan headed north to Damascus. Out of the funds allotted him by Ziba "after expenses," he purchases a second mule for Kissara, and a third one for her mother. He pays the head of the caravan his fee.

"All right, everyone!" the caravan leader shouts, "out there, I am your master, your god, your everything. If you want to get to your destination in as good shape as you are today, you will listen to me and follow my every order. You do not question me. Anyone who does is out of the caravan and with no refund. I do not care if your uncle or brother or neighbor is a caravan leader. I am the one leading this one, and you will follow my instructions at all times without question. Is that clear?"

He waits for ascension, but the response is weak.

"I said, am I clear. Well?"

This time the response is loud and strong.

They head out of the plain north of Jerusalem, turn east, and cross the Jordan River. Now they are headed straight north.

On one mule, Sett has an extra robe and tunic, an extra pair of protective boots, his crutches, and extra clothes for Kissara and her mother. On the second mule, he carries plenty of barley for the mules, cheese and bread and dried fruit for himself, and water in abundance for all. He rides the third mule, with his usual step stool tied to the rump.

Two days before arriving in Damascus, they smell smoke. Sett looks around to see where the fire is. He cannot find it but knows it is growing.

The caravan leader rides fast to a nearby rise to see where it is coming from. He rides back down and shouts, "Follow me!"

He directs his Arabian horse to the east off the highway. Sett can see now that the smoke is from a forest fire in the Ante Lebanon Mountains to their west.

The fire moves fast. Sett begins to choke. He puts his head down and covers his mouth and nose with his hand.

The caravan turns and follows the leader out of the foothills where the highway is and toward the desert where there is nothing to burn. People whip their animals into a run. All struggle to control animals, beginning to panic. Some on foot camels break ranks and rush past the others.

Sett hangs tight to the reins of his three mules and follows the others out of danger. He looks behind him. The fire has crossed the highway where they were moments earlier. On they rush into the desert. Now the fire is in the brush. Moving fast.

Still in danger, Sett and the others urge their animals on. Some lose control of their pack animals that now run in sporadic directions, panicked. The burros are slower, the flames nipping at their heals.

Still the galloping and rushing and choking. Choking from the smoke behind them and the desert dust being stirred up in front of all but those in the lead.

Hurry. Escape. Live.

Sett notices people in the front stopping. He slows his three mules and is grateful he has been able to maintain control of them.

When he comes to a stop, he turns and watches as the flames grow smaller and finally burn out for lack of fuel. The desert has stopped them.

"We will spend the night here," the caravan leader announces.

The next morning, they return to the highway and head straight north, then veer west toward Damascus. The day after that is spent replenishing supplies that had fallen off in the frantic rush to escape the fire.

They turn northeast toward their next destination

Sett's mind wanders. *Will they replant those trees, or let the desert take over there too? Will they be there for my grandchildren? Well, I have to marry Kissara first, don't I?* He smiles to himself.

For two weeks, they travel.

Sometimes people ride, sometimes they slip off their mounts and walk beside them for exercise. Sometimes they talk, sometimes they just think.

*I wonder what she is doing right now?*

Another day passes.

*Is she still making gold jewelry?*

Two more days.

*Did she have many customers today?*

When they stop on the sixth night at the oasis, the caravan leader announces the spring has dried out.

"There is no water here. You will have to drink your emergency supply. And may the gods help whoever failed to follow my orders and bring an emergency supply."

For two more days, they pass through the desert,

hoping for an oasis that is not dying. It does not happen.

"Did he bring us out into this desert to die?" someone near Sett complains.

"He doesn't know what he is doing."

"We need to get rid of him."

"Out!" It is the caravan leader. "Gather up your stuff and get out."

The startled men look up at the leader, eyes squinting as though they had heard him wrong.

"Now. You have until I count to fifty to be gone. I do not need people like you in my caravan."

"But there is no water out there," one of the men complains.

"Since you're smarter than me, you will find water on your own. And I am almost through counting."

The leader pulls out a whip. "Or do you prefer fifty lashes?"

The men ride off into the darkness. The leader turns and looks at the others who had heard the complaints.

"Anyone else? Now I suggest you take a small swig of water and go to sleep. Then you can have all the water you want in your dreams."

The next morning is the third day without water. The animals trudge slowly. Many of the people are now off their animals and walking next to them or leaving them beside the road. One step at a time, hoping for water soon before they die.

Sett's tongue is swelled, he is dizzy, he sometimes wonders where he is, his heart races. He determines to keep going. Some drop out and stop beside the highway to wait for death.

Sett had not noticed when the caravan leader had left them. But now their leader makes his way back toward the caravan shouting with a hoarse voice, "Found water. Euphrates River. Just ahead. Brought back enough for everyone. A little for your animals. A sip for each of you."

Each one takes his turn until he has had his sip.

"Follow me now," he says though most do not hear his weakened voice. "Thank the gods."

Renewed, they sleep on the banks of the Euphrates River that night, the river that descends out of the mountains far to the north and spills into the sea many days journey south on the other side of Ur.

*Did my sweetheart drink out of these same waters today? Is she now touching the drops of water I touched earlier?*

The next day, the recovering caravan makes its way to the other side of the Euphrates along its branch called Bilakh. They enter through the western Aleppo Gate of Harran on the twentieth day, two days overdue.

Here they stop for a day of rest due to changing caravan leaders. It is hot here, but the trees offer shade. He sees many stumps and people pulling them out for farming.

Sett puts his horses and baggage in a stable and goes for a walk. He is curious about the cone-shaped houses. He smiles. *They look like beehives. Wait until I tell Kissara about them.*

Past these houses, he sees a temple to Nanna, the same kind as in Ur.

He stops at the booth of a pottery merchant.

"Do you know where the palace of Harran was? You know, the founder of the city? He was brother to one of my ancestors, Abraham."

"Sorry, don't know about any old palace."

He goes to another merchant.

"Do you know of a palace here that might be a thousand years old?"

"There are some old buildings, but they are in another part of the city."

"Do you know of an ancient palace?"

"There is a palace up that hill. It looks pretty old. That may be where your ancestor's brother lived."

Sett works his way up the street and up a hill until he arrives at the ruins of what Sett believes might have been a palace two thousand years before. He goes to the opposite side of the road from the front gate and squats to watch it and imagine. *I wonder if Abraham walked this street and lived in that palace?*

The next day they are back on the highway. They have a new caravan leader who goes down the line, meeting everyone, and making sure everyone knows he is in charge. He stops and chats with Sett.

"I'll bet you are glad you stuck with your mules," the leader tells Sett. The caravan leader I replaced is a fan of Arabian horses. Did he try to sell you one?"

"Yes, he did. But my mules are larger than most horses, and are stronger."

"And can stand heat better too," the leader adds. "Well, we'll be headed southeast toward Nineveh now."

"How long will it take us to get there?" Sett asks.

"About two weeks. Unless we run into something unexpected, of course."

*Is Kissara okay? Lord God of heaven and earth, protect her. She is not very strong. Besides, she does not know how to use a spear or sword or....*

*Come to think of it, I don't either. Maybe I can take lessons from someone tonight.*

That night when the caravan stops, Sett makes his way down the row of tents being set up near camels, horses, mules, and donkeys, looking for someone who might be handling a weapon. He sees a man making arrows.

"Hello, sir. Are you an expert archer?"

"Some people would say no, but I think I'm pretty good. I'm an expert at the Parthian Shot."

"What's that?" Sett asks, leaning hard on his crutches.

"It's where you ride your horse one direction, but you twist around in the saddle and shoot arrows at people coming at you from behind."

"Amazing. Without hanging on to the reins?"

"That's the idea."

"Do you think you could teach me? Not the horse trick,

but just shooting arrows. I can pay you."

"Well, I don't know in your condition and all."

"Please give me a try."

"I guess I can start teaching you how to make your own arrows. Sit over here."

Another six days pass, and the caravan continues southeast until it reaches the Tigris River. They camp there for the night.

*Lord God of heaven and earth and all things. You can see everywhere. Look down on my Kissara. Watch over her. Protect her. Keep her safe until I can get to her. I love her, Lord God. I love her.*

On they travel. Though many in the caravan are new arrivals picked up in cities and villages along the way, some have traveled all the way from its beginning in Jerusalem.

For the most part, Sett has tried to stay to himself. Too many questions could put him in danger, especially from someone loyal to King David. *Well, they should be loyal to him. He is our king now.*

More days traveling along the banks of the Tigris.

"At least we do not lack for water now," Sett tells his mules. "I'll bet you're happy for that."

On day nine, it rains. All day it rains. The caravan moves on, grateful for the blessing of the gods.

Sett bows his head to shield his eyes whenever the winds shift the rain around, and it comes at him from the southeast. Now and then, he looks up and sees most everyone else with their heads down. *What about the caravan leader? He has to know where to take us.*

They stop earlier than usual for the night. Everyone struggles to put up his tent and get under its shelter. Some have goat-hair tents that grow more waterproof as more water pours down on them. Some have leather tents.

Sett's is a goat-hair tent. As usual, he kneels and works his way around, securing it with pegs along the corners and between. Finally, he puts up the long pole that raises it in the middle and crawls inside. As always, his blanket has remained dry because of it being rolled up inside the tent when stored.

"Sorry, you three. You're going to have to stay out in the rain tonight," he tells his mules. "My tent isn't big enough for you and me both."

He grows cold and pulls out his small bow drill and some dry cotton. At the entrance to his tent, he builds a small fire. He falls asleep.

Morning comes, and he hears yelling. He crawls out of his tent, dragging his crutches with him, and lifts himself up with strong arms.

He looks around. Water from the Tigris has overflowed its banks. Though it has not reached any of the tents, he knows it still poses a problem for them. The rain has reduced to a drizzle but is still coming down.

Each man wades around in the mud, taking down his tent and trying to keep what he can dry by rolling it up inside his tent. Animals are repacked and fed, then lined up.

The caravan veers away from the fast-flooding Tigris and continues southwest. Not too far away is the Euphrates. They are between the two great rivers, and their road has become a marsh.

People who have brought carts and wagons with them struggle to free wheels from the mud, only to do it all over again after just a little bit of progress. Temperamental donkeys sit in the mud and refuse to go on. Grouchy camels refuse to drink the water because it has "things" in it. The mules do not seem to care one way or the other. They plod on.

"I am so proud of you," Sett tells his three mules.

The drizzle continues all day, and so does the flooding. The caravan leader works his way back. "Let's just stop where we are. We have to give the water a chance to soak into the ground. We may be here two or three days. So just settle in the best you can."

*Oh, my darling Kissara, I am coming. Even if it takes me a year, I will come to you. Wait for me, my darling. Wait for me. I am coming.*

The next day, the sun comes out. It is a welcomed sun that will draw the moisture out of the ground. But it is a hot sun. People set up their tents, and those with hides spread them on the ground inside so they do not have to sit and sleep in the mud. Sometimes Sett goes over to the archery expert and takes a lesson.

Three days later, they resume their journey south. Seventeen days after leaving Harran, they arrive at Nineveh. Sett has been traveling nearly a month and a half.

They cross over to the east side of the Euphrates and travel along the River Khoser, one of its branches flowing east. Being a procession of mud-caked, tired, disheveled travelers, they enter the grand city through the side Watering Gate.

On their left is the temple to Nabu, son of Marduk. Sett, despite being tired, slides off his mule and goes inside to see what yet another statue declared to be a god looks like. Nabu wears a horned cap, and his hands are clasped in front of him in the same manner Sett remembers his neighbor, Yassib, newly-made priest of Dagon. He has a long, curly beard like all good Assyrians do, and fringe on his long shawl as do all wealthy Assyrians. *Humpf. Doesn't look any different than a human.*

As he exits the temple, Sett sees across the street another temple—this one dedicated to Ishtar, the name Assyrians call Inanna of Ur, both the goddess of love and fertility. He does not go into that temple

As always, they stay in the city a full day to give everyone opportunity to replenish their supplies and replace any equipment that has been ruined in their travels.

They leave Nineveh and head farther south. On their first night, Sett finds his archery tutor.

"Thank you, my friend, for helping me pick out a bow back in Nineveh," Sett says.

"All bows are a little different. Sit, and I'll show you how to hold your bow."

More days pass as the caravan slowly snakes its way south. Closer to Sett's Kissara. Closer to the woman he loves and wants to be his own the rest of his life.

*I am coming, Kissara. I am coming.*

Despite the rain three weeks earlier, the desert has settled back to normal—dry, desolate, unfriendly, challenging. They see miniature dust cyclones now and then on either side of the highway. The sky is a mixed blue and brown. But that is the way of the desert.

Sett now notices small animals scampering around the desert floor in a frenzy. They are funny looking, and Sett laughs at them.

The wind, formerly concentrated around the miniature cyclones, lifts and seems to disappear. All is quiet. Sett feels safe.

Then they see it. Rolling across the desert to their right is a cloud of dust higher than twenty ziggurat towers like the one in Ur. Horses and mules rear up on their hind legs, their eyes wild. The camels close one set of eyelids and squat where they are.

Sett and the other riders slide off their animals and urge them to lie down by whatever means works. The wind grows stronger, then it hits. Sett lies between two of his mules, head down, and robe brought up over his head.

He does not know how long it takes for the mountain of dust to pass through them. He waits as the wind whistles, and the dust particles ram into anything in their way.

On it comes, and on. Wind, dust, and the debris it has picked up along its path. Sometimes he is hit by the branch of an acacia tree out in the desert somewhere. Sometimes he is hit by a rolling ball of a dead desert bush. Often, he is hit by gravel picked up by the strong gale.

It stops. The wind leaves them behind as it makes its way farther east in search of more victims.

Now in the quiet, Sett stirs and gradually sits up. Sand falls off his head. His mules stand and shake the sand off their backs. He smiles in relief, climbs back onto his mule, and waits for the caravan to begin again.

Once more on the highway, farther and farther south. *I am coming, my sweet Kissara. I am coming.*

They cross back over the Euphrates River so they are on the west bank. Then they shift over to one of the branches flowing southwest. The week after, they arrive in Babylon.

They enter the city through the Lugalgirra Gate. They could have entered through the Ishtar Gate, but are too dirty and not allowed in through it.

Sett sees the temple to Ishtar to his left, along with other temples. What is most striking is the tower in the middle of the city. It looks to Sett to be sixty or seventy man-lengths high.

"What is that?" he asks the man behind him.

"This is old Babel. This is their famed tower."

Sett cannot take his eyes off it. "I never saw anything that high before," he says to whoever can hear him. "It reaches nearly to the clouds."

They come to the temple to Marduk and stop. The bazaar is right there next to it. Travelers disburse to where ever they need to go to replenish supplies or do a little sightseeing.

The following day as the caravan reassembles, Sett rides up to the caravan leader. "How far are we from Ur?"

"Ur is our next stop. It will take us two weeks to get there. Is that soon enough for you, son?"

# MAP 2:  UR IN 1000 BC

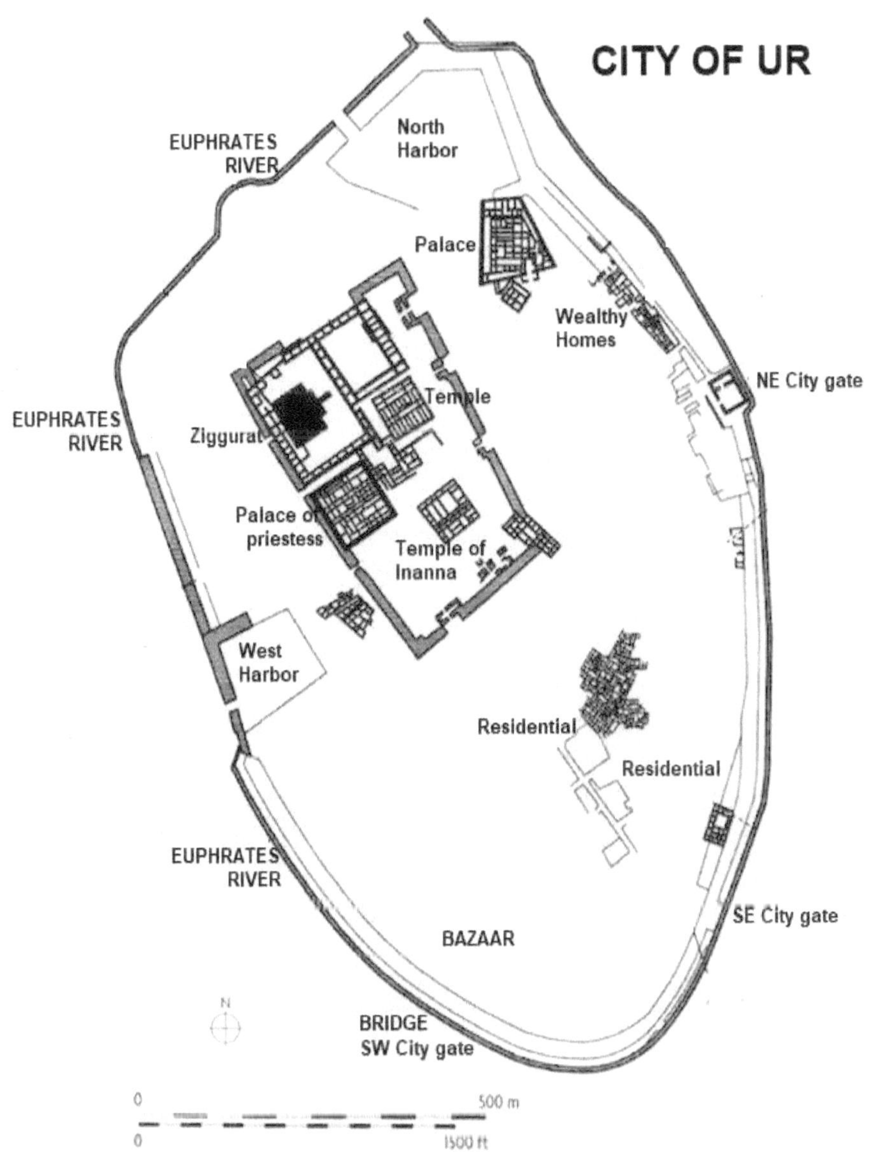

# 14 ~ HIDING PLACE

**B**ack on the highway, Sett and the others work their way ever south. The day is a hot one. Hotter than any they have encountered thus far.

Wind. Where is the wind? Too much wind a week ago. Now not enough. Hot, steamy, stifling. Trying to breathe. Drinking more water. Pouring water onto their robes and hiding under them.

The animals move slower. Sett dismounts, as does many others, and makes his way with his crutches beside his animals to help them preserve their strength.

One step at a time. Then another. And another.

The caravan leader stops the procession.

"All right, everyone," he says. "We're stopping to sleep. From now on, we ride at night and sleep during the day. Otherwise, we'll kill our animals in this heat. Well, I don't suppose we'd kill the camels, but it will be easier on them. And easier on us humans. We want to arrive alive."

Sett puts up his tent, crawls inside to find shade from the heat, though he leaves openings at both ends for even the slightest breeze to flow through and give a little relief.

He tries to sleep but cannot.

*Oh, Kissara, my sweet. I am almost there. Wait for me, my darling. Smile. Be brave. I am coming.*

Sett smiles to himself.

*How arrogant can I be? She is perfectly fine. There is nothing to save her from. Lord God, keep her that way. Keep her safe. And, let her answer still be yes.*

Somehow it is now dark and time to get back out on the highway. Sett is surprised at how busy the highway is in the middle of the night.

They pass Nippur where Machir had met his wife, but do not enter with the gates closed all night. They pass Uruk,

Finally, Sett arrives at his destination. They stop outside the gates of Ur to wait until they are opened.

*Thank you, Lord God, for keeping me safe so I can be reunited forever with my Kissara.*

Relying on his strong arms, he paces back and forth in front of the gates with his trusty three-footed crutches until they are opened.

Now back on his mule, he makes his way across the bridge over the Euphrates River, through the North Harbor Gate and into the city of his dreams.

The palace is on his left. Just ahead and on his right in the middle of the city is the walled temple complex dedicated to Nanna, god of the moon, and his deified daughter, Inanna, goddess of love and fertility.

At the far end of the complex are the royal tombs. He continues on until he comes to the house of his former slave master, Garash. He does not stop. He passes other homes not near as nice until he finally comes to the bazaar.

He stops, puts his mules in a stable, pulls out a comb, and grooms himself. He reaches for a waterskin on one of the mules, pours some in his hands, and splashes it onto his face. He wipes it with his sleeve.

Satisfied, he moves on, looking for his beloved's shop. *Now, which way was it?* Frustrated that, after only two years, he does not remember, Sett makes his way down several narrow lanes. His heart beats faster.

Finally, he spots it. The shop of golden jewelry. The shop of Kissara and memories of golden moments. And there she is. His Kissara.

After all the planning, and months on the road, and anticipating, he realizes he does not know what to say. He stands facing Kissara. She is looking down at a necklace on the counter. He clears his throat.

Kissara raises her eyes, a broad grin comes to her lips, and her sparkling eyes flood with tears. "Ohhh."

They stand before each other, hearts at last reunited. Sett smiles at her, still not speaking.

She lifts the end of the counter, pulls him in, and reaches up, holding on to his neck and burying her head in his chest.

Supporting his crutches with his elbows, he reaches around his love and embraces her. Still, they say nothing. For a long while, they say nothing. He bends low and kisses the top of her head. She looks up into his eyes, her own still flooded with tears.

"When? How? Where did you go?" she whispers.

"Didn't you get my letter? I wrote you right after I arrived there. Well, no matter. I am here now and ready to take you home with me."

"What about my mother?"

"Your mother too. I brought three strong mules, one for each of us to ride."

She lays her head back onto his chest. And his arms embrace her closer.

"When can you be ready?" he whispers after moments of silence.

"Well, I don't know. There is so much to do."

Sett holds her at arm's length. "Like what? Take your jewelry and supplies with you, and bundle up your clothes and some food. I'll ask Garasa if he will take possession of your house and shop and sell them for you. You can be ready by tomorrow."

"I have one more customer coming later in the day," she says, pulling gently away. "Then, I will gather up everything, lock up, and we will go to my mother's home."

"I have to go back to where I stabled my mules and rent a room for the night," Sett says. "By the time I get back here, your customer should have come and gone."

He raises the counter again and backs out of the booth. Their happy eyes lock for a moment of bliss, and he pulls away.

An hour later, Sett is back at the shop. It is closed up. He looks at it, his brows pushing down, and furrows forming between his eyes. Then he laughs. *Oh, nothing to worry about. Her customer came early, and she went on home. Let me see now if I can remember where she and her mother live.*

He heads in the direction he remembers Kissara always walking when going home. He progresses a few blocks but decides he is going down the wrong street. He turns and tries another street. Still, nothing he recognizes.

*Perhaps I remember her gate wrong.* He stops at a shop. "Excuse me. Could you tell me where Tilha and her daughter live?"

"Sorry."

He goes on down a little farther and stops again.

"Excuse me. Do you happen to know where Tilha and her daughter live?"

"No."

More stops. No more smiling. Now hard to breathe. Now squinting to see. Now straining to find and hold on to his forever.

"Excuse me. Do you happen to know where Tilha and her daughter live?"

"Do you mean the gold jeweler? They live next door to me. I am just now closing up. You can follow me."

He has reason to smile again.

Less than an hour later, Sett knocks on the gate of his beloved. Harder, he knocks. And faster. He hears a soft voice on the other side and stops to listen. The gate is opened by a little lady Sett recognizes as Kissara's mother, Tilha.

"It's me, Mefiboset," he says.

She opens the gate wider and lets him in. She smiles.

"Well, when did you arrive?" she asks. "Kissara will be thrilled to see you. She talks about you all the…what's wrong?"

"You haven't seen her?"

"What do you mean?"

"I arrived in town three hours ago. I saw her at the booth. She said she had one last customer before she could close up, so I went to find a room to rent at an inn. When I got back, she was gone."

Tilha stares up at the tall Sett, her eyebrows furrowed, and her lips curled as though preparing to cry. "How long ago was it?"

"Half an hour."

"Oh, no. They started out a few months ago, asking when she was going to arrange everything, but we refused. Then they started telling her when to show up, but we still refused. Apparently, they have taken her by force."

She sits on a wooden bench in her courtyard and puts her hands up to her face.

"They who?" Sett asks, sitting opposite her.

"The priests of the temple to Inanna. You may remember Inanna is the deified daughter of Nanna of our city. The temple to Inanna is in Uruk, a day's journey north of here."

"She's gone?"

"Well, she is still here in Ur. They take the maidens to the palace of Nanna and prepare them."

Sett looks at the sky above. The veins in his large neck pulse. He clenches his teeth. He does not want to ask the next question.

"What are they preparing her to be?"

"Oh, they aren't preparing her to be a priestess, if that's what you are thinking. But they are preparing...they are preparing my little girl...to offer her body as a sacrifice to at least one man before releasing her."

"What?" Sett responds, his face turning red. "No!"

"Every woman in the kingdom is required to do this at least once in her life. But she is not necessarily freed right away. The women sit in rows, and the men walk between them to select the one they want. The woman has to wait until she is selected by a man, whether it be three days or three years. If she disfigures herself to avoid ever being selected, she will be there the rest of her life."

Sett rises and works his way around the courtyard, the veins on his neck throbbing. Tilha weeps.

He returns to her. "We've got to get her out."

"That's impossible. The temple complex is surrounded by thick walls in the middle of the city, and every gate is heavily guarded. She's gone forever."

"Let me think," he says, sitting back down.

Silence.

"I know what I will do," Sett says, standing again. "I will go to the gate and tell them I could not go up to Uruk to worship Inanna because my ship bound for the Indian Sea is getting ready to leave. I have enough money on me to give as a bribe that they will not refuse me."

"But how will you get her out?"

"I don't know," he says, his voice lower now.

They think longer. They do not speak. Tilha leaves for a moment and returns with some cheese, barley bread, and dipping yogurt.

They each eat a little, then return to their thinking.

The sky turns red. They both know this will be Kissara's first night in the priestess's palace, and she will be weeping in fear.

"There is only one thing that can be done," Tilha finally says in a low voice.

"What?"

"I will spend the night taking apart three of my late husband's robes and sewing them on to each other. You are a very tall man. If you weighed more, it would not look unusual. That extra weight will be me."

"But what about your feet showing?"

"You have crutches. When you walk, you keep your feet up off the ground. I will put on my husband's large shoes and provide you with feet. You will just be temporarily injured and need the crutches a few days, you will tell them.

"We will wrap a long sash around both you and me, so we do not accidentally separate from each other. My part of the sash will be under my arms, then we will wrap your part over your shoulders. It will work."

He thinks.

"But what good will that do? You certainly cannot get her out of the priestess's palace."

Kissara's mother looks into Sett's eyes. He does not understand. She tells him. "I do not plan to leave."

"What?"

"I am about her same size. I will take her place. If we do it in the early morning shadows, no one will be able to tell the difference."

"But what will you do when they discover you are not Kissara?"

"You will not worry about that. You need to figure out how you will get my daughter out of the city and away from here. Ur is an evil place."

They are quiet a while longer.

"Well, I guess I could go see Garash tonight, tell him where my mules are, and ask him to have at least one of them somewhere near the gate out of the temple complex so we can make our escape."

"That is perfect. You go do that, and I will start putting together a large robe for you and me to wear."

She stands and takes a few steps to the bench opposite her, where Sett is seated. She puts his face in her hands and looks into his eyes. "The gods have brought you here for such a time as this.

"Now go. We must be ready by daybreak."

# 15 ~ THE IMPOSSIBLE

*J*ust before dawn, Sett returns to Tilha's house. She is ready and lets him in.

Tilha looks at him and whispers, "Thank you for doing this. Oh, and here is money to pay for her."

She backs up to his chest, and they wrap a large sash around themselves, part under her arms and part over his shoulders. Her head comes up to Sett's chest. Then he puts on the large robe she had made and hides all but her feet behind it.

They open their gate and head toward the middle of the city where the Nanna temple and palace complex are. When they arrive, they see Garash standing across from the gate with all three of Sett's mules. Garash nods at them briefly, then turns away.

As planned, Sett knocks on the gate into the Nanna complex. The plan goes into action. Garash across the street with the three mules beats them and makes them rear up on their hind legs.

"Help!" he cries, and the guards rush over to him.

By now, the gate has been opened, and the gatekeeper is at the entrance.

"Please, may I come in and worship Inanna? My ship is going to leave within an hour, and I wanted one last time to worship her."

"No. That is done up in Ukur, not here."

Tilha thrusts her foot in her husband's big shoes

forward in the way of the gate being closed.

"I have money," Sett says. He pulls out his money pouch. "How much do you want? I will give you thirty pieces of silver."

"No."

"Forty."

"No"

"How much?"

"One hundred."

"That's fine. Take the entire pouch. You can have it all."

He pushes the gate and enters. The gatekeeper nods to the soldiers in the courtyard, and the soldiers return to their positions.

"Follow me," the gatekeeper says. "You will have to wait a few moments while we gather them together. You understand we just give them beauty treatments here before sending them on up to Uruk.

"Have a seat."

"Uh, no. No, thank you. I will stand and wait."

The gatekeeper disappears.

*What is going on back there? Has she run away? Did they figure it out and kill her?*

They continue to wait. Then a door in the back of the room opens. Young women file out and sit. Many are crying and have their heads down. They are all dressed alike.

*Look up, Kissara. I cannot tell which one is you.*

"All right. Take your pick, go to that room over there, and when you are done, leave. And it had better be quick."

Sett slowly makes his way down the rows of women. "Look up so I can see you," he tells each one. His heart beats faster as he anticipates finding her. *But will I be able to get her out of this hell?*

Then he sees his Kissara. When she looks up, Sett quickly cautions her. "Shhh." He turns to the gatekeeper.

"I will take this one." He throws the required coins into her lap, she gathers them up and stands. He leads her to the assigned room.

As soon as they close the door, Sett throws open his robe.

"Mother?"

"Now change clothes with me," Tilha instructs, "and take my place under the robe. Here are your father's shoes. Put them on quickly."

Once Kissara is in place, Tilha wraps the sash around them both to keep them from getting separated enough they are discovered.

Tilha leans over and kisses her daughter, then leans up and pulls Sett's head down so she can kiss him also.

"Have a good life."

With that, she sits on the floor on a mat, her head down, and Sett opens the door with a large smile.

"Thank you," he says, calling over to the gatekeeper.

The gatekeeper leads him back to the gate and opens it. They see scuffling and yelling on the street. Garash is still there, drawing attention away from the holy palace gate. Garash looks up at Sett, and his eyes point to a camel. "Go!" he shouts, then returns to his arguing with the guards.

By now, Kissara has wiggled free and is out from under the large robe so she can see. "Do you know how to get a camel to kneel?" Kissara calls out, trying to keep up with Sett and his crutches.

"I saw it done once," he says.

When they arrive, there is another man with a stick. "Can you help us get on?" Sett calls out.

The man hits the camel's knees, and the camel goes down. The two climb on and the camel man says, "Up." As the camel rises, he calls up to Sett while handing him the reins.

"The other three words she knows are down, go, and stop. Oh, and one more. Run, Jamil, Run."

By this time the sun is up far enough in the pink morning sky that the gates to the city are open. The camel heads toward the closest water, the gate next to the west harbor, and gallops through.

"Hang on!" Sett shouts.

Not sure how to handle a camel, Sett holds onto the reins loosely, and hangs on to the horns of the saddle. Kissara leans forward and does the same.

Jamil does not slow down for an hour. Then he goes into a trot.

"Where is he taking us?" Kissara shouts, looking up at Sett.

"I have no idea," Sett calls back. "But when he gets tired, I guess he'll stop. And I believe he is a she." He kisses Kissara's hand.

After two more hours, the camel takes off into a run again. They arrive at an oasis, and the camel comes to a halt so abruptly Sett and Kissara almost tumble onto the camel's long neck and down to the water below.

"Down, Jamil," Sett says. "Down."

Jamil continues to drink.

"Down, Jamil, down."

This time, the camel thinks a moment, then bends her front legs. As she goes down, Kissara and Sett lean so far forward, they have to grab hold of the saddle just to keep from falling over the beast's head.

When she finally bends her hind legs, Sett shouts, "Now!"

The two young people jump off the camel and roll on the ground, laughing. When they finally stop rolling, they face each other and draw close.

Kissara snuggles up to Sett, and he puts his strong arms around her.

They become quiet.

"It was her idea," Sett finally whispers.

"Do you think she was able to escape?"

"No."

Silence.

"She has a quick mind. Do you think she was able to talk them into letting her go free?"

"I really don't think so."

Silence.

"Mother? Mother?"

Kissara hides her face in Sett's chest and weeps. "Mother. You gave your life for me."

They stay where they are until they notice Jamil sniff the air and break out with a half whinny and half snort.

"I think she's ready to go again," Sett whispers. "We'd better get to her before she takes off across the desert again, but this time without us. They are very independent, I always heard."

Wiping her eyes, Kissara gathers up the crutches thrown from the camel and hands them to Sett. "I like riding in front. I shall climb on first, then you," she says.

Once settled on, Sett announces to the camel, "Up, Jamil," and Jamil pulls her front legs up, while Sett hangs on to the back of the saddle, and Kissara hangs on to him.

Again, Sett holds on to the reins lightly, knowing the camel knows more about what she is doing than does Sett."

Once completely up, Sett says, "Go, Jamil," and Jamil goes. They continue to head west.

Sett and Kissara adjust their seating positions so that the back-and-forth swaying of the camel does not jar them loose from their saddle.

"Hey, sit still," Sett chides her.

"I'm just crossing my legs," Kissara says. "I've seen camel riders put one or both legs up when they ride. Seems like a good idea. She is too broad for me to be stretching my legs that far."

They ride on.

"Ah. This is much better. You should try it, Setty."

"Okay. You talked me into it," he responds. With that, Sett takes hold of one leg and puts it in front of Kissara's, then does the same with his other leg."

"Hmmm. I think you are right."

Jamil stops and sniffs the air. She raises her voice in a slobbery snort, toots, grumbles a song, and takes off again trotting.

Kissara is the first one to see it.

"Look, Setty. A caravan. She has smelled out a boyfriend."

Jamil catches up with the caravan and falls in line. Four hours later, they arrive at an oasis, and everyone stops.

"Well, now is when we find out if they plan to kick us out."

"Do you have any money, Setty?"

"I gave it all to the gatekeeper at the priestess's palace, my peach."

"Uh, oh."

"Well, we may as well get it over with. Down, Jamil."

Before they have a chance to climb off, the caravan leader arrives.

"Don't know where you came from, but you'll have to keep going. I don't provide my expertise for free. I have to make a living like everyone else. So, begone. Both of you. Get out of here."

"Sir, I have money back in Gibeon."

"Gibeon, what? Never heard of it."

"Have you heard of Jerusalem? I have money there."

"Sounds like you've got money scattered over everywhere but here. Now get going."

"But, sir," Kissara says, putting on a pouty face, "We promise to give you your fee—whatever it is—as soon as we arrive."

"Well, I don't know where either city is, which means I am not going there. So leave now."

"But, sir..."

"Go. Get out of here."

"Up, Jamil," Sett says with a low voice. "Right, Jamil."

The camel veers to her right around the caravan and toward the barrenness surrounding them.

"Do you know where we are, Setty?"

"No. Do you?"

Jamil's walk is slow. She takes a few steps, then stops.

Another few steps, then stops. Sometimes she looks back at the other camels and wheezes and whines.

"Wait," Kissara says. She turns in her saddle and calls back to the caravan leader. "Wait. We've got money!"

"We do?" Sett asks.

"Back, Jamil," she commands. "Back."

Not sure what she is supposed to do, the camel takes a few steps backward, then turns around the way she came from, breaking into a happy trot. "Good, Jamil," Kissara says.

They get halfway back to the still-resting caravan when Kissara calls out to the caravan leader again, this time waving her hands. "We've got money. We can pay you. How much do you want?"

"You had better not be lying to me," he says when they arrive next to the leader. "Let's see your money."

"Turn your head," Kissara says to the caravan leader.

"What?"

"Turn your head. It's hidden, and you are not allowed to see our hiding place."

"It is? He isn't?" Sett asks.

Grumbling, the caravan leader turns his camel around to face the other way.

Kissara holds the hem of her father's enlarged robe up to her mouth, and she tears at it with her teeth. A gold earring falls out.

"Okay, you can turn around now," Kissara says. She holds out the earring. "Would this be enough?"

The caravan leader takes the earring, bites into it to test the softness that real gold has, and smiles.

"This earring will be just fine. How far do you want to go?"

Kissara looks up at Sett.

"Uh, we need to go across to Bozrah, then up to the Dead Sea."

"Never heard of the Dead Sea, but I know where Bozrah is. It's the king's city. We have several merchants headed there. Where did you get this gold ring, anyway?"

Sett and Kissara smile.

"Well, tomorrow, get your camel in line with the others. I think she has picked out a boyfriend to follow. We shouldn't have any trouble with her."

"Why tomorrow?" Kissara asks."

"We are going to spend the day here sleeping. Be ready to get up as soon as it is dark, and we will move on then."

"What should we do?" Kissara asks Sett. "We're not married yet."

"Your mother gave us her blessing. We are legally betrothed. In my society, a person cannot break a betrothal without a divorce. It is a period when the husband makes arrangements for a place for his bride to live in. Since I have a place for us to live, we're almost married."

"Well, we still must be proper. Why don't we attach my father's very large robe to the top of your crutches and set some rocks down on the other end? It will give us a little shade to sleep under, but we can be seen by everyone and maintain our honor."

"Very good," Sett says. "Very honorable."

The trip across the desert is long, just as it had been when Sett had crossed it when eleven years old as a new slave, and again just two years earlier with Machir at age 18.

They travel a week. Then two. Then four. Then seven. Sometimes Kissara is morose and speaks of her mother. Sometimes she quietly weeps. Sett gives her the time to mourn.

Now in their eighth week, and having passed Bozrah and left the caravan behind, they are on their own. They work their way up the Arabah and finally to the Jordan River close to where it empties into the Dead Sea.

"We're almost home, Kissara," Sett says, taking a deep breath in an effort to relax for the first time in nearly half a year.

Sett looks at the river ahead, and tears of relief come to his eyes. "We're almost home," he whispers.

"Stop!" Kissara shouts.

"Back to reality, Sett jerks his head around to see if they are suddenly in danger. "Why? What's wrong?" Sett asks.

"I want to clean up at the river."

"We're still a day away from home."

"You just said we were home."

"That's not what I meant."

"What if we meet someone we know?"

"You won't. I may. But you won't."

"And it wouldn't hurt for you to clean up yourself. Your hair and beard are full of sand. They're dry and windblown and look terrible."

"Yes, ma'am," Sett says. "Down, Jamil. Down."

The two dismount and make their way down the steep embankment to the water. Jamil follows them, sniffs the dirty water, and refuses to drink.

Sufficiently cleaned up, they climb back on Jamil, she takes them across the river, and up the other embankment.

"Jericho is up here. We could spend the night here and buy some decent clothes. These we've had on since leaving Ur are worn through and smelly."

"Why didn't you say so?" Kissara asks, wrinkling her nose at him.

"You were so insistent that we clean up, well, and true, we might meet someone I know on our way to Jericho."

"Setty, what am I going to do with you?" she growls.

"Marry me is what you're going to do."

They arrive in Jericho, sell Jamil's saddle, rent two rooms at an inn with a vat to bathe in, and a stall for Jamil. They meet at the front of the inn after cleaning up and head for the market nearby. Luckily they see a weaver's shop soon after they arrive.

"Sir, do you sell tunics and robes?"

"Yes, we have a few. By the looks of you two, you need them. But we do not have your size, sir."

"We will wait and come back. How long will it take?"

Sett asks.

"Come back when the sun is lower."

Just before sunset, the couple returns to the weaver and make their purchase.

Morning comes, and they meet at Jamil's stall.

"Well, my darling, are you ready?"

They mount Jamil, make their way out the west gate of the city, and begin the long winding trip up out of the Jordan Valley.

"There's a fork in the road here," Sett explains. "The one on the right would take us to my palace. But it is not ready for us yet. So, we will take the left fork to Jerusalem and King David's palace."

"Go, Jamil. Go."

"You're friends with the new king? Isn't that dangerous?"

"He and my father were best friends. He would never hurt me."

"What do I call you when we get there?" Kissara asks. "King Mefiboset? Prince Mefiboset? What?"

"Just call me by my name. But be sure to call David King David."

They ride along in quiet.

"I'm nervous. What if they don't accept me?"

"They will accept you."

"How do you know that? What if they don't?"

"You will be so sweet, they will have no other choice but to accept you. Now, do not worry."

Closer, they come to their destination.

"Well, here it is. The north gate into Jerusalem." As they go through the gate, the guards salute Sett. They work their way through the main street up the side of what is Mount Zion. They pass the fortress on their right.

They see a large and steep retaining wall and ride around to the other side of it.

"Well, this is it, my sweet. We are home. Down, Jamil."

Sett and Kissara dismount. She walks beside him as

they approach the guards wearing the sky blue uniforms at the gate of the palace.

Sett stands without saying anything. He waits as the guards figure out who he is.

"I'm nervous," she whispers.

"Mefiboset? Is that you?" one of the guards asks. "We thought you were dead. That's what Ziba has been telling everyone. His son, Lechy too. Well, welcome home, Mefiboset. Welcome home."

The guard takes the reins of the camel, and the couple walks into the king's outer courtyard with its blue-and-white tile and columns with clouds painted on them. Sett looks around for someone he recognizes. He sees the servant who had always looked out for him.

"Elza, do you know if King David is here?"

"Yes, he is."

"Would it be possible for me to see him?"

"I will ask," he says, taking a quick glance at the woman beside him.

Sett leads Kissara over to a marble bench in the courtyard. He and Kissara sit and wait. He takes her hand and squeezes it. With her other hand, she twists a strand of hair around her finger.

"Master Sett. He said he will see you."

Just as Sctt and Kissara stand, they see someone walking toward them.

"Bow, Kissara. Bow. That's the king."

# 16 ~ ALL THINGS NEW

Sett drops to the tile and bows his head to the floor.
Kissara watches him out of the corner of her eye and does the same.

"Rise, you rascal, you!" David says, rushing up to the pair. He embraces Sett, then stands back. "And who have we here? Aren't you a beauty? This must be the maiden you told me about."

"Yes, Your Majesty."

"Is she yours yet?"

"We were betrothed by her mother."

"Then we shall have the wedding banquet as soon as possible. Will tomorrow be soon enough for you two?"

"That would be wonderful, sire. Uh, would it be possible for her to stay with my grandmother tonight? And could my family come to the wedding?"

David pauses, looks at the floor, over to an empty bench, then smiles. "By all means, they shall attend."

David leaves, and Sett leads her across the courtyard and through a door leading down a long corridor.

"Where are we going?" she asks.

"David has blessed my family by allowing all of us to live. He did not have to do that since he usurped my grandfather's throne. But he is a good man. I am taking you to their quarters, my peach."

"Behind the palace?" she asks.

"Shhh. This is a wing of the palace for special guests.

My grandmother is the queen mother, but you must not bow down to her because David's is now the official queen mother. You will like her. You will like my whole family."

They arrive at the back wing, and a guard lets them in.

"We are here to see my family. I am Mefiboset, grandson of King Saul and son of his son, Jonathan."

"Yes, sir. I will bring them out to you."

"I'm nervous," Kissara says, looking up at Sett and hugging herself.

"My family will love you. Just you wait and see."

The first one to arrive is Queen Mother Ahinoam. She sees the girl standing next to her grandson and knows. She smiles and walks forward.

"My child, how charming you are. And such beautiful long hair. Does it go all the way to your waist? Let me see. Turn around. Yes, it does. How beautiful, and I know all of you is beautiful."

She looks up at her grandson. "You did well, Sett. She will be a delight to all of us." She looks over at Kissara. "Welcome to our family, my dear. Oh, here is Rizpah. I guess you could say we shared our husband."

Rizpah walks forward and gently takes hold of Kissara's shoulders. "How beautiful you are, young lady. Do I detect a little shyness? You will get over it before you know it."

"Your hair is beautiful too," Kissara says, daring to speak. "I haven't seen much red hair."

"I'm afraid some of it is turning gray. But thank you. Oh, and I would like you to meet my two sons—Armoni and Mefiboset."

Kissara giggles. "That's the same name as my Setty."

"Indeed, it is. Your Setty, as you call him, was named after him. They are very close to each other despite their age difference. I suppose my Mefiboset has always been kind of a substitute father for your Setty. So, here they are."

Armoni steps forward and tips his head to Sett's bride.

Mefiboset does the same. Kissara is not sure what to do. Sett notices. "Just smile and ask them a question," Sett whispers.

Uncle Armoni grins. "Remind me one of these days to tell you the silly things Sett did when he was little. I know it's hard to believe he was ever little considering he looks like a giant now, but he was.

"Oh, here is Merab, Sett's aunt."

"Hello, dear," Merab says. I have five young, healthy sons, but they could not come. I hope you will understand."

"Yes, ma'am," Kissara replies.

Ahinoam walks forward and takes Kissara's arm. "I understand the wedding is tomorrow. We are going to have to get you into something elegant," she says, motioning to the guard.

He opens the door and lets the family and Kissara back through to their quarters.

"I love you, Setty," she calls back as Sett stands in the middle of the room, feeling empty.

He turns, goes back down the long corridor, and out into the courtyard. He opens the door to his old room and sees that his belongings are still in it after his long absence.

He goes back out into the courtyard and requests that someone ask King David if he can speak with him before the wedding banquet the next day.

The following morning his request is granted.

"You wanted to see me, Jonathan?" David asks.

Sett bows low then stands. "I do not have any right to ask you this since you have already been so kind to me. But, when you gave my grandfather's estate back to me..."

"Ohhh. Of course. Why didn't I think of that? Yes. Yes. You may take your bride up to your grandfather's palace to live. Since old cranky Ziba is your servant, that makes his sons and his slaves yours also. Now, you'll need some maids for your bride. I believe your income should be enough that you can hire a couple of cooks and ladies in waiting. Consider the palace my wedding gift to you. Is there anything else?"

"No. Thank you, sire. As the grandson of your enemy, I do not deserve your favor like this."

"Oh, but you do. You have brought my Jonathan back to me."

With that, David rises from his throne and disappears out a back door.

When Sett returns to his room, he sees a new outfit of wedding clothes laid out for him. Someone is waiting for him—someone he does not recognize.

"I am your barber. My, you need fixed. When was the last time you trimmed your beard? Your thick hair is beautiful when cared for properly, but, well, I heard you have been out in the desert for months. Sit here on this bench, and let me fix you up. I have also brought scented oil for your hair. You certainly need it. You will be a proper groom this afternoon."

Sett cleans up and dresses. He has on a yellow tunic, blue robe, and a small groom's crown. He spends the rest of the day pacing in the courtyard. The servants smile. Even some of David's relatives smile.

The wedding banquet finally arrives. Kissara wears a long yellow linen veil over her hair and white tunic that reaches the floor. It is held in place with a garland of daisies.

Sett and Kissara walk into the banquet hall and kneel before the king. He takes their hands and joins them. "You are officially recognized as married." They smile and are seated together.

A harp plays in the background as everyone enjoys the wedding banquet.

"There is someone here who wants to sing a wedding song for you," David says. "I believe you remember Egglah, the singer in our family."

"My son, Ithream, is now twelve and is going to sing a duet with me," Egglah says.

"How delightful," Kissara says in one of her daring moments of saying something.

The song flows throughout the banquet hall, soothing, exciting, entertaining, and full of genuine love for the newlyweds.

The song over, Sett thanks the singers, then stands.

"Come with me, my little one. I am going to take you home."

They leave the banquet, but not unnoticed.

"God bless you both," someone calls out.

"May you have many little ones," someone else says.

"May there be nothing but laughter and happiness in your home."

The couple makes their way to the door. A girl with thick, long black hair, blue eyes, and ivory skin approaches them. She has a large grin.

"You don't remember me, do you? My name is Tamar. We met at my grandparents' palace up in Gesher when I was eight years old."

Sett stares at her a moment. "Are you that little girl who kept running around their reflecting pool?"

"Yes, I loved that reflecting pool. I'm twelve now. Can I come see you sometimes? My father is the king, and he will let me."

"Of course," Sett says. He turns to Kissara. "Isn't that right, my love? It will be nice having little Tamar visit us sometimes."

"I'm not so little now."

"Indeed, you are not. And do come see us."

Now out in the courtyard, they see a chariot waiting for them. It is decorated with daisies. They board the chariot, and Mefiboset skillfully takes the reins and guides it out the gate of the palace, then north through Jerusalem, and out into the countryside.

Just as the sun turns bright red. Sett and his bride approach his palace.

"Oh, Setty. This is home?"

"Yes, this is your palace, and you are my queen."

Sett pounds on the gate, and it is promptly opened by

Lechy.

"Lechy, please take care of my horse and chariot. Are my apartments ready?"

"Yes, sir," Lechy replies, not smiling.

Sett sees several brothers of Lechy standing in a line nearby, none of them happy either. In another line are Ziba's slaves and the maids that have been hired by David for Kissara.

"Everyone," he announces, "this is the new lady of the palace. You will obey her every command. Make sure she is always happy."

"Come with me," he whispers.

Sett makes his way up the same steps he had fallen on fifteen long years earlier and brought his life to a halt as some have said. This evening, as Sett climbs those same stairs, he is reborn.

The days and weeks go by.

"Today, we are leaving on an adventure," Sett announces one morning. "We are going to visit a couple of forests down south. We will wander under the trees and listen for the birds and watch the squirrels and rabbits scamper."

"Where are they, Setty?"

One is in Herath down around En Gedi. Then we will go over to Beersheba to enjoy the Forest of the Negev. That will take another day. Then we'll come back home and maybe stop to see friends on our way. So we need to take along at least four days of food and other supplies."

Sett goes out to the courtyard. "Oh, Lechy. Make sure you pack my goat-hair tent."

"Yes, sir."

"And do you have the three mules ready?"

He returns to Kissara. By now, she is seated by the reflecting pool.

Sett leans over and kisses her on the forehead and touches her nose. "It will be fun."

"Why do you get so excited about the forests? I don't

understand it."

He sits next to her. "The forests are disappearing, my little one. People are cutting them down and not replacing the trees. They are turning our beautiful world into a desert. Do you remember people talking about the forests in Arabia?"

"Well, I guess so."

"They're not there anymore, are they? We cannot let our kingdom become like that. Well, I guess we do not have any control over it. That's why we need to visit them. So we can tell our children and grandchildren how beautiful our land once was."

He stands, takes her by the hands, and encourages her to stand.

"I'll bet you have never seen a doe running through the trees, her little fawn behind her. Have you ever seen a waterfall? Forests have them; the trees protect the streams. Have you ever swung from a vine dangling off tree branches high above? I'll bet you have never heard the breeze whistle through the leaves reaching for the heavens or watched the clouds peak in and out at you with the high branches turning them into lace. Oh, my darling, I feel so close to the Garden of God when I am in a forest. Go with me. Have fun with me."

"My dear, dear Setty. You are such a poet and lover of all things. I shall go with you if, for no other reason than to watch you become enchanted. Then perhaps I shall become enchanted with you."

The weeks and months go by. The crippled prince and love of his life share the delights of each other and of the world around them.

It has now been a year.

"Darling," Kissara says one day. I have a little surprise for you."

"How little?" Sett replies.

"Pretty little."

"As little as a camel?" he asks.

"Oh, much littler."

"As little as a mule?"

"Littler than that."

"Ummm, as little as a chariot."

"Littler."

"I know. As little as a goat."

"Oh, no. Littler."

"Just how little are you talking, my dear?"

Kissara puts her arms together and rocks them. "This little."

Sett grabs his crutch and jumps up. He forms a large grin and his eyes sparkle.

"Kissara, a baby? You are going to give us a baby?"

They embrace.

"I never knew a good woman could bring a man so much happiness. Sometimes I thought I would never be completely happy. I was wrong. You have become my rebirth, my light, my life."

Two months later, they are breaking their fast together in the grand dining hall, just the two of them. Lechy glares at them as he serves their meal. Sett chooses not to notice.

"Oh!"

Kissara drops her spoon and grits her teeth. She scoots back and crosses her arms over her middle.

"Little one," Sett says. "What is wrong?"

"I just had a sharp pain."

"You will go right to bed. I will send for the midwife at David's palace. She is the best there is, and I have already paid for her services for you.

"Oh, Lechy," Sett says. "I need you to ride fast to the palace in Jerusalem and bring back the midwife. Hurry now." Sett then turns his attentions back to Kissara.

The midwife arrives and talks to Kissara at length. "Here are two teas I want you to drink regularly—chamomile and coriander. Also, I want you to stay in bed from now on. Agreed?"

"Yes, ma'am," Kissara says. She begins to weep.

The midwife puts her hand on Kissara's cheek. What's wrong, child? You are not going to lose this baby."

"That's not it. My mother. I wish so much my mother were here."

"Would you like for me to send for her?"

"That is not possible."

"Then may I stand-in for your mother? I do not look or speak like her, but I can pretend."

Kissara wipes her eyes. "Forgive me for acting like this."

"When you have some of this tea, you will feel a little better. I will return tomorrow."

Sett makes his way out with the midwife. "Thank you for coming."

The next day when the midwife returns, she has someone with her.

"Hello, Aunt Kissara."

"Tamar. How nice of you to come. You certainly have brightened my day."

"She has looked through my grandfather's and father's scrolls in our library," Sett explains, "and would like to read to you sometimes."

"Oh, how delightful," Kissara says.

"Sett says I can come see you every time your midwife does. We will read lots of things."

The weeks go by.

"What are you going to do about this situation?" Sett hears Lechy say to his aging father in the office Ziba set up in the storeroom. The door is ajar.

"Sett stops where he is, and the clomping of his crutches ceases. He stands still and listens.

"I cannot stand that man interfering with our lives and taking over our palace like this," Lechy continues. "He expects us to cower to him."

"Keep your voice down, Son," Ziba warns. "I will figure something out. We will get the palace back one of these days. It will happen. Just be patient."

Sett smiles to himself and shakes his head. *They are always threatening. But they are harmless.*

"Ahhh." The scream echoes from the royal apartment and out into the courtyard. "Ahhh."

Sett manipulates his crutches up the steps and hurries to his wife's apartment.

"Darling. What is it?" he says, throwing his crutches aside and falling onto the bed near his wife.

"It's coming, Sett. It's coming. Send for the midwife."

Sett grabs up his crutches again and rushes to the door. He calls down from the balcony. "Get the midwife. Hurry. Get the midwife."

"Yes, sir," one of Ziba's servants says, heading toward the stalls to ride their fastest mule into Jerusalem.

"Sett returns to his beloved's bed. "Are you okay? Is the baby okay?"

Kissara forces a smile. "Of course, I'm okay. And the baby is okay."

"Whether it is a boy or girl, I will love it as much as I love you. I will protect it as I have protected you."

"That you are an expert at, my dear Setty," she says just before screaming again.

Sett squints his eyes and presses his lips together. "What can I do? What can I do to help, my little one?"

"You can hurry the midwife along," she groans. "Is my birthing stool here?"

Sett looks around. "Yes, it is here. You will be fine. Right? You're going to be fine?"

He lays his head next to her, and every time she screams, he takes her hand and kisses her on the cheek, the nose, the eyes, the forehead.

"I am here, my darling. I am here."

Three hours later, the midwife arrives.

"It is time for the father to leave," she tells Sett. "The king has allowed your grandmother to come with me. Send up one of the maids, please, and be sure she brings plenty of water."

"Yes, ma'am," Sett says.

Ahinoam reaches the top of the stairs with her arthritic legs and smiles at Sett.

He looks into the eyes of the woman whose apartment this had been long ago when she was the young wife of tall, handsome King Saul.

"Thank you, Grandmother, for coming."

The former queen embraces her grandson, then closes the door behind him.

He makes his way back down to the courtyard. When he arrives, he realizes his Uncle Mefiboset is there.

"You shouldn't have to go through all this waiting by yourself. I shall wait and groan and wonder with you."

"Oh, Uncle Mefiboset. You have always been there for me."

"You have me to thank," now 13-year-old Ithream says. "I had to do a little begging to my father, but he finally consented to two members of your family coming.

"Thank you, young sir," Sett says. "Thank you very much."

"Well, let's get started pacing," Mefiboset says. "That's what we men are supposed to do."

The screaming in the upstairs apartment comes and goes. Each time, Sett looks up, grits his teeth, and says a prayer.

Four hours later, the door opens. Ahinoam walks down the steps with a bundle in her arms. Sett approaches her.

"Here is your son," she says, handing the baby to his father.

"Micah. Your name is Micah," Sett says, staring at his own flesh and blood. Your life will belong to God. It may be a hard life, but in the end, you and God will win."

He looks at his grandmother. "When do you have to go back to Jerusalem?"

"David has given you a special gift to celebrate your son's birth," she replies.

"What?"

"Me."

"You?"

"I can stay."

## 17 ~ UPSIDE DOWN

"Micah, you must be quieter," Kissara says to her five-year-old son, coming out onto the second-floor landing. "Your Great-Grandmother is very sick."

"Is she a queen?" Micah asks from the courtyard below.

"She used to be a very long time ago."

"Was she mean?"

"Oh, no. She was a very nice queen. She has been very nice all her life. But I'm afraid her life here on earth will not be much longer."

"If she isn't on earth, where will she go?"

"She will go to heaven. The God we believe in is not like the make-believe gods and goddesses I was told about when I was your age. They do not promise a happy life after we die, which doesn't matter anyway since they aren't real."

"Is heaven nice?"

"God is there and loves everyone very much. Angels are there too. After we get to heaven, we will never die again."

"Can I go to heaven, Mother?"

"Indeed, yes. Now, I must return to your Great-Grandmother's apartment and sit with her. You run along and play, but whisper."

She re-enters Ahinoam's apartment. It is the same one she had had long ago behind her Saul's apartment with adjoining doors.

"Oh, Grandmother. I cannot lose you," Sett says,

sitting by the elderly woman's bed. When he looks at her, he sees the energetic, beautiful woman of years long past.

"I have lived a long life," she whispers. "It has been a hard life, but it wasn't that way always. I had my early years with your grandfather when we were so happy together, and he wasn't so worried about enemies. I lost all my sons, but I have had you, the delight of any grandmother's heart. Now I have Kissara and Micah. Thank you for the brightness you have added to an old woman's life."

Sett leans down, gently pushes the stray strands of gray hair away from her face, and kisses her on the cheek.

"Remember when you made me king for a day? I shall never forget it," he says. "Thank you for giving me my day."

"You at least had the opportunity to experience what you have deserved all along—to be the King of Israel."

"But David has been good to us."

"Yes. He allowed me to come here and die in my home. He has been better to us than any other king has been to his usurped predecessor. We have your father to thank for that. Jonathan did love David."

She closes her eyes and groans.

"What is it, Grandmother?" He waits. He presses his lips together. "Grandmother? Grandmother?"

"Oh, I'm not gone yet," she whispers. "But I'm growing very tired. Is it okay if we don't talk for a while?"

There is a knock on the door. Sett looks up as it opens.

"Darling, the rest of her family is here," Kissara says.

"Did you hear that, Grandmother? David let them out to come see you. Wake up, Grandmother."

The former queen mother opens her eyes and smiles. "How lovely."

"Hello, Mother. It's Merab. I brought my sons with me—all five of them."

Ahinoam lifts her hand with the crooked fingers, and one by one, Merab and her sons bow and kiss it.

"You know, I never saw you very much when the boys were small. You always seemed to be so busy with your family," her mother says.

"And I regret that, Mother." She and her sons step to the other side of her bed.

Mecal comes in next. Though David's first wife, she is not wearing her queen's crown. She kneels by her mother's bed and weeps. "Thank you for being there for me."

"You were not treated fairly by David, the man you dearly loved. But you are strong."

"I am strong only because you are, Mother."

When she steps aside, Ahinoam notices a woman with partly red and partly gray hair walk to her bed.

"I guess we have been rivals all our life," Rizpah says. "Ever since your husband took me to be his mistress. But I always admired how you handled yourself with me around. I really did."

"Oh, Rizpah. We should have leaned on each other more when our Saul died."

"My sons came with me. I hope you do not mind."

"Of course, I do not mind," Ahinoam whispers.

Armoni steps forward, bows, and kisses the queen mother's hand. Mefiboset steps forward and does the same. They walk to the end of the bed.

"We are all here, Grandmother," Sett says.

"I am pleased," she whispers. "All of you have brought me joy." She closes her eyes.

There is silence a while. And sniffing and wiping of tears.

Ahinoam opens her eyes. "Saul was the love of my life, you know," she whispers. She closes her eyes one last time.

They know. They all know. Their mother has died.

The funeral is the next day. Ahinoam is buried in the Mountain of Olive Trees Cemetery across from Jerusalem, the new cemetery of royalty and anyone of any importance.

David's sixth wife, Egglah, attends with her son, Ithream, now nineteen years old. Tamar, age eighteen, also attends. She brings her brother, Absalom, with her.

"I will speak to the king on your behalf," Ithream tells

them just before they return to the secured wing of David's palace. "I will ask my father to spare your lives."

Sett, Kissara, and Micah return from the funeral to Saul's palace. They exit the chariot, hand the reins to one of the servants, and walk to the courtyard. They sit around the reflecting pool.

"Micah, you need to know we have set aside something for you to live on if anything should ever happen to us."

"What do you mean, Mother?"

"I brought a lot of pure gold jewelry with me from my former home in Ur. I have put it in a special place in my apartment. Some day when you are older, I will show you where it is."

"Can I wear some of the jewelry?" Micah asks.

"You can do whatever you like with it," Sett replies.

"Can I play now?" Micah asks.

"Yes, and I guess you do not have to be as quiet as you were when your Great-Grandmother was here."

Life returns to normal in Sett's household. Six months later, there is a rapid knock on their gate. As soon as the gatekeeper answers it, Ithream runs in.

He is two hand-spans shorter than Sett but weighs about the same.

"Sett! Kissara!" he shouts. "Where are you? Come quickly."

The couple hurries to the courtyard.

"What's wrong, Ithream?" Sett asks.

"It's Tamar. She has been raped."

Kissara raises her hand to her forehead. Tears rush to her eyes. She trembles.

"We've got to get over to her. Where is she?"

"She is at Absalom's estate. Hurry. She is cowering in a corner, and we're all afraid what she will do to herself."

Sett and Kissara climb into their chariot and follow Ithream back to Jerusalem and to Absalom's estate, horses in a gallop.

Handing the reins over to Absalom's gatekeeper, they

rush in. Ithream takes them to his older brother, Absalom, who is walking the floor.

Absalom motions for a maid standing by to take Kissara to Tamar's apartment.

"I cannot imagine how you feel," Sett says when they are alone, not really knowing what to say.

"How dare he!" the big man says. "I will kill him for this." He pounds his fist into his other hand.

"Who? Who did it?" Sett asks.

"Amnon."

"No! You cannot kill him. You're not thinking straight."

"Why not?"

"You cannot turn a wrong into a right that way. Amnon is David's oldest son, the next king."

"Not if I can help it. He does not deserve to be king. He does not deserve to live. The conniving snake!"

"If you kill him, people will think you are only doing it to be the next king yourself. They all know you are next in line. You cannot get by with it."

"No one treats my sister like that," Absalom booms. "No one!"

Sett sits and watches Absalom pace. He realizes there is nothing he can say to assuage his anger.

"Why, Amnon?" Absalom calls out, raising his arms over his head and looking up at the ceiling. "How could you do this thing? Would you want someone to do this to your wife?"

"He doesn't have a wife yet," Sett replies.

Absalom glares in response, and Sett wishes he had kept his mouth shut.

Tamar's brother sits, bows, puts his head in his hands and shakes. He stands and paces again. "He has just ruined her life," he bellows.

"She has always been such a sweet, innocent girl," Sett says.

"Well, she isn't sweet and innocent anymore. She will never be the same. He has ruined her."

After two hours, Kissara appears at the door. Her eyes are red. "I need to go home," she whispers to Sett. "I promised her I would return tomorrow."

She looks up at Absalom. "Give her a little milk or juice to drink. Don't force her to eat. Make sure someone is always with her, but don't force her to talk. Let her mourn."

Absalom looks down at Kissara. "Thank you for coming," he says quietly. He turns to Sett and shakes his hand. "And thank you for coming. I know I have been ranting, but having someone to rant to has helped. Well, a little."

Sett rises, makes his way to Kissara, and she clings to his arm. They make their way out to the chariot and head back north to Gibeon and their palace.

"You didn't say a word all the way home," he tells Kissara as they go over to the reflecting pool.

"Sett, I guess there is something I need to tell you," she says in a whisper.

"What is it, my little one? Tell me. What can I do to help you?"

She looks up at him, her eyes still puffy from crying with Tamar. "You have already done it. You rescued me."

"From what?"

She sits next to the pool. "A few months before I met you, I was raped."

Sett stares at her, takes her hand, and holds it to his chest. He looks up at the sky overhead. "Not you too. What is wrong with those men?"

"He was hardly a man. We were both fourteen years old. He was my neighbor, who I had played with as a child. I had known him all my life."

She pauses and weeps anew.

Sett draws her close, and she leans her head on his big shoulder. He waits.

"What right do they have to do anything to someone else's body they want to?" she groans. "What right do they have to think their body is more important than anyone else's?"

He remains silent.

"They destroy women just as much as if they cut their hands off or set fire to their body."

He leans over and kisses the top of her head.

"They steal from women just as much as if they stole their house from them. They are kidnappers just as much as if they took them from their families and shut them up in a hole."

"I am so sorry," he whispers, rocking her back and forth.

Kissara looks up at her husband.

"You came along at just the right time. I no longer had a father. I had no brothers. I needed to believe all men did not treat women like a piece of lifeless wood.

"When you came toward me on those crutches that first day, I thought I could be safe with you. I thought I could relax around you and not be afraid of you. Those crutches were like a flag over you: 'I am gentle and will not hurt you.' It was because of you that I began to come alive. Not many women get that second chance to be able to live again. I will love you forever for what you did for me."

"Oh, my little one. I am so sorry." Still, they rock.

"Do you know what Tamar is thinking right now? She is thinking she is no more human than some grains of sand and no better than that. Her soul has been yanked out of her, and she feels only like a lump of lifeless clay. She no longer feels human. Poor Tamar. Poor, poor Tamar."

"She will never be the same again, will she?" Sett whispers.

The next day, they hear a knock on the gate. It is Ithream again.

"Can Kissara go back to see Tamar? No one knows what to do for her? She just squats in a corner rolled up like a ball."

Kissara stands and looks at Ithream with puffy eyes.

"I am sorry, Kissara. You seem to be the only one she

will listen to."

He looks over at Sett.

"By the way, there is a man standing on the edge of your property. He looks like some sort of priest or monk. But he is dressed, well, odd. It's like he cut open a large fish and almost climbed inside. The fish's head is like his turban, and the fish's body is like his cloak. The fish's tail drags the ground behind him."

"What is he doing?" Sett asks.

"He has a wand that he is waving over your land and shouting. I don't even know if they are words from a real language. But he looks very angry."

"Don't pay any attention to him," Sett replies. "That is just my neighbor, Yassib. He does not like anyone in King Saul's family. So he is cursing the land. I do not know why he hates us so, but he does."

Sett looks over at Kissara.

"I think I need to go back with you. Absalom is still in no shape to be left alone. He is like a mad dog."

"You are right about that," Ithream says. "He is throwing things, he's out in his courtyard swinging his sword in circles, he's growling. He is shouting at his brother, Amnon, as though he is standing in front of him. He is completely out of control."

Sett and Kissara spend much of the following week at Absalom's estate.

Finally, both Tamar and Absalom become quiet. They withdraw into themselves. They pretend things are back to normal, but Sett and Kissara know better and wonder how long it can last.

Oblivious to everything that is going on, Lechy announces he has just gotten married. Sett digs out one of the gold rings his wife had brought with them when they escaped Ur and gives it to Lechy as a wedding gift. Lechy keeps his wife away from Sett and his family.

Sett and Kissara sometimes go to visit Absalom and Tamar. Still, nothing changes the strange atmosphere in

Absalom's home. The undertone is always present. The rape of Tamar keeps her family and close friends reeling.

Two years later, they get the word.

Absalom has killed Amnon.

# 18 ~ SURVIVAL

*L*echy is smiling.

"What's going on in your life that is so good, Lechy?" Sett asks.

"My son's birthday. He is three years old today."

"Well, congratulations. We don't see him very much. Let me see if I can find one of Micah's old toys to give him."

Lechy's smile disappears. "My son gets only the best," he says, walking away.

Three days later, Sett begins to pack his traveling supplies.

"Sett, don't go," Kissara says. "We need you at home. Micah is nine years old and needs his father. What if something happens to you on the road to Gesher?"

"You worry too much, my peach," Sett replies. "I have survived two trips across the Arabian desert and a trip up and around the north country. I have survived permanent injuries and slavery and even riding a camel for two months. Or was it three? I will survive this."

"But we need you more than Absalom does."

"David banished Absalom because he would not even say he was sorry for killing David's oldest son. It's been three years. We have to try to pull that family back together."

"It's not your problem."

"It wasn't Machir's problem when he found me as a slave at the other end of the world. But he bought my freedom and took me to his house for two years. What would

I have done if he had not made me his problem?"

"I guess there is no talking you out of it, is there?"

"No, my little one. But Ithream and I will not be long. I know the king and queen of Gesher, Absalom's grandparents. Maybe Ithream and I can think of some way they can smooth things over with King David, and Absalom can return home."

Kissara looks down at the floor. "When are you leaving?"

"Tomorrow. The sooner we leave, the sooner we will be back home."

The next morning, Ithream knocks on Sett's gate. Lechy answers it.

Ithream stays with his mule, so Sett joins him outside.

"Come back soon, my love," Kissara calls out to him.

As the gate is closed back, Sett hears Lechy mumble, "Stay gone forever."

The two men ride up the highway heading east mostly in silence. Sett is now thirty-two years old. Ithream is twenty-three. Both in line for the throne at one time, and both with no hope of ever having it. Though different in age, they have this in common.

They wind their way down the steep road to the Jordan Valley and arrive in Jericho in time to rent a room at an inn for the night.

"Do you think it will work?" Ithream asks.

"I don't know," Sett replies as they finish with a meal fixed by the innkeeper's wife. "I barely remember my father, so know what it is like to not have one."

"My father has ten sons by his wives and nine sons by his mistresses. And that's not counting his daughters, my half-sisters. So, even though I have a father, he doesn't have time for me. I doubt he even misses Absalom. Absalom is now his oldest son and legal heir to the throne. My father needs to make up with him."

The next day, Sett and Ithream leave Jericho out the east gate, cross the Jordan River, and head north.

"Should we stop in Mahanaim?" Ithream asks. "I think both our families have used it as a royal stronghold when things were bad back home."

"No, I think we should get to Absalom as soon as possible," Sett says.

As they ride along on their mules, Sett notices Ithream wagging his head back and forth.

"What are you doing?" Sett asks.

"Oh, that? I'm singing on the inside. My head keeps the rhythm."

That evening, they stop in Succoth for the night.

"I have changed my mind," Sett says. "We shall go east from here along the Jabbok River and spend tomorrow night in Mahanaim. We will get fresh food there, then head straight north to Ashtaroth."

"What's in Ashtaroth?" Ithream asks, taking out a fresh tunic to wear the next morning.

"Your brother. That's where the King and Queen of Gesher live."

"Oh, I thought they lived closer to the Sea of Galilee. Well, I should have listened to you. You have been there, and I have not."

They ride farther east where the Forest of Gilead begins. The third day just before sundown, they arrive at the stronghold at Mahanaim. They make their way through the town past the barracks and parade grounds until they arrive at the palace. They knock on the gate. A servant opens it.

"Sir, does Barzillai still live here?"

The servant does not reply.

"Would you tell him that Mefiboset is here? Also, Ithream? He should remember at least one of us."

Still, without saying a word, the servant closes the gate back. They hear him talk to someone. Soon the gate opens again. This time, a man with gray hair opens it. The man looks first at Sett.

"Ohhh... You still have your crutches, Mefiboset. I tried, I really did try."

Sett offers a slight smile, his head nods just a little, and his eyes say, "I understand." He takes a deep breath. "May we come in? It's good to see you again, Barzillai. This is my friend, Prince Ithream, one of King David's sons."

Barzillai brightens. "Of course. Of course. Welcome. Come in. I'll bet you are hungry."

Sett looks around but remembers little. The tiles covering the courtyard pavement are still black and coral. The walls and columns supporting upper floors are still plain.

He leads the travelers to a circle of benches in the courtyard, motioning for the gatekeeper to take charge of their guests' mules.

"Have a seat. Give me a moment to send word to the cook to bring out extra food."

A few moments later, Barzillai returns and sits on a third bench near his guests. He sees Sett looking around.

"Nothing has changed since you were here. That was a hard three years, trying to heal you of your foot injuries. I'm so sorry. We tried everything, and we put you through so much pain. I have never seen a braver boy than you were." He pauses, looks up toward the room the boy had been in, and back to Sett.

"I see you have grown into a fine man. Are you doing okay?"

Sett smiles. "I do not remember those days very well. I guess my mind blocked them out. I just remember that you were kind and tried to help me."

"Those are words of comfort for me."

Barzillai turns to Ithream. "So you are one of our king's sons. How is he?"

"He is doing well."

"Strange how the son and grandson of enemy kings are friends."

They sit in silence.

"You know your brother, Prince Absalom, came through here a few years ago," Barzillai says. "He did not look happy."

"No, he has not been happy for a long time," Ithream says. "We are going up to spend some time with him. Hopefully, he will be returning with us."

"Something tells me I should not ask any more questions. Oh, here is our dinner. I have a nice rug spread out over in that corner. Let us eat over there where we will be more comfortable."

The next morning, Sett and Ithream leave, once again heading north.

"We should be able to spend the night in Ramoth," Sett explains.

The sun is now high in the sky. They stop to feed their mules and let them drink from a spring alongside the road. They eat some cheese and grapes they had brought with them from the stronghold.

"What was that?" Ithream asks, his eyes darting around.

"What was what? I did not hear anything." Sett takes a swig from his waterskin.

"There it is again," Ithream says, standing.

"I tell you, nothing is out there."

Suddenly, two men jump down from a high point above them. One lands on Sett, the other on Ithream.

They roll into the legs of the mules, the mules whinny and stomp their hooves, and the men roll the other way.

Sett grabs one of the crutches that had been knocked out from under him. With his strong arms, he crashes it down on the back of his attacker.

The attacker, arches his back, calls out in pain, then glares down at Sett, teeth clenched, beating on his head.

Sett rolls over and now is on top of his attacker.

"What's wrong with you?" Sett demands. He twists around so that he is sitting on his attacker's chest.

"Get off me," his attacker says.

"How are you doing over there, Ithream?" Sett asks.

Ithream pulls on his attacker's hair and sticks his

fingers in his ears. Other than the slight discomfort, it does not stop the blows.

Ithream grabs hold of one of the attacker's hands and bites into it deeper and deeper until his opponent cries out in pain and stops pounding on Ithream long enough for his good hand to grab his bitten hand.

Taking advantage of the slight break, Ithream reaches up and digs his fingers into his attacker's eyes. The attacker reaches up with his good hand to grab Ithream's.

"You had better quit beating up on my friend," Sett tells Ithream's attacker from atop his own. "He's got connections you would not believe. You do not want to make him mad."

Ithream's attacker notices his partner still pinned down by Sett's knees. He looks back at Ithream and beats on his head with his good fist.

"If I were you, I would leave while I had the chance," Sett continues. "Otherwise, we will be forced to tell all your friends how you were beaten by a cripple and a guy who almost bit you to death."

Ithream's attacker looks back over at his friend and Sett. He stops beating on Ithream.

"If you promise to be nice," Ithream says, "we will let you up, and you can go on your way. Agreed?"

"Do you promise?" Ithream's attacker asks.

"Would the son of King David lie to you?"

"Let's get out of here," Ithream's attacker says, jumping up.

Sett shifts his weight off his attacker, and the two would-be robbers take off running up the road and disappearing into the woods.

"Well, that was refreshing," Sett says, crawling over to Ithream.

Ithream stares at Sett a moment. "You should have been king."

That night they stay at an inn at Ramoth of Gilead on the border of Gad's land to the south and Manassah's land to the north.

They nurse their scratches and hope they do not show too much when they arrive at the palace.

"We should be there by tonight," Sett says on the road the next morning. "I have enjoyed going through these woods in the Bashan Mountains. I hope people do not cut them down. The oak trees, junipers, sycamores. I hope our grandchildren grow up to enjoy them like we can."

That evening when they can no longer see the sunset because of the forested mountain peaks surrounding them, they enter the city of Ashtaroth. At the palace gate with the thrones of Goddess Ashtaroth on each side, Sett explains to the guard on duty who he and his companion are.

Soon they are admitted and taken to King Talmai's courtyard where Sett delights once again to enjoy the green and white tiles laid out to resemble a forest and the cedar trees used as columns. They are led from the courtyard to the king's receiving hall.

"Welcome, my friend. It has been a few years."

Sett and Ithream immediately bow to the floor.

"Rise and tell me about your trip."

"It has indeed been a few years, Your Majesty," Sett replies. "May I introduce to you Prince Ithream. I suppose you know why we are here."

The king frowns. "I can guess. Prince Ithream, this family is really suffering right now. I do not see how it can be solved. Prince Absalom, my grandson, says he had his choice of accepting exile or being speared to death for killing the crown prince, the next king, his brother."

"Well, those were not his only choices," Ithream says. "Our father just wanted him to show remorse for killing Amnon. That's all he wanted."

"Oh. I see. So our daughter's husband is not as heartless as our grandson makes him out to be."

"I'm right here. You can speak to my face."

At the sound of Absalom's familiar voice, Sett and Ithream turn and watch Absalom walk forward.

"If you have come to get an apology from me, it will never happen. Amnon killed the spirit of my sister. She has lost all the life she used to have in her. He has destroyed her. Moses said, 'Eye for eye, tooth for tooth, life for life.'"

"But now you can never go home. That means you will never see your sister again," Ithream says.

"She can come here. Amnon could have gone to one of the cities of refuge where I could not touch him. But he was so arrogant, he thought he was untouchable. I showed him different."

"Our father would stop this exile business if you would just…"

"…say I'm sorry? But I am not sorry. I will never be sorry for destroying my sister's destroyer."

Sett looks at the king. "Your Majesty, do you think you could talk to King David. He might listen to you."

"I am only his wife's father, not his father. I am afraid it would do no good for me to even try. Pray to your God for this family. That is all I can suggest. Pray. Well, it is nearly time for bed. Have you eaten, Ithream?"

"Yes, we have. Thank you, Your Majesty."

"Then I will bid you goodnight. We will talk more in the morning when we are fresh." The king leaves the throne room.

Morning comes. The men meet again.

"All I want to do is put my family back together again," Ithream says.

"You are wasting your time," Absalom says. "Why did you even bother to come here?"

"Absalom, think about Father. He isn't growing any younger. He is over sixty now."

"He didn't think enough of his own daughter to defend her honor."

"He threatened Amnon."

"Threatened him how? Threatened to cut his allowance in half? Threatened to not let him sit on the throne next to the king's throne for a month? Threatened to cut the number of wives he could have? Just how did he threaten Amnon?"

"I don't know, but my mother told me he did."

"What does your mother know? She's ten years younger than my mother."

"Absalom, please." Ithream looks over at the king.

"I can kind of understand Absalom's point of view. His mother is my daughter, and I think I would kill anyone who raped her."

"Go home. Go back to Jerusalem. You tried, and it didn't work," Absalom says. "I appreciate your trying. But go home now."

The men take walks in the woods surrounding the palace, they watch a waterfall, they see signs of bear tracks, and they fish in a mountain stream. But they no longer speak of Amnon and Tamar.

On the third morning, Sett and Ithream leave the palace and head west. They spend their first night on the banks of the Yarmuk River. At the end of the second day, they arrive at the home of Machir just outside of Lodebar.

"Come in, come in," Machir says when they arrive.

The two travelers enter, and Sett sees that, after all these years, the floor tile is still green and his columns blue.

"How have you been, Sett? And who is your friend?"

"I have been fine, and my friend is Prince Ithream, son of King David."

"Your Highness," Machir says.

"As to how I am," Sett says, "I went back and got Kiuuuru and married her, and we now have a nine-year-old son. Or he may be ten by now. I lose track."

"Good for you, Sett. You deserve a little happiness after all you went through in your youth. It looks as though your adult years are going to outshine your childhood. Good for you. How long can you stay?"

"We are on our way home," Ithream says.

Indeed, two days later, Sett and Ithream leave, cross the Jordan River at the intersection where Sett had sold gold jewelry and met the King and Queen of Gesher the first time and head south.

They spend the next night at an inn in Beth Shean.

"Do you always go through that routine every night with your feet?" Ithream asks.

Sett, sitting on the side of the bed, looks up at his companion.

"I have to. I have no feeling in them. If they were injured, I wouldn't know it, and the injury could grow fast. My feet do not heal very well, and if the wound grew until it was out of control, they might have to cut my feet off. I would like to keep the little bit of dignity I have of at least having feet."

"You amaze me how you get around, Sett. I really admire you."

"Well, thank you, friend. But I have no choice—survive or don't survive."

The following night is spent at Tirzah, and the night after that at Shiloh.

"Let's rest for a day here," Sett suggests. "This is a very historic city for us. I'd like to see where the tabernacle stood that Moses made."

The next morning, the two men get directions and walk over to where the tabernacle had stood for three centuries. They stand and stare at the bare ground.

"I cannot describe how I feel, standing before this holy spot where the ark of God was," Sett says, "and where the tabernacle was wherein Moses spoke to God."

"My father keeps talking about building an actual temple to place the ark of the covenant in," Ithream says. "He is already having the stones cut and assembled at the quarry."

"Where does he plan to build it?" Sett asks.

"On Mount Moriah."

"Where is that?"

"Jerusalem is on Mount Zion with my father's palace at the top. On the other side of my father's palace is a ridge, then a higher mountain. That's Mount Moriah."

"I still feel holiness here," Sett says. "Kind of like what I felt when I found where the Garden of God once was."

The next day, the two men return to the highway, and that night are in Bethel.

"I love Bethel and all the trees here. I hope they protect their trees. The forest here is so beautiful."

"I agree with you there," Ithream responds.

"You know, my hero lived here and even had a vision here," Sett says.

"Who was your hero?"

"Jacob. He was lame in his hip after he wrestled with an angel all night. That is when God renamed him Isra-El—Prince of God. He spent the rest of his life hobbling around like me. A crippled prince like me. Well, not as bad as me, but he still hobbled and was still a prince of sorts like me."

Morning comes.

"We will be home later today. We will arrive at Gibeon first. You may as well spend the night with us there."

"No, I want to go on home to Jerusalem. My mother will be worried about me."

Late that afternoon, they arrive at King Saul's palace. Sett pounds on the gate. "My darling I am home," he announces through the gate in a sing-song voice.

A servant opens the gate, and Kissara is right behind him. She is crying.

"What's wrong?" Sett asks, hurrying to the arms of his wife.

"It's our son. It's Micah. He is missing."

# 19 ~ MISSING

**S**ett stares down at his wife

"No. That couldn't happen. We have too many guards here."

Kissara dabs her eyes with her handkerchief. "But it did happen. He has been kidnapped."

"How do you know he was kidnapped? Maybe he is somewhere on our property with a snake bite or something."

"We've already searched the property. He is not here."

"Where is Lechy? How could he let this happen?"

"Lechy has disappeared. His son too."

Sett steps away from his wife, looks up into the sky overhead, and runs his big hand through his thick hair. He looks back to her.

"Ziba!" he bellows. "Ziba, where are you?"

Ziba comes out of his office.

"Did you call, sir?" he says, almost joyfully.

"Where is my son? Where is your son?"

"I do not know, sir. I am as mystified as you."

Sett turns away from him, and Ziba returns to his office.

"What is going on around here? I am gone a month, and my world turns upside down. We've got to search some more. Have you searched all over Gibeon?"

Kissara looks up at her husband without replying.

"Of course, you have. I don't mean to sound like I'm accusing you. I'm not. Oh, my darling."

Sett draws her to him again. They embrace and sway back and forth, his cheek on her scented black hair, both weeping silently.

"I will go see David and ask that some of his soldiers help in the search for Jonathan's grandson. I will go right now."

As Sett breaks away from his wife, he hears a knock on his gate. He watches as the gatekeeper answers it. The person at the gate leaves promptly, and the gatekeeper turns toward Sett.

"Sir, he delivered this scroll for you."

Sett takes it and goes over to a bench in the courtyard. Kissara sits next to him as he unrolls it. He reads aloud.

You have killed my son. Therefore, I will kill your son. But I will give you a chance I did not have. My son was four years old. Therefore, I give you four years to prove me wrong and bring my son back to me alive. If you do, you may have your son back alive. If you do not, at the end of the four years, I will kill your son as you did mine, and dump his body at your damnable gate.

"What is he talking about?" Sett asks, dropping the scroll.

Kissara looks up at Sett, her eyes swimming.

"Yesterday, Lechy was running around here mad at the whole world. He wouldn't tell me what was wrong. All he would say is, 'He will pay. He will pay.' Then, this morning he did not come to work. At first, I did not connect that with Micah not being in his bed this morning. Oh, Sett, what are we going to do?"

She brings out her handkerchief and weeps anew.

Sett rises. "What does he mean I killed his son?" he wails, turning in circles. "Where would he come up with such an idea? I wasn't even here yesterday." He grits his teeth. "Ziba! Come out of that hole of yours and tell me what is going on."

Ziba appears. "You called, sir?"

"Where is my son?" Sett barks. "Where is your

grandson? Did you know anything about this?”

“This what?” Ziba asks.

“Stop that. You are not ignorant. Why is Lechy accusing me of killing his son?”

“Because you did. We have an eye witness. And by the way, my grandson had a name—Iptur.”

“You’re fired,” Sett says.

“You cannot fire me. You need me to be your arbitrator with Lechy until this matter is resolved—until you prove you did not kill Iptur, and that he has just run away.”

“Four-year-old children do not run away,” Sett says.

“Precisely. If you present his son back here alive, your son will be returned to you alive. I must see my grandson myself as proof. If that happens, I will send word to Lechy to release your son.”

“Where are Lechy and Micah?” Kissara screeches between sobs.

“In a place where you will never find them. I would suggest you begin now to find my grandson. The sooner you do, the sooner you get your son back.”

“How do you know your grandson is dead?” Sett asks.

“Because he disappeared two days ago. That is the only logical conclusion.”

Ziba walks back to his office and closes the door.

“What does he do in there all day?” Sett asks.

Kissara does not reply.

Sett paces. Clop. Clop. Pause. Clop. Clop. Pause. Clop. Clop. Pause. His feet never touch the floor. His crutches do it for him.

“We must start looking immediately,” he says. “You have already searched our property and the city of Gibeon. Where else can we look?”

“Dear, we are going to have to search for both boys. Both are missing,” Kissara says. “We’ve got to prove one is alive in order to get the other back alive.

“Unless we find Micah first.”

He paces still. He stops.

"Of course. The secret passage. That's where he has Micah."

"What secret passage?"

"When I was a kid, I discovered a secret passage from my father's apartment that led behind the walls of all the other rooms. I'm sure I can still find it."

Sett makes his way up the side steps to his father's and his third-floor apartment. Kissara follows.

They arrive, and he feels around the walls.

"Here it is. Right where I knew it would be. Stay here while I go in."

"No, I will go with you," Kissara says. "I can carry the lamp to light our way."

They enter the passageway.

"It was much bigger when I was in here before."

"No, dear. You are now much bigger."

They crawl until they are behind another room. Sett listens but does not hear anything. He pushes the secret door into that room open and enters. He looks around.

"They are not in here," he says as he re-enters the secret passage.

They work their way all the way through the passage, down the narrow steps to crawl behind the second-floor apartment, then back up again.

They crawl out and sit on the side of his father's bed, still in the same place where he had slept in it as a child.

"This was too easy. He must have Micah somewhere else."

"And whoever took his son would not have kept him here in the palace."

"I will go see King David right now and ask for his help."

Sett is gone the rest of the afternoon.

"Well, what did he say?" Kissara asks upon his return that night after dark.

"I waited all afternoon. A servant finally came out and said he was gone, and they did not know when he would return."

"Do you think that was the truth?"

"Yes, I think so. Well, it is dark now, so there is nothing we can do until tomorrow. May God give courage to our Micah this night."

"And to his Iptur."

"Why did Lechy name him that? That's a Canaanite name. It's not Jewish at all."

"I do not know, dear. Let's go to bed and rest while we can. Micah needs us. Iptur too."

"We shall pray they are both still alive."

Morning comes.

"I am going to search through Gibeon today," Sett announces. "I know you already have, but twice wouldn't hurt."

Sett spends the rest of the week searching every place he can think of in Gibeon, and offering rewards for finding either boy.

"When the Sabbath is over, I will return to David to obtain his help."

On his next attempt, Sett is allowed a brief audience with the king.

"Your Majesty, my son has been kidnapped. I know who kidnapped him, but his kidnapper is missing also."

"Who would do such a cruel thing to a helpless child?"

"Ziba's son, Lechy, Your Majesty."

"I never trusted Ziba completely. I trust his son even less. What can I do for you?"

"If your soldiers could keep on the lookout for a ten-year-old boy in whatever city you send them, I would most appreciate it."

"Done. Anything else?"

"Only that, well, I was just a year older than him when I was sold as a slave in Ur. Do you think that is what happened to my son?"

"Let us pray for the best outcome. May the Lord be his watchtower and strength, where ever he is, and keep the breath of life in him.”

“Thank you, sire.”

Sett returns home and spends the rest of the week trying to think of somewhere else to search for Micah and Iptur. He paces around the blue-and-red tiles of the courtyard. Two hours later, he ascends the steps to his apartment.

“Why didn’t I think of this earlier, Kissara? Where is the most unlikely place Micah could be hidden? In the temple to Dagon. Lechy has always gotten along with Yassib, one of their priests.”

The next day, Sett takes some of his guards with him. He must be careful which guards he chooses, with several of them being sons of Ziba. They go to the temple on the outskirts of Gibeon and on a hill.

“You cannot come in here,” he is told.

“I demand entrance.”

“You cannot defile our temple. Leave.”

“Never! I know what you are up to. You are hiding my son in there.”

“We do not have your son. He is an unbeliever.”

“He is not old enough to be an unbeliever. Let me in.”

Two priests stand together at the entrance into the temple. Sett charges forward, raising one crutch toward the head of the two priests. They duck and move out of his way.

Sett rushes into the temple and looks around. All he sees is a large statue of a half man half fish in the middle of an otherwise barren room. The temple has only the one room.

He makes his way around the statue and rages at it. “Why?”

With that, Sett leaves the temple and fumbles down the high steps. He sits on the bottom step and tries not to let the guards with him see him weep.

He returns home and dismisses the guards.

“You didn’t find him,” Kissara says. “What are we going to do?”

They sit side by side alone in their apartment. The eyes of both are red and swollen.

"I don't know. But we will keep trying to think of places. We will not stop trying until we find both boys."

A month goes by. Kissara is becoming thinner. Sett is in the courtyard watching her. She is working on her embroidery but does not progress to any degree.

"What are we going to do?" she asks her husband.

"Keep looking," he groans. "He has to be someplace around here. Lechy did not have time to take him far and get a message to me so fast."

He stands and looks out a window facing the property of Yassib.

"Of course," he says. "Why didn't I think of it? Who resents us more than Ziba's family? Our neighbor, Yassib. I never understood why Yassib resents us so much, but he does. They are friends. That's why Micah wasn't in the temple to Dagon. Lechy is paying Yassib to hide Micah in his own house."

Sett calls out his chosen guards and leaves. They gallop toward Yassib's house. They arrive and Sett pounds on the gate with his crutch.

"Let us in, Yassib. I know you are hiding him."

"Hiding who? Go away, Sett. I'm not hiding anyone," Yassib calls back through his still-closed gate.

"You know well who I am talking about. You are helping Lechy hide my son. How much is he paying you?"

"Your son is not here."

Sett signals his guards, and they force their way into Yassib's house. They search the courtyard and every room. They return to the street in front of the house.

"We did not find either boy," one of them says.

More months go by.

"We have been through such a terrible year. How can we endure three more years of this?" Kissara asks her husband as they eat their evening meal together in their apartment.

She drops her bread into her plate.

"Please, dear," Sett urges. "You have lost so much weight. You need to eat. Try, Kissara. Try."

Finding the two boys never leaves their thoughts.

"Have you checked with David's troops lately?"

"Yes," Sett replies. "Still nothing. Just dead ends."

Sett sometimes meets with Ithream to see if he can think of any place the boys could be.

"My father had all the houses in the city searched," Ithream says one day.

"They have to be somewhere nearby. But where?"

Sett sometimes goes to see his family in the political-prisoner wing of David's palace. They give him ideas. He tries them all. But all are to no avail.

"Caves. There are a lot of caves on the Mountain of Olive Trees," Sett tells Kissara one afternoon.

"They've turned that mountain into a cemetery. Surely, neither boy would be there this long.

"We cannot rule out anything. Some caves are large enough for entire families. Tomorrow I shall go there."

"Then I shall go with you," Kissara says.

"Do you think we should take an extra mule just in case?"

"The boys can ride with us."

The next morning, the childless couple rides on two mules to Kidron Valley on the outside of Jerusalem, then up the Olive Tree Mountain and to the cemetery.

They start at the top and travel in a circle to check out caves on all sides. Late that afternoon, they are at the bottom, and still childless.

They go to Absalom's estate in Jerusalem and spend the night with Tamar.

The next morning they head back to Gibeon and home.

More months pass.

"Maybe we have been wrong all along. Maybe he did take Micah far away. Where could that be?"

Sett checks Hebron to the south and Bethel to the north. No sign of either boy.

"I'm going to check the royal stronghold at Mahanaim," Sett tells his wife.

"That's too far. It doesn't make sense," Kissara objects.

"Nothing makes sense. Not since the beginning. We cannot rule out anything."

Sett notifies Ithamar, who agrees to travel with him.

The next morning, they head west down the mountain and to the Jerricho Valley. They spend their first night in Jericho, then cross the Jordan River. They spend their second night in Rabbah. They travel through the Forest of Gilead and arrive in Mahanaim the third night.

"Barzillai, it's me," Ithream says. "Let us in."

Once Sett explains the problem of the two missing boys, Barzillai agrees to have the guards search the entire stronghold, including the palace.

"They're just not here," Barzillai says at the end of the week. "The guards have searched everywhere."

"Sett, I have another thought if you are interested in considering it," Ithream says.

"I am out of ideas. My son has been missing well over a year and a half. I cannot find him, nor can I find Lechy's son to prove his son is not dead. How can I go back and face Kissara?"

"This may not be worth the trip, but didn't you say Machir travels everywhere buying gold jewelry?"

"Yes, but he is another two days away, and Lechy does not even know him."

"Hear me out, Sett. True, it is doubtful either boy is in Lodebar. But he is world traveled. I assume he knows different languages and different cultures. With such a wide background, he might be able to come up with ideas for more places for us to search. We need an outsider's thoughts."

Sett does not answer.

"He may have a point there," Barzillai says. "As you said, you have run out of ideas for places to search. This is your flesh and blood. You cannot give up. You can never give up."

"You are right. I cannot. I will spend the rest of my life searching for Micah if I have to."

"But there is a deadline. Remember. You have only two and a half years left to find him."

Sett sits and looks at the floor. He puts his elbows on his knees and his face in his hands. He looks up at Ithream, then runs his hands through his thick hair. He locks his fingers on his head, squints, grits his teeth, raises his arms and shouts, "Why?"

No one says anything for a long while.

Sett looks at the other two men. "Then, to Machir we will go."

Three days later, Sett and Ithream arrive on the outskirts of Lodebar and Machir's house.

"Look who's here," Machir says, answering his own gate. "What a pleasure."

Sett and Ithream do not smile.

"What's wrong? What has happened?"

After hearing the details of Micah's and Iptur's disappearances, he sits quietly with the younger men. He stands and paces, then reseats himself.

"Do not overlook the obvious. Do not overlook the easy. They may be next door to either of you."

"I've tried that," Sett says. "I searched my neighbor's house."

"You know what I mean. Who do you consider your neighbors? You, too, Ithream. Look high into the trees. Look under your feet. They are probably nearer than you think."

Two days later, Sett and Ithream cross the Jordan River and start up the precarious winding road back up toward Gibeon.

It takes them four days to arrive back home. They struggle to maintain hope.

"Spend the night with me, Ithream. Then I will ride the rest of the way with you on to Jerusalem."

Around noon the next day, Sett and Ithream arrive back in Jerusalem, trying to give rest to his heavy thoughts.

"Absalom has a nice estate of his own," Sett says. "Has David provided you with your own house?"

"He has been talking about giving me Amnon's estate," Ithream says. "So far, he has not been able to bring himself to allow Amnon's things to be moved out. It's exactly the same as it was when he walked out of it five years ago. Would you like to see it?" Ithream asks.

"You have been on the dusty roads with me once again for over two weeks. The least I can do is go a short distance out of our way for you. Of course. I'll be happy to go with you."

Amnon's estate is between David's palace and Absalom's estate. They ride their mules up to it, and Ithream addresses the guards outside the gate.

"I am Prince Ithream. I need you to open the gates and let me in to look around."

The guards step aside, and the two men guide their mules inside. They dismount and look around.

The tile covering the pavement in the courtyard is coral and white. The columns supporting the second floor are green. The walls are scarlet.

"What's that on the wall?" Sett asks.

# 20 ~ ALL THE SONS

"Where?"

"Under that window," Sett says, pointing with his crutch. "Is it a crack? Looks like you are going to have to do some repair work before you move in."

They draw closer to the crack to further inspect it.

"Huh? Huh?"

"What do you see, Sett?"

"That's not a crack. That's...."

He looks at Ithream, his eyes wide.

"Help me, Ithream. Help me. It's my son!"

Ithream takes the steps to the second floor two at a time. Moments later, Ithream looks out the window.

"He's here! He's here!"

In a realm of time that both races and stands still, Micah, now twelve years old, rushes down the outside steps to his father.

The two embrace. They weep. They rock back and forth. They fear to let go in case it is a dream. They cling to each other in order to cling to reality.

"Let me see you, Son," Sett says, finally pulling back from him and trying to smile. "You have grown so tall. You're as tall as your mother."

"Let's get out of here before Lechy gets back," Ithream urges. "Guards. Open the gates."

The men mount their mules. Micah climbs on behind his father.

They race out of the gates. They gallop back out of Jerusalem. They rush north toward Gibeon. They do not allow the animals to stop and rest.

Speeding.

Running.

Racing.

On they go.

Escape. Escape.

They reach the bottom of the hill where the city of Gibeon begins its sprawl.

Micah slides off the back of his father's mule.

"What are you doing, Son?"

"You said yourself I am taller than my mother. I can run faster than your tired mules. I'm going to run the rest of the way home. I can't wait to get home and see Mother."

With Micah suddenly aware of actually being alive for the first time in nearly two years, the men guide their exhausted mules into a walk behind him.

The tall twelve-year-old boy stretches his long legs, eyes wide, wind in his hair.

Even before they reach the gate of the palace, Sett calls for the gatekeeper to open up. They see Micah race through the gate and hear him cry out, "Mother! Mother! I'm home, Mother," then collapse in her arms.

The men dismount and slowly walk their mules through the gate, giving Micah and his mother a moment of treasured reunion.

Sett joins his wife and son in a family embrace. Finally, Sett remembers Ithream and turns to his loyal friend.

"I think we have had a very good day," Ithream says, grinning. "Now, I really do need to get home."

Alone again, the three sit in a circle. "How did you like my signal, Father? I knew you would find me someday."

"Tearing your belt down the middle and hanging it from the window was brilliant."

"Remember, Mother, how I wanted it to be purple, and

you had it dyed special for me?"

"How lucky that I listened to my son for once," Kissara says, still weeping and grinning at the same time.

"What's all the noise out here?" Ziba calls out from his hiding place, which he claims as his office.

"Micah, you and your mother need to run up to your mother's apartment and lock the door. I have something to take care of."

Sett motions for the gate guards to follow him—not the ones who were Ziba's sons, having fired them the previous year. He works his way over to Ziba's still-closed door, and one of the guards bangs on it with the handle of his sword.

Ziba opens it. "What is..."

"Ziba, you no longer work for me. My guards will escort you out."

"Oh, no, you don't. You need me."

"I no longer need you. Now, do not turn around and go back into this room. Walk immediately away."

"What about your son? You need me."

"If you do not leave voluntarily, I will have you chained and thrown out. It is your choice."

Ziba looks at Sett, looks around the courtyard, then at the guards. He steps between them and leaves. The gates of Saul's palace are secured behind him.

As the guards head for their posts in the four towers, Sett announces, "He is never to return." He looks at the gatekeeper. "Is that clear?"

Kissara appears at the top of the steps. "Is it safe to come down? Both of us?"

"Yes, both of you. We are finally free of that detestable family."

That evening, they eat together for the first time in nearly two years. Sett explains the disappearance of Lechy's son, Iptur. "He has been accusing me of killing him. Did you ever see him while you were being held prisoner?"

"No, Father."

"Did you hear anything?"

"Well, Lechy did say that the last time he saw his son, he was in the market near the Jericho Gate of Gibeon."

"If he wasn't with you," Sett says, "maybe he really was killed by someone, or his father was lying to make me suffer."

A week later a messenger arrives at the gate and leaves a clay tile to be delivered by the gatekeeper to Sett.

"I am being summoned to David's palace," he tells his wife, smiling.

"Maybe he is planning a banquet in honor of Jonathan's grandson who has been returned to us safely," Kissara says.

"That's probably it. But I'm not sure I am ready to let Micah outside these walls yet."

"You will have to eventually. Otherwise, he will be as much of a prisoner here as he was with Lechy."

The following day, Sett mounts his mule. "I will be back this afternoon probably. Perhaps while I am in the city, I can check around for someone to hire as my new steward, now that Ziba and his family are gone."

Sett rides into Jerusalem whistling. Micah is on the mule behind him.

"Isn't it a blessed day?" he says to people at the market as he heads his mule up toward the palace. "God bless you. And you."

Once inside David's palace, he notices a boy around six or seven years old pointing to him and laughing. Then the boy pretends he is on crutches and swaggers back and forth, hanging his tongue out and panting as though out of breath.

"Father, look what that boy is doing?"

"He will get over it. He is just young." Sett makes his way on, taking up his whistling again

He and Micah climb the grand stairs at the far end of the inner courtyard, walk down the long corridor, and arrive at the doors into the throne room. A sky blue-clad guard lets them in, and the boy follows beside them.

Sett notices David smiling at the boy they had seen earlier. "Get along now, Eliphelet."

The king motions for Sett and Micah to come forward. Sett lowers himself onto his knees and touches the marble-tiled floor with his head. Micah imitates his father.

"You may rise, friend. Now come forward. Isn't he some boy? That Eliphelet? He's my youngest. Got a lot of spunk like me."

Sett stops two man-lengths from the throne. Micah does the same.

"So, this is Jonathan's grandson we have all been so worried about. He looks more like Jonathan than you do, Mefiboset."

David pauses, looks toward a side door, and mumbles, "Now, where is he? Oh, there he is.

Sett stares, squints, and juts his head forward as though doing so will bring what he sees into better focus or make it disappear.

"I believe you know each other. Now Ziba here tells me you have fired him. You cannot do that, Sett. He has been with the palace since long before you were born.

"But, Your Majesty, he and his son conspired in the kidnapping of my son."

"Is that right?" the king asks Ziba.

"I never knew anything about it. This is the first I have heard of it. I just thought the boy was visiting his mother's parents in Ur for a while."

"No, he's..."

Sett pokes Micah in the side. "Shhh."

"There. You see. Ziba knew nothing of it. Now, you will reinstate Ziba today."

The king looks over at the old man who, by now, is smirking. "Ziba, I never liked you, but sometimes you have to keep your enemies nearby when they can serve you."

"Uh, sire," Sett begins, "about Absalom."

David jerks his head back.

"You are dismissed."

Ziba works his way around so he is beside Sett and Micah, and walks backward with them until they reach the door out of the throne room.

Once outside in the corridor, Ziba glares as Sett and walks on ahead of him.

They hear a small voice. Young Prince Eliphelet walks behind them, stomping his feet in tune with Sett's crutches.

When they arrive at the palace courtyard, the boy disappears. Micah stops. His father stops with him. "Why do you let people run over you like that?"

"Don't worry about it, Son. It is not important. Let's go home."

They ride past Absalom's estate and see people gathered in front of it.

"What's going on here?" Micah asks.

"Shhh. Listen."

"Hail, Absalom!" they hear.

Sett looks up at a window overlooking the street. He sees Absalom in the window, waving to the people."

They ride out of Jerusalem and back to Gibeon and their own palace in silence.

A month later, Sett's gatekeeper announces royal guests. "Presenting Prince Absalom and his brother Prince Ithream," the gatekeeper says.

"Welcome. Welcome," Sett says. "Come sit here in the warm air."

He turns toward a servant, then calls up the stairs. "Kissara. Come. Look who is here."

Kissara joins the guests in the courtyard, and the four sit on benches facing each other.

"It is so good to have you back, Absalom," Kissara says. "How is Tamar?"

"Thank you, Kissara. Tamar is just Tamar. She has no life left in her. She helps the cooks and the maids. She embroiders a little and walks around my courtyard as though in a trance."

"I am so sorry. At least she has you back."

"Yes, at least she appreciates me."

"So, you finally convinced your father to end your exile."

"He did," Ithream says. "But it is only for appearances. He still refuses to see Absalom."

"He has sent word to me that, as far as he is concerned, I am as dead as my brother. Well...."

"Brother, let us not speak of it now," Ithream interrupts. "We are with friends."

"Yes, and I have sent word to our cooks to prepare extra for you," Sett adds. "You will join us for our evening meal."

"And we expect you to spend the night with us. You can return to Jerusalem in the morning," Kissara adds. "I wish you had brought Tamar with you. She needs to get out sometimes. I shall go see her in a few days."

"Were you ever able to find little Iptur?" Ithream asks.

Sett and Kissara both shake their heads.

"No one has ever found his body. He has to be somewhere, but I cannot imagine where. Micah said Lechy last saw the boy while they were in the market here in Gibeon."

"Let us pray you find the answer to this mystery someday and that it ends well after all," Absalom says.

"Personally, I think Lechy just hid him so he could accuse my husband of something bad enough he could justify kidnapping our son."

"I don't think so, dear," Sett says.

"Whatever happened to Lechy?" Ithream asks.

"I hired him," Absalom interjects. "Didn't I tell you? He is a good steward. His father trained him well."

"You did what?" Sett says, glaring at Absalom.

Ziba walks out of his office.

"Do I hear friendly voices?" the old man says.

"Good to see you, Ziba," Absalom says.

Sett and Kissara watch the two men as they greet each other with embraces. The hosts look at each other a moment, then look over at Ithream.

Ithream shrugs his shoulders.

"Well, I must get back to work now, Absalom. We will talk more the next time I get to Jerusalem." With that, Ziba returns to his office.

The next morning while Sett's family says goodbye to their overnight guests, a farmhand approaches.

"Sire," he says to Sett as Absalom and Ithream ride away on their royal white mules, "there are dead vultures all over your land."

"All of it?"

"Well, not exactly. They are over on the west end of it."

"How many?"

"Probably fifteen or twenty. Maybe more."

"It's that Yassib again, Father," Micah says. "You've got to do something about him."

"Just put them all in baskets. Take the baskets out of town and throw them off a precipice somewhere."

"Yes, sire."

"That's all, Father?" Micah demands. "You can't let him get by with it. Dump the dead vultures back on his land."

"I am more worried about these meetings Ziba is having with Absalom. What is he up to?" Sett says as they walk back into their courtyard, and the outer gate is closed.

Time passes. Whenever Sett goes to see King David, he reports the same thing: "I worry about David," he tells Kissara. "He has aged a lot since he brought Absalom home."

"Are they talking to each other yet?"

"No. The king's bitterness toward Absalom killing his oldest son and taking over as the crown prince is tearing away at him. He is as bitter toward Absalom as Absalom was toward his sister's rapist."

"Didn't you say great grandfather became bitter toward David when he became too popular?" Micah asks.

"I hadn't thought of it like that, but I think you are right. David isn't as violent toward him; he isn't trying to kill

Absalom. But he still refuses to acknowledge his existence. I shall go see the king tomorrow. We will talk about my father and maybe sing a few songs together. I will try to get them talking to each other again. Would you like to go along, Micah?"

Micah, in his thirteen-year-old hoarse voice, says he does.

They arrive at the palace and are met, as usual, by Prince Eliphelet, who is now nine years old and still imitating Sett.

"How does he know to be nearby whenever we arrive?" Micah asks his father.

They make their way through the outer courtyard into the inner one.

"I suppose he tells the gatekeeper he likes us, and be sure to send word to him so he can be around to greet us."

"Doesn't the king ever discipline his sons?"

They go up the wide steps at the far end of the inner courtyard and head down the long corridor.

"It seems he underdoes it with some and overdoes it with some. Now say no more. Someone may overhear us. Here we are at the throne room now."

They notice the corridor outside the room is empty. "Where are all the people wanting to get in to see the king?" Micah asks. "Has their allegiance gone to someone else?"

"Shhh," Sett warns.

A servant opens the folding doors. Sett and Micah see the king on his throne. They bow to the floor.

"Come! Come! Both of you. How good it is to see you again. And what may I do for you today, Jonathan?" David's voice is scratchy.

"Your Majesty, we have come for a time of enjoyment with you," Sett says. "You and I love to sing, and my son seems to be following in our footsteps."

The king's eyes light up. "Ah! In that case, follow me."

David leaves his throne, goes to the entrance from whence Sett had come, and rushes down a back stairway.

They arrive at the room with the balcony facing the Kidron Valley.

He turns and sits on a bench. "So, what shall we sing?"

"You choose, sire," Sett says. "Didn't you used to be a shepherd?"

"Ah, yes. They call me the Shepherd King, and I guess that I am."

"Have you composed any songs about sheep?" Micah asks.

David looks out and up to the sky. "Yes, it is one Jonathan, and I used to sing together whenever he joined me out in the pasture.

*The Lord is my shepherd,*
*I shall not be deprived of anything.*
*When I am tired, he lets me lie down and rest.*
*When I am thirsty, he gives me pure water to drink.*
*He makes my soul live again.*
*He leads me to paths of goodness.*
*I praise his name because of his kindness toward me.*

David's voice falters. It is not as strong as it had been the first time Sett sang with him eighteen years earlier. He clears his throat.

*Even when I am forced to face death,*
*He walks with me through the valley*
*And I fear no one because*
*The Lord is there beside me.*
*His rod is always there to protect me.*
*Right there while my enemies watch*
*My Lord sits me down at his table.*

As he sings, David looks over the valley below and beyond to the Mountain of Olive Trees where the graves are. Sett wonders if he has forgotten he is not alone.

*He washes my sins away and gives me all I desire.*
*Indeed, his goodness and mercy will remain with me*
*To the day I die.*
*Then I will live with him in heaven forever.*

It is quiet now. David lifts an arthritic finger and wipes an eye.

"Uh, sire, that is a beautiful song. Did you say you used to sing it with my father?"

David turns. "Oh, indeed, yes," he says with a fresh smile. "What a man he was. Did I ever tell you that you look just like Jonathan?

"Well, we must be going now, Your Majesty."

"No, Jonathan. I need you."

Sett stares at the old man David has become.

"I need you to move back here. It is for the best. I need you. Ziba will continue to watch over Saul's estate and give you the proceeds to live on."

Sett tips his head and squints.

"Oh, I don't mean for you to go to the wing the rest of Saul's family is in. I trust you more than I do them, though these days, I sometimes wonder who I can trust. But, Jonathan, I need you here. Sometimes I feel a little lonely. Do you understand?"

"I will move my family here within the week," Sett replies.

David brightens. "Besides, we can sing together more often. There is one I especially want to teach you. It's about the majesty of the heavens."

On their way out of Jerusalem, Sett and Micah see a crowd gathered at the city gate.

Absalom is sitting in a stately chair on a small platform, a princely crown on his head, and royal robes.

"What is he doing, Father? I thought David was still the king," Micah says.

"As the oldest living son and heir to the throne, he is

within legal right to hear cases of the people," Sett replies.

"Come to me, my people," they hear Absalom say. "Come and let me bless you, my people."

# 21 ~ DOOMED

"We have been back with David three years. I don't like it here. Why won't he let us go back to our palace in Gibeon?" sixteen-year-old Micah asks.

"Son, count your blessings that we are still alive. Your great grandfather tried to kill David many times. They were mortal enemies."

"I know. I know. Our family was saved because David was best friends with your father. But, well, it's that Eliphelet."

"What has he done this time?"

"He put a dead rabbit in my bed. The last time it was a dead squirrel. How did he get in here, anyway?"

"Well, there is nothing we can do about it."

"The king dotes on all his sons—well except Absalom—and lets them have anything they want. You should see what he gave Solomon the other day," Micah retorts.

"He is only two years younger than you. I thought you and Solomon were friends."

"He gets anything he wants. His father gave him his own white mule for his birthday. I don't even have a black mule of my own."

Sett shakes his head. "And yet he still refuses to acknowledge Absalom as his son. You would think he would be over the whole mess by now."

"Dear, Ziba is here at the palace again," Kissara says. "He has been coming more often. The king hasn't been inviting you to sing with him as much since Ziba's trips here have increased."

"David is just tired. He is growing older, and it is harder for him to… What's going on down in the street?"

Micah rushes to a window of their apartment overlooking the street. "Father, some people are shouting 'Long live King Absalom'."

"They'd better be careful talking like that," Sett says.

It is night now. King David's palace is quiet. Everyone now in bed—Sett and his family, David and his family, the day-time servants.

"What was that?" Sett says, rousing himself. He sits up.

Running and shouting out in the corridor. Pounding on his door.

Sett grabs his crutches and goes to his door just as his servant, Elza, in his nightclothes, opens it. "What's going on out here?"

"Absalom has his own army, and they're just a little way out of Jerusalem to usurp the throne," a servant and friend of Elza says. "The king has left the palace in his nightshirt and is headed toward the stronghold in Mahanaim."

"Hurry. Saddle my mule," Sett tells his old servant.

"What's going on?" Kissara asks, joining her husband by the door.

"Absalom has declared himself king, and David is on the run," Sett says. "I must get to him. He stood by me all these years. I must stand by him now."

Sett dresses and goes out into the corridor to hear the latest news while waiting for his mule. He sees Ziba headed toward him. Ziba is smiling.

*What is Ziba doing in the palace in the middle of the night, and in my wing?* "What is the latest, Ziba?" Sett asks.

"Oh, it's nothing. People are getting excited over nothing. Absalom isn't doing what they say."

"But your son is Absalom's steward now. What has

Lechy been telling you?"

"People are exaggerating. That's all. Now, just go on back to bed."

"What about David?"

"He has already gone back to bed. Everyone is beginning to calm down. It was a false report. Go on back to bed."

Sett's servant arrives. "Your mule is ready."

"Never mind, Elza. It was a false report. Put the mule back in its stall."

With that, Sett returns to his apartment and goes back to bed.

"Father. Are you up? Father." It is Micah on the other side of his parents' door.

Sett rouses himself and sits up on his elbows. It is morning.

"We had a hard night," Sett calls out to him. "What is it now that is so important?"

"The palace is almost empty. Everyone is gone but a few of David's servants and his mistresses," he says through the closed door.

Sett stares in the direction of Micah's voice a moment, grabs his crutches, hurries to his bedroom door, and opens it. "Are you sure?"

"Yes, sir. Everyone is gone."

Sett works his way to his apartment door and opens it. He goes out into the corridor and looks both ways. All is quiet.

"No! No! David needs me. Ziba, why? Why do you keep betraying me?"

He returns to his apartment. Kissara joins him. "Perhaps you can still catch up with him, dear."

He sits and leans back against the wall. "No, I can't."

"Why?"

"First, because I do not know for sure where he went, and second, because Absalom will be here within the hour, and his soldiers may mistake me for the enemy."

"Father, what's that noise out in the street?"

Sett does not go to the window to find out. He knows.

"Hail, King Absalom."

"Long live King Absalom."

"Hail, King Absalom!"

Sett puts his face in his hands.

"No. This cannot be happening. Oh, David."

The rest of the day, as commotion grows outside their window, Sett sits and stares.

"He needs me. David needs me." Tears streak down his cheek and into his beard. "He needs me."

Another day goes by. A week.

Sett wanders around their apartment on his knees, his feet dragging, his hair down in his eyes, his bushy beard growing wilder.

"Setty, you are worrying me. You're hardly eating. You haven't cleaned up and put on clean clothes. Worst of all, you are not taking care of your feet. Here, let me do it for you. What if you get injuries you cannot feel?"

"No. Leave me be. I don't want to eat and clean up or change clothes. I don't even want to check my feet. I don't care anymore. My father's best friend is wandering out there, not knowing who his friends are. Probably thinking I have turned against him too. Oh, Kissara. I feel so helpless."

They hear marching down on the street going through the middle of Jerusalem.

"Father, it looks like most of the kingdom has decided to recognize Absalom as king. Look."

"I cannot look, Son. I cannot look." He stares at the bare ceiling. "Oh, David. I have wished most of my life I could have had my father. What has happened between you and Absalom?"

Sett crawls toward the window, then stops. He puts his head down onto the carpet and weeps.

"Maybe this will wake David up," Kissara says.

"It could be too late."

They hear a knock on the door. Kissara answers it.

Ziba walks in, smiling.

"Well, Lechy finally got his revenge for you killing his son. He has managed to direct Absalom's rise to power, and I have managed to direct David's hatred for his son. Divide and conquer. And it worked. You no longer have a home. David has given me the entire estate of Saul. You now have nothing."

With that, Ziba grins, winks at Sett, and leaves. They hear him out in the corridor. Whistling.

"That evil family," Micah says. "Why didn't you get rid of them while you could?"

"Ziba is wily," Kissara says. "All along he must have been telling David he was his only true friend. Apparently David believed him. No wonder he felt lonely."

"Father, what are you going to do?"

"Nothing, Son. Nothing."

Another week goes by.

Micah wanders out in the corridor to see if there is any news. He reports to his parents. "David is at the royal stronghold in Mahanaim now."

Still Sett refuses to clean up, change clothes or check his feet.

"Dear, at least let me check them for you."

"No."

"You have been scraping them on the floor. What if they're infected now?"

"I don't care. I care about nothing. David is going to think I betrayed him."

Sett's eyes are swollen. He crawls around the apartment, refusing to use his crutches. His desire to live is gone. He weeps. He stares.

They hear troops outside.

"I see Absalom. He is at the head. He's leading his troops out of the city," Micah says.

"The inevitable will happen soon now," Sett says. "Will they kill each other?" He weeps yet more.

Another week of wondering and praying and dying on

the inside. Sett sits and crawls and lies down, and bows prostrate on the floor.

A loud voice on the other side of their apartment door. "Absalom is dead!"

Micah opens the door and walks out into the corridor. "Did you say Absalom is dead?" he asks the servant.

"He is dead and his army is appealing to rejoin David."

The following day, Sett calls his servant to him. "Saddle my mule, Elza. David will be coming home shortly. I will meet him."

"Me too," Micah says. "I'm sixteen years old and am a man. I should be able to go with you to meet the king."

Sett looks back at the servant. "Saddle two mules."

A while later, Elza returns. "Your mules are ready."

Micah walks slowly with his father as they work their way out of their wing of the palace and down to the stables. Sett still has no protective boots on his paralyzed feet. His toes drag the pavement. His hair is still in his eyes. His tunic is dirty. His eyes swollen.

Sett attempts to mount his mule but is unsuccessful. Without a word, Micah, now as tall as his father, helps him up.

Slowly they make their way down to the bottom of the mountain that is Jerusalem and out through the gate.

"Do you know where David is?" Micah asks one of the guards.

"I heard he is near Gilgal, just north of Jericho, but still on the other side of the Jordan."

"Let's hurry," Sett calls to his son in a sudden burst. He puts his mule into a gallop, his hair and grimy robe flying behind him. They rush down the precarious winding road, heedless of its dangers.

They arrive at Jericho and go around it, heedless of the exhaustion of their mules. They head north to Gilgal, where thousands of David's subjects have gathered. They cross the Jordan River and see a large encampment.

"I've got to get to him," Sett keeps saying. They slow

the mules and head into the camp. They see a large tent with the royal banner over it. Sett and Micah go to David's tent. David is sitting outside of it.

Micah helps his father off his mule, and gives him one crutch, putting his father's other arm over his shoulder.

David, as red-eyed as Sett, looks up.

"You show your face? You stay behind to take my throne from me just in case Absalom fails? Now, you come to me to offer support because you failed?"

Sett collapses to the ground, his head touching the carpet laid down for David.

David makes him wait but finally gives Sett permission to rise and speak.

"Your Majesty, I was ready to go with you, but Ziba came and told me it was a false report and that you were safely in bed." Sett takes in a hoarse breath and continues.

"By morning, when I realized everyone was gone, it was too dangerous for me to catch up with you. So I stayed behind and have prayed for you day and night." Sett bows his head into his hands and shakes.

"Oh, sire, I love you as my father loved you. I would give my life for you. Do not accuse me of betraying you. Kill me if that is your wish. But do not call me a betrayer."

"That's not what Ziba tells me."

"Don't you know Ziba by now?" Micah says, interceding for his father. "He has been manipulating everyone so he can take over my father's estate once and for all. He manipulated Absalom into taking over as king in hopes you would kill each other, and my father would be killed along with you."

"That cannot be," David says, shaking his gray head. "Ziba helped me on my way, and is back here now to help me return to Jerusalem."

"He is wily. You know that, Your Majesty," Micah continues. "Look at my father. Is that a betrayer?"

David is silent a moment. He stands and turns his back on Sett, then returns to his portable throne.

"I thought you, of all people, would have been the first to go with me. Your father would have. And why haven't you cleaned up to see me? You look terrible."

"I tried," Sett replies softly.

"How could he when he has been grieving for you since you left?" Micah says, interceding again.

"Ziba told me you convinced Absalom to take my throne so we would kill each other, and you could get Saul's crown back for yourself," David retorts.

"That's right," Eliphelet says, having arrived at the tent moments earlier. "You can believe Ziba. He is your friend, not that Mefiboset and his fool son, Micah." He looks over at Micah and smirks.

"No, Your Majesty," Sett says, still on his knees, still in tears. "All I want is you. You took me in when I had nothing. That was nearly twenty years ago. We have been friends since then. I could never betray you."

"Your Majesty, my father, is telling you the truth. You have not been with him watching him crawl and cry and grieve for you all this time," Micah says. "My father has neglected his feet, and they are so scraped, he may never recover. He loves you like the father he longs for, your Jonathan."

David stands again and walks away. He stares at the sky, turns back around. He returns to his throne.

"I'm tired. I don't want to hear any more excuses. I just want to go home," David says. "You are all lying to me. Well then, divide up the estate. You can have half of it back, but Ziba gets to keep the rest. Now, leave me alone."

"I do not care what you do with my grandfather's estate. All I care about is that you are safe. I would live in the desert if that is what it took to keep you safe."

"Go away," David says.

Micah leads his father from David and sits him on the ground. "Stay here, Father. I will be back shortly."

Sett does not know how long Micah is gone, but when he returns, he has a leather tent large enough for four people. He sets it up for them to sleep under that night.

The next day when Micah wakens, his father is sitting up.

"Where did you get this tent, Son?"

"I traded my saddle for a tent, traveling supplies, and some food. There is a clean robe for you somewhere in these things."

Sett looks at his son. "Thank you for standing by me. You are more of a man than I thought."

"Do you think you are going to be okay now, Father?"

Sett sighs. "David is safe. I will be fine. Shall we go over to the Jordan and clean up?"

The tents in the encampment are taken down, and Ziba shows up to help David recross the Jordan and return to Jerusalem.

"What is Ziba up to now?" Micah asks his father.

"It seems he is never satisfied," Sett says. "He must have heard David took half of Saul's estate back from him and gave it back to me. Perhaps he hopes to win David's complete confidence again and get all the estate for himself again."

"He will never be satisfied. He is the most greedy man I have ever known," Micah says.

"We shall say nothing. If Ziba gets it all back, so be it."

"But, Father. It belongs to you."

"As long as David knows I will always be his friend, I am satisfied. Even if we are exiled and must live in a tent in the desert, I will never stop loving the man my father loved. So speak no more of it."

On the other side of the river, only David's tent is re erected. He enters, and two hours later, reappears cleaned up. He is wearing his royal robes, and the crown is on his head.

With bodyguards in place and loyal representatives of all twelve tribes of Israel lined up behind him ten across and one hundred in each of the columns, the procession slowly makes its way up to Mount Zion and Jerusalem.

Sett is toward the rear, just ahead of the soldiers guarding the end of the procession.

"Why do you do this, Father?" Micah asks. "You should be up at the front, not back here."

"Be quiet, Son. This is my decision."

Just as the sun turns red for the evening, the gates to the City of David are opened.

Sett stays outside the city where the representatives of the people and many of the soldiers in their sky blue uniforms set up tents to spend the night and guard the city for their reinstated king.

"Mother is going to be worried."

"She will be fine. We will return to David's palace when all has settled down. Then we will resume our life as it had been before."

"Father, no. We got your palace back and part of the land. We need to go home."

"Not now, Son. David needs our reassurance. He needs to know that Jonathan's son is still his forever friend."

"Father, you are always letting people run over you. Just because you are crippled, they think they can get by with it. Prove them wrong, Father. Stand up for yourself. And for Mother and I."

A few days later, Sett and Micah return to David's palace. Kissara puts salve on Sett's feet and thanks God their injuries consist only of scrapes. Sett stays in bed until they are healed.

"I need to go see my family in their wing," he tells Kissara. "They will wonder what happened to us."

"I will go with you, Father," Micah says.

"Not this time, Son. I need time alone with them."

Sett makes his way to the other wing of the palace and waits for his family to join him in the waiting room. A guard escorts them in.

His Aunt Merab and her five sons—Sett's cousins—come. Merab is thin and drawn, her gray hair is unkempt, and some of the strands fall into her eyes. She does not try to brush them out of the way.

Rizpah, Sett's step-grandmother, and her two sons come too. "You're safe," Rizpah says for the others. "We were worried about you."

"You've lost a lot of weight. Did they starve you?" Aunt Merab asks.

"No," Sett replies. "I guess I starved myself. I just could hardly eat with everything going on with David and his son."

He looks over at his uncles. "You were bereft of your father when you were young. You remember what it was like. Why couldn't David have forgiven Absalom? Well, it's all over, and Absalom is no more."

"At least you are safe," Merab says.

"Oh, we heard Ziba betrayed you again," Mefiboset says. "He was a lying rascal even when he was young."

"At least you got the palace back. When are you returning there?" Rizpah asks.

"I don't think I am for now. David needs me. When things settle back down, maybe I will then."

"But what is going to happen to our palace? That Priest Yassib hates you. He could burn down the palace next. Did you ever find out why?"

"Why he hates me? No. I think Ziba and Lechy know."

## 22 ~ OLD ENEMIES

"**Z**iba is dead," Sett announces to his family. "He's been dead two weeks, and I am just now hearing about it."

"Good," Micah, now twenty-one, says. "I never knew such an evil man. Didn't even know what a conscience was."

"Do you think his son, Lechy, will inherit his father's half of the estate now?" Kissara asks.

Sett touches his wife's cheek. "You are still beautiful. How did I ever deserve you, my peach?"

Kissara smiles. "You're changing the subject."

"Remember the day we met? When I first saw you, I thought I was looking at the face of an angel."

"I'm going riding," Micah announces, twisting his nose around at his parents.

"How have you been feeling, my little one?" Sett asks, not paying attention when the apartment door opens and closes back.

"I'm okay. Sometimes I have a pain up here, but it never stays long."

Sett reaches over and puts his hand where her hand is. "Let me take the pain away, my love," he says.

They sit in quiet a while.

Micah returns and slams the door shut. "Guess what I just heard? Oh."

He looks over at his parents, who have fallen asleep, his mother's head on his father shoulder, and his arm around her."

"Wake up. Wake up. Guess what I just found out? We would have never known about it if it had been left up to fat Eliphelet. Why does he resent us so much anyway?"

"He is the king's youngest son, the youngest of his nineteen sons," Kissara says, rousing herself. "How would you like to have eighteen brothers all bigger and more important than you?"

"He's not mad at us, Micah," Sett says, untangling his arm from Kissara's shoulder. "He is just mad at the world."

"Well, Ithream met me outside and asked when we were moving back to our palace. When I didn't know anything about it, he said the king had told Eliphelet right after Ziba died, and instructed him to get the message to us."

"What did David tell him?"

"The king said we could have all of Saul's estate back."

"Oh, that's wonderful," Kissara says. "It's been nine long years since we were allowed to live there. It will be good to be back in our own home again."

"Yes, I have missed the old place," Sett says.

A week passes. Sett, Kissara, and Micah stand just inside the gate of Saul's palace. They stare at the blue-and-red tiles in the courtyard and see that some of them are chipped. There are more hairline cracks in the columns surrounding the courtyard.

"Welcome home," the gatekeeper says.

A servant walks up. "Welcome home. I trust we have kept it in good condition in your absence." Sett recognizes him as one of Ziba's sons.

Micah rushes across the courtyard and ascends the steps toward the third-floor apartments, taking two at a time.

The stonework comes loose on one of the steps, and Micah tumbles back down to the courtyard. He stands, wipes his knees, and looks up at the step.

"Be careful, Son. It's a good thing you weren't very far up. Those steps can be dangerous. I know."

"Which one was it, Father? The one that killed your feet?"

"I do not remember. It must have been halfway down. I was only five at the time."

The servant comes running up. "I do not understand it. I requested someone fix that step just before you returned."

"Well, we have survived. Micah can skip that step, and Kissara and I will go to our apartments by way of the front steps and through the throne room. Are the doors into the throne room working okay?"

"I am sure they are. No one ever goes up those steps. I guess they did when the king lived here, but not now."

Sett and Kissara ascend the wide front steps, and the servant opens back the folding doors far enough they can enter the throne room.

They walk toward the copper-colored alabaster throne that has been empty for so long. Sett envisions his grandmother sitting in the lesser green alabaster throne next to it as queen. He envisions his father, as crown prince, sitting in the other lesser throne on the other side.

"It is just as well that these doors be closed all the time," Sett says softly.

He makes his way over to the throne. "Come, my dear. We may as well sit in them when no one is around to see us make fools of ourselves. Here is the queen's throne next to mine. You will be beautiful in it."

They seat themselves and do not speak.

"When I was eleven years old, I was hailed King of Israel by my relatives. They were all down in the courtyard in full view and called out, 'Hail to the King. Hail King Mefiboset.' My grandmother made sure I knew what it felt like. She made me king for one day. I miss her."

"I do too, Setty. Well, we need to go on into our apartments."

Two days later, Sett and Kissara walk outside to look over their land.

"Looks like ole Yassib is behaving himself," Sett says. "No dead vultures."

He greets the farmworkers.

"You are doing a fine job."

"Thank you, sire."

"I am proud of you."

"Thank you, sire."

"Let's go back to the house," Kissara says. "I'm getting a little tired."

They work their way back up the road to the palace.

"I love it here, you know," Sett says. "I never allowed them to cut any more trees than were needed for the crops. I never let them cut any for lumber.

"Woah. What was that?"

Sett is knocked off balance by something dropping onto his head and falls to the ground.

"Setty, are you all right?"

He looks up and notices a missing tile from the edge of the roof.

"That was close. We've got to get that fixed before it kills someone," Sett says, lifting himself back up.

"Was that Lechy I just saw behind that tree?" Kissara asks.

"No, of course not, dear. He has no reason to be up here anymore."

They return to the palace. A few days later, Sett and Kissara are in their apartment talking about Micah's future.

"Eeek!" Kissara points and freezes.

"A snake. There's a snake in that corner by my clothes basket."

Sett steps forward, pushes her clothes out of the way with one crutch, and spots it. He pushes a tunic back over the snake, then traps it with his three-footed crutch.

"Be careful, Sett," Kissara squeals.

He leans over and picks up a basket. He throws the basket over the snake, then moves in close enough, he can pick it up and throw the basket lid over it.

Sett makes his way to the window and dumps the snake out.

"He was poisonous," Kissara objects.

"There are poisonous snakes everywhere. Haven't been bitten by one yet," Sett responds, making his way back to his wife. She is trembling.

"You were lucky it was a black adder and not one of the vipers," Sett explains.

"Eeek," Kissara cries out.

"What now? The snake is gone."

Kissara stands, pointing at Sett's foot. "A scorpion. There's another one next to your crutch."

Kissara grabs two mugs from a table holding their water pitcher.

She slides the scorpions into the mug, covers them with the other mug, then goes to the window and drops them to the ground below.

"Mother! What is going on?" Micah says from the balcony above them. "Are you all right?"

He rushes down to their room. "What's all the screaming?"

"Well, first, it was a poisonous snake, then two scorpions."

"That's too much for a coincidence. Either Lechy or Priest Yassib is at it again. Nothing is going to stop them short of putting them in prison."

"But we cannot prove it was them."

Sett now realizes his wife is sitting on the floor. "Kissara, what is wrong?"

"Oh, it is nothing. Just that old pain."

"We cannot stay here," Sett says. "We need to go back to Jerusalem."

"No, Father. We belong here. I will inspect the entire palace and make sure everything is safe. Father, we must stay here. It is our heritage."

The following week Sett and Kissara hear a yelp. It is Micah. They hurry to him. By the time they arrive, he has pulled his foot back through the hole in the floor of his apartment.

"We cannot stay here," Sett says. "It is too dangerous."

"But we know who is doing it. They will get tired and stop one of these days."

"No more. We go back to David's palace."

"But, Father."

"I have ruled."

"Let me go talk to our neighbor. Maybe he will take a bribe," Micah suggests.

"What could you bribe him with?" Kissara asks. "Other than these four walls and floor, we have hardly anything left."

"What about the gold jewelry you said you were leaving me when you die?"

"You do not touch that, Micah."

"By the way, you never did show me where you hid it."

"Good point," Sett replies. "We have moved it a couple times. I will show you right now. But you are not to use any of it. Grab a lamp. We're going into a tunnel."

Sett leads his son to his father's old apartment on the third floor.

"I discovered this secret passageway when I was ten years old, and they had me loc... Well, they had me stay in my father's apartment a long time."

Sett feels along the wall, then pushes. The panel moves.

"Father!" Micah says with a large grin. "You really do have a secret passageway. I had heard there was one, but thought everyone was just teasing me."

"All right. Is your lamp lit?"

Sett gets on his knees and climbs over the threshold and into the darkness. Micah holds the lamp high.

"It's tight in here."

"It wasn't when I was ten."

The two big men squeeze through two man-lengths, and Sett stops.

"Okay now, Micah. Reach up with your left hand and feel around for a box."

"Ahhh!" Micah shouts. "There's a snake up there."

Sett laughs. "That just a branch I put up there to scare anyone who finds it who shouldn't have. Scoot it out of the way. Do you feel the box now?"

"I think so."

"Pull it down, then we'll take it back into my room."

"It's heavy. What's in it? Gold bricks?"

Once back in Sett's boyhood apartment, he instructs Micah to sit with him on the bed to look over the contents.

"This is ours, and all the times we needed money, you never got it out? Where did it come from?"

"It came from Ur over by the Euphrates River. Your mother made this jewelry. It is pure gold. Now, after you have looked at it, you are to put it back in the ceiling where I showed you. And you must vow to me by the name of the Lord God that you will not touch it until both your mother and I are dead. Promise me, or I will move it to someplace where you will not be able to find it."

"I promise, Father."

A few days later, servants load up the pack mules again, and Sett, Kissara, and Micah once again move out of their family palace.

"Father, how are we going to stop Lechy and Yassib?"

"Well, I could always give them a yearly bribe."

"Not with my gold jewelry, you don't."

Sett smiles and winks at Kissara. "I finally showed it to him."

"How did you get it all the way here from Ur?"

"Aboard a camel, my son. Aboard a camel."

They each mount their mules and go out through the gate. Micah heads down the hill that is Gibeon and realizes his parents are not with him.

"Come along, Son. This way."

"No. We would have to cross Yassib's land."

"Exactly."

"Never!"

Sett and Kissara continue on. Micah finally catches up with them.

"Why? What are you up to?"

"You will see."

They arrive at Yassib's house. Sett knocks on the gate from his mule with his crutch. The gate is opened.

Kissara hands something down to the doorman.

"Make sure Yassib gets this," she says with a smile.

"Okay, what was in that basket? Did you return his snake and scorpions to him?" Micah asks as they make their way south toward Jerusalem.

"Actually, no. It was a big batch of baklava."

As they make their way down the hill that is Gibeon, people come out and stand by their gates, glaring. Or they wave fists at them from their flat roofs.

"Sett waves at them and smiles."

"Father, you're just making them madder."

Two hours later, as the gates of Jerusalem come within view, an arrow flies past Sett's head. The guards in the watchtowers see it and call down to the guards on the ground. The gates into the city are slammed shut.

Sett and his family urge their mules into a run and head toward a wagon full of bricks near the gates. They dismount and hide behind the wagon.

Micah takes out his sword and stands.

"Get back down here," Sett shouts.

Arrows fly from the top of the wall onto a gang of thugs. They divide up into three companies and shoot at the guards at the top of the wall, down on the ground, and over at Sett's family.

"Those are Gibeonite arrows," Sett calls out.

Another arrow. One strikes a guard on the wall in his throat. He falls forward.

Micah scrambles to grab the bow of the stricken guard, along with his quiver of arrows.

"Hand me those," Sett instructs his son.

Using the skills he had learned long ago while with the caravan going down to Ur, Sett gets on his knees and sends an arrow back toward the Gibeonites.

He struggles to move away from his family to avoid arrows shot at him, hitting Kissara instead.

He scoots on his knees, scraping them and making them bleed. His paralyzed feet too.

Another guard on the wall falls. Micah grabs a board off the top of the wagon and holds it between him and the Gibeonites as he scoots back out to grab the bow and quiver of arrows from another fallen guard.

The arrows fly down from the wall to the ground. Some fly up from the ground toward the guards and Sett. Others fly from Sett to the Gibeonites. Some hit their marks, others do not. All fight to conquer the enemy.

A ladder is produced and positioned on the wall of Jerusalem. Two Gibeonites start up the ladder. Sett's arrow hits one of them in the leg, and he falls. A guard at the top of the wall pushes the top of the ladder with a long spear, and it falls, temporarily trapping the Gibeonite under it.

Still, the arrows fly. Blood flows. From arms, necks, torsos, legs.

Now spears. Clearly at the advantage, the sky blue-uniformed guards at the top of the wall hurl them down on their Gibeonite attackers.

The battle lasts until there are only four Gibeonites left. They turn their horses around and head north into the hills.

Once Micah sees they are gone, he stands and goes over to his mother to help her up.

"Are you okay, Mother?"

"Yes. But we lost our pack mules and all our belongings. I guess they'll eventually turn up back at the palace in Gibeon."

Micah turns to help his father up. Sett is already situated on his crutches, his knees and feet bleeding.

"What's wrong with those Gibeonites?" Micah asks.

"I intend to find out."

# 23 ~ BROKEN VOW

three-year drought and no hope of coming to an end. The ground parched. Wadis just cracked clay. Vultures flying over, looking for weakened creatures scampering along the floor of formerly food-bearing land looking for water.

The Jordan being bled dry. Irrigation opening its veins to slower moving water. The steep banks of the river now dropping down to parched gullies.

Farmers digging for water that is not. Hoping. Praying for the impossible.

People dying. Being buried in hard ground. Others leaving. Deserting. Going elsewhere. Emptying Israel.

David sends for Sett. He is in his music room with the balcony overlooking dry Brook Kidron and the Mountain of Olive Trees.

"Your Majesty," Sett says, bowing his head to the floor.

"Come in, Jonathan," the aging king says. His hair is now a steel gray. His once firm jaw is now sagging. His fingers arthritic. His strong sword arm not so strong anymore.

"It is always up to the king to solve the problems of his kingdom. That is why they pay him taxes and provide soldiers for his army. But this latest problem is in the realm of God who controls the rain, and I do not know how to solve it."

Set does remains silent.

"Let us sing a while," David continues. "Perhaps as I sing, God will inspire me to understand what I do not understand."

Sett sits on the floor on a purple linen cushion. David sits on a stool a little above him. They look out at the cloudless sky.

Silence at first. Then it comes.

*I sing my song to God.*
*I sing my praises to him.*
*I lift up my voice,*
*and it rides across the arid land.*

David's song is melancholy. His old voice quivers.

*Still, I will exalt him, Lord of lords, King of kings.*
*A father to the fatherless, a protector of widows,*
*He sets the homeless in homes.*

Always hope amid despair. But where is the hope now? He sings on, and Sett sings with him.

*But to those who rebel against God*
*He sends only parched land.*
*Land with no hope.*

Both men are quiet again. David finally speaks. "I have my answer."

"Answer to the drought, Your Majesty?"

"Yes. To the drought. We have rebelled against God. But what is it that we have done? We must find the answer, so God will bless us again."

"How will you do that, sire?" Sett asks.

"I will call for one of my scribes to read to me. My eyes aren't good like they used to be. But my hearing is still good. I will have them read the Law of Moses to me. If the answer is not there, I will have them read of Adam and Abraham,

243

Moses and Joshua, and Samuel."

"You will find the answer, sire. It is in there somewhere. You will find it. God will help you, and I will pray for you."

A week goes by. There is another message delivered to Sett. "Come," the clay tablet says. "I found the answer."

"This is a happy day for our country," Sett tells Kissara. "He has found a way to end the drought. We will have happy prosperity once again. David is a good king."

This time Sett is taken to David's throne room at the end of the corridor leading from the grand stairway. Bathsheba is seated on one side of him as his favorite wife. Sett's Aunt Mecal is on the other side of him as his first wife.

Sett acknowledges his aunt with his eyes, then bows to the floor. He wonders at her presence. Though his first wife, she has never, to his knowledge, sat on the queen's throne.

David tells him to rise. His voice is strained. Sett is confused. David does not smile. No one smiles.

"I believe you know Priest Yassib," David begins.

"Uh, well, yes, I have known him since I was a young man. He is a priest of Dagon."

Yassib walks into the throne room. He wears his usual tunic of blue, white robe trimmed with gold fringe, and cone-shaped turban. He has lost some of his curly hair. He stands with his hands folded by his waist.

"Of course, you knew he is a Gibeonite."

"Yes, I always knew that. A strange man. He always hated my family. I never understood why."

Yassib stands by, not saying anything.

"I know why," David replies. His voice is low. Sett strains to hear him.

"Your grandfather broke the vow."

"He did?"

"It was the vow made before God between our ancestor, Joshua, and the Gibeonites."

Sett does not understand.

"The Gibeonites tricked Joshua into sparing their lives," David recalls with Sett. "Joshua did not consult God first, so he vowed before God, he would always protect the Gibeonites, even though they were not believers in the only true God. God always keeps his promises, no matter who they are to."

David lets Sett think. He motions for a scribe to come forward and read the account from the inspired writings of Joshua. Sett listens to the end of the account, still confused.

Yassib stands where he is, still silent.

"Your grandfather, Saul, broke the vow. He decided to exterminate all Gibeonites. Your grandfather slew Yassib's family. He was the only survivor. Your grandfather, along with his sons, were the only ones involved in the massacre. The blood of the massacred Gibeonites rises up from the ground, demanding vengeance."

An intake of air rushes into Sett's lungs. His eyes widen. He stares at Yassib, David, the scribe, Mecal, and back at David as he begins to understand.

"The Gibeonites have agreed to sacrifice our lives in exchange for theirs," Sett says in a low voice.

"Yes. I have to allow it, so the anger of God for breaking his promise is assuaged, and he will bring us rain again. I have no choice."

Sett looks up at his aunt, Queen Mecal. She has tears in her eyes.

"When?"

"Tomorrow. I have convinced Yassib here, as their spokesman, to spare you because of my vow to your father. The rest of the men in your family will be sacrificed tomorrow."

Silence.

Yassib exhibits a rare smile.

"May I go see them?" Sett asks.

"Yes. I have a guard standing by to take you down there. They have already been told."

Sett swallows hard and grits his teeth. He bows low

and backs out of the throne room.

Soon he is at the door to the waiting room. "They are waiting for you," the guard says.

Pressing his lips together, Sett enters the room. Queen Mecal enters at the same time through a different door.

He sees his aunt Merab and her five sons, Sett's cousins, who he never knew very well. He sees his step-grandmother, Rizpah, and her two sons, Armoni and Mefiboset.

Without words, he kneels at their feet. Mefiboset leans forward, and the two embrace. They move over to a bench.

"You were the father I never had growing up," Sett tells his uncle. "You were always there for me."

"I did not love you as much as your father did. I could not. But I loved you mightily."

"Oh, how I will miss you, Uncle."

"I have lived a long-enough life. Look, even my red hair is gone," he says with a slight smile. "I'm seventy years old now. I am content."

"We were never as close as you are to my brother," Armoni says. "But I always admired you. You were so brave when you were first injured. You are still brave. One of the bravest men I have ever known."

"Thank you, Armoni. I do not feel brave, but thank you for your confidence in me."

"Did you know your father tutored the two of us?" Mefiboset says. "Not being legal heirs, we didn't get the special tutoring. But Jonathan was a good teacher. We also sang together."

"My father was a singer?"

"Oh, yes. He and David used to get together and sing often."

"I am forty-five years old and never knew that," Sett responds.

The men laugh, then grow somber again.

Sett looks at Rizpah sitting between her two sons and holding their hands.

"Did you know I loved your red hair when I was young. I couldn't figure out why I couldn't have red hair too," Sett says with a forced smile. "Thank you for being there for me when my grandmother died."

Rizpah, now nearly ninety years old, tries to smile but does not succeed. Her tears reveal her heart.

Still kneeling, Sett moves over to his Aunt Merab and his five cousins.

"I always admired the way you picked up techniques used with different weapons," he tells his cousins. "Commander Abner was a good teacher. I guess you knew Abner was our grandfather's cousin."

"I think Father was a little afraid of Abner," Merab says with a forced smile.

"I do not remember Abner much, but it seems he did look a lot like Grandfather."

"They were both tall and husky like you."

Sett stands and returns to Mefiboset.

"Oh, my soul. What am I going to do without you to give me advice? I will be lost without you."

A guard opens the door to the waiting room.

"You are not allowed to visit after dark."

"Yes, yes. Of course," Sett says. "May I come back at dawn and ride with them?"

Queen Mecal, who has said little, steps forward. "I will make sure you can," she says.

Sett stands in the middle of the room with his three-footed crutches invented by him and his nurse when he was ten years old, and accepts the embraces of his uncles and cousins, his step-grandmother and aunt, then leaves.

It is now dawn. The procession forms at the gate of David's palace. David stands in a balcony and salutes the sons and grandsons of his predecessor, Saul, King of Israel.

Micah is on a mule next to his father.

The gates are opened, and the funeral procession begins. Gibeonite and Israelite guards are interspersed with each other.

Slowly they make their way north across the hills until they see on a higher hill before them, Gibeon. They go to the large flat rock known by everyone in the city. The sacrifices will be made there.

One by one, the two sons and five grandsons of King Saul, hands tied behind their back, are taken over to seven trees.

Time passes so fast as a shooting star.

They are fitted with nooses.

The moments race by.

The other ends of the nooses are attached to high tree branches.

Time refuses to stand still.

Sett's eyes fill with tears. Micah reaches over and puts an arm on his father's shoulder.

Old Mefiboset looks around for Sett, finds him, and their eyes meet.

Sett tries to smile.

The beloved uncle—his namesake--s smiles one last time at Sett.

And dies.

Sett returns to his apartment

Everyone knows the seven bodies will be left as examples to anyone who passes near them.

Two weeks go by. A knock on his door. A clay tile has one word: **Come**. Pressed into it is King David's seal.

When Sett arrives at the throne room, David invites him to come forward.

"How are your aunt and step-grandmother? They are the only ones left down there now, you know."

"I have not been there since, well, since the sacrifice," Sett replies. "I guess I should go see them."

"You need to be aware of what your step-grandmother is doing."

"Rizpah?"

"Yes. She is still out there on the rock. She has a pallet, and someone sends food to her every day. Every time a vulture or wild animal gets close to her sons' bodies, she scares them away."

Sett stares at the king. "I am nearly speechless. I had no idea a mother's love could reach beyond the grave like that. I must go to her."

"It is time to give your family a state funeral," David says.

"What do you mean?"

"The bones of your grandfather, your father, and two of your uncles who all fell on the same day forty years ago, have never been honored.

"The men of Jabesh Gilead on the other side of the Jordan River stole back their bones from the enemy and buried them outside their city. I have sent for their bones.

"When they arrive, we are going to have a grand funeral at Zela. Kish, Saul's illustrious father, is buried in a large cave there. The bones of Kish's son, grandsons, and great-grandsons will be laid to rest there.

"Sire, may I go with your men to Gibeon to help take down the bodies from the trees and put them in their coffins?"

"If you can be ready within the hour."

"I am ready now. I would like to take a chariot, so I can bring Rizpah back in it."

By mid-afternoon, Sett has arrived at the rock on the hill. The rock he dreads to return to. He looks up at the seven trees. Two of the men are almost recognizable. The robes they wore still nearly the way they were on that day.

He sees his step-grandmother, thin, bent over, waving with crooked, arthritic fingers at the vultures. One of them lands on her head, and she fights it off.

Sett hurries the best he can to her aid. Putting all his weight on one crutch, he waves the other one at the vultures until he can no longer balance himself, and falls at her feet. She crumples to the ground with him, and the two embrace as they never had before.

They weep.

"I loved your sons," Sett whispers.

"I know you did. They loved you too."

Her voice breaks. They embrace again.

Sett pulls away. "You do not need to protect them any longer."

"No, I must. This is the last thing I can do for my sons. I must do this," she says through small weeping eyes.

"Look, Grandmother. Those men are taking their bodies down now. And over there on the wagons are their coffins. You can rest now, Grandmother."

"What did you call me?" Rizpah asks, pulling back, strands of her thin gray hair hanging close to her tears.

"I called you Grandmother. After my other grandmother died, I realized I also love you. My grandfather loved you. I am certain of that. He took care of you and loved you."

"And I loved him. He was so big and tall and handsome. He was always king of my heart. You look so much like Saul."

"Come, let us try to stand," Sett says with a grin. "Perhaps, once we are up, we can support each other and get to that chariot over there. It has a seat in it for you, and the horse is very gentle. We will lead the procession back to the palace."

Slowly, the two make their way over to the chariot. As they do, the caskets are loaded onto wagons. Sett expertly maneuvers the horse around so that he and Rizpah lead the funeral procession back into Jerusalem and to David's palace.

When they arrive, they are taken to a reception room off the great courtyard. In the reception room is Merab, Sett's aunt and Rizpah's step-daughter, and also Queen Mecal.

"You will no longer be in the wing of the palace for political prisoners," Queen Mecal explains to her sister, Merab, and to Rizpah, her mother's former rival. "I have never had much influence with David, though I loved him with all my heart in our youth. But he has agreed for you to have an apartment next to Sett and Kissara."

Merab embraces her sister, the queen. Rizpah embraces her royal step-daughter.

"The funeral procession will begin tomorrow. The bones of my father, Saul, and my brothers, who fell in battle with him, have arrived."

The next morning, Micah knocks on the apartment of Great Aunt Merab and Great-Grandmother Rizpah, relatives he hardly ever knew. They are ready. They join him, Sett and Kissara, all dressed in refinery fit for former royalty provided to them by the king.

When they go down to the courtyard of the palace, King David is there with his first wife, Mecal, and his favorite wife, Bathsheba. He rides on a fine white mule. On either side of him is a litter for each wife. They leave first. Then Rizpah and Merab follow in their own litters. Then the royal wagon carrying the ossuaries of King Saul and his family. Then Sett, Kissara, and Micah. And behind them are bodyguards and a guard of honor.

They make their way slowly to the cemetery. The honor guard places the bones in the cave with the ancient patriarch of the family, the illustrious Kish.

Sett recites one of the blessings of Moses. He, David, and Micah sing the song David had composed for them so many years ago:

*Saul and Jonathan were lovely and pleasant in their lives,*
*and in their death, they were not divided:*
*They were swifter than eagles,*
*They were stronger than lions.*

*How are the mighty fallen in the midst of the battle!*
*O, Jonathan, you have been slain.*

*I am distressed for you, my brother Jonathan:*
*Very pleasant have you been unto me:*
*Your love to me was wonderful,*

*Passing the love of women.*

*How are the mighty fallen.*

It is nearly dark by the time they arrive back at the palace.

The following morning, David sends once again for Sett.

"You need to take your family somewhere for a while. I want to make sure the Gibeonites are satisfied with the sacrifice we gave them. Do you have any idea where you will go?"

Sett stares at the king a moment. "I think I would like to go north and east and see the Forests of Assyria before they are all cut down. Then, over to uh, a place in Ephraim."

"You mean the Ephraim Wood where Absalom was cut down," David says, his voice low. "You were close to him. Thank you for that. I just did not know how to handle the situation. I could handle entire armies, and I could handle an entire nation. But sometimes I was at a loss how to handle my own family."

David's voice becomes almost a whisper. "What happened was unthinkable. I will weep for Amnon and Absalom the rest of my life. And little Tamar."

He realizes he is talking to a cloud out his window. David sighs.

"By the way, how is Kissara?" David asks. "I heard she is sickly sometimes."

"Yes, sometimes. But she has a strong body and a strong will."

"When you get back, if I judge the Gibeonites to be satisfied, I think you should return to your grandfather's palace. After all, your family will start growing again one of these days."

Sett smiles.

"How old is that son of yours anyway? Isn't he getting close to marriage age? Has he fallen in love yet?"

"Micah is twenty-two now, Your Majesty."

King David stands. "I am tired," he says.

Sett bows with his head to the floor.

The king turns to leave, then turns back. "Did you know I am seventy years old now? Of course, you didn't. How could you know that?"

Sett hears a few more words, but they are said too far away to be understood. He hears a door open and close and lifts his head slightly. The room is empty now except for Sett. The King of Israel is gone.

Thunder. He hears thunder. The air smells of rain. Blessed rain. Oh, yes. A drink now for the thirsty kingdom.

Sett imagines people out in the street in celebration, holding their heads high, their hands reaching toward the sky, their mouths open to receive God's returned blessings.

The drought has been broken. One last time, King Saul has served his kingdom.

Sett manipulates his crutches—always never far from him—lifts himself up to his knees, then with his strong arms, raises himself up to nearly full length.

He turns to leave, working his three-footed crutches around expertly to take steps for him, his feet always completely off the ground. The toe end of his feet are held up by a strap from his ankles so they do not drag. He smiles at himself as he passes the guards. *I am still taller than them.*

As he makes his way down the corridor and up the steps leading finally to his apartment, his thoughts return to Kissara. His beautiful Kissara. His peach of Ur.

He remembers the pain in her chest that returns more often now.

*How was I ever lucky enough to have her for my wife? She has been my rock through all these hard years. She is the gold of my sunset, the beating of my heart. How could I ever live without her?*

# 24 ~ OVERCOMERS

"Are you ready to go?" Sett calls out to his family.

"Elza has taken everything down to the pack mules, so I guess we are," Kissara says.

"Assyria, here we come," Micah says with a grin.

"When we get down to the stables, I want him to add one more pouch that I arranged for a couple days ago. It's been stored in the stalls. Then we will be ready."

He stares at his son. "Micah, what's all that stuff?"

"Well, I have my bow and a quiver of arrows. And a sword. And a dagger. A spear. A couple of slings. A club. An ax."

"We're not going to war, Son. Get rid of them."

"But what if we run into robbers or slave traders? You yourself said it's dangerous on the highway, especially if we're not in a caravan. We're going to have to defend ourselves."

"Get rid of half of them then," Sett says. "Now, are we ready?"

Shortly, they are down in the courtyard. Sett goes into one of the stalls and brings out a large leather pouch. It has a strap long enough to put over his head so he can carry it on his back.

"What's that, dear?" Kissara asks.

"Just a little surprise."

The three mount their respective mules. Sett takes the

reigns of one of the pack mules, and Micah takes the reins of the other.

"Let's do it," Sett says.

Just before leaving the courtyard of David's palace, Sett looks up and sees David on a balcony looking down at them. Sett dips his head, and David does the same.

They leave through the palace gate, go past the fortress, work their way down Mount Zion through the city of Jerusalem, and out the city gate. They arrive at Jericho and spend their first night at an inn. The next morning, they cross the Jordan River, then turn north.

"It is going to take us close to two months to get to our final destination—the Forests of Assyria. I have been in part of Assyria, but there is more I want to see. Thank you, family, for going with me. By the time I die, I want to have seen all the forests of the world."

"Well, dear, I don't know if we can go with you to all of them, but we will for the next few months."

Sett smiles and winks at his Kissara. "I love you."

They spend their next night in Succoth on the east side of the river, and the following night at Jabesh Gilead.

"Father, what did you do before we left Succoth, and this morning at Jabesh? I saw you go to the river and do something."

"I planted a tree, Son."

"Are you sure they'll grow?"

"I have the pods with me, so they're pretty fresh. They are from acacia trees that are hearty in both arid and marshy regions."

"We're not going to any marshes, are we?"

"Once we get between the Euphrates and Tigris Rivers, that's about all there is."

Late in the afternoon of the fourth day, they arrive at the crossroads near Lodebar. Sett is pleased the international traders are still set up in booths there.

"My booth was right over here. Or was it over there? Well, it was one of them. This is where I first met the King and Queen of Gesher."

They turn east where the Jordan branches and creates the Yarmuk River.

"There is someone special I want you to meet here. He saved my life thirty years ago. I hope he is still alive."

Sett leads his family up the road, and just before they arrive at the city of Lodebar, he stops and knocks on a gate.

They wait. Sett knocks again. After a while, they hear shuffling feet and a cracked voice.

"Yes? Who is there?"

"I am Sett. Remember me, Aviva? I lived with you for..."

The gate swings wide.

"Of course, I remember you. How could I ever forget? The crippled young man who could do tricks with his crutches."

"You did tricks with your crutches, Father?" Micah mumbles with a wide grin, winking at his mother. *And what else did you do when you were young?*

Kissara and Micah enter the courtyard after Sett, all leading their animals.

"This is my wife, Kissara, who I met in Ur where your husband found me."

The women embrace. Kissara admires the green and white tiles covering the pavement, and the blue columns. "Your décor is beautiful," she tells the older woman.

"The tiles are old and getting chipped, but I still love the home my husband and I have shared so many years."

"And this is my son, Micah." Micah bows at the waist to the elderly lady.

"Uh, about Machir."

"Yes, he is still alive. He is rather weak and sleeps often, but he is alive. He stays in the room down here that you had."

The family spends the evening with Machir and Aviva, remembering days when they were all much younger and full of much more energy.

Early the next morning, Sett's family leaves. They guide their mules through the city of Lodebar and continue northeast, following the watercourse.

Just as they go out of sight of Lodebar, Sett rides a little closer to the river's edge, reaches into the leather pouch on his back, brings out a pod, breaks it open, and drops an acacia tree seed where the water splashes up toward its bank.

"We will not have to do that for a little while now. We are headed into the Forest of Bashan. It is beautiful up there. It's part of the Kingdom of Gesher, which goes west all the way to a huge lake everyone calls the Sea of Galilee."

Although the road is on an incline, their mules are seasoned and strong and have no problem reaching Ashtaroth by the end of the day.

They go through the city gate just before it is closed for the night. Sett looks ahead and sees the palace on a peak in the middle of the city.

"See that round temple over on the other peak? That is a temple to their goddess. They believe Ashtaroth protects them. We will be seeing a lot more such temples as we travel farther away from Israel."

At the palace gates are still the two gigantic empty thrones ready for their goddess, Ashteroth. Sett tells the gatekeeper who he is, and they are welcomed inside.

"Didn't I tell you his palace was unique and magnificent," Sett tells his family as they admire the tiled forest under their feet and the columns of cedar trees along the perimeter. He says nothing about the statue of Ashtcroth in the ccntcr of the reflecting pool.

King Talmai comes out to the courtyard to greet them.

"Welcome, welcome," he says.

At his appearance, Sett drops to the pavement to pay homage. His family follows his example.

"Rise and tell me who this beautiful lady and handsome young man are."

"I am anxious to see both the queen and you," Sett

says.

The king looks down. "I am afraid I lost the only woman I will ever love last year. She would have been so pleased to see you again after all these years. At the time you said you were going to find the love of your own life and marry her. Is this the lucky lady?"

"Indeed, she is. This is my Kissara, and this is our son."

The evening is spent in reminiscing. Once again, early the next morning before the king rises, they leave and head farther north.

It takes the family three days to arrive at Damascus in Syria. After that, it is six more days to Ebla.

They enter through the Dagon Gate.

"I wonder if our neighbor, Yassib, has been here," Sett says.

"Dagon has temples everywhere, I think," Kissara says. "He is sometimes called Enlil, where I grew up."

"I don't like this city," Micah says.

"I don't either," Kissara says. "It has a temple to Ishtar."

"We will leave right now and not purchase food here," Sett says as soon as he sees the old fear in his wife's eyes. "We will get by without Ebla. It may be a great city full of palaces and temples and libraries to some people, but not to our family."

They turn around, go back out the southern Dagon Gate, and go around the city.

As the trees from the mountains thin out and they reach more desert, Sett resumes dropping his acacia tree seeds along either the Orontes Riverbank or an oases.

"We are following the path our ancestor, Abraham, took when he left Ur. He came up and around to here, then down to Israel. In fact, our next stop will be Harran, where he stopped and lived until his father died."

At the end of nearly three weeks, Sett, Kissara, and Micah arrive at Harran in Anatolia.

"I like it here," Sett says. "Let's stay here a few days and rest. There are forests all along the north of the city that provide relief from the heat.

On the third day, they resume their journey toward the Forests of Assyria.

Not far south and east of Harran, they come to a fork in the road.

"If we take the right fork, we will go along the Euphrates River to Babylon. If we take the left fork, we will go along the Tigris River to Nineveh in Assyria, and finally to Ashur. Between the two rivers is marshland. But my acacia tree seeds will take hold there too."

"Someone back in Harran said this is where the Garden of Eden was. What do you think, Father?"

"Well, the two rivers begin near each other here and end near each other south of Ur. It sure looks better here. Perhaps someday I will return and trace the beginnings of the rivers north of here. Who knows? You may be right, Son."

On the third day out of Harran, things change. Assyrian soldiers patrol the highway toward Nineveh and Ashur.

Each man's uniform consists of a short tunic tucked in a short wrap-around fringed kilt with a wide leather belt. His armor is a leather vest and coned helmet. He carries a long spear and curved sword. His round shield hangs from his waist. Some have bows and quivers full of arrows on their back.

"Father, I don't like this."

"Just be on the alert, Son. Are you okay, Kissara?"

"It's a good thing I brought my weapons."

"Do not jump to conclusions, Micah," Sett says in a low tone.

"We have been lucky so far," Micah says. "It looks as though that luck may not last much longer."

"Do not touch those weapons, Son," Sett says while keeping his eyes trained straight ahead. "Keep away from them. Cover them if you can. Then keep your hands where the soldiers can see them."

Micah brings his mule next to his father.

"Who do you think they're after?" he asks.

"They're usually at war with the Babylonians," Sett replies, his eyes darting to the left and right as well as ahead of them.

"Who is their king?"

"The last I heard, it was Ashur Resh Ishi. Are you okay back there, Kissara? Come up here and ride between Micah and me."

As they approach Assyrian soldiers, they move to the side of the road out of their way.

"This is a trade route to India," Sett says. "Maybe the soldiers are after someone from India. There are many villages between here and Nineveh. We shall stop at each one and pay for a night in one of their homes if they do not have an inn."

"How brilliant, Setty," Kissara says, trying to put her two men at ease. "We will develop friendships along the way. They will help look out for us."

It takes over two weeks to arrive at Nineveh. They break away from the Tigris and progress east on its branch, the Khosr River. They go over a bridge across the moat and enter through the Quay Gate. It is south of the Khosr, which winds eastward through the city.

On their left on the other side of the Khosr are temples to Nabu, prophet son of Marduk, sun god of Babylon. Another temple is to Ishtar, goddess of love.

"Don't look at it, Kissara," Sett says. "We will stay away from it. Don't be frightened. I will protect you."

Sett looks at his wife and reaches his hand over to her. "Just as I did before."

Micah looks over at his mother and notices her tears. Sett stares at his son, Micah recognizes the look and remains silent.

On their right is a temple to the Sibitti. "That's the one I am worried about," Sett says.

"Do you know about the god Sibitti, Father?"

"Not the god. The Sibitti are supposedly seven gods that carry weapons of war, the deadly bow and arrow. The people here claim the gods fight against evil demons, but whoever the king does not like is considered an evil demon."

The soldiers are everywhere in the city. Some stand guard at the intersection of each street. Some stand guard at what appears to be local government buildings.

Some patrol along the narrow streets of the bazaar. Some patrol between each of the eighteen city gates and alternate with the sentries who guard the city gates.

"What is going on, Father?"

"Not now, Micah."

Sett puts the reins of one of the pack mules in his teeth, then reaches over once again and takes Kissara's hand briefly.

"Should we try to stop, or keep going?" she asks.

"Uh, Father."

Sett looks over at his son, then at the soldiers who have lined up across the street in front of them. They are holding round shields in front of them, and their spears are pointed toward the strangers in their city.

Sett hands the reins to his pack mule to Kissara, put the reins of his own mule back in his teeth, and holds up his hands.

Not sure what to do since he has no one to hand one set of reins to, Micah quickly winds a set around each wrist and holds up his hands.

One of the soldiers steps forward.

"Get down," he orders. "Her too. She is needed in the temple."

They dismount. Sett grabs his crutches and supports himself with them.

The soldier stares at Sett, glaring, his eyes squinting.

"Arrest them. Arrest them all. They are spies."

Micah, now hanging on to the reins of his mules again, holds up one hand above his head to get the soldier's attention and permission to speak.

"Micah, what are you doing?" Sett mutters.

"Uh, sirs, may I say something?"

"Not now, Micah," Sett warns under his breath.

The soldier standing in front walks up to Micah, smiles, and pushes the wooden end of his spear into Micah's middle.

The young man doubles over. "Ughhh."

"Stop!" Sett says. "We will go quietly with you. The old woman too."

He glances over at Kissara. "Act old," he mutters between his teeth.

Immediately Kissara bends over and reaches around to her lower back. "Ohhh," she groans. As she shuffles forward, she limps. With her other hand, she pulls back the hood of her cloak far enough they can see the roots of her newly graying hair.

"Turn around!" the leader of the unit orders.

Micah turns the five mules around, then returns next to his father.

Half the soldiers who had blocked their way in the street march forward and lead the procession. The other half stays where they are to bring up the rear.

The three are marched across a bridge over the river that travels down the middle of the city and proceed to the temple to Ishtar.

"No!" Sett shouts.

"Shut up!" a soldier behind him orders, pushing him with his shield.

Sett steals a look at Kissara.

Kissara is crying.

*I've got to protect her. How am I going to do it? Not the temple to the love goddess. Jehovah, help her!*

They pass the temple and go to a building with no windows. The leader pounds on the gate with the blunt end of his sword. A man opens it. They stand out in the street, arguing and pointing at Sett and his family.

"Forgive me for bringing you out here," Sett whispers to Kissara.

Eventually, the soldiers lead Sett and his family into the courtyard and through to another door in the back of it.

The accused prisoners enter a dark room, the guardhouse. They turn around in time to see iron bars swing in front of them.

Sett immediately calls out to the guards. "We are personal friends of Talmai, King of Gesher in Bashan."

The guards do not respond.

"Probably our friend, the king, is already sending out..."

"Shut up!"

Sett looks at his wife and son, each sitting in a corner with its own filth.

"Father, I just want you to know," Micah says, "I do not hold you responsible for any of this."

The eyes of the older man and younger man meet. Sett silently tips his head in response.

The stench assaults the nostrils and stifles the breath.

Kissara clutches her heart and screams.

"Please!" Sett cries out. "My wife is dying! Do you have a healer here? Hurry!"

A guard comes back and looks at Kissara, then returns to his corner at the other end of the guardhouse where he resumes talking with the other guards.

"Take her to a healer," Sett shouts again.

Kissara lets out another scream.

"What for?" A guard calls out. "She's going to die anyway." He laughs.

"Take us to Ashur-Resh-Ishi. If he is a god, he will be able to heal her, and I will pay him."

"Save her so he can heal her? Shut up." Other guards nearby laugh.

"I can pay you."

"No, you can't," the guard calls back. "We took all your money."

"We had some hid."

Sett hears the wooden legs of a bench scrape along the pavement. The guard walks up to the jail gate. "Oh, you did, did you?"

"Two silver coins. You can have them if you take us to King Resh-Ishi."

The guard grabs the coins out of Sett's hands and walks away, laughing.

"So, when are we going on down to Ashur where the king is?"

"Tomorrow, the guard says. "We were taking you there anyway. Ha, ha."

"Anyway? But why? What did we do? We were newly arrived in the city."

# 25 ~ IMPOSSIBLE

*T*he guard looks back at Sett behind the bars. "It was you. You are the reason why. You have no feet."

"Yes, I do."

"Well, they don't look like feet. Cutting off people's feet is what we do to spies running around in our kingdom. Maybe they stopped your feet from working. Either way, you were punished as a spy. Next, you will be executed as a spy."

"But I'm not a spy."

"You're lucky. The leaders of enemy armies we capture are skinned alive. Be glad it's only your feet. After that, your death is quick. Or fairly quick.

"But I just arrived."

"They all tell me the same lie. Doesn't work.

"By the way, I don't know how your wife and that boy over there missed out on their punishment. When we get to Ashur, we'll cut their feet off too. Then you will all be executed along with the other spies we have caught."

Sett stares at the guard. His brows are heavy over his eyes.

"Ha, ha," the guard says from the other end of the guardhouse. "I just got paid extra to do what I was already paid to do. Ha, ha."

Sett sits in the middle of the cell, legs crossed, and his head almost touching his knees. Kissara crawls over to him. She says nothing. She lays her head on his shoulder.

Micah crawls over and sits behind his parents.

Sprawled-legged, he puts his arms around them both, and they lean their heads on his big chest.

Sett quietly sings.

*The Lord is my Shepherd*
*Never shall he deprive me*
*Of what I need.*

Somehow, they sleep. Somehow, they survive the night. Somehow, it is morning.

"Okay," the guard says as the keys rattle the jail door open. "Get out here."

The three make their way out of their cell and wait, but do not know for what.

A rope is thrown over each one's head.

"We're going for a little ride. Well, I am. You will be walking."

Out in the street are ten soldiers waiting. Their guard takes the lead. He hands the leashes of the three prisoners to three soldiers immediately behind him. Three other soldiers are posted behind Sett's family, and two on each side of them. There is no sign of their mules or supplies.

They head south out of Nineveh. The sun beats hard on them. They are surprised Sett can go as far as he can in a day.

Gradually Sett realizes there are more and more trees. By the end of the second day, they are in a forest.

"It is wonderful in here," Sett says.

"Shut up," one of the guards says."

"Assyria is indeed blessed. Protect your blessings."

"I said, shut up."

On the evening of the sixth day, the trees begin to thin out again. By the seventh day, there are only a few scattered ones.

The procession of foreign spies arrives at Ashur, capital city of Assyria, on the eighth day.

Built on the Tigris River, its waters surround the city

to create for it a moat. They cross the bridge and enter at the Tebira gate.

The city is not as large as Nineveh but supersedes it in opulence. They pass the guard tower on the left. On their right are three temples. One for Nabu Marduk, god of writing and wisdom. One for Ishtar, goddess of love. A dual one for Siun and Shamash, gods of wisdom and justice.

On their left is the palace, and beyond it is a high earth-filled ziggurat, whose presence dominates the city even from a distance.

Sett realizes time is fast running out. He stares at the heavy door with bars across it, which he knows will lead to the cells and death within days, if not hours.

"King Ashur-Resh-Ishi!" Sett calls out. "Would you like to see a footless man walk? Hey, King Resh-Ishi!"

Sett's booming voice echoes off the walls of the great gods that do not exist and which are worshipped. He breaks out in song.

*Resh-Ishi, oh mighty king*

Sett bellows. Micah joins him with his tenor voice. Kissara joins the others with her beautiful clear soprano.

*Resh-Ishi, oh mighty king*
*Wonder of wonders come.*
*Let praises for you ever ring.*
*From morn to setting sun.*

"Father, look!" It is a voice from a balcony of the palace. It is a child's voice.

A nurse runs out to the balcony and grabs up the boy. The child's screaming can be heard from the street below.

"Again," Sett says. "Again."

*Ashur-Resh-Ishi, might king*
*Wonder of wonders come.*

*Let praises for you ever ring.*
*From morn to setting sun.*

The child rushes back to the balcony, a tall man following close, grabbing at the boy's hand.

When the tall man stands straight, Sett can see he is wearing a cone turban on his head, a long purple shawl trimmed with gold fringe draped across his shoulder, and a long square beard that has been tightly curled.

Still holding the child's hand, he looks out over the rail of the balcony.

"Ha, ha. Who has come to entertain my little Tiglath Pilesar?"

He looks down and sees the three strangers surrounded by guards.

"Bring them up!" he commands. "I have a birthday soon. I just might invite them to sing for my birthday guests."

"Your Majesty, these people are set for execution."

"Then, execute them after my birthday."

The front gate is opened, and Sett's family, along with the original arresting guard, enter. The others march in the opposite direction.

The gatekeeper lets them in and looks at the three foreigners.

"You cannot be allowed to see the king like that."

"But," Sett begins, "he ordered us to see him. We must."

"Go into that room over there."

"But..."

"You cannot appear before the king smelling and looking like that. You will be bathed in there and given decent clothes."

"Oh."

"The woman will go through that other door."

"Oh, no, you don't," Sett objects.

"Don't worry. You can have her back when we're done

with her."

With that, the guard pushes Sett in the direction of the first door, almost knocking him over. By the time he has restabilized himself, Kissara is gone.

An hour later, Sett and Micah emerge from the room wearing short tunics made of white linen.

"Kissara. What about the woman?"

Just as Sett asks about her, she comes out wearing a long white tunic and a shawl over her head. "I talked them into letting me have the shawl," she whispers to her husband.

The three follow another servant across the courtyard and up a long flight of stairs. They go down a long, wide corridor with floor and walls of marble tiles in all bright colors arranged in geometric patterns. The ceiling, Sett judges, is five man-lengths high.

"When the door is opened, you bow your head to the floor and wait for him to acknowledge you," the servant instructs.

The door is opened, and all three take one step inside, then bow to the floor. They wait. They hear giggling and little bare feet running in their direction. Sett hears a scraping noise.

*Oh, no.*

"Look, Father," the boy says. "A play stick."

They hear a man's footsteps approach the boy. "Where did you get this stick?" he rumbles.

"From that funny-looking man over there with no feet."

"What? Stand up. All of you," the rumbling voice commands.

With Sett's strong right arm, he pulls himself up to his knees, then full length, that same right arm holding all his weight on his one crutch. He shows a strained smile.

The king stares. "Are you the singers?"

"Yes, Your Majesty," Micah says, holding on to his father's elbow.

"What's this?" he bellows, holding Sett's crutch in the air. "I repeat. What is this?"

"Sire, it is my trick crutch," Sett replies.

"Your what? You two, back away from him."

Once again, Sett shifts his weight, so his one strong arm is supporting his entire bulk.

"You're not touching the floor," the king says.

"Yes," Sett grunts. "This is one of my tricks." *Lord God, sustain me and give me your strength.*

"Can you switch arms and do that?" the king inquires.

Sett, holding the lives of his family in his hands as well as his entire weight, strains and gradually switches to his left arm on the only remaining crutch.

"It has three feet on the bottom. Can you do it with just one?"

"I am sorry, Your Majesty. I cannot."

The king stares at Sett longer. He bends over to his young son. "Do you see what that big man is doing? Do you like it?"

"He's funny, Father."

The king stands. "Take this other crutch over to the man before he busts his insides out."

Little Tiglath-Pilesar pads over to Sett, dragging his other crutch behind him.

Sett reaches out for it, but the boy suddenly turns away from him and giggles.

"Tiglath, don't tease the man. Give him his crutch."

Now settled on both crutches, Sett watches the king. The king walks to the other end of the room and sits on his throne.

Sett and his family wait.

"I do not know what to do with you. You have no feet. That means someone has cut them off because they proved you are a spy. Was it someone up in Nineveh? I am going to have to warn them again not to do such things without my written consent."

He leans his elbow on the throne arm and puts his

chin in his hand, careful not to disturb his long, square, curly beard, which Sett has by now decided is artificial, perhaps made of horse-tail hair.

"I am going to have to execute you, you know."

"Yes, I know," Sett replies.

Micah jabs his father in the rib. His eyes glare at his father. Sett knows what he is thinking—*What did you go and say that for?*

Kissara, standing on the other side of Sett, tugs on the back of his tunic, winks, and mouths the words, "I love you."

"Your Majesty, your son has enjoyed us so much, perhaps we can perform for you tonight. Then tomorrow, you can execute us."

King Resh-Ishi smiles. "You are being a good sport about this, I have to admit," he says. "Okay. Why not? Tonight you shall entertain us during our dinner, and tomorrow I shall execute you. Do you prefer before or after dinner?"

"Whatever is your pleasure, Your Majesty."

"Well, we do not have to decide now." The king rises, and Sett's family drops to the floor in obeisance.

Sett hears the king walk away from him, a door opens and closes again. They wait still.

"You may rise." It is the servant who had delivered them to the throne room.

Night comes. Sett has requested costumes of various colors for his family to periodically change into in order to give the king the illusion of doing many new tricks and singing many new songs.

"We will sing my song about my father, which I made up at age six," Sett instructs his family. "We will sing it in Hebrew, so the king will not understand it is a child's song. We will also sing David's *How the Mighty Have Fallen*, but instead of Saul and Jonathan, will substitute the names Micah and Mefiboset.

"Kissara will sing David's *The Lord Is My Shepherd* as a solo, and also join us men in singing my childhood song."

Sett shows Micah how to walk on the crutches with his feet up in the air, just as Sett had done as a boy to save his life.

The evening goes well. The king and his family have a grand time. He drinks his wine, joins in the songs on occasion, and stands on the table one time to toast the guests.

Now the performances are over. It is time to go. Two guards march forward to escort Sett and his family to the dungeon.

"Uh, Your Majesty. I know I am a cowardly foreign spy who does not deserve to even be in the same room with you."

The king nods his head in agreement.

"May I have just one request?"

"Certainly. I am in a good mood. You may have anything you wish as long as you are dead by dinner time tomorrow."

"Your Majesty, I would like to bequeath to you one dozen healthy slaves."

"You are richer than I thought, spy," the king replies. "Where do you have them?

"Sir, give me one month—not eternity, just one month—to turn your devious spies into such slaves, you will wish all your other slaves were as good."

"That is not possible. But I always enjoy talking to you. So, let me get this straight. You want to turn my twelve worthless, no-good spying prisoners with no feet into valuable slaves for me. Is that it?"

"Yes, Your Majesty."

"And you want a month."

"Yes, Your Majesty."

"Accomplish it in a week. Then I will decide how valuable they are. If they fail—which they will—they die. You too."

"Yes, Your Majesty. May I present them to you on the same street that your balcony overlooks?"

"That's a good idea. After your failure, we will have a

public hanging right then and there."

Sett and his family are in the dungeon. It is morning. Sett rattles his chain on the bars of their cell door.

"Shut up," a guard bellows from a nearby room.

"I believe the king has ordered the other prisoners be allowed to go into the torture chamber," Sett calls out.

"Yes, but I cannot imagine why you would want to be in there."

"Also, he has ordered that I be given whatever supplies I need within reason," Sett continues.

"How did you know that?"

"I need twenty-four firm tree branches from the forest we passed through between Nineveh and here. They should be the width of a man's leg and waist-high.

"Also, I need twenty-four large copper bowls."

"No! You are out of your mind."

"You do not need the king's wrath on you, sir," Sett says. "Send word to him. Ask him if I will be allowed to have these things."

Sett sits in the filth that is the floor of the dungeon and leans his head against the mold-infested damp wall.

Later in the day, the guard walks back to Sett's cell. "The king laughed and told me you get whatever you want. Well, none of my men are going to cut your branches for you. That young man of yours will go out to do it, and I will hold you two as hostages.

"What about the copper bowls?"

"The king said to sell your costumes and pay for the bowls with that. Young man," he says, turning to Micah, "come with me."

Days pass. Sett goes into the torture chamber every day with the dozen condemned men with no feet. At the end of each day, he comes out with them. Then the week is over.

"Well," the guard says to Sett the morning following the deadline. "You will be dead by noon."

"Sir, I am ready to deliver the king's new and most valuable slaves to him. I believe we are to go out to the street in front of the palace."

"Yes, that is the agreed-on place. We already have the gallows in place there."

# 26 ~ ESCAPE

The guard leaves. Kissara and Micah follow them out. Then Sett.

Behind Sett are one dozen footless prisoners manipulating tree branches that have been pushed through upside-down copper bowls. Sett puts forward one of his crutches with three short legs, then the other, swinging his feet between them. The prisoners put one of their branches forward, then the other, swinging their footless legs between them.

Clang. Clang. Pause. Clang. Clang. Pause. Clang. Clang. Pause.

Sett looks up toward the balcony. There is the king as he had promised.

"Your Majesty, may I present to you twelve of the finest slaves in your kingdom, all of which can personally serve you in a unique way. As I give the name of their service, they will step forward.

"Scribe." The scribe steps forward. "Basket maker." The basket maker steps forward. "Potter." The potter steps forward.

Sett continues to give their occupations, and the men step forward: "Weaver, musician, grinder, tailor, incense maker, dyer, fisherman, perfumer, tanner."

The king laughs. "Yes. Yes. I can use most of their skills. Why not?" He looks down at the men whose arms are beginning to tremble, holding up their entire weight with the branches.

"You may sit," he says. "I get tired standing a long time myself. Now, Sett, what am I going to do with you?"

"Your Majesty, I am the oldest grandson of Saul, King of all Israel, and son of Jonathan, oldest son of the king. Though the kingship has gone to another, I am close personal friends with the new King of Israel, David. Is there anything I can do for you?"

"Never heard of King David. I guess you and your family are going to have to stay here and be executed for spying for King David."

"Your Majesty!"

Sett turns in the direction of the voice. He wrinkles his brow. "Not now, Micah," he hisses at his son.

"Your Majesty!" Micah calls up again.

"Please pardon my impetuous son, Your Majesty," Sett says with a forced smile.

"No, let him speak," the king says. "I'd like to know what this young man—who is about to die because of his father's spying—has to say."

"Your Majesty, I have something I believe you will find of value. I would like to give it to you in exchange for my father's life?"

Sett stares at Micah. "What are you talking about?" he mutters.

"Your Majesty, may I have permission to bring my gift to you?" Micah calls up.

Sett glares at his son, but Kissara touches his elbow. "Setty, he is no longer a boy," she whispers.

The king motions to the guard who had led the procession out of the dungeon. The guard approaches Micah and escorts him inside the palace. Soon, Micah and the guard are seen on the balcony with the king. Sett and Kissara watch as Micah puts something small in the king's hand. The king smiles.

"Okay," the king calls down. "Sett, your freedom has been bought. But your wife and son will still have to be executed."

"No! Kill me," Sett calls up. "Keep them alive. They did nothing against you. Kill me."

The king looks down on the street a moment, then turns back to Micah. "What? What do you want? You have bought your freedom, haven't you?"

Micah holds up two more very small things, and the king looks closer to see them better. They say a few words Sett and Kissara cannot understand.

"Really?" the king finally says. He turns and looks down at Micah's parents.

"Well, it looks like your son has bought your freedom too. You may go. But I want you out of my city within the hour. My son will miss you, but you complicate my life too much. Oh, and if you ever come back, you will be executed."

Micah disappears from the balcony and reappears on the street without the guard. He rushes up to his parents and the three embrace.

Some of the bystanders smile. Others look confused. Still others scowl, stick out their lips in disgust, and grumble, "Ruined a perfectly good execution."

They turn to leave, but Micah directs them over to the palace stables.

"The king told me he wanted to get rid of some kind of strange animal he wants nothing to do with. He thought his people would enjoy the joke of seeing us out on the road riding it. One last laugh, he called it. I cannot imagine what kind of animal it could be."

Shortly the gate is opened, and an animal is led out to the street. They strain their necks to see the top of it.

"Ha, ha, ha, ha!"

"What in the world is it, Father?" Micah asks in confusion.

"Ha, ha, ha, ha!"

"Well?" Micah looks back and forth between his parents. "Well?"

Kissara stops laughing and wipes her eyes. "It's a

camel, Micah. It's a camel."

"Huh? Where did it come from?"

"The Arabian nomads have been using them for years," Sett says. "Ha, ha, ha, ha. They're good for long-distance travel in the desert."

"But, how do you get on this, this monster?"

"Ha, ha, ha, ha. Let's get this thing out of the city, Son. Then we will show you. Take the reins and let us be going while we can."

As they make their way up the main street toward the northern Nineveh gate, people they pass stop and point. Most guffaw.

"This is embarrassing, Father," Micah says.

"Let them laugh. Some day they will be riding camels too. You will be seeing more and more of them here in the north."

"Get going there." Micah looks behind them and sees two soldiers following them.

Now they are outside the gate on the other side of the moat and free of the soldiers. "Is it safe to stop yet?" Micah asks. They stop beside the road.

"We've got to figure out in what language our transportation was trained," his father says. "He will probably know the word down, up, forward, backward, and stop. He might even know run. He might know go instead of forward. Do you have any idea where this camel came from?"

"Someplace south of here is all I heard."

They are interrupted with a combination of honking, sputtering, and gurgling.

"What's he doing?"

"Ha, ha. He is arguing with us," Sett says.

"Camels love to express themselves," Kissara says.

"He sounds like a cross between a mule, a donkey, and a goat," Micah says.

"Ha, ha. That's about it. Let him talk. But don't walk in front of him when he's mad. He could spit at you. Or even reach over and take a bite out of you."

"We've got to figure this out quickly before the guards get suspicious and force us back into the city," Micah says.

"I wonder if he knows my native language," Kissara says. She steps closer to the camel and looks him in the eye. "*Jals,*" she says.

"Look out, Mother. He's moving."

Kissara steps back and watches as the camel lowers itself to its front knees and sits.

"Yes. He knows my language. So, from now on, when we want him to sit, we will say *jals.* Let me test him on another word," she says.

"*Mawqaf.*"

The camel stands.

"I don't dare test him for go or run yet. And telling him to stop when he has already stopped would only confuse him."

"Okay, Son," Sett says. "You did well. Your mother and I will ride on the camel. You may continue to lead it. You are a good leader, after all."

"Which way, Father?"

"We need to stay away from Nineveh. I asked some of the spies I trained where cities were between here and Anatolia. It seems the next nearest city, if we go around Nineveh, is Razama. They said it is on a trade route that goes north past Harran."

"We will be fine in Harran," Kissara says.

"Well, let's walk until we come to a fork in the road, and let's hope it is soon. Let's get out of here."

"If I'm going to lead, I need to at least know what to call this, this animal," Micah says. He pauses. "What about Dipti?"

"That sounds good to us," Sett says. "Now, let's get out of here, Dipti."

Micah moves over to the front of Dipti, staring up at the animal's eyes, and Sett and Kissara mount it.

"*Mawqaf,*" Kissara calls out. "*Mawqaf.*"

Dipti raises his hind legs. Sett and Kissara hang on.

Then he raises his front legs.

"Ready?" Micah calls back to his parents.

The camel ambles along heading north while the parents get settled on Dipti.

Sometimes Micah looks behind them. "We're not being followed yet. But maybe we should put Dipti into a run."

"Camels are fast, Son. You wouldn't be able to keep up with him. Let's just keep praying to the Lord God. He did an amazing thing for us in Ashur. Only the Lord God of heaven, the only real God, could have arranged for our escape like that."

"Oh, there is the fork in the road," Kissara announces. "I wonder if Dipti knows the word for left. "*Alyasar*, Dipti. *Alyasar.*"

Dipti veers to the left.

"Hey, we have one smart but strange-looking animal here," Micah says.

"He will look even stranger to people as we work our way farther north. Too bad, we're not going to be able to go back to the forest we went through outside of Nineveh. But, the forests were beautiful around Harran too, weren't they?"

Silence now.

The camel sways sideways, and Kissara falls asleep, leaning her head on her Setty's broad shoulder behind her. After a while, she brings up both knees and snuggles her head and shoulders in her husband's chest. Sett holds her and thanks God for her.

"Uhhh," he hears. Sett looks down at her and knows she is asleep. "Uhhh," he hears again. This time, it is a little higher pitched.

"Are you okay, my little peach?" he whispers. She does not answer.

"Son, I'm getting worried about your mother. Some of those screams in the dungeon may have been real. Can you run?"

Micah stops. Having gotten used to following him, the camel stops also.

"He looks up at his parents. "Yes, I can run."

"*Yajri*," Kissara whispers.

"*Yajri*, Dipti. *Yajri*," Sett calls out.

Micah rushes forward, the camel right behind him in a trot.

After two hours, they stop.

"*Tawaquf*," Sett calls out. "*Tawaquf.*"

"*Jals* now, Dipti. *Jals.*"

The camel bends his front knees, then his back knees.

Micah walks around to help his parents off the camel. By now, Kissara has awakened and is smiling.

"Where are we, dear?" she says in a still-groggy voice.

"We're almost there. We just need to let our son rest. Dipti, of course, could trot half the day and not get tired, but our son is not a camel."

Micah sits on the ground and leans against Dipti. His parents go a short distance away.

"It should not be much farther," Sett says. "They told me the cities were closer together over here on this trade route."

"Okay, I'm ready to go again," Micah says.

"But first, your mother and I would like to know what you gave King Ashur Resh Ishi that was worth the lives of three people."

"Are you sure you want to know, Father?" Micah replies.

"Of course, we want to know."

"Do you promise to not get angry at me?"

"Son, just tell us."

"Okay. I gave him three gold earrings."

"Where did you... Your inheritance, wasn't it?"

"Father, we were going on a trip that would take months, and you didn't know if we would be in a caravan any of the time. We needed protection."

His parents look at him and smile.

"You are so much like your father," Kissara says.

"Mother, why was there an earring without a match? I

picked out two gold earrings and saw the one without a match, so—luckily—brought it too.

"That other earring, Micah dear, saved the life of your father and I when your father was your age. He escaped Ur with me, but we ended up on the edge of the Arabian Desert and had nowhere to run but right into it.

"We didn't know what we were doing, but spotted a caravan. The caravan leader refused us until I noticed my mother had sewn gold jewelry into a robe we had with us. I offered a gold earring for him to guide us across the desert. Little did I know the match to it would someday save our lives again."

"Guess what we were riding on out in that desert?" Sett asks with a gleam in his eye.

Micah grins. "Really? You escaped on a camel?"

"That's when we learned the hard way how to control those things. Her name was Jamil. She could sputter and spout and argue and laugh and growl with the best of them," Kissara says.

Despite being her old self again, Sett notices how tired Kissara's eyes look. "Let's go on, my peach. We should be almost there."

The parents climb back onto Dipti, Micah returns to the lead, Kissara whispers *"Adhhab"* and Sett calls out, "Adhhab, Dipti. *Adhhab."*

Micah runs, and Dipti trots.

By the time the sun is nearly down, they see city gates ahead of them.

"We're here, little one," Sett tells his wife. "Wake up now. We're here."

Kissara opens her eyes and whispers, *"Abti."* Sett calls out, *"Abti,* Dipti. *Abti,"* and the camel slows to an ambling walk.

Micah turns and walks backward in front of the camel.

"Father, what do we do now? We do not have any money to buy a tent or rent a room. We do not even have a blanket."

"You are going to get a job, Son."

"I thought it was too dangerous to stay here very long."

"It is. We just need enough money for a room at an inn or to buy a tent. When we enter the city, there should be a bazaar near the gate, and a city square near it. Stop there."

As predicted, they go through the city gate of Razama, pass a bazaar, and stop at a city square where other people are lounging. Sett assumes they are either transients like them or local job seekers.

"What kind of job am I looking for, Father? I never had to work before. The money from great grandfather's estate always supported us."

"You will think of something, Micah. You saved the whole family from execution, didn't you? You will think of something."

Micah hands the reins of Dipti up to his father and heads back to the bazaar. Sett guides the camel to one edge of the square, Kissara tells it "*Jals*" and they climb off.

"Little one, I know you are hungry. Micah is too. He will come back with something for us. If not today, then tomorrow. We have been hungry before."

"Yes, in our youth, we were hungry several times. We did it then. We can do it again." She smiles.

They sit on the ground and lean next to Dipti. He grumbles and spits, though Sett wonders if he is flirting with a mule filly also in the square.

Suddenly they become alert. They hear a crowd. *What's going on? Did they catch us?*

"Look!" Kissara says, standing and pointing toward the bazaar. "It's Micah, and he has a crowd of people behind him. They're laughing. We haven't been caught, Setty. They're laughing."

Sett works his way over to his son. "What is going on?" he asks.

"Camel rides. A few people have seen camels, but not all of them. I offered them camel rides. One ride around the city square for a copper coin."

"Ha, ha, ha, ha," Sett says. "Good for you. Your mother and I shall move over to the center of the square out of your way."

When the sun is all the way down, Micah turns the rest of the people away and leads Dipti to his parents. He sits with them and counts his coins.

"So, how much did you make, Son?"

"What will twenty copper coins buy us?"

"There is an inn over there," Sett says, pointing at a building bordering the north end of the city square. Do a little bargaining. Ask for two rooms and three meals a day for three people for a week. When they get you down to one room, two meals for three people, and for one night, take it."

"I've never bargained before."

"Go. And do not let them think you don't know what you are doing."

It is completely dark by the time Micah returns.

"Did we get it?"

"We got one room, two meals for each of us—that would be tonight and in the morning—but also a stable, water and barley for Dipti."

"Good for you, Son," Sett says, slapping the young man on the back. "Now, let's get your mother to bed. She has had a long day."

"And you haven't?" Kissara says with a smile.

The next morning, after eating a hearty meal and putting part of it in a kerchief, Kissara has washed and tied up at the corners, they leave out the gate of Razama. A few merchants at the edge of the bazaar and the guards at the city gate wave a happy goodbye.

"Where to next, Father?" Micah says, walking backward in front of a refreshed Dipti who is squawking, gurgling, and having a generally good time.

"From what the innkeeper said, we can keep going along this highway and should easily be in Qattara by night. Then the next day, we should be able to go to Andarig.

"At Andarig, I will get directions to the cities between

there and Harran," Sett continues. "Once we are in Anatolia, we will be safe. Lord God, Creator of the heavens and the earth, continue to bless us."

"I heard there is quicksand the way we are going."

# 27 ~ SAFETY

*I*t is morning in Andarig. The farther north they go, the stranger their camel looks to the people, and the more money Micah is able to make for their travels.

"Were you able to find a tent? What kind?"

"Yes, Father. It is a black goat-hair tent."

"Good. We can slow down and stop between cities now that we're almost out of Assyria. The next city is Kahat. We will take two days to get there.

"What about food and water for Dipti?"

"I took him to the city well, and he drank thirty jugs of water," Micah says. "I thought he would never stop drinking. He ate enough barley to fill a small cart stacked tight. I suppose he stores all that in his hump and other places."

"Well, he's all set for the next few days. Did you get enough food for us?"

As they progress north, the highway traffic grows.

"It is certainly hard to hide when our transportation is higher than everyone else's," Sett tells his wife as they amble along, heading toward final freedom from re-arrest. "We're sticking up like a tree among bushes. We shall just keep praying for..."

"For no one to notice us?" Kissara says with a grin. "Only God can make us invisible. Perhaps that is what he has done so far."

After two days' travel, Sett and his family arrive in Kahat. They spend the night at an inn where they can get a good meal.

"How far is Kahat from the Assyrian border?" Micah asks just before stuffing a large piece of barley bread soaked in yogurt into his mouth.

It is morning, and the family is being served breakfast along with other guests. The room is dark and crowded with travelers, most of whom are suspicious of one another.

"I think it is a half-day walk, Son. We could reach the safety of the border by noon today."

A strange man appears and leans on their table. His dirty hand almost tips over one of the mugs.

"Are you the ones with the camel?" the stranger asks them.

"Yes," Micah says, looking up and smiling.

The stranger is of average height, wears a brown tunic, and smells like manure.

"Did you want me to take someone on a camel ride before we leave?" Micah asks.

The stranger looks at Micah briefly, then Kissara. Finally, he looks at Sett, frowning. He lowers his voice and leans in.

"I work at the stable where you had your camel last night. Some men came by this morning looking for you."

Sett drops the sop of bread in his plate, presses his lips together, and tries not to reveal any of his anxiety.

"Thank you for informing us," Sett replies.

"They said they were friends of yours," the stable hand continues.

"Oh, uh, maybe they were. How many were there, and what did they look like?"

"There were four of them. They rode magnificent black mules, and well, looked like they were soldiers. They didn't look like anyone's friends to me."

"Oh," Sett replies.

"I didn't trust 'em. Their story didn't make sense. You have a woman here to protect."

"I see what you mean."

Sett hands the stranger a copper coin. "Thank you for letting us know, kind sir."

The stranger turns to leave. Sett watches him disappear out the door of the inn.

"We'd better get out of here, and fast," Micah says. "The king must have changed his mind as we thought he would."

"Wait, Son. We need to wait until he is back at the stable. And... Annnnd that should be just about now."

Sett throws three copper coins on the table and rises.

"I'll bring Dipti up to the door," Micah says, running between the tables and out.

By the time Sett and Kissara are outside, Micah has arrived. Dipti kneels, they climb on, and Micah leads them out through the south gate of the city.

"Good thinking," Sett calls to his son. "They may be waiting for us at the north gate."

"Father, you need to outrun them," Micah says, walking backward so the camel will keep following him. "You need Dipti to go full speed. I would hold you back."

"I know what you are about to say, Micah, and we are not going to do it."

"Father, even though I don't run as fast as camels, I can run almost as fast. I'm healthy. If Dipti ran, you could make it to the Assyrian border in probably an hour. I could be there to join you an hour later. I know I can."

Sett notices Kissara already with heavy eyes and bobbing her head.

Micah walks around and hands the reins up to his father. "For Mother. Do it for Mother."

"Well..."

"I'll be safe. I'll run over beside the road and look back sometimes. If I see them, I'll hide somewhere. Really, Father. I'll be safe. I'll meet you at the border in less than two hours. Go, Father. For Mother, go."

Sett presses his lips together and shakes his head. He hears a noise and jerks.

Micah throws the reins across the camel's neck. "Hurry, Father. Do it now. I will catch up with you!" He steps back from his parents and smiles.

Sett takes one last look at his son, nods his head, and takes up the reins.

"*Yajri*, Dipti, *Yajri*," Sett calls out.

Though Dipti has soft padded hooves, his heaviness pounds the earth. People on the highway jump out of the way or quickly steer their animals to the side of the road.

"Hang on, my peach," Sett says, one arm around his wife's waist, the other extended with the reins.

The wind whips through their hair and presses against their clothes. Sett wishes for the forests that he knows are in the mountains behind Harran. Forests with trees to hide in. But Harran is still far away.

Dipti strains and stretches his long legs forward.

*Just get to the border. Get to the border.*

Dipti huffs and honks, his eyes wide, his muscles straining.

Pounding the earth below, challenging the unknown ahead and behind, beseeching the heavens above.

Sett strains to hear mutual pounding behind. *Are they getting closer? Is that them? Go faster, Dipti. Don't let them catch us.*

"Hurry, Dipti. Hurry!"

Still, the pushing and thrusting and challenging.

Dust flying. Birds scattering. People rushing out of the way.

Up ahead. What is that? Men. Uniformed battle-ready men. Men on fine mules. Across the road. A wall of soldiers stretching away from the road and across the countryside.

"*Yahri*, Dipti. Just a little farther. *Yahri*, Dipti. *Yahri*"

Sett pushes on. He does not veer to the left or the right. He does not slow his animal down. Closer to the wall of guards. Closer. Almost on them.

Hooves pounding.

Closer.

At the last moment, the guards at the border dive out of the way, and Sett pushes on through them. He keeps going until he is out of their sight, then lets go of the reins to give Dipti a chance to slow down at her own pace.

"*Abti*, Dipti. *Abti.* It's all right now. Good Dipti. Good Dipti. It's all right now." Sett reaches over and pats the camel's neck. "It's all right now. Good Dipti."

Once the camel is at a slow pace, Sett tells it to kneel. Sett and Kissara slide off.

"I'm going to have to cook something special for Dipti," Kissara says. She scoots down and leans her head on Dipti. Dipti snortles.

Sett stares behind them. "I'll be back," he tells his wife.

He makes his way back down to the curve in the road from whence they had come and carefully looks to see if he can see the soldiers. He can. He drops to the ground and watches.

*Come on, Son. You can do it.*

He strains to see any sign of the young man. He waits. *He should be almost here.*

The sun reaches the pinnacle of the sky. *He should have been here by now.* Sett scoots a little way, then stands and makes his way back to Kissara.

When he arrives, she is on her side, her head snuggled into the camel. Both have their eyes closed.

Sett reaches for the waterskin, then sits next to his wife. He takes a drink. "Are you thirsty?" he whispers, not willing to wake her out of a deep sleep.

"Oh," she says, lifting her head. "When did Micah catch up with us? Are we ready to go now?"

"He hasn't yet. I'm getting worried."

Now fully awake, Kissara looks in Sett's eyes. "We can't lose him. We cannot lose our son."

"We will just keep praying."

A smile forms on her lips. "You know, he is so much like you. He will think of something. You always did when you were trapped in a situation."

"Yes, he will too. He is a lot like me, isn't he?" Sett says, trying to smile back. "Do you need anything?"

"No, Dipti and I are getting along fine. Except that Dipti snores. And sometimes I think he is dreaming about chasing a mule or something. He dips his head up and down and snortles and chokes and hisses, then settles back down to his dream."

Sett smiles. "Well, when we get him home, we are going to have to give him a pasture all his own and spoil him the rest of his life."

"Unless our grandchildren run him to death," she retorts.

"We don't have grandchildren," Sett objects.

"We will. I've noticed Micah looking at the young ladies. We will."

Silence for a little while.

"Well, I need to get back. I know watching does not really help him. But I need to do it."

"Yes, I understand."

Sett is now back at the curve in the road on his front, watching for his son. *Come on. You can do it. Come on, Micah.*

The day grows hotter. Sett reaches around and takes out the extra waterskin he had brought along. He takes a swig, pushes a wooden plug back into the opening, and wipes his brow.

*Lord God of heaven, be my boy's shepherd. Be his lifeline. Be his watchtower. Give him wings to fly over the heads of the enemy. Make him invisible to his enemies and visible only to you. Lord God of heaven, be with my boy, my Micah.*

A few clouds wander by, pushed around by the hot breeze. He watches the birds, large and small, float on waves of air.

Shadows now form. Shadows off rocks and shrubs and an occasional tree. Shadows cast more heavily by the soldiers patrolling the border of Assyria.

Sett strains to see. Each person who walks through is

searched and questioned. Some are detained. Some return the way they came. Some proceed in Sett's direction.

When someone passes him along the road, Sett puts his head down on his arms and pretends to sleep. They walk on by, most having never even seen him.

Long shadows now. Long and heavy shadows. The sky turning pink, then red. Blood red. *My son, my son. Be courageous. Come home to us. Come home, Micah.*

Still, he watches. Just after the sun dips below the horizon and the last remnants of day disappear, Sett sees a lone man walking with a limp approach the guards. At first, they do not notice him.

The lone man works his way toward the edge of Assyria. One slow step at a time. Step. Shuffle. Step. Shuffle.

Sett raises himself up to his elbows. He hears voices now. He cannot hear what is being said. Then the yelling.

"You cannot take me. I am a personal friend of King David!"

*It's him. It's him. He needs my help!*

Sett hurries back toward his wife and the camel. "*Mawqaf,*" he shouts as he makes his way closer. "*Mawaqf,* Stand up. Come here, Dipti. Hurry. *Yajri!*"

Dipti raises his head. Kissara moves out of the way, and Sett thrusts himself sideways across the camel. "*Yajri. Yajri!* Run!"

As the camel raises its big bulk, Sett twists around so he is straddle of it. He grabs the reins. "*Alyasar,* Dipti. Turn left."

As Sett and the camel rush to the curve in the road, Kissara runs behind them.

Sett heads the camel directly at the border guards as he had done that morning. Dipti huffs and honks and chortles and snorts. "Hurry, Dipti, hurry."

The lame man sees what is happening and, while the guards are watching Sett, he slips past them and toward Kissara.

Sett charges at the guards, gets almost to them, and

swerves. He circles around and charges again. The lame man continues to run toward Kissara and she toward him.

Charge again. Keep charging. Keep the guards distracted enough, they cannot even reach for their bows. Charge, circle, charge, circle.

When Sett can no longer see the lame man and Kissara, he turns Dipti toward the curve in the road and goes around to the other side.

"*Tawaquf*," he shouts. "Stop, Dipti, stop."

The camel slows and stops. He kneels when ordered to, and Sett slides down.

Kissara and Micah rush over to Sett and the three, kneeling under a foreign moon, embrace each other and laugh and weep.

"What happened, Son?" Sett finally asks when they break apart.

"Here, have some water," Kissara says. "You haven't eaten all day either. Wait while I go get some cheese for you."

"Mother, I am okay."

"How did you injure your leg? What happened?" Sett asks.

"Oh, there is nothing wrong with my leg," Micah says.

"Your foot then. You injured your foot. Or your hip."

"I didn't injure anything. I ran for a little while until I realized I was attracting too much attention. Then I heard hooves behind me and knew the soldiers had spotted me. So I pretended I turned my ankle and sat down in the middle of the road, hoping everyone would swerve in time to miss me.

"The soldiers stopped and came back to me. When they spoke, I spoke Hebrew back to them, slobbered a little, and acted like the sun had stopped me from recognizing anything, including myself. They got disgusted with me and rode on.

Sett grins, reaches over, and pats his son on the back. Kissara takes his hand and smiles.

"So, anyway, I decided I had hit on a good disguise. Why would the king of all Assyria want a crippled man who couldn't speak his language?"

"And here you are. Do you know how much you worried your mother?"

Micah looks directly at his father. "I know, Father. I know."

"Well, we've kind of settled in here, so why don't we spend the rest of the night where we are?" Kissara says. "You men put up the tent while Dipti and I see what we have to eat."

Later, before they all fall asleep, Sett says in a low voice, "This is not what you bargained for when you came with me to visit the Forests of Assyria. Thank you. And I'm sorry."

"We wouldn't have missed this for anything," Micah replies.

"Oh, my! Now I've got two of you to keep tamed," Kissara says.

It is morning. They gather up their tent and supplies.

"Someone on the road I limped with a while yesterday said Gozan is the next town," Micah says. "It is on the Habur River."

"Is Gozan in the right direction, Son?"

"Yes, it is on this trade route headed toward the territory of the Hittites and then the Greeks."

Micah stops what he is doing and stares at his father. They grin.

"Oh, no, you don't," Kissara says. "Neither one of you. The Hittites and Greeks can keep their forests for now. Dipti and I are going home. You two can tag along if you want to."

It takes two days to arrive at Gozan, a fairly new city. The local people say it was built for the traders, so they do not have to travel too long between places to spend the night and buy food.

Sett and his family appreciate having a bed to sleep in.

Another day on the road. "We should be back at Harran by noon tomorrow," Sett announces. "Let's stay a few days there as we did before. You know, when we were there before, I heard people say that the Tigris and Euphrates Rivers come back together up there, and this is where the Garden of God was. I guess we will never know. But I would like to look around and imagine maybe it was here instead of down below barren Ur."

When they arrive in Harran, Micah sets up business at the city square.

"Come see the strange creature from the deserts of Arabia. Come ride him if you dare. One copper coin is all it takes for you to get a ride on the monster."

Sometimes when he has the crowd of children following him around in a good mood, he announces, "And if he bites you, I will pay you the copper coin."

The people in the old city of Harran take to Micah. Sett and Kissara sit nearby, watching and proud.

"That's some boy we hatched," Sett says.

"Indeed, he is. We are so lucky."

They watch a while longer.

"Setty."

"Hmmm?"

"Do you think he will ever give us grandchildren?"

"Give him time, my peach. He will someday."

After a while, Micah approaches them.

"I think I need to give poor Dipti a little rest," he tells his parents. "Why don't we go for a walk toward those mountains behind us and see if we can find some trees to wander through?"

"I am a little tired," Kissara says. "I think I will go to the enchanting cone house you rented for us tonight and rest. You two men go on."

After three days, Sett and his family begin their final southward trek toward home. They stop for the night in Irridu, then Carchemish, then Halab, and finally Ebla, all cities in Syria. It has taken them five days.

"I don't like this city, but we are tired."

They enter Ebla though the Sipish Gate. On their right

is a fortress. They walk through the bazaar and into a residential neighborhood. Many houses built a thousand years earlier have caved in. But there is much of the city still alive and well.

It is a city of kings, a city of former glory when Ebla was not just a city, but an entire kingdom stretching all the way to Assyria.

They pass another fortress on their right. Opposite it is a palace complex and a complex for the temple to Ishtar.

"Don't look at it, little one," Sett urges Kissara. "The pain has never left you, has it? Well, you are safe with me. You are always safe with me."

Kissara does not reply. She looks away.

They see yet another palace on their left, and a royal cemetery across from it on their right. They come to a sanctuary of dead kings beyond the second palace and a temple to Dagon.

Finally, they come to another bazaar near the southern Dagon Gate and some inns.

"This is the strangest city I have ever been in," Sett tells the innkeeper.

"This is the city of kings," their host replies. "We have five palaces. But our city has been here for thousands of years and gone through a lot of kings, many of which wanted to outdo the previous king. And each king built a temple to his favorite god or goddess."

"Some of the temples look run down."

"Not the ones to Ishtar, Dagon, and Hadad. They are the popular ones right now."

Sett looks over at Kissara, standing next to him. "I'll be okay," she assures.

"We will just stay in our room."

He turns to the innkeeper. "We want one room to spend the night, a meal right now, and another meal in the morning," Sett replies.

The next morning, Sett continues to lead his family south through Hama, Qatna, Nazala, and Damascus.

Everyone agrees they need to just go on home. But there is one stop they must make.

It is a one-day trip south into Gesher. They climb up through the mountains of Bashan, enjoying the forest once again. Early in the evening, Dipti takes them through the streets of Ashtaroth, and they arrive at the palace with its green-tiled forest underfoot and cedar tree trunks for columns.

King Talmai greets them enthusiastically.

"So good to see you again. Come in. Come in. Did you have a successful journey? Too bad about what happened while you were gone."

"Why? What happened? We haven't heard anything."

"Then you don't know? King David is dead."

# MAP 3:  JERUSALEM 1000 BC

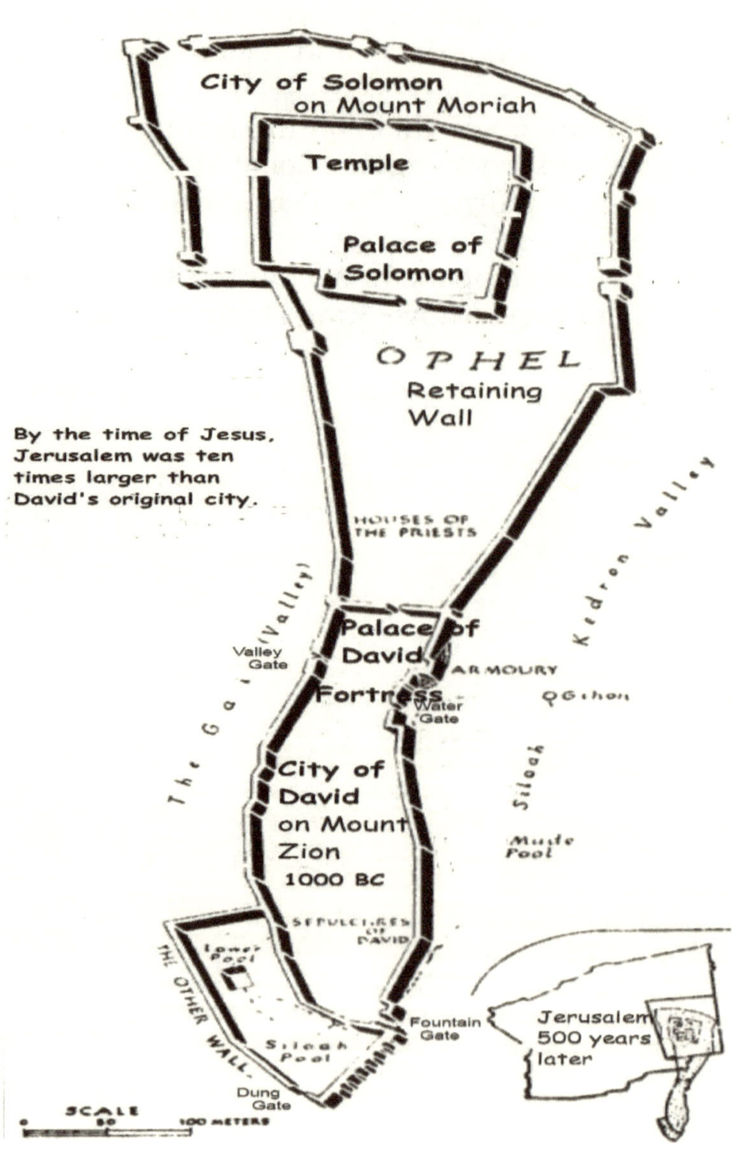

# 28 ~ CONFUSION

"**I** was looking forward to spending a couple days with you, Your Majesty. But I must hurry on home. I have a step-grandmother and aunt still there, the only survivors of King Saul besides me."

"Oh, my," the king responds.

"And I do not know what has happened to my family's estate or whether my family will be allowed to stay in David's palace. I don't even know if we will be allowed to live."

"I understand, Sett. By the way, if you would like a mule for Micah to ride and another for your supplies, I will be most happy to give them to you. My daughter speaks well of you. And you were always good to my grandchildren, Absalom and Tamar."

"Your Majesty," Micah says, "thank you for the offer of a mule for me, but I have grown rather accustomed to walking all day. It has become very invigorating to me."

"Thank you for taking us in," Your Majesty, Kissara says. "I wish we could have stayed longer. We love it up here in the forested mountains. Especially Sett does."

"Perhaps you all can return after you have settled things for yourself in Jerusalem and Gibeon," the king says. "Do at least take the pack mule. I have a sufficient supply of water and food for it to carry that should see you through until you arrive home. May your God keep you protected."

Sett and his family work their way down the other side

of the mountain and arrive at the Yarmuk River. They follow it southwest until they arrive in Lodebar.

"Welcome, friend," Machir says when they arrive at his house with the green-and-white floor tiles and blue columns. "So, how was your adventure?"

"Machir, friend. What are you doing out of bed? I thought you were…"

"You thought I was about to die? Well, I didn't. It must have been some of that new kind of tea Aviva began serving me after you left. I believe she said Kissara told her about it. Thank you, Kissara," he says, turning to Sett's wife.

"And where is Aviva?"

"Here I am," Aviva says, walking into the courtyard, a slight limp in one hip. "Welcome back."

"I always feel as though I am home when I am here," Sett replies. "You two were the father and mother I grew up without."

"You were an amazing young man, and always full of surprises. It was all our pleasure, Sett," Machir says. "Too bad about everything that has happened while you were gone."

"Yes. We knew nothing of it until we saw King Talmai. Do you know any of the details? How did he die? Was he assassinated?"

"No, King David died in his sleep."

"How the mighty have fallen," Sett says.

"Have I heard that before?"

"When my father and grandfather were killed in battle, David composed a song dedicated to them. It began and ended, 'How the mighty have fallen.'"

"Yes, indeed. David was that all right. Sometimes he was a complicated man. But he was a good man."

"Have you, well, have you had a chance to…"

"To go down and check on your family estate? Yes, I did. I was not allowed inside, but on your land, things seemed to be normal. And the palace is still standing. I assume it is being taken care of."

"Thank you, friend," Sett says.

"I see you have picked up a camel along the way."

"You know what a camel is?" Micah asks.

"Of course. I have traveled on one myself going across the desert to Ur. So, how was your trip? I believe you wanted to see the Forests of Assyria. Did you make it to Assyria? How did you like it?"

Sett looks at Kissara. Micah clears his throat and stares at the ceiling.

"I see. And do all your looks mean it was good or bad?"

"A little of both," Kissara says.

"Father was brilliant," Micah says.

"Micah was innovative," Sett says. "Someday, when we have more time, we will come back and tell you all about our adventures and misadventures in Assyria. Or better yet, you will have to come see us at our home."

"If we have a home," Kissara says. "By the way, I would love to see some of your recent stock of gold jewelry. Are you still selling it? Do you get back to Ur very often?"

The next day, Sett, Kissara, and Micah resume their journey, heading south along the long-familiar Jordan River. After three days, they arrive at Jericho.

They take a room at the familiar inn, and are served an evening meal.

"Keep your ears open, everyone. Hopefully, we'll find out whether we should go on to Jerusalem or straight home to Gibeon. Things may begin to get dangerous."

As they eat, they hear the name of Solomon mentioned often.

"Do you think Solomon is the new king?" Micah asks. "He is about two years younger than me. We did things together sometimes."

"If so, Ithream, who was next in line to the throne, was bypassed," Sett says. "Well, I think we should go to Jerusalem first. Perhaps the new king will see us."

"So, this time tomorrow, we could be dead?" Kissara asks.

"If he finds King's Saul's heir to the throne a threat, yes. I will be dead, though he may save you. But I have lived with this possibility since I was five years old."

"Do you ever get used to it?" Micah asks.

"No, but you learn to live with it."

The next morning, Sett and his family go to the market and buy fresh tunics and robes. They bathe at the inn, wash the dust out of their hair, and put scented oil on their chafed, sun-dried skin.

Sett and Kissara climb on to Dipti one last time, and Micah mounts the black mule given to them by the King of Gesher. They ride slowly toward Jerusalem. As they draw closer to the gate and after they enter the city, people run beside them.

"Are you here to claim your throne?" some ask.

"You're going to die this time," some say.

"Solomon may spare your life," some say.

Either way, the word spreads that the oldest son of the oldest son of the dethroned king of Israel has ridden into the capital city of the Kingdom of Israel.

They pass the fortress and arrive at the gate of David's palace at the top of Mount Zion. The guards recognize them.

"We will have to check with King Solomon," a guard says. "Please wait here."

While they wait, Sett, Kissara, and Micah dismount and stand in front of the closed gate into the palace as dignified as they can.

"I see our new king is already making changes. The guards now have uniforms of gold."

A stable hand takes the reins of the animals for them.

Still, they wait, heads high, looking straight ahead. And wonder.

At last, the gate opens. Standing before them is young King Solomon himself. "Well, welcome back," he says, his arms stretched out to them.

Solomon is tall like his father. He has curly black hair and a short, neatly trimmed beard. He has high cheekbones, and his nose is turned down on the very tip. He is wearing a long gold tunic and emerald green robe.

Sett and his family immediately fall to the pavement in obeisance.

"Rise. Rise," he says. "And follow me."

They work their way across the magnificent courtyard, made more magnificent by the new king with statues of different animals between each column. The tall, handsome son of David bounds up the steps three at a time.

Sett and his family follow at Sett's pace. At the top of the steps, a servant meets them and leads them down the corridor to the throne room. The door has been left open for them. Solomon's mother, Bathsheba, as queen mother, is in the lesser throne next to him.

Bathsheba has a long neck and brown curly hair that falls gracefully down her back. Her eyes are large with a delicate lift to them on the outer edges, and her lashes are long. She is wearing a long white tunic and royal blue robe. She has a ring on each finger.

As soon as Sett sees the king and his mother on their thrones, he once again falls prostrate to the floor, his family following his example.

"You know, Mother, I used to play with Micah sometimes," Solomon says to Bathsheba. "He is a little taller than me, so used to beat me at foot races. However, he did sometimes let me win. You may rise," he says. "Come forward. I believe we have some things we need to work out."

Sett leads his family forward a few more steps. He stares straight ahead.

"First, I am sure you are wondering if I am going to let you live," the new king says. "Of course, I am. Your father loved my father in their youth. I want to honor the pact they had with each other."

Sett smiles and nods his head yes, though he is careful not to interrupt the king's speech.

"Yes, I did keep your apartment for you. I believe your step-grandmother and aunt are not much longer for this world, but they are still there. I am sure they will be happy to see you."

Once again, Sett smiles and nods his head in gratitude.

"Finally, I am sure you are wondering what I have decided to do with your grandfather's estate. As you know, your grandfather hated my father and chased after David, trying to kill him. But Jehovah God protected my father.

"You never did show anything but respect for my father. In fact, my father talked often about the two of you getting together sometimes to sing. How he loved to sing."

Solomon looks over at his mother and realizes she is weeping. He moves his hand over to hers.

"This has been very hard on my mother. She and my father loved each other very much. They were almost inseparable."

"I understand," Sett says.

"Well, I am going to let you keep your grandfather's estate and all the proceeds that come from farming your land."

Sett smiles and dips his head in appreciation.

"However, this next part, you may not like. But I could see no other solution. You have been gone several months. I did not want the palace to sit empty without anyone to care for it, or the servants in the field, not knowing what to do.

"Therefore, I appointed Lechy, the son of Ziba, to be steward over the estate."

Sett maintains his composure, though he clenches his teeth. Kissara gulps air, then pretends to cough. Micah squints his eyes, jerks his head around to look at his father, then glares at the king.

"This is not to your liking, Micah? Well, this is the way things are going to be. Lechy is about your father's age and has been working at the palace all his life."

"Forgive my son's youthfulness, Your Majesty. He has become rather, well, uh, protective of me, though I do not normally      need      protecting.      He      is      a      good son and will be cooperative."

"Good. I am new at all this decision making. But I had a good example from my father. Now, is there anything else you would like to know?"

"Uh, Your Majesty, I am concerned about my step-grandmother and aunt. After their sons and my grandmother died, there was no family left for them on the wing where they lived. Your father allowed them to move into an apartment next to mine. Would it be possible for me to take my step-grandmother and aunt back to the palace with me?

"Great idea, Sett. Great idea. Of course. They are getting to be pretty old, I guess."

"Yes, my step-grandmother is over ninety now, and my aunt is around seventy-four."

"Fine. Now, is there anything else?"

"Nothing, Your Majesty. I just want to wish you a long and successful life, and the same for your mother." He looks directly now at the queen. "Queen Bathsheba, I offer you my deepest sympathies over the loss of your husband."

Bathsheba nods but says nothing.

"Do I have any other judgments I need to pass down this afternoon?" Solomon calls out to a servant standing by the door to the throne room.

"None, Your Majesty."

Sett backs toward the outer door and his family follows his example. By the time they arrive at the door, Solomon and Bathsheba have left.

Out in the corridor, Sett, Kissara, and Micah stand in a small circle.

"We are going to be fine," Sett says. "Shall we go up to see Rizpah and Merab and tell them the good news?"

"Then we shall go home," Micah says.

"Let's spend the night here to give your great-grandmother and Merab time to gather up their things," Kissara says. "Then we will leave in the morning."

As the three head for their third-floor apartment,

Micah forms a large grin, bounces, swings his arms, and rocks his head back and forth.

"Stop that swaggering, Micah."

No one sleeps well that night. A new beginning for them all. What will it be like this time?

Sett's thoughts remain on Lechy. Will he be any more cooperative now that his father is dead? Will he become his father? Will he begin acting like a servant as he should? What will life be like back in the same living arrangements with Lechy?

*I was never able to find his missing son. I cannot imagine losing Micah. Let me see. He would be fifteen years old by now. I need to start looking for him again. What was his name? Iptur. I think that was his name. I've got to find out what happened to Lechy's son. Is he dead or alive?*

Morning comes. Sett's old servant, Elza, walks next door and gathers up the older ladies' things. The little bit Sett, Kissara and Micah had left behind during their trip to Assyria is taken down by Micah.

A cart is arranged for Sett to load everything on. The two women are helped into a chariot to be driven by Micah. Sett and Kissara climb on to Dipti. Micah leads the way. He grins and swaggers as he goes.

"What are we going to do with that boy?" Sett says.

Kissara smiles. "We have already done it, and he has turned out just fine."

It is mid-afternoon when they arrive at Gibeon. They make their way up the hill through the main street. Town people rush to see them and wave. The family waves back.

Dipti snortles, gurgles, and wags his tongue back and forth, expressing his own feelings.

One man in the back of the crowd throws rocks at them.

"It seems Priest Yassib, our neighbor, is still mad," Sett whispers to Kissara.

"We will not let him ruin our day. We are having a fine homecoming. Don't you think, Setty?"

"Overall, little one, yes, we are." *And I hope it stays that way when Lechy opens the gate to us.*

Finally, they are at the palace. Saul's old palace. Palace of the former great Warrior King of Israel.

Sett orders the camel down and dismounts. Micah is the first to the gate and knocks on it.

Soon, they hear scraping of the security bar across the gate, and squeaking of hinges. The gate is opened. A stranger stands before them.

"Yes? What do you want?"

"We want in," Micah declares, a large grin on his face and pushing out his chest a little.

"And may I tell the master who you are?"

"You are wrong," Micah says, pushing the gate open himself. "I am the master. And my father is the master. There is no other master."

The gatekeeper steps back and looks around the courtyard as though wondering what to do.

Micah looks up at the two guardtowers in the front corners of the palace and recognizes two of Lechy's brothers.

"Uh, I will tell the uh..."

"You just tell Lechy that he has to the count of one hundred to get his stuff out of my apartment," Sett announces, then wishes he had said it a little kindlier. *He has been through so much.*

Micah goes over and helps Rizpah and Merab out of the chariot. They walk slowly toward the center of the courtyard, each holding one of Micah's strong arms.

The women look around at the old familiar blue and red tiles they had walked over back in the years when they had been royalty. Tears come to their eyes.

"It has been so long."

"Yes, so very long."

"Just how long has it been?" Rizpah asks, brushing back her wispy mixture of red and gray hair.

"I think thirty-five years, Mother," Merab says to her step-mother, mistress of her father.

"Well, we're finally home."

The door to Ziba's office opens. Lechy walks out and stops dead.

Sett makes his way toward him. Lechy does not move.

"Thank you, Lechy, for looking out for our estate while we were gone."

Sett smiles. Lechy does not.

"Father, why do you take it?" Micah whispers.

*It has begun. Again it has begun.*

# 29 ~ CONFRONTATION

"**M**icah, I'm ready to go for that ride through the property. Are the mules ready?"

"Yes, sir," his son replies.

"Lechy, how long have we been back from our trip?" Sett asks, passing his steward in the courtyard on his way to the stables.

"I think two years now."

"You mean, 'two years now, sir,' Micah says.

"Uh, Lechy," Sett interjects, "I just want to thank you once again for how well you oversaw the workings of the palace and farm while we were gone."

"I just do what my father did."

"Ziba was a very efficient steward also," Sett replies. "Well, if Kissara comes down asking for me, tell her where my son and I will be."

"At least you have a son," Lechy replies.

"I am so sorry, Lechy. It is not fair what happened to you."

"Not that again. You are the one who killed him," Lechy says, watching Sett and Micah walk away from him. "I just couldn't convince King David to have you executed for it, but your day will come," he shouts after them.

"Why do you put up with that, Father?" Micah mutters as they walk toward the stables.

"He has been through a lot in his life."

"Not as much as you. But you do not hate the whole

world as he does. Why don't you fire him?"

"You know I cannot do that. Even though my grandfather's estate has been given to me by the king, the king is the actual owner, and the king decides who will watch over it."

They reach the stable on one side of the large palace courtyard. Two large black mules stand ready. With Sett's strong arms, he raises his knees to a small stool he keeps on his saddle, grabs hold of the saddle horn, and hoists himself up.

"I don't know how much longer I'll be able to do this. I'm forty-seven years old now."

"You will always be able to do that, Father."

"We can't be gone long, you know. Not with the banquet tonight."

After an hour, Sett and Micah return. They dismount, hand their mules over to the stable hand, and proceed across the courtyard.

"What? Ughhh!"

Sett's crutch slides sideways and falls to the pavement. He tries to balance himself on his one remaining crutch, but it too slips.

Micah lunges at his father to break his fall. He reaches out his hands to grab him under the arms, but is too late.

Sett falls on his back and hits his head. Micah drops to his knees. "Father!"

Sett opens his eyes. "Whew. What happened?"

"Are you all right, Father? Don't try to sit up."

Sett pulls his elbows around and sits up. He looks around. By now, Kissara, Aunt Merab, and Grandmother Rizpah have come. They stand around, looking down at him.

"Well, somebody, help me up," Sett says. "Where are my crutches?"

Micah moves over to pick up his father's crutches. "This one has been cut. See the marks, Father?"

"Well, it was bound to happen someday. They are old crutches."

"No, Father, someone has deliberately weakened it."

"No harm done. I'm okay."

Micah hands the one good crutch to his father and stands behind him to help lift him up. Kissara stands to one side of Micah.

"Come, dear," Sett says. "Let's go over to that bench by the reflecting pool. I love watching the little fish in the pool. Don't you?"

Micah watches his parents. He looks at Rizpah and Merab. "Why does Father let him get by with it?" he asks them.

"Your father is too good. He has always been too good," Rizpah says.

"He has always handled things by laughing them off," Merab says. "He lives in a dream world, not a world of reality."

Micah and the women return to their apartments. Lechy stands outside the door of the storeroom his father had turned into an office. He is grinning.

"I believe I am going to be a little sore tonight when we hold our banquet," Sett tells Kissara.

"Afterward, we're going to have to inspect your feet with extra care. You may have to spend the next few days in bed to give the scrapes on your feet time to heal," Kissara says.

"Until then, we shall enjoy our banquet. Now, how many people did you say are coming?" Sett asks, reaching over and touching Kissara's cheek and noticing it is more hollow than it used to be.

"Well, we have invited every one of our farmhands," Kissara says. "I think we have thirty of them. Maybe forty."

"How is Lechy handling it?"

Kissara grins. "He is definitely not happy. Sons of kings do not fraternize with the servants."

"How easily he forgets he is one of those servants," Sett replies, inspecting his one good crutch.

"He lives in a strange world of his own making. He

would be master of heaven and earth if he could. How long has he been like this?" Kissara asks.

"As long as I can remember. His grandfather enslaved himself to my grandfather for debts he could not pay because he was a drunk. Ziba was part of the deal, and being just a boy then, had the dirtiest jobs like handling our smelly waste. His resentment apparently rubbed off on Lechy when he had a son of his own."

Kissara shakes her head, looks down at the ground, then back up at her husband. "How did his father manage to work his way to the steward of the estate if he started out so lowly?"

"Lying," Sett says, sliding his hand through the cold water of the pool. "He would just lie about a person whose job he wanted, then be given the job of whoever he lied about."

"But what about Lechy? He didn't go through that."

"At first, he was just imitating his father. That's all he knew. But now he has his own reasons for his bitterness: The death of his son."

"He blames you for killing him. Do you think his son is really dead?"

"I don't know. But I think I want to rest the remainder of the day so I will be fresh for the banquet. "Uh, Lechy," he calls out, knowing he is never far from the central courtyard where he can keep an eye on everything.

Lechy steps out from the kitchen area. "Did you say something?"

"Come here, Lechy." Sett waits as his servant walks leisurely to him. "I seem to have broken my crutch. Would you kindly have another one made for me by the time of the banquet tonight?"

Lechy looks at Sett, says nothing, and walks away.

Evening comes, and the guests begin to arrive. House servants, most of whom have been hired to replace Lechy's brothers, stand at the gate to greet the farmhands.

"Come into the chariot house," they say. "We have

water for you there to wash up with, and a fresh tunic."

Everyone is then escorted to the large banquet hall under the broad staircase leading to the usually-closed-off throne room.

When everyone is seated. Sett, Kissara, and Micah arrive and seat themselves at the head table. After them, Rizpah and Merab come out and sit on either side of them. The older women wear the small crowns of princesses.

Still, without his replacement crutch, Sett rises, one hand on Kissara's shoulder and the other on Micah's.

"The descendants of mighty Saul, Warrior King of Israel, welcome you. Many of you have been loyal since the days of my grandfather and remember him well. This banquet is just a token of our appreciation for your loyalty all these years."

Applause.

"Now for the entertainment."

Silence. Everyone waits.

"Uh, Lechy," Sett says, turning and addressing Lechy standing behind and to one side of him. "Where is the entertainment?"

"I thought you told me to cancel it."

"Of course, I didn't," Sett whispers. "So, does this mean we have no musicians?"

"I am afraid so. I am sorry."

Sett turns to face his guests again. "While the first course is being brought out, my son will sing a song for you."

Micah turns to his father. "I'm going to do what?"

"You're going to sing. It doesn't matter what. Just sing."

"But, Father..."

"Sing, I said. Sing."

By the time Micah's song comes to an end, the first course has been served.

"Enjoy the stew, everyone. It is a special recipe my wife brought back from the wife of Talmai, King of Gesher."

"Eeuggh!" someone says, standing and pushing his

bench back.

"Eeuggh!" another says.

Sett watches his guests either jump back from their bowls or push them away. He looks down at his own bowl. "Oh, no."

"Oh, no is right," Merab says. "It is full of worms."

Sett turns in his chair. "Lechy, have the bowls of stew taking up immediately."

"As you wish," he says, completely expressionless.

"Then, run into Gibeon and buy all the bread you can." He turns to Kissara. "Can you salvage this?"

Kissara scoots back her chair and leaves. A few moments later, she returns with a smile.

"We have extra cheese and honey that can be served. You are going to tell the guests to dip their cheese in the honey for a new taste that everyone these days is trying."

As the cheese and honey are distributed to the guests, Merab volunteers a song. The rest of the evening proceeds as planned.

It is now the next day.

"Do you know what Lechy said last night after the banquet?" Sett asks his wife in their apartment.

"I can imagine."

"He said, 'At least you have a family.'"

"His family is bigger than yours. He has fourteen brothers."

"He does not live in reality. All he can think of is his one great loss—his son."

Two months go by. It is morning again. There is a loud knock on Sett's apartment door.

"Hurry. There are threats to the palace. You must escape."

Kissara opens the door to hear Lechy's warning better.

"I know I have not always treated you right," he continues, looking over at Sett still on his bed. "But I want to make it right. You must leave the palace at once."

"How do you know all this?"

"This clay tablet was just delivered. Someone intends to break in by noon and kill you."

"I guess we had better heed the warning," Sett says.

"Go into Gibeon out of danger," Lechy says. "The overseer of the farmhands has agreed to take you in. I will let you know when the danger has passed."

Sett, his wife, son, aunt, and step-grandmother rush to the courtyard where five mules have been saddled.

As Sett prepares to mount his mule, he looks back at Lechy. "Thank you," he says. Lechy smirks.

The following day, Sett receives word that the danger has passed, and he can bring his family back.

"Whew," Sett says as Lechy meets him at the front gate. "Just what happened? Who was the culprit?"

"I do not know."

"You 'do not know, sir,'" Micah corrects.

"Well, you have made a lot of enemies through the years," Lechy says. "Your grandfather made even more."

"I wonder if Yassib made the threat. Even though my uncles were all hung to satisfy his lust for vengeance for my grandfather killing off his family, he still hasn't forgiven us."

"Could be, Sett. Could be."

"It's a good thing we got the anonymous warning."

Three weeks go by.

"Sir, Sir," Sett hears through his apartment door. He recognizes Lechy's voice. Kissara opens the door.

"Sir, there has been another threat on the palace. A volley of arrows will be sent over your wall at the time of your morning exercises in the courtyard."

"But we were already threatened, and it didn't happen."

"Perhaps the one who warned you before was able to thwart their plans. I wouldn't take any chances, sir. Hurry before the sun goes down. You can stay with the farmhand overseer again."

Once more, Sett and his family escape danger at the palace. At noon the next day, one of Sett's servants arrives to tell him all is well, and he can return to the palace.

"Well, I don't think it was Yassib. He normally writes on papyrus, not clay," Sett tells Lechy upon their return. "What I do not understand is why this person—whoever he is—sends me warnings. Why doesn't he go ahead and kill me?"

"He must want you to suffer before he kills you," Lechy replies. "Perhaps like being tortured before being executed."

Three weeks go by. Sett hears the distressing knock on his apartment door and Lechy's warning voice once again.

"Sir, your life is in danger. You must leave immediately."

"Well, Lechy," Sett replies, having answered the door himself. "Why don't you run and I will stay here to guard the palace?"

"No, sir, you must escape."

"Lechy, you have had your fun. We are not going anywhere. So you can stop your game."

Lechy stares at his master. Sett stares back. Their eyes lock. Micah walks up and stands outside the open door.

"What? Another one of Lechy's scares? Lechy, my father told you to forget it and go back to work. If I were you, I would do just that."

Without saying more and without looking at Micah, Lechy turns and goes back down to the courtyard and his office.

"Father, is there no way to get rid of this man? He has gone mad. He makes no sense anymore."

"If he gets worse, perhaps I will go see King Solomon about him. But, until we have proof..."

"Don't we still have the clay tablets with the threats on them?"

"I don't know. Even if we did, they are not signed, and we cannot prove who wrote them."

"Well, we women are going to station ourselves in the courtyard all day, just to celebrate the enemy not coming," Kissara says, smiling.

Through the day, Sett enjoys watching his wife, aunt, and step-grandmother sit in the courtyard, giggling much of the time.

"Father, you need to confront Lechy," Micah says.

"I think you are right. I cannot prove I did not kill his son, but perhaps I can somehow convince him."

Three days later, Sett has the folding doors opened to the throne room. He stands at the top of the wide steps leading from the courtyard to the second floor, King Saul's copper-colored alabaster throne behind him.

When Rizpah walks out to the courtyard on Micah's arm and sees it, she gasps. "Oh, his throne. My beloved's throne. How I longed to sit in the queen's throne next to his."

"Great-Grandmother, would you like to sit in it now?"

"Oh, may I?" she asks, looking up at Micah.

Sett, having heard, nods his consent.

"I am ninety-two years old now, you know," she says to Micah as he assists her up the grand stairs. "If I could just sit on the throne one time, I would be ready to die."

They arrive at the throne room, and Micah escorts her to the smaller queen's throne made of green alabaster. "Your Highness," he says as he holds her hand and she pivots around to sit.

Rizpah puts both hands on the arms of the throne, smiles, pats the ivory inlay, and looks off into the distance.

Sett, standing nearby, smiles.

Micah bows to her. "Hail to the queen," he says softly. "Long live the queen."

Tears come to her eyes. "Oh, you precious boy," she says to Micah.

The men watch her form a smile with her trembling lips.

She lifts her head and looks around as though acknowledging her subjects.

She looks down at the courtyard below and turns her head this way and that.

She lifts an arthritic hand and tips it toward her

would-be admirers, scattered from one row of grand columns all the way across to the other.

She puts her hands back in her lap, her smile fades as she returns to reality, and she dabs her fresh tears.

She looks over at Micah. "Well, I guess I have had my turn. Take me back to my apartment now."

As Micah and Rizpah descend, Lechy walks over to the bottom of the stairs.

"I got your message. Well, I'm here. What did you have to say that is so important?"

"Come. Let's talk here," Sett calls down.

As Lechy ascends the steps to the throne room, he continues talking. "You really know how to show how superior you are. You have had everything. You had a grandfather who was a king; my grandfather was a drunk. You had a father who was a hero; my father was a stinking slave. You were born in your family palace; I was born in one of those shacks on land my family can never own."

By now, Lechy has reached the top and is standing a few paces from Sett.

"Do you know how much I hate you?"

"Yes, I do."

"I have always hated you."

"I know."

"You had everything, and I had nothing."

"Not always."

"Okay, so you broke your feet. And you wandered around many times to escape your enemies who, by the way, you deserved."

"You have lived in palaces all your life," Sett responds. "If it wasn't mine, it was Absalom's. And your father trained you well to be a steward."

"But I had no son to train. You do everything with that son of yours, but you killed mine just to deprive me. He was six years younger than your son. Iptur would have been eighteen years old by now."

"Lechy, I did not kill your son."

"Then where is he if you didn't kill him? Hmmm?"
Lechy's face turns red.
"Tell me that."
His breathing grows rapid and loud.
"Tell me if you dare. Tell me!" he bellows.
Lechy steps back. His eyes are wild.
He clenches his teeth. An otherworldly growl emits from deep in his throat.
He raises his hand above his head. In it is a knife.
"You killed my son. Now I kill you."

# 30 ~ LOSSES

**S**ett raises one of his crutches, suspending his body now completely with his right arm and crutch.

Lechy's arm comes down. The knife glistens.

Sett crosses his crutch under the knife, and it goes flying.

Lechy lunges at Sett. He knocks him over.

The two men wrestle on the floor of the throne room.

"No!" Lechy continues to shout, his voice like a frenzied oxen searching for her lost calf. He pounds Sett on his chest but is no match for Sett's strong hands that grab hold of his.

"No! You cannot get by with it. I have no son. I have no son. I have..."

Lechy screams at the ceiling stops wrestling and breaks out in sobs.

He grows limp, and Sett sits up. He cradles Lechy in his arms. Two fathers, but one now bereft of his son. Two fathers whose sons should have played together, but were never given the chance. Two fathers, only one son, the other forever gone.

Sett holds Lechy a long time, sometimes rocking him. Lechy groans. It becomes dark. They are quiet but still cling to each other.

Finally, Lechy raises his head and looks at Sett. His eyes are red and swollen. He stares as though he does not know what to say. Sett does not force him to talk.

"I am going to find your son," Sett whispers, "if it is the last thing I do."

"You cannot. He is dead."

"Did you see him actually dead?" Sett asks.

"No, but I know he was killed. A father knows those things."

"Why don't you take a few days off? Go up into the Bethel Woods for a while."

"I can't. I have too many responsibilities here."

"They will be here when you return. Now go on your vacation. You deserve it."

Lechy stumbles down the stairs and leaves. Sett remains where he is.

"Father, where are you?"

"I'm up here, Son," Sett replies.

Micah climbs the steps to the throne room, the doors still wide open.

"What have you been doing up here?"

"Talking with Lechy."

"It looks more like you were wrestling with him."

"Well, maybe I was."

"You cannot allow that. You must report him to King Solomon."

"Now is not the time."

"When is it the time? Father, you let him run over you and disrespect you all the time. Why?"

"When you are older, perhaps you will understand. Now, did you need me for something? Is your mother okay?"

"Mother has gone to bed early again. Seems as though she sleeps a lot these days."

"Yes, she does that," Sett whispers.

"What I came about is Great-Grandmother, Rizpah. Great Aunt Merab came to my apartment and said Rizpah is not doing well."

Sett and Micah go out to where they pick up the steps to the third-floor apartments, the apartments originally built for King Saul's children.

When they arrive at Rizpah's door, it is wide open.

"Oh, thank you for coming," Merab says. "She is not doing well."

"What do you mean?"

"Come and see."

Rizpah is curled up in her bed, her knees and elbows bent and her hands behind her cheek. Her breathing is deep and fast.

"She sounds as though she is running," Merab says.

Sett sighs. "Yes, she is running. She has decided to let go. She is running toward the angels, and the angels are running toward her.

"Micah, go see if you can wake up your mother. She may want to be here."

"Are you sure?"

"Yes, I think she would not want to be left out."

After a while, Sett and Merab hear a soft voice at the door.

"Micah told me what is happening," Kissara says. "Is she still with us? Am I in time?"

"Yes, my little one, you are in time."

Micah brings in a comfortable chair for his mother, and another for himself. They sit on one side of Rizpah's bed while Sett and Merab sit on the other side."

"Should we send for my sister at the palace," Merab asks.

"Don't you remember?" Sett replies. "She passed away the same year her husband, King David, did."

"She had such a sad life," Merab says. "When we were teenagers, she fell so madly in love with David. Though they were legally married, he never lived with her. Then, when she was finally happily married to another and David became king, he insisted she come to the palace with him. What did he think she was going to do to him? Usurp his throne? Her father, King Saul, was dead. She was no threat."

"Life is often hard," Kissara says. "It is only in hoping for what is better in the next life that sometimes keeps us going."

Rizpah opens her eyes.

"Mother Rizpah? Are you okay?" Merab says.

The mistress of the great Saul, King of Israel, forever deprived of her queenly crown, looks briefly at Merab, closes her eyes, and breathes her last.

A funeral procession is formed. What is left of Saul's family makes its way to Zela, the family burial cave. They decide to move Ahinoam's bones from the Mountain of Olive Trees to the family cave at the same time to be laid next to the man they both loved.

What is left of Saul's family stays and mourns. Merab mourns for her parents and for her five sons hanged because of the sins of her father. Sett mourns for his beloved grandmother, Ahinoam, and his father, Jonathan. Micah wonders what it will be like to bury his own mother and father here someday.

The four arrive back at the Gibeon palace and hear music.

"What is that?"

They enter and see Prince Eliphelet, David's youngest son, now age twenty-two. He greets them. "I thought you would like some music to cheer you up," He tells them as they make their way in.

"How do you know we need cheering up, you little thug?" Micah says.

"C'mon. It's all over my big brother's palace. The mistress of the great and notorious King Saul, who hunted down my father like a lion and rabbit, is dead. Everyone is celebrating. That is one less threat to my father's—David's—dynasty.

"You are welcome to come here," Sett says, "but we are not much in the mood for your music."

"Did you notice how I can blow on the trumpet and handle the cymbal and tumbrel with my feet? I'm gifted that way. Sometimes I just need something to celebrate. Being the youngest son out of nineteen sons of my father... Well, it seems I have always been lost in the crowd. I sometimes thought my father forgot I was even alive."

"I'm sorry," Sett says.

"One adjusts. I have my music. I love to wait until the middle of the night to play something. Solomon doesn't mind. He's always up there on the site of the temple he is building at the top of Mount Moriah. Well, Solomon has his thing, and I have mine. Right now, my thing is to cheer all of you up."

"Eliphelet, we do not want or need to be cheered up," Micah says.

Eliphelet looks across the courtyard at Lechy. "See, I told you they didn't want to be cheered up." Lechy grins.

Two days later, Kissara has a suggestion, "Setty, let's take a ride up to the Bethel Woods, just the two of us."

"That is a great idea, my peach."

"I already ordered some food packed in a small basket," she says with a glint in her eyes. "Maybe we can find a big flat rock up there; we can spread a blanket out on to sit and eat."

"I always did know you enjoyed the woods as much as I do. You just never admitted it. Well, now, I've caught you. So, let's go."

The couple leaves their apartment and heads to the stables next to the grand courtyard. When they arrive, Sett asks the stable hand to put their tent on Sett's mule.

"Or we could put it on Dipti," Kissara giggles.

"Let's not bother poor old Dipti," Sett says, laughing. "We put him through enough escaping Assyria. He deserves to stay in retirement."

The stable hand brings out two mules. Sett and Kissara climb on, and they head west and then north out of Gibeon.

It is sunset by the time they reach the edge of the woods.

"I think I remember a little clearing just inside," Sett says.

They ride into the woods, the smell of bark and rustle of leaves filling their senses. They arrive at the clearing, and the two work together to put up the tent.

That done, Sett builds a fire with his bow drill, and Kissara spreads out their food.

"Oh, you brought my favorite cheese," he says, settling down next to the growing flames of the fire.

As they eat, the evening breeze moves in.

"Let's see if we can scare a squirrel," Kissara says.

They wander into the woods a little way.

"You can't see the stars in here, but you know they are there," Kissara says.

"Uh-huh."

"Sometimes on a really clear night when the leaves are gone," she continues, "and all that is around you is you and the branches reaching up, you can see a star."

"I think that is when stars glitter the most," Sett says.

They are quiet a while.

"It's cooling off faster than I thought it would, Setty."

They work their way back to the clearing and sit on their blanket by the fire.

Kissara giggles. "Remember when we escaped out into the Arabian Desert,, and we weren't married yet?"

"And night arrived?" Sett says, grinning.

"And we needed a place to sleep and maintain our honor?" she says, poking him in a rib.

"And we propped up your father's huge robe on the top of my crutches, and stretched it out to the ground on the other end?" he says, touching the tip of her nose.

"And slept under it?" she giggles.

"You have no idea how hard it was for me to lie beside the most beautiful woman in the world and not make her mine."

"Well, you have me now, Setty."

He puts his arm around her, and they lean their heads on each other.

"Setty?"

"Hmmm?"

"How long have we been married?"

"Thirty years, as you know," he whispers as he reaches over and kisses her forehead.

"They have been good years, haven't they, Setty?"

"With you to share them with, yes, they have been good years."

Silence.

"Oh, look!" Kissara jumps up.

Sett rises and tries to see what she sees. "Oh, I think I saw the tail end of it," he says.

"A shooting star." She turns, puts her arms around his neck, and smiles.

They return to their seat by the fire, dreaming once again.

"Kissara, when I saw you the first time that day, you were like an angel from heaven to me."

"Did I have wings too?" she teases.

"Oh, indeed, you did. They were so wispy and shimmery, they were almost invisible. But they weren't invisible to me. I saw them right away."

"I wish I had flown away with you then."

"We were so young at that time. Too young. I was just sixteen, and you were fourteen."

"We thought we were grown up, though."

"Yes, we did."

"Remember how I wanted a gold neckless for my mistress like the peach I was eating?"

"Somehow, you thought that would impress me," she giggles. Her smile fades into wistfulness. "I missed you so while you were gone, Setty."

"Well, I went back and got you, and we have not been separated since," he says, kissing her on her cheek.

Sett and Kissara grow tired, crawl into their tent, and fall asleep. The next thing they know, they hear something hitting the tent.

"Oh, no! It's raining, Sett."

He grins, looks over at his wife, and draws her into his arms.

It is a gentle rain. After a long while, its tapping stops. They peek outside. The sun is chasing white clouds around a deep blue sky, and a rainbow floats in distant clouds.

Kissara crawls out, dragging her basket with her. She sits near the now burned-out fire of the night before and takes out their breakfast.

"I always enjoyed those times David and I sang together," now sitting next to her.

"Yes, I know you did. You had a lot in common."

"I suppose so. He was almost king while my grandfather chased him, I was almost king forever. He composed songs, and I sang them. He loved my father, and I loved my father too."

Silence.

"Did you know David used to call me Jonathan?"

"No, I did not know that."

"He had too many wives and mistresses," Sett says. "He missed the opportunity to belong to just one woman who would fill his life with everything, as only a woman can do. I was the lucky one. I had you."

He pops the last grape in his mouth and puts his arms around Kissara. "And I still do!"

"The sun seems to have dried everything out sufficiently. Shall we go on back?" she asks.

They take down the tent and store it on the rump of Sett's mule. Just before mounting their animals, Sett embraces his wife.

"We need to do this more often."

It is late afternoon when they arrive back at the palace.

"Look whose back," Micah says with a large grin. "My parents look very happy. Just what were you up to in those woods? No, don't tell me. You embarrass me sometimes."

"Well, we gave the mules exercise, for one thing. Have you been exercising Dipti lately?"

"Ha, ha. That scoundrel camel. Did you know he talks

to himself? Sometimes I go by his pasture and hear him gurgle and squawk and honk and whinny."

Now down off their mules, Sett watches Kissara walk slowly toward their apartment.

"Your mother grows weaker all the time."

"Does she get those pains in her chest still?"

"I think so. But she has become an expert at hiding them."

The next day, Kissara comes down to the courtyard with her embroidery work. She sits with Aunt Merab, and they talk.

Sett watches Kissara, trying to absorb everything about her—the tip of her nose, the laugh lines that have formed beside her eyes, her pointed chin, her dainty ears, her beautiful long hair turning gray.

After a while, she sets her cloth onto her lap and drops her limp hands with it. She stares at Sett across the way. He rises and makes his way over to her.

"Come on, little one. I think you need a nap. Then you will feel better."

Kissara clings to Sett's still-strong arm as they make their way across the courtyard and to the steps to their second-floor apartment.

She ascends the steps alone while he watches. She closes the door, and he returns to his seat by the reflecting pool.

He has taken up whittling, and resumes his project, though he is unsure what it will end up being. He wishes he could make an image of his wife.

The next day, Kissara rises and goes down to the kitchen area. By the time Sett is ready to eat, she has flour all over her hair, hands, and clothes.

He sits down at his table.

"Guess what I made you today, Setty?"

Sett grins wide, and his eyes sparkle as he watches his Kissara. "I cannot imagine, my little peach. What did you make me?"

"Baklava. I worked on it for hours."

"You did, did you?"

She sets the plate down in front of him, seats herself across from him, puts her elbow on the table and her chin on her hand and leans forward. "Well?"

He takes a bite. "This is indeed the best baklava you have ever made."

"It's the first baklava I have ever made, silly."

"So, I was right. The best."

He takes another bite. "So, what shall we do today?" he asks.

"I think I would like to go see Dipty. I kind of miss him."

"Then that is what we shall do."

After breaking their fast and cleaning the sticky honey off their fingers, Sett and Kissara board a small chariot and make their way out the front gate and turn toward the pasture.

It does not take them long to arrive. They stand close to the stone wall.

"I see him," Kissara announces, grinning. "*Tati*, Dipti, *tati*."

The camel looks up, sees Kissara waving at him, and gallops toward them.

"He remembers me," she says, her eyes dancing.

When Dipti arrives, Kissara holds out her hand with chunks of salt in it. Dipti wiggles his nose, quickly consumes it, then honks in delight.

"Hu, hu."

"I don't know if he likes you more or the salt more," Sett teases.

"*Jals*, Dipti. *Jals*."

The camel promptly sits.

"What are you doing, Kissara? You cannot ride him."

"Oh, I'm not going to ride him. We are."

She giggles and climbs over the wall. Sett follows her. Sett climbs on Dipty first. Kissara follows and snuggles in front of him.

"Are we ready?"

"Do we remember how?"

"*Mawqaf*, Dipti. *Mawqaf*."

The camel raises its back legs, then its front legs. "A*dhhab* now, Dipti. *Adhhab Haq*."

Dipti turns to his right and begins to walk.

"Hey, I forgot how bad he sways. Hang on. If we fall off, we have a long way to go," Sett laughs.

They cross to the other side of the pasture, then back where they started.

"Okay, it's out of my system," Kissara announces.

The camel sits and lets off his beloved passengers. He rises, looks at them, nuzzles his nose in Kissara's hair, and takes off running to the other side of the pasture, honking.

Sett and Kissara make their way back to the palace. When they go through the gate, they see Micah.

"Come help your mother," Sett says. "I think she is tired now."

Kissara sleeps the rest of the day.

The next morning Sett wakes up and realizes Kissara is not there with him. He rises, splashes water on his face, dresses, and returns downstairs.

Kissara is sitting by the reflecting pool. Sett watches her slide her fingers through the water a moment, then joins her.

"The water in the pool sometimes looks gold when the sun is just right," she says.

"I remember the gold jewelry you used to make," he replies. "I wanted to buy all of it to make you rich."

"How could you have done that, silly? You were a slave."

"It didn't stop me from wanting to. I wanted to give you the world."

"You did, Setty. You gave me you."

They sit in silence a while. She snuggles her head under Sett's chin. He smells the perfumed water she always washes it with.

Micah watches his parents from his balcony on the third floor and smiles.

"Setty?"

"Hmmm?"

"Do you know what I would like to do today?"

"What's that, my peach?"

"I would like to go for a little walk. Just in here. A little walk."

"That would be fine, little one. Are you ready?"

They stand and cross over to the side of the grand courtyard, where the stables are hidden behind the marble columns. They walk across the front where the guard towers and front gate are. They turn and make their way past the side of the courtyard, where the chariots are kept behind more marble columns.

"We'll have to go for a long chariot ride one of these days," Kissara whispers.

"We shall do that soon, my little one."

They turn and pass one of two entrances into the grand banquet hall. They walk past the broad, expansive steps leading up to the throne room. They walk past the other side of the steps where the other entrance to the banquet hall is.

"That was fun," Kissara says. "I think I shall rest now."

Micah sees his mother approach the steps to the second floor and hurries down to her.

"Let me help you, Mother."

Sett stays at the bottom of the steps and watches his Kissara make her way up to their apartment.

It is quiet. Even the servants speak in hushed voices.

After a while, Sett makes his way up to the apartment he had inherited from his grandfather so long ago. He lies down on the bed next to his Kissara and talks to her about times gone by.

It is now the next morning.

"I don't believe I will get up for a while," Kissara says.

"I will get up a little while later."

"Then I will stay here with you."

Sometime later—Sett does not know how long—there is a knock on their door.

"Come in," Sett says.

Micah and Merab stand in the doorway. "May we come in?"

They sit with Kissara as they had sat with Rizpah earlier in the year. Hours go by. It is almost evening.

"Remember the stars?" Kissara whispers.

"Yes, my little one. I remember the stars."

"Even when you cannot see them, they are there."

"Yes, my peach, they certainly are."

Quiet again.

And Kissara dies.

# 31 ~ NEW BEGINNING

"**I** do believe my son is falling in love."

Micah grins. "Maybe. She is so beautiful, Father, I cannot take my eyes off her when I see her, and when I am away from her, all I can see is her face."

"Oh, you definitely are in love. Would your mother approve of her?"

"She is a lot like Mother." He pauses. "I miss her so much, Father."

"Yes." Sett sighs. "I miss her more than you can imagine. She was the light of my soul."

"She hadn't reached fifty yet. It was not fair."

"What is fair is that we had her as long as we did. She added gentleness to our life. That's what a good woman does."

"Nina adds gentleness to my life, I guess."

"Yes, you are a calmer man than you used to be."

They hear a knock on the gate and wait for the gatekeeper to answer it.

"Micah, ole boy," they hear.

Prince Eliphelet dismounts from his white mule and swaggers over toward them while Micah rolls his eyes toward the heavens.

Sett grins. "I think I spoke about your calmness too soon," he whispers.

"Hello there, Eliphelet," Sett calls out.

"Don't encourage him, Father."

"So, how is the least favorite and most forgotten son of King David doing today?"

"Ha, ha. Sett, the man who couldn't be king, how are you?"

"Why do you encourage him, Father?" Micah mutters.

"Because he is just that—the least favorite and most forgotten."

Sett rises. "Welcome. Welcome. So, what are you up to today?"

"Oh, nothing. Big brother Solomon got himself another girlfriend. And he's working away on his new palace, now that the temple is completed.

"I hear it is going to be grand," Sett says. "Have a seat."

"Yes. Gold, marble and brass all over the ceiling and floors, and the walls lined with cedar. From what I hear, his largest room is going to have huge cedar trees holding up the ceiling instead of marble columns.

"Oh? And where is he getting his cedar?"

"Over in Lebanon. Our father made arrangements for all the materials for the temple before he died. All big brother had to do was put it together. Now he is going back to the same places for materials to build his palace. He wasn't satisfied with the palace our father built. Nooo. Not big brother Solomon."

"Well, number one, I hope the king over in Tyre replaces all those trees he is cutting down. Number two, I am amazed at what he did with the temple. People all over the world will come to see it. And I hope decide to worship the only real God."

Silence.

"Too bad about your mother, Micah. She was nice."

"Yes, she was," Micah says, glad Elipelet's bragging session is over.

"I still have my mother," Eliphelet says. "I guess I'm lucky that way. She's from Arabia, you know. She was her parents' only child like you are, Micah. So, when she dies, I will inherit whatever she inherits."

"Is she close to her family?" Sett asks.

"I suppose so. She goes to see them sometimes. I have gone a couple times and was bored."

Micah and Sett do not respond.

"Well, I guess I'll be going. Just thought I'd drop in and few moments. Bye for now."

Elipelet remounts his white mule and rides out of the courtyard.

"That was fun," Micah says, twisting his mouth around and glaring. "Do you have any special plans for today, Father?"

"I thought I would like to go out and check on the crops, and maybe tell the farmhands how good they are. And you?"

"I'm really into this pottery thing. I think I'll work on my latest project today. I'm trying to see what the biggest urn is that I can make."

"A worthy goal, Son. I will see you when I get back."

Sett whistles, and the stable hand opens the stable doors at the signal. He saddles Sett's mule and puts down the small knee-high stool next to the animal. Sett puts his knees on the stool, then pulls up with his arms that are not as strong as they use to be, and straddles the mule. The stable hand moves the stool aside, attaches it to one side of the saddle, the gatekeeper opens the gate, and Sett leaves.

"The air is fresh today after yesterday's rain," he tells his mule. They work their way down the road through their property. Sett stops by the wall where old Dipti grazes. He whistles. The camel comes galloping to him, and Sett leans over to hand him a few lumps of salt. Dipti nibbles and slurps, then honks and wheezes, raises his head, and gallops back the way he had come.

"She sure had a way with you, Dipti, didn't she?" Sett says. "I'll bet you miss her almost as much as I do."

He flips his reins, clicks his tongue, and the mule moves on down the road. Suddenly his mule bends his knees, shakes its head, whinnies, struggles, and finally regains its balance.

"What is wrong with you?" Sett asks. "It's not like you to stumble."

Sett guides the mule around so he can see what it stumbled on. "What is that rock doing on the road? It wasn't there before. Well, maybe it fell from somewhere."

He guides the mule back around and continues on his way. A few moments later, his mule bends his knees, almost goes down, struggles, then regains its balance again.

"What's going on?"

Sett turns the mule so he can see, and realizes another rock is on the trail that had not been there before.

"There is mud piled around it to conceal it. Who did this?"

Sett looks over his crops and visits a while with the farmhands. The overseer wanders over.

"We do not want to take them from their work too long chatting, do we, sire?"

Sett smiles. "You are as much of a pusher as you always have been," he says. "What would I do without you?"

"It looks like that will not happen. Micah comes to our little house quite often now."

"Yes, I heard. This situation will bear watching."

Sett turns his mule to head back to the palace. Halfway there, his mule falls to its knees and rolls over onto his side. Sett jumps off just in time to avoid being pinned under the large animal.

He looks at his mule's leg and sees that it has dropped down into a large hole. The mule whinnies then is quiet.

Sett touches the animal's side and realizes his heart is racing. He manages to get his crutches off the animal and heads back to the palace.

As he approaches, he calls for the gatekeeper who opens the gate before Sett has to wait.

Micah stands. "What's wrong, Father? Where is your mule? Did the workers take it from you?"

"No, Son. We have been sabotaged again. Walk down

the trail, and you will see it. Don't take your mule. Walk it."

Sometime later, Micah returns.

"How could he? Eliphelet pretends to be our friend only so he can get close enough to take his anger out on us. Every time he shows up, something goes wrong as soon as he leaves. We can't help it if he is not appreciated by his family. Why does he take it out on us?"

"I guess because we are the only royal family, he knows with no power to get back at him."

"Father, you are not to allow that man on our property again!" Micah shouts.

"I am what?"

"Oh, Father, I didn't mean to tell you what to do. It's just that... Well, Father, why don't you report him to Solomon?"

"Report what? He does nothing provable."

"Can't you punish him yourself then?"

"No."

"Father, why do you take it?"

Weeks and months pass with no further incidents. Even Lechy seems calmer.

"I had a visitor while you were gone into town this morning," Sett tells Micah, smiling.

"That's nice, Father. Did you have a nice visit?"

"You should be asking me if we had a successful visit."

Micah looks up. "Huh?"

"Your future father-in-law came by."

"He did? He is?"

"Well, I have known Cheber a lot of years. He is a good overseer out in the field. I have seen him with his children a few times working out there with him. He is a solid man, and I think his daughter would make a fine wife for you."

"Yes!" Micah shouts at the sky. "When?"

"Of course, first you must be betrothed. Once you are betrothed, neither of you can back out without a divorce. The betrothal will give you and her time to prepare for married life. Now, do you want to move her into the apartment you have always had?"

"Oh. I never thought that far ahead. Well, of course, I will bring her to the palace. Uh, let me think now."

Micah paces while Sett watches and grins. He turns toward his father. "You know, there are so many empty apartments up on the third floor. Four large ones and four smaller ones total. I have one, and Great Aunt Merab has one. Great-Grandmother Rizpah used to have one next to me. Do you think I could have both hers and mine? We could put a door between them.

"That is fine, Son. Now, what else do you want to do to prepare? Think about your future wife."

Silence.

"Oh, I see what you mean. To fit into a royal family— well, we used to be royal—she needs some training how to act in different situations. And she needs some new clothes. Do you think Great Aunt Merab could help with that?"

"I would be honored to, Micah."

"Oh, I did not see you sitting over there," Micah responds. "That is great. So how long do you think it will take you to train her?"

"She's not an animal, my dear Micah. I shall tutor her."

"Yes, that's what I mean. And the wedding banquet."

"Slow down, Son. First, we have to have the betrothal banquet. What about next week?"

"Oh, Father. I am so happy."

"I remember those early days with your mother. I will never forget them, and you will not either. They will be some of the best memories you will ever make. Guard them and cherish them."

Sett becomes quiet and looks up at the apartment he had shared with his Kissara.

"She is the one who should be tutoring young Nina and planning the banquet," Merab says. "Not me."

"She liked you a lot. And relied on you for more than you realize," Sett says.

"I am eighty-two years old now. Little Nina needs someone younger than me to tutor her."

"You are a young eighty-two, Aunt Merab. Besides that, you are daughter of King Saul, and therefore Princess Merab. You will do fine."

The following week is the betrothal banquet and ceremony.

The banquet hall is full. The front half is filled with the children of King David by his mistresses and his youngest son by his last wife, Ithream. They bring their wives and grown children—all princes and princesses.

The back half of the hall is filled with the farmhands that the bride's father supervises.

Merab arranges for a harpist to play in the background.

Sett enters from one side of the banquet hall with Micah behind him. Cheber and his wife, Talya, enter from the other side of the banquet hall with Nina behind them.

The two families meet at the head table.

Micah steps forward and looks at Nina's parents. "I hereby promise to provide a suitable home for Nina, along with many rooms for our children to live in. I will provide her with fine clothes, food to eat, and every desire of her heart. I swear this by God in heaven."

Cheber steps forward. He embraces Micah, and Micah kisses him on both cheeks. Cheber steps back and says, "I accept."

The parents move aside so that Micah and Nina may sit together.

Now able to see Nina more clearly, everyone sees that she is wearing a long white tunic with a long yellow shawl that drapes from her head to the floor. It is kept in place on her head by a garland of flowers.

Micah wears a long tunic of yellow, matching her long shawl, and a robe of royal blue. He dons a turban of mixed red and blue. His dark beard is trimmed close.

Sett stands. "It is now official. Our children are

betrothed to each other. Today, there is a star in heaven looking down on them and smiling. I anticipate that we will be able to finalize the wedding in a month or so."

The men around the banquet hall pound the table in front of them with their open hands in approval while the women, seated on the other side of the hall from the men, clap their hands and trill their tongues.

The food is served, and Princess Merab, wearing her princess crown, is complimented for the menu, decorations, and background music.

Small talk follows around the hall as everyone waits for the first course.

A scream is heard. It is coming from the kitchen behind the banquet hall. Merab motions for a servant to find out what is happening. The servant returns shortly.

"Madam, it seems a rat has been discovered swimming around in the barrel of wine."

Merab clutches at her throat. Micah and Sett notice. "What's wrong back there?" Sett asks.

"A rat in the wine. What are we going to do?"

Sett motions to the servant.

"Take a cart and rush into town. Buy all the wine you can find. Tell them they will be paid tomorrow."

Micah looks around the banquet room from the elevated head table. He spots him.

Eliphelet salutes Micah.

"Father, why did you have to invite him?"

"Without us, I believe he would be completely friendless. He is a lonely young man."

"He deserves to be. He has been mean all his life. Now he comes to ruin my betrothal banquet?"

"Everyone! Attention, everyone!"

It is Lechy, dressed in his finery.

"I did not invite him," Sett whispers to Micah.

"I would like to offer my blessing on this couple before you today. May they have the kind of happiness I have had. May they have each other as long as I had my wife. May they have as many children as I had. May what happened to my son happen to their son."

The guests look over at Micah and Sett. They are not smiling. There is something wrong with this strange blessing. The guests do not smile, either.

Lechy sweeps his arms across the table in front of him, and his dishes fly to the floor. In a rage, his eyes flashing hatred, he walks out.

Immediately Eliphelet stands and follows Lechy. He does not close the door out of the banquet hall. Everyone remains quiet. They listen. What will they do now?

"You insulted my friends," they hear Eliphelet shout. "Go back in there and apologize. Now!"

"Never! They are not your friends. They are no one's friends, and I hate them for what they did to me."

"What can be so terrible?"

"They killed my son. That's what."

Sett motions for the doors to the courtyard to be closed. He rises. "Everyone, join me in a song that my dear friend, David, composed.

*Come, let us sing for joy to our Lord;*
*Let us shout aloud to the God of our salvation.*
*Let us come before him with thanksgiving*
*and praise him with music and song.*

"Come on, everyone. Sing! Sing louder. This is a joyous occasion. Within the year, I am going to have grandchildren! Sing, everyone! Stand and sing!"

Micah watches as Eliphelet re-enters the banquet hall.

# 32 ~ NEW AND OLD

"He's at it again," Micah tells his father.

"Who? Eliphelet or Lechy?"

"Neither. This time it is Yassib. Or Priest Yassib, as he prefers to be called. He's at it again."

"The last time, he was throwing rocks at us. Now what?" Aunt Merab says. They're in the courtyard.

"Another curse," Micah continues. "When I passed him on the way back from town, he was standing on the border of his property and shouting at our property."

"Was he wearing his fish again?"

"Yes, his monster fish. It's so big, even when he puts his head inside the fish's head, the tail drags behind him."

"I wonder if it made him feel better," Merab says with a wink.

"He was all in a frenzy, as usual. Waving his arms and jumping up and down. He even had a knife in his hand this time."

"He just cannot let it go," Sett says. "My grandfather killing his family was a long time ago. He was too young to even remember it."

"Sweetie. Micah," Nina says, sitting next to Merab and tearing squares of cotton into swaddling bands for the baby. "Would you bring the mid-sized basket in our apartment down for me to put these bands in? Oh, and bring the large basket down. And a pillow. I want to fix it up to put the baby in."

Micah bounds up the steps to their third-floor apartment, two steps at a time. He is grinning.

"Finally, I am going to be a grandfather. I wish Kissara were here. She would love to spoil him."

"Or spoil her," Nina adds.

"Here comes Micah now," Merab says. "He's so proud of you and the baby."

"Ohhh! Ohhh!"

"What is it, Nina?"

"It has started."

"Send for the midwife, someone," Micah calls out.

"I believe that is the father's job," Sett says, smiling.

"Oh, uh. Don't have the baby until I get back," he tells his wife, rushing toward the stables.

"I wouldn't worry about that. Babies take their time, especially first babies. Of course, when you have five like I did, each one comes faster." Merab pauses to think about what she just blurted out and is no longer smiling.

"I am so sorry," Sett says. "I was never around your sons much, but I heard they were good, and everyone liked them."

"Well, Yassib got his revenge for their part in killing his people."

"What color do you think I should cover the pillow with inside the baby's basket?" Nina asks.

Sett and Merab turn their attention back to the living.

"What about the color of trees?" Sett suggests.

"In the summer or autumn?" Aunt Merab asks.

"Their blossoms or their leaves?" Nina asks, giggling.

The following morning, Sett becomes a grandfather to a healthy boy.

"So, what are you going to name him, Son?" Sett asks.

"Pitthon."

"What an amazing name. I like it. I really like it."

"Yes, I want my son to always be harmless and honest."

"With you as his father," Sett says, "your son is going to grow up to be a man of integrity. Good for you. I like that name."

A month later, there is a knock on their gate.

"What brings you here, Eliphelet, the most overlooked youngest son of David in the world?" Sett calls out.

"Hello there, show-off grandson of Saul, who gets all the attention."

The two men laugh.

"I heard about the baby and wanted to see it for myself. Oh, could I take my mule into the stable while I'm here? I forgot to feed him this morning. I hope you don't mind him eating some of your barley."

"Help yourself, Eliphelet."

"Do I hear voices down here?" Micah says from the third-floor balcony. He looks down. "Oh, it's you, Eliphelet."

"Yes, it's me. I've come to see that son of yours. Where is he?"

"Since when are you interested in babies, Eliphelet? He is in our apartment, but we were just preparing to bring him down so he can get some sun."

Eliphelet walks around the courtyard. "You should see the courtyard big brother Solomon is putting in for his palace. Well, actually, he is going to have three or four courtyards. Never does anything halfway. Always has to outdo everyone else."

Nina walks over to her usual bench near the reflecting pool. She sits and calls Eliphelet over.

Eliphelet takes one look at the baby and smiles. "Well, I've got to be going now. My horse should be well fed."

He goes into the stables.

"What are you doing in there?" Micah calls out after a few moments.

"Oh, after that nice meal of barley you gave him, he wanted a drink," Eliphelet says, leading his white mule out of the stables and mounting it.

"See you later," he says as the gate is opened for him.

"Why does he even bother to come here?" Micah asks. "He is so jealous of us, you'd think he would want to stay away."

"Because he wants what we have—real family experiences. He gets that while he is here."

"Then punishes us for it when he leaves," Micah says, finishing his father's sentence.

"He is a sad and complicated young man," Sett says. "Well, I think I'll ride out and inspect the new crops. It's been about a month since they were planted. I'll bet the rain last week helped them significantly."

The stable hand opens the doors to the stables and brings out Sett's mule.

Sett makes his way over to the animal while the stable hand puts the stool in place for his fifty-five-year-old master.

He brings his knees onto the stool, reaches to the top of the saddle, hefts himself up with his strong arms, and gets almost all the way up. Suddenly the saddle is falling and Sett with it. He and the saddle tumble onto the stool, then slide from it down to the blue-and-red tiled pavement.

"Father!" Micah shouts, running toward Sett.

The stable hand glances at Micah with wide eyes then reaches down to take the saddle off Sett.

Micah arrives and begins to pull his father to a sitting position.

"No. Don't do that. Let me lie here a moment, Son. Just let me..." He sighs, leans his head back, and stares at the sky above. Sett takes a deep breath. "Okay, now slowly. Just help me sit up. Then we'll decide what to do from there."

Now in a sitting position, Sett rests again. "Okay, I think I haven't broken any bones. Where are my crutches?"

"It looks like this strap was cut most of the way through," the stable hand says. He hands the crutches to Micah, who helps his father up.

"Well, I don't guess I'll be inspecting the crops today. I think I'll just sit on this bench over here for a while. Then maybe I'll go up and take a little nap."

As Micah helps his father to the nearby bench, tears form in his eyes. "He could have killed you. Doesn't he know that? You're the only friend in the world Eliphelet has, and he treats you like this."

Sett is now seated. "I guess he's just testing to see if I'll reject him as everyone else does."

"Can you blame them? He started harassing you when he was six years old. He's been doing it for nearly twenty years. Father, this has got to stop."

"If my pain eases his pain a little..."

"But it doesn't, Father. He is just plain mean."

"Speak no more of it, Micah. Speak no more of it."

"Well, I guess I'll have to inspect the crops. I can take you up to your room before I go."

"No, I decided I want to sit out here a while."

By now, the stable hand has Micah's mule out and is inspecting the saddle.

Micah mounts and leaves. He is gone an hour.

Sett hears galloping. "Let me in!" Micah shouts, still a little distance away from the outer gate.

The gatekeeper opens it, and Micah rushes in.

"What's wrong?" Sett asks. "Who's after you?"

"I am so mad, I could kill him."

"Kill who?"

"Priest Yassib. Remember how I caught him cursing our land a month ago? Well, he did more than that. He planted weeds among our barley seeds."

"Oh, no," Sett says. "We cannot afford a setback like that."

"Does my father know?" Nina asks.

"Father, you have to stop him. Buy his land so he'll have to go somewhere else. Do something. Get rid of him."

"You know he won't sell his land. Besides, what would we buy it with? Even if we salvage the good growth, we'll destroy some of it getting the weeds out."

"I'm growing sleepy," Nina says. "I'm going back upstairs and take a nap while the baby is sleeping."

Micah and Sett watch the two new additions to their family ascend the steps to the third floor.

"She has been good for you, Micah. You seem to be more content now."

"Yes, she has. I just wish she could tell me what to do to get rid of our enemies."

"Turn them into friends, my son."

"But people don't change. You should know that. Your enemies will never stop being your enemies."

"Eieeieeigh!"

"What was that?" Micah says, his eyes darting up toward the third floor.

He bounds up the steps, three at a time.

"I'm coming. Hold on. I'm coming!"

He enters his apartment and moments later comes out again. He leans over the railing. "No. No. No."

Sett rises and heads toward the stairs. Aunt Merab does too.

"What happened to Nina?" Sett calls up.

"It's not Nina," Micah says.

"The baby?" Merab asks.

"It's our baby. It's Pitthon."

Merab starts up the steps.

"What is it, Son. Tell us."

Micah holds up a dead crow. "This was in the baby's bed."

Sett looks over toward Lechy's supply-room office.

Lechy opens the door, looks out, smiles, then goes back inside.

By now, Merab has disappeared into her apartment, and Micah is back in the courtyard, carrying the dead bird by one wing. The gatekeeper takes the bird from him.

Micah goes to the bench where his father has just reseated himself. He puts his elbows on his knees and lowers his head into his hands.

"Father, I don't think we can take much more of this. They're getting more aggressive all the time."

"Maybe God is testing us."

"Testing us for what? This family has been tested more than any family I have ever known. Your grandfather, father, and all your uncles killed. Then my uncles were executed. You have been unable to put your feet on the ground to walk most of your life. You were made a slave. Mother died."

Micah stands and lifts his face to the sky. "God! What do you want from us? God, answer me!"

"Sit back down, Son."

Micah crumples to the pavement and puts his head on his father's lap.

"Oh, Father. I cannot take anymore."

"But you can. And you will."

"Why does God pick on us? We have always been faithful to him."

"It isn't God, my son. It is Satan. We are strong. He knows that. He keeps trying to break us. Every time these things happen, and we blame God, he laughs at us. Every time Satan convinces someone to hate us, and we don't hate back, Satan cringes. Don't give in to him, Micah. Never give in to him."

Micah looks up at his father but says nothing.

"Stand up now, Son. Stand up. Be a man."

Micah rises and sits next to his father. He wipes his eyes and takes a deep breath.

"That is good, Son. Now smile. There is still much good in the world. Just look over there coming toward you. You are the luckiest man on earth."

By now, Merab, Nina, and the baby are back down in the courtyard.

"It is such a beautiful day, Micah, sweetie," Nina says, approaching her husband. "Let's walk down and show Pitthon to Dipty. I wonder what Dipty will do when he finds out he's an uncle."

Nina giggles and Micah forces a smile. She looks over at her father-in-law, and Sett winks.

"When you get back," Aunt Merab says, "I have a

surprise for everyone."

An hour later, the young family returns.

"Ha, ha, Father. You should have seen Dipti take to our Pitthon. He sat down without being told and jibbered and squawked away. When that didn't bring the results he wanted, he laid down on his side, and looked back at us whining and squeaking."

"Yes," Nina continues. "And it almost sounded like a question. Almost like Dipti was asking if little Pitthon could ride on him and promising to be gentle."

"So, what happened next?" Sett laughs.

"Well, what could we do?" Nina continues. "We climbed over the stone wall into the pasture."

"You didn't!" Merab says, also smiling.

"Yes, we did," Micah says. "I laid little Pitthon right on Dipti."

"He never let go of the baby, you understand," Nina adds.

By now, Sett is laughing so hard, he has to wipe his eyes. "And what did Dipti do?"

"He raised his head and squeaked and squawked like he was singing a lullaby."

"Ha, ha, ha."

"But we were afraid he might decide he was the father and not me, so I took Pitthon off him, and we climbed back on the other side of the wall."

"And, did he object?"

"Of course, he did," Nina says. "He sputtered and honked and lifted his head, and went galloping to the other end of the pasture to pout."

"How funny. I should start a journal called *The Antics of Pitthon*. Or perhaps I should call it, *The Antics of Dipti*," Sett says.

"But there was one person Dipti was no match to. Your mother. Whenever Dipti disobeyed, he had to face the wrath of Kissara, and could she ever hand it out."

"What did she do? Beat him into submission?"

"No. Nothing like that. She made him go all day without a treat, the treat usually being salt. Would he ever honk and snort at her, but it never worked. She stayed firm. And the next time she told Dipti what to do, Dipti obeyed."

"Ha, ha, ha."

"Well, I told everyone I had a surprise for you when you got back."

"Oh, that's right, Aunt Merab," Nina says. "We're ready."

"I don't think I can outdo what Dipti does for you, but, well, here it is."

Merab leans over to a basket at her feet. She holds up a square of linen. Embroidered on it is an image of Kissara.

"Oh, Aunt Merab. It's beautiful. How can we thank you?" Sett says.

"That's not all."

"There's more?"

"Much more." She sets Kissara on the bench beside her and leans over to the basket again. This time, she holds up a square of linen with the image of Sett on it."

"Hey, Father. That's you."

She sets it on the bench next to her and reaches down to the basket again. This time, she holds up an image of Micah. Then Nina. Then baby Pitthon.

Everyone applauds and ahhs and oohs.

"This next one is special for you, Sett. It is of my brother, your father, Jonathan."

She holds it up. Sett reaches over and takes it. He stares at it and tips his head to one side, then the other, then sets it on his knee.

"Father," he tells the image, "I have always tried to make you proud of me. Now I have a whole family for you to be proud of."

"I had a hard time making it different from the one I made of you. You look so much like your father, Sett.

"This last one I made for me," she says, picking up the last linen square from her basket.

She holds it up. The image is of a man wearing a crown. "My father, King Saul."

"Where is the one of you, Aunt Merab?" Micah asks. "You must make one of you."

The others join in. "Yes, one of you."

"Well, maybe," she replies.

Sett leans over and goes through the pile until he comes to the one she had done first. He takes it and puts it on his other knee. As he smiles, tears come to his eyes.

"Kissara, you have a fine family. My dear little one, Kissara. My gold maker, family maker, and dream maker. My dear little one, Kissara."

"We all loved her, Father. She was the dearest woman in the world."

The family smiles and looks through the pile of linen images to admire them again.

Lechy stands outside his office and glares. He walks into the courtyard with a long pole. He pounds on the columns supporting the upper floors encircling the courtyard.

"What are you doing, Lechy?" Micah calls out.

"I'm testing them. If it rains again, we need to make sure the columns do not fall down and collapse the entire palace."

"Well, do it some other time," Micah says. "You're interrupting us."

"Oh, but there are many things wrong with the palace's structure. It is very old. We must be vigilant that it does not fall down around us."

## 33 ~ THE PAST

Sett comes out of the old mostly-unused-since-the-days-of-Saul barracks between the stables and the front watchtower, which he has turned into an office.

"I need to send this message to Princes Ithream and Eliphelet," he tells one of his servants.

"Does it require a reply?"

"Yes, it does. Wait for an answer. It may take them a day or two to decide."

Three days later, the servant arrives back with replies from both men.

From Prince Ithream to Mefiboset, grandson of Saul: Not if Eliphelet goes.

From Eliphelet, the youngest to Mefiboset, the oldest: Not if Ithream goes.

Sett smiles to himself. *Hmmm. Looks like I've got some work to do.*

Sett returns to his spacious barracks-turned-office and comes back out some time later. He calls his servant back. "Take these messages to Ithream and Eliphelet."

"Wait for their replies?"

"Yes, wait."

Three days later, the servant reports in to Sett. "They have refused to answer."

"That's odd. They had their choice of yes or no. How

hard could that be? I just may have to go alone. Well, maybe I will try one more time," Sett hears.

Two days later, Sett hears a knock on the gate.

"Ithream, my old friend. Did you decide to go with me, after all?" Sett asks with a large grin.

"I cannot have you traveling that far by yourself. Of course, I'm going with you."

"I'm planning to leave tomorrow," Sett says. "You can have one of the empty apartments on the third floor for tonight."

"That will be fine."

"What changed your mind, Ithream?"

"What you said about Eliphelet. I had never thought of him being smart, energetic, and innovative. Those aren't bad traits to have on a long journey into the unknown. Just don't tell him I said so."

Just before the evening meal, there is another knock on the gate. The gatekeeper opens it, and Eliphelet stands in his saddle, his arms raised to the heavens, and shouts, "Here we come, wherever it is."

Sett waves Eliphelet in and follows him to the stables.

"I didn't think you were coming. What changed your mind?"

"You said my big half-brother was the youngest of our father's wives' sons, just like I'm the youngest of our father's mistress's sons. He's twenty years older than me, so I never thought of it that way. Maybe he can give me some tips on being a successful youngest."

"Well, come into the dining hall. We are just preparing to eat. You can spend the night in an empty apartment on the third floor."

Morning comes, and the three men are ready.

"Father, I hope you find what you are looking for," Micah says.

"I've been wanting to go there since it all happened. I need to do this. I am fifty-eight years old. This will probably be my last trip."

"Maybe you should have taken Dipti with you," Micah laughs.

"Ha, ha. I think his long neck and hair would get tangled up in..." Sett stops laughing.

"I understand," Micah says. "Don't take any chances. And don't get yourself accused of being a spy."

Micah winks, father and son embrace, and Sett climbs onto his mule.

Micah watches Prince Ithream, and Prince Eliphelet on their royal white mules and his father between them on his black mule go through the outer gate.

On the rump of Ithream's mule is the tent. On the rump of Sett's is barley tied in a tight bundle for the animals, and a large leather pouch for watering them. On the rump of Eliphelet is a large basket of supplies.

"How far are we going?" Eliphelet asks.

"It should take us three to four days. We have strong mules. I think three days," Sett says.

As they make their way east, winding down the steep road toward Jericho, Ithream wags his head back and forth.

"Still singing in your head after all these years, Ithream?"

"Yes, I guess I was born with a thousand songs in my head, and I have spent my whole life trying to get to them all."

"Are you singing in the new temple now?"

"Oh, yes. Years ago, my mother convinced David to let our Kohath clan of Levites be in charge of the music. We were in the tabernacle tent and now in the temple. I love singing there. Our voices just echo off those high walls."

"Eliphelet, what nationality is your mother?" Ithream asks.

"She is Arabian. They live down by a seaport on the Red Sea. Well, they also spend a lot of time in the desert. They're kind of important, but I do not understand how. They don't look important to me."

"How many times have you visited them?"

"A couple when I was a kid. I haven't been interested in going back, and my mother is getting too old to go back.

"Eliphelet, your grandfather, from what I hear, is sheik over one of the largest Bedouin tribes in Arabia," Ithream says, "if not the largest. Do you remember a lot of tents and camels?"

"Well, yeah."

"Then, my information is correct. Be proud."

Eliphelet sits higher in his saddle. "Really? I'm important? Wow!" He raises both arms to the heavens and lifts his face to the sky. "I'm important, everyone. I'm important."

Sett looks over at Ithream. "Thank you," he whispers.

They arrive at Jericho in the Jordan Valley and rent a room for the night for themselves and a stable for their mules. The next morning, they have a hearty meal, ride out the east gate, and cross the Jordan River. Here they turn north.

Just before arriving at the mouth of the Jabbok River, they stop for the second night. They set up their tent, build a fire, feed and water their mules, and eat cheese, dried figs, and barley bread.

"Is that all you brought for food?" Ithream asks. "Well, I have a treat for everyone. I brought a large slab of baklava."

"How did you pack that sticky stuff, so the honey didn't go everywhere?"

Ithream smiles. "I put it in a clay box I'll throw away. Here, have some."

"I don't like sweets that much," Sett says.

"I'll take some," Eliphelet says, shifting around to sit next to his stout older step-brother. "I just may like you after all," he says, licking his fingers.

After eating the full supply of baklava, the men watch the fire in silence.

"Sett, how do you do it?" Eliphelet says.

"Do what?"

"You know. Get around like you do."

"You get used to it. I almost don't remember walking on my feet."

"Your crutches are funny looking with those three feet at the bottom," Eliphelet adds. "But I guess they work. They can stand on their own."

"I noticed you have a kind of rhythm when you walk, well, when you swing your feet between your crutches," Ithream says.

"Yes, I guess I do. I just don't notice."

"You're really strong," Eliphelet says. "I'd like to be as strong as you."

"Well, get yourself a couple of crutches and start swinging your feet," Ithream says, punching his younger step-brother in the shoulder.

The next morning, they gather up their supplies, load them on their mules, and head north again. When they arrive at the Jabbok River, they turn and follow it away from the Jordan heading northeast into the mountains.

At Succoth, they stop just long enough to pick up more fresh fruit and bread to add to their remaining supply of cheese and dried fruit, then continue on.

"We're almost there," Sett says when they arrive at the edge of the Gilead Forest.

They stop, set up their encampment, and eat.

"What are you doing, Sett?" the curious Eliphelet asks. "You do it every night."

"Inspecting my feet. I have to. I have no feeling below my ankles, so I would have no way of knowing if I got a scrape, a cut, a bruise or anything."

"Wouldn't they just heal on their own like ordinary feet?"

"Not really. My feet are not as healthy as yours. Whatever it takes for healing to occur, does not do very well in paralyzed feet. If they get injured in any way, I have to go to bed and stay there until they heal."

"That sounds boring. What do you do in bed day after day?"

"Ha, ha. I think of ways to pester you and convince you that no one loves you because you are David's youngest son."

"That, little brother, is what you get for asking so many questions," Ithream announces, slapping the younger man on the back.

"Oh, yeah? Well, that's what you get for making me eat so much baklava. I was sick all day."

Eliphelet pushes Ithream over.

"You're not getting off that easily, little brother." Ithream grabs Eliphelet, rolls him over, and gets on top of him.

"I can't breathe, you big lug. Let me up."

"Oh, yeah?"

"Yeah. So, let me up before I lose my dinner all over you."

The two half-brothers sit back up while Sett laughs at them.

"I never had a brother," Sett says. "I think it would have been fun. Well, I am through inspecting my feet. I'm ready to go to sleep. How about you two?"

The next morning, they load up their things.

"Are we going on up to Mahanaim now?"

"No. we're not too far from our destination," Sett says. "Perhaps we will on our way back. Today, we go deeper in the Gilead Forest until we come to Ephraim Wood."

"Oh," Ithream says.

The two men stare at each other a moment and become serious. Ithream presses his lips together. "That's where it happened."

"Yes, that's where it happened, and I have never been there to memorialize him. He was a haunted man, but the good side of him deserves it."

"What's in Ephriam Wood?" Eliphelet asks.

"That is where our brother, Absalom, died," Ithream says.

"Way up here?"

"Yes," Ithream replies. "He had amassed an army down in Jerusalem, then had headed north chasing after Father. He picked up more men as he progressed. I guess he decided he would be at an advantage among the trees north of Mahanaim where Father had fled to. But it was his downfall."

"How come I never knew all this?"

"You were only ten at the time, and our father refused to let anyone ever speak of it again."

"I have long wanted to go there," Sett says. "I need to pay my respects to him. Let's mount up."

They make their way deeper into the Forest of Gilead headed north. About noon, they come to a meadow.

"There it is on the other side of the clearing," Ithream says.

They cross the clearing and enter Ephriam Wood. Their mules walk slowly. Sett looks up at the different kinds of trees. He sees a low-hanging oak and stops.

"This could be the one. Let's stop here."

They dismount, and Sett sits on a fallen log.

Ithream looks around and gathers up stones, piling them up under the oak. Eliphelet sees what he is doing, understands, and helps. Sett watches quietly.

"Eliphelet," he says when they have piled up all the rocks they can find, "I have a leather pouch on the back of my mule. Would you bring it to me?"

Still seated, Sett opens the leather pouch. He pulls out a square of linen cloth and a clay tablet. He holds up the square for the others to see.

"That's Absalom's image," Ithream says.

"Yes, I asked my aunt to make it for me. Eliphelet, would you set it in front of the rocks and put these four spikes in each corner to hold it down in the wind?"

The men remain silent as Eliphelet solemnly arranges the image of the fallen brother he hardly remembers. He stands and salutes it.

"Ithream, do you remember this song your father

composed? He wrote it for my grandfather and father. But, perhaps he loved Absalom enough to think it was for him too."

Ithream walks over and picks up the clay tablet. He reads it. "Yes, I remember it."

"Will you substitute my father's name for David's son's name?"

Ithream leans the tablet against the pile of stones, then stands next to it and sings.

> *I am distressed for you, my son, Absalom.*
> *Very pleasant have you been unto me:*
> *Your love to me was wonderful,*
> *How the mighty has fallen.*

Ithream sits next to Sett. They weep together. Eliphelet sits on the ground next to the memorial and watches.

A drop of rain. Then another.

"Hey, let's get out of here," Eliphelet says, "before we get stuck in the mud."

The three mount their mules and head back toward the clearing. The rain comes down harder. They gallop through the meadow and enter the larger Forest of Gilead.

Thunder now. The horses slow down to maintain their footing and keep from running into low-hanging branches.

Still, the rain comes. Heaver now. Harder to see. Keep going. Keep going.

Then it stops—the rain. Nothing else.

The thunder now closer. It booms and explodes around them. The eyes of the mules grow large and dart everywhere. The men struggle to keep their mounts from panicking.

Now lightening. Flashing and crashing. Behind them. In front of them. Cracking. Ripping through the sky and the trees below.

The wind. Rushing, swirling, howling, screaming.

Fierce. Unrelenting.

They smell smoke.

They know.

Keep moving. Escape. The thunder. The lightening. The wind. The treacherous fire.

The mules stop in their tracks, not knowing where to go. They smell the smoke. They know. They rise up on their hind legs in hopes of trampling what they fear. Their riders hang on to them. They pat them on the neck, but the mules cannot feel it for the pelts of dirt and loose branches swirling at them.

They turn in circles.

"It's over there!" Eliphelet shouts.

The men turn their mules in the opposite direction, disoriented now and hoping they are not going deeper into the forest.

Still, the thunder, the lightning, the fire.

Hurry, but don't hurry. Run, but don't run. Escape. Escape.

They see a clearing ahead and hope they have not run in circles, and it is not the one they had just come from. They see the Yarmuk River ahead. The mules break free of the forest and gallop toward the river where the men finally manage to bring them to a halt.

Dismounting, they hang on to their mules' reins and turn in the direction from whence they had just come. They watch. Helplessly they watch. The fire.

The circling wind continues relentlessly, pushing and spreading the fire in every direction. The flames rise above the forest in victory.

Still, the men watch in complete helplessness.

The lightening eases. The thunder more distant.

After a while, they hear only an occasional rumble and see an isolated flash in the distant black clouds.

It is almost quiet now. Everything now gone. Lightening gone. The thunder gone. The wind gone.

The fire, not so. The fire still raging and still devouring.

Roaring and attacking and eating alive.

The rain returns as a light shower from the few wispy clouds hanging back. It gently chides the flames. "Slow down, now," the rain says. "Don't hurry so. Don't be so angry. Slow down."

Now, just black smoke. Black smoke drifting to the sky above and beyond.

"No!" Eliphelet shouts. "No!"

He raises a fist above his head. "Everything I do is destroyed. Now, this. No!"

Eliphelet digs his knees into the side of his mule and gallops toward the forest that is no more. Galloping and shouting and cursing. His fist still in the air.

"No!"

He pulls back tight on the reins, and his mule slides to a stop.

Eliphelet slips off his mount and picks up stones. He throws them at the forest that was and the monument to his brother that is no more. Bending. Picking up. Cursing. Throwing.

"Take that. And that!"

Up and down in front of the blackened trees.

"God, why? Why do you destroy everything I try to do? I hate you, God."

He whistles for his mule, and it comes galloping to him. Eliphelet races toward Sett and Ithream. He pulls back hard on the reins and faces Sett.

"I hate you, Sett. You tricked me. I hate you and Ithream and Absalom and my father and my mother. I hate God."

With that, Eliphelet takes off galloping west along the Yarmuk River, his hair and robe flying behind him.

Sett tries in vain to catch up with him but finally stops.

"I cannot help him anymore," he tells Ithream when he arrives at his side.

By evening the two older men are back in Succoth.

They rent a room at an inn and spend the night.

"Did you see a young man on a white mule come through here?"

"No, we haven't."

The next day they resume their return journey home. As they do, they look for signs that Elipelet has stopped and camped. There are no such signs.

They work their way farther south along the Jordan, and camp the second night.

"Those trees. All destroyed," Sett says. "Do you think anyone will ever replant them?"

"I don't know," Ithream replies.

Just before dark ten days after having left, Sett and Eliphelet arrive at Saul's palace in Gibeon.

They do not smile. And they are tired.

"Oh, Father," Nina tells Sett when they bring their mules into the courtyard. "Something terrible has happened."

# 34 ~ BLESSINGS

"**I**s it Micah? The baby? Aunt Merab?"

"No. Follow me."

Sett hands the reins to his stable hand, slides off his mule, and follows Nina.

She arrives at the bottom of the steps leading to his apartment on the second floor behind the throne room. "The damage from the rain is worse in your apartment."

Sett presses his lips together and grits his teeth. He looks up the long stairway. *Do I want to know? Do I really want to know?*

Sett is slow to make his way up to the door he dreads going through. But he is tired. Rest is on the other side of the door. What else?

He arrives at the top of the steps. He takes a deep breath. He presses his lips harder together. He lowers his brows, and swings open the door.

By now, it is nearly dark, and he cannot see inside. Nina is right behind him with a lamp. She scoots around Sett and enters his apartment before him. She uses her lamp to light a few others, then stands in the middle of the floor watching her father-in-law.

"Over by that outside wall," she whispers.

Sett makes his way in that direction, then stops. He lowers himself to the floor and stares at the baskets he had stored Kissara's clothing in.

He leans over, picks up his wife's favorite tunic, and holds it up. The dirty water drips from it. No longer is it the lively yellow it had always been. He sets it aside with as much care as if he were setting it out for her to wear the next day.

"I will leave you now," Nina says. He does not hear the soft closing of his door behind her.

He picks up the red-and-blue robe she always wore with it. Again, the dirty water. The colors have run together. *Oh, she cannot wear that tomorrow. She must select something else.*

One by one, he picks up the clothes he had stored in the basket with such tenderness six years earlier and lays them out on the floor to dry.

He makes his way over to the corner of the same wall. There he sits on a straw mat on which is a smaller basket. He opens it, and with misty eyes, he touches Kissara's embroidery work. Again, he takes out one piece, lets some of the dirty water drain from it, and lays it on the mat.

There is the one she did of his likeness. There is the one of Micah when he was twelve. This one is of Uncle Mefiboset. This one of Queen Mother Ahinoam. Some have flowers on them. He smiles when he sees the one of her mother and one of her father.

When he is through laying everything out, he moves over to the end of his bed and looks at them until the wicks in the lamps burn out.

Sett wakens to knocking on his door.

"Come in," he says, rousing himself.

It is Lechy.

"I am sorry, Sett, but the rain came down too hard. I knew there were cracks in the walls, as you recall, and tried to find and patch them all. But the rain was too strong for the patches. Too bad, you lost everything that ever belonged to the one you loved."

With that, Lechy leaves.

Sett swings around to sit on the side of the bed, and realizes he had forgotten to check his feet the night before.

There is another knock on the door. Micah enters and looks around at his mother's things.

"He did it on purpose, you know. There were no cracks in these walls. He is the one who put them there."

"Come help me with my feet, Son."

Micah sits on a low stool by his father's bed and looks over his feet. "Father, you have your proof now. Go to King Solomon and have him fired. We have tolerated him..."

"Say no more, Son. It will not bring back your mother's things. He is feeling a pain we can only imagine. I must try harder to find out if his son is really dead."

"After all these years? I was ten when it happened, and I'm thirty-four now. There is no way to find out. Why do you do these things, Father?"

"Can we talk of something else?"

Micah brightens. "Oh, I meant to tell you. While you were gone, Nina brought another grandson for you into the world. We named him Melech."

"That is wonderful, Son. Your mother and I are so proud of you. Bring the babe to me as soon as I go downstairs."

They are quiet a moment.

"I think I would like to move down to the old barracks by the other front tower. You know, next to the carriage house."

"Well, it's true I have been worried about you making this long climb up the stairs. You fell on them once and..."

"Is Prince Ithream up?"

"Yes. He has already left for Jerusalem. He said he had a bitter young man to try to salvage. Do you know what he was talking about?"

"Yes. Help me get dressed. After I eat a little, I would like you to get several of the servants to move my things down to my new apartment."

"What should I do about Mother's things?"

"Leave them here."

Sett makes his way down to the courtyard and is served fresh grapes, figs, and cheese while he sits on his bench near the reflecting pool. Nina brings his new grandson to him for his blessings.

A knock on the outer gate. Shortly, a servant approaches. "Someone delivered a letter to you, sire."

Sett takes the scroll and reads it.

Greetings to the only survivor of the innocent Gibeonite family and the one who hates you, Priest Yassib.

It has come to my attention you have been spying on me. Did you think your visit to Ebla, the city dedicated to the great god Dagon, father of Baal, would go unnoticed?

I have proof you were there just before Kissara died. Too bad about Kissara. At least now you know what it is like to lose someone in your family.

Sett puts the scroll down and works his way around the courtyard. He stops and looks up at the door to the apartment he had shared with the love of his very soul and being. The door that never opens anymore. His brows lower, and his lips tremble. He goes back over to the bench and the scroll.

I understand you have had problems with your crops and even your palace. Too bad. Too bad, you have not been punished with more calamities. You deserve them all.

May Dagon, god of all that is right and good, curse you. May he bow your old head in tragedy after tragedy until you think you can take no more. Then, may Dagon send you more.

I will break you someday, Mefiboset. Mark my words. I will break you.

Sett lays the scroll on the bench beside him and stares at it. After a while, he tosses it in the reflecting pool, then watches as the servants work to get his large king's bed into the barracks, now his new apartment.

"I think I will go for a short ride," he tells the stable hand. "No, not my mule. I am kind of tired. Would you get out one of the small chariots for me?"

Sett settles himself on a bench in the chariot and guides the horse out the front gate. He goes through his property all the way to the back where it adjoins Yassib's.

He stops and stares at Yassib's property a long time. "Lord God, help him let go of Dagon and worship you. But how?"

Now back at the palace, he calls one of the servants over. "Go to my office and bring me a small scroll, and whatever else I will need to write a letter."

Sett returns to his favorite bench and waits. Shortly, the servant returns with his writing supplies and a small table.

He writes his reply to Yassib with a fine hand.

From your neighbor, Mefiboset, a mere man, to Yassib, my friend from long ago.

> The LORD Jehovah bless you
> and hold you.
> the LORD Jehovah make his face shine on you
> and be kind to you.
> the LORD Jehovah turn his face toward you
> and give you peace.

He seals it with the seal of the house of Kish and Saul and calls his waiting servant over.

"Will you please deliver this to our neighbor, Yassib?"

A week goes by, and Sett has heard nothing from his neighbor.

Life goes on. Weeks. Months. More than a year. His third grandson, Tarea, is born. Then Sett celebrates his fifty-ninth birthday.

"It seems someone has sent you a birthday greeting," the servant says, handing a scroll to Sett sitting by the reflecting pool.

To my neighbor, Mefiboset, grandson of the cruelest king known to history. From Yassib, who will never tire of hating you and all you stand for.

Today is the fifty-fourth birthday of your grandfather's well-deserved death. I rejoiced on the day it happened. All of Gibeon rejoiced. Every Gibeonite family rejoiced, for none had been left untouched by the vengeful, vow-breaking, bloody sword of King Saul.

The high priest of Dagon was there the day Saul was stricken down and beheaded. He was there the day they hung his body on the wall of the temple to our great Dagon. He never stopped rejoicing over our great victory that day.

We have since then been blessed by our great God Dagon, while your silly invisible God gets a puny temple built on top of a hill too high for anyone to climb to.

Cursed be you, your family, and that ridiculous god of yours. Dagon curses you all.

Sett notices the handwriting is larger than his previous message a year earlier. He puts the scroll down on the bench next to him, and, as he had done before, he calls to his servant.

"Get my chariot ready for me. I am going for a little ride."

And, as the year before, he rides through his property to the border with Yassib's property. He stops and stares a long time at the land of his neighbor.

"Lord God of heaven and earth. Bring your blessing to this man who is hurting beyond words."

Sett returns to the palace and to his bench by the reflecting pool. A pillow has been placed on it for ease of sitting with old bones.

He sits and watches the scroll a while, then throws it into the pool. He watches it a while, then calls to a servant. "Please bring out to me a small scroll and all the supplies I will need."

He picks up his pen to write once again with his fine hand.

May the Lord God, Jehovah, give you increase,
May you be blessed by the Lord God, Jehovah,
Maker of heaven and earth.
The heavens are the heavens of Jehovah.
But the earth He has given to us.

He seals it with the seal of the house of Kish and Saul. Once again, as he had the previous year, he asks that a servant deliver the message to neighbor, Yassib.

Another year goes by. Aunt Merab dies—the last of King Saul's children and sister of Jonathan. Princess Merab was ninety years old and the last of that generation.

They bury her in the tomb with her parents and grandparents, her five sons sacrificed to the Gibeonites and the rest of her family.

Sett wonders if he will ever live to be that old. *Kissara, I want to see you again. I do not want to live that long.*

Time goes by, and as is his custom, he is on his bench in the red-and-blue tiled courtyard with the cracking columns surrounding it. "What's that smoke? Does anyone smell smoke? Check the upstairs apartments."

One of the servants runs up to the northwest tower and looks out.

"It's your fields, sire!" he calls down.

The gates of the palace are shoved open. Micah orders all the servants to grab shovels from the ground floor of the guard towers and follow him. He mounts his mule barebacked and gallops toward the assaulted field. Sett follows him in a chariot.

When the servants reach the outer edge of the field, they begin digging a trench. Micah joins them. Sett watches as frantically they dig while the flames bear down on them.

Dig faster.

Deeper.

Wider.

Stay ahead of the flames.

Stop the flames.

Don't let the smoke choke you. Keep digging despite everything. Stop the flames. Save the crops.

After two hours, they stop. The flames have gone out for lack of fuel.

Part of the field is saved. Not all. "It is not too late to replant," Sett tells the overseer of the farmhands, Nina's father.

Sett looks around for his enemies but does not see

them.

Exhausted, Micah returns to the palace with his father.

A year after, there is another addition to the descendants of Saul, Jonathan, and Mefiboset.

"You have another grandson, Father. We named him Ahaz."

"I am pleased. We are finally using the children's apartments on the third floor again. The palace is filled with the voices of happy children once more. That is good, Son. That is good."

Then comes the letter on Sett's sixty-first birthday.

To the infamous grandson of the more infamous King Saul, disgrace of Israel and loathsome to all of Canaan. Greetings on yet another birthday from your neighbor who has tolerated you for too many years.

Did you like the fire? I am getting a little old for such things, so got help from a young man, actually one of the sons of former King David. He did well, don't you think?

May you burn someday in the underworld. May your palace burn and everything and everyone in it. You are the enemy of all that is right and good that comes forth from the great god, Dagon. May Dagon be praised now and forever. Amen.

Sett stares at the scroll, noticing how large the handwriting has become.

"Poor man. He must be losing his sight," he tells whoever is in hearing distance.

Once again, Sett works his way around the red-and-blue tiled courtyard thinking.

Ten-year-old Pitthon nearly runs into his grandfather leading in a race with his brother, Melech, two years younger than him.

"Oh, excuse me, Grandfather," Pitthon says, looking behind him. "You cannot catch me," he shouts in a sing-song tone to his little brother.

"Stop right there, young man," Sett says. "Go into my

apartment and bring out a small scroll and everything I need to write a letter."

A few moments later, Pitthon comes out, assisted by brother Melech carrying a small table. They set it in front of their grandfather, hitting his knees.

"Thank you. Now for my writing supplies," Sett says.

Moments later, he is writing. As always, it is a brief reply.

> The earth has yielded its produce;
> God, Jehovah, blesses us.
> God, Jehovah, blesses us,
> That all people of the earth
> may be amazed by Him

Sett seals it with the seal of Kish and Saul, then orders his chariot be brought out.

He makes his way through his farmland, then onto Yassib's land. Yassib is not there though his farmhands are. Sett had not really expected him to be.

Sett progresses into the city of Gibeon and finds Yassib's house. He does not leave his chariot. Instead, he draws it close to Yassib's gate, leans over, and knocks on it. A servant opens the gate.

"Sir, would you kindly give this to your master, Priest Yassib?"

"And may I tell him who delivered it?"

"His neighbor. He will know."

With that, Sett turns his chariot around and rides back up the hill toward his palace. When he arrives at the border of Yassib's property and his own, he stops. He faces Yassib's side.

"Lord God, Jehovah, the only God that exists, bless this man in a special way. Ease his broken heart and bring him to you."

Sett heads back to the palace.

His chariot back in place, he goes over to his office on the opposite side of the courtyard from his downstairs apartment.

Micah stops by Sett's office. "We will be eating soon. I promise to make the boys stay quiet during the meal."

"How old are you now, Micah?"

"I'm forty-two. Why?"

"I do not know how many more years I will have. I need to see some more forests before they disappear. I think I'll take a ship up to see the Forests of Lebanon."

"Father, you're not serious. You are sixty-five years old."

Sett pulls on his gray beard. "So?"

# 35 ~ CEDARS

"*O*kay, I have secured passage aboard the corn ship *Amir*," Sett tells Micah.

"No, Father. This is a big mistake. You are not as strong as you used to be. You scrape your feet more than you used to, and you heal slower."

"You are just jealous I am not taking you along," Sett says with a large grin.

Sett is back at his favorite bench by the reflecting pool.

"That's not it. You just cannot visit all the forests in the world."

"Who said so?"

"Father, quit joking with me. I am serious."

"I'm serious also. I am going."

"Not alone."

"Yes, alone."

"Is there any chance I can talk you out of it?"

"None at all."

Two days later, early in the morning, Sett sits on his courtyard bench, watching the servants load his baggage into the chariot.

"Can I go with you, Grandfather?" eight-year-old Melech asks.

"Of course, you can't," Pitthon tells his younger brother. "He is going on an important trip to see important people, and kids can't go see important people."

"Are you, Grandfather? Are you going to see important

people?”

"Yes. I hope to have an audience with Hiram, King of Tyre and all of Lebanon. And I hope he will take me on a tour of his cedar forest."

"Wow. You're going to see a king?"

"We used to be a king," Pitthon says. "Isn't that so, Grandfather?"

"Indeed, it is. Your great-great-grandfather, Saul, was the king of Israel. In fact, his throne room is right here in this very palace."

"It is? I never knew that."

"Perhaps I will show it to you when I get back."

"Well, hug your grandfather goodbye," Nina says.

Pitthon and Melech, already at his knee, give him tight hugs and kiss him on each cheek. Six-year-old Tarea is next. Sett hugs and kisses them all back.

And finally, there is four-year-old Ahaz who Sett takes to his lap. "Are you going to be a good boy while I am gone?"

"Uh-huh."

The two embrace.

Everyone backs out of the way while Sett lifts himself up onto his three-footed crutches, and makes his way to the chariot. He seats himself. Nina reaches over and embraces him. Then Micah.

"Father, I wish you wouldn't go. I have a bad feeling about it."

"You just put that worrying side of you away, Son. I am going to be fine. Do not weep. Be happy for me."

The gates out of the palace swing wide, Sett clicks his tongue, and the horse heads out the gate. They progress through the family farmland, down the hill that is the city of Gibeon, and west toward the coast of the Great Sea.

Now in the plain, he eases up on the reins to let the horse go at its own pace. Three hours later, Sett arrives in the city of Ashdod.

"Sir," he asks one of the city guards. "Could you tell me where the great temple to Dagon is?"

After being given directions, he works his way to the highest part of the city. *That's where it happened.*

He stops, ties his horse to a ring in the wall, and makes his way to the threshold.

"You cannot come in here. You are not a priest. Back away from the threshold. No one is allowed to step on it."

"That's okay," Sett says. "I just wanted to take a quick look. Dagon ended up falling down and bowing to the Ark of Jehovah here, didn't he?"

Sett grins and quickly pivots to head back to his chariot, knowing he has insulted the priests and their Dagon. *Wait until they tell Yassib about this,* he thinks, still grinning.

Back in his chariot, he goes down the sacred hill, through the city, and to some stables.

"Here is enough money for a week. I do not believe I will be gone longer than that. Someone will deliver my horse and chariot to you as soon as I find my ship."

Sett progresses out of the city and on down to the harbor. He guides his chariot slowly down the pier, reading the names of the ships until he comes to the *Amir*. He hails a sailor walking back in the direction of the city.

"Sir, I would like to pay you to take my horse and chariot to the stables just inside the west gate of the city. You will receive this amount again when you deliver them."

The arrangements are made, and the sailor takes Sett's things out of the chariot. Sett waits until another sailor passes him on the busy dock.

"Sir, here is a copper coin if you will take my baggage on board my ship for me."

"I will for two copper coins."

"That is fine."

Sett makes his way to the gangplank of the ship and looks up, analyzing how he will have to angle his body in order to stay upright on the precarious slanted plank. As he does, an officer calls down to him.

"You're not coming on board this ship if that's what

you're thinking."

"Sir, I have purchased passage."

"You still cannot come on board. You will injure yourself and probably everyone around you. The ship rocks too much, and you have no feet."

"Sir, I have feet."

"You know what I mean. You cannot come on board," the officer says.

"I tell you what I will do. I will make you a wager. If I can make it up your gangplank without falling into the sea, you have to take me on as a passenger, and I will personally pay you an extra bronze coin. If I fail and do fall into the sea, you get to laugh at me. Fair enough?"

"Ha, ha. This is going to be fun. Come on. Hey, men. Come watch this."

Sett figures out the sway of the ship on the waves, the angle of the gangplank, and the number of steps his crutches will have to take. He wags his head at the sailors on deck with a grin and commences.

"One. Two. Three. Four. Five. Well, here I am, sir, and I am afraid I have disappointed you," he says to the officer. "Would you like me to go down and do it again?"

The officer shakes his head, rolls his eyes, and holds out his hand. "That will be two bronze coins."

"Well, that is twice as much as I offered you, but I am in a good mood. You may have your two bronze coins."

Sett is nudged by the sailor with his baggage and moves out of the way. He looks at the officer.

"Would it be all right to settle on the deck in front of the bridge?"

"Do what you want."

Sett goes over to the bridge, pays the sailor his two copper coins, takes a quick look back at the city, then north up the coast, and squats next to his baggage.

A bell is rung, and they set sail.

Sometimes he sings. Sometimes he reads his scroll of David's psalms. Sometimes he sleeps. Sometimes he dreams of his Kissara.

*Oh, my darling. I wish you could be on this trip with me. We did so many wonderful things together. Well, and sometimes not so wonderful. But you stuck with me all those years. How I miss you, my little one.*

The ship docks at Tyre the following day.

"Are you sure this is where you want to go?" the same officer asks him.

"Well, yes. I am going to meet King Hiram, and he is going to take me on a tour of his cedar forest."

The officer grins and shakes his head. "Good luck," he says in a sing-song tone and a wink.

Sett makes his way down to the pier and looks around for someone he can hire to take him to the palace of King Hiram. Shortly he sees a man with a small cart.

"Excuse me, sir," he calls out.

The man comes over, they decide on a fare, and Sett climbs onto the cart with his baggage.

*I wonder why he is grinning. The ship's officer did the same thing.*

They arrive at the front gate of the palace, and Sett climbs off. He goes closer to the gate.

"Excuse me," he tells one of the guards. "I am wondering what it would take to have an audience with King Hiram."

None of the guards reply. Sett repeats himself. They still do not reply.

"I am not expecting to be admitted today. But if I could have some idea. I am, by the way, the grandson of the great King Saul of Israel."

Immediately the guards cross spears in front of Sett.

"Step back," one of them says.

Sett shifts back.

"Wait here," the guard says, then disappears through the door leading into the watchtower. A few moments later, he returns through the main gate with two other guards.

"You are under arrest."

"For what? Saul is no longer the king," Sett says. "In fact, he is long dead. I am not a spy."

"Follow me."

Sett follows the guard with the two others on each side of him. They go through a door into a lower part of the palace. He sees an impending predicament.

"No. Wait. All I came for is to admire your king and your cedar forests."

They lead Sett through a second door with bars. He is taken down a corridor and into a room with more bars. The gate clangs shut.

"Wait!" Sett calls out. "King Solomon. He is my friend. Contact King Solomon. Or even Prince Ithream. They will speak on my behalf."

He hears the outer door slam. It is quiet. He looks around, though he cannot see much in the dark. His senses are assaulted by the stench only a dungeon can have.

*Kissara, it isn't as bad this time. At least he didn't threaten to cut off my feet. Lord God, be my guardian, my keeper, my savior. And be with my family back in Gibeon. Is my time to rejoin Kissara now?*

He falls asleep. The only way he can now tell whether it is day or night is when the outer door is opened, and a guard enters or exists.

The days go by. Sett wishes he has his scroll of David's psalms, and wonders what happened to his baggage. He sings sometimes. He sleeps sometimes. He dreams of Kissara sometimes and has her back for a while.

*We had a good time in this last dream, didn't we Kissara? We will again soon, my little one.*

He worries about his feet. He keeps his high boots on, hoping they will keep them protected from the poison air. He has his crutches with him and sometimes walks in circles in his cell a while, trying to keep the strength in his arms.

Sometimes he thinks it is night, and he imagines the stars overhead, though he cannot see them. He remembers once again her last words to him:

"Remember the stars. Even when you cannot see them, they are there."

*And you are there among them, the brightest star of them all, my little one.*

Days merge into nothingness. Is it dark or light out? Is it rainy or sunny? Is the wind blowing, or is it calm?

*What is Micah doing today? And Nina? And my four energetic grandchildren? Oh, Kissara, you would love them so. And they would love you.*

The outer door opens, and a guard unlocks Sett's cell. *Will it be my doom?*

Taking up his crutches, he makes his way out of the dungeon, and through a different door than he had come in through. From there, he is taken to an ornate room, though definitely not the throne room. It has no other doors.

"King Solomon sent word you are harmless," the senior guard says, sitting behind a table. "So, what are you doing here?"

"I was hoping to meet King Hiram, and for him to take me on a short tour of your famous cedar forest."

The senior guard lowers his head and shakes it. When he raises it again, he is laughing. "You want the king of all of Lebanon to take you on a hike? Not only take you on a hike but allow you onto his royal barge to cross over to the mainland, then cross the plain, then climb the mountains so you can see our cedar forest? Ha, ha, ha."

"What do you mean, barge?"

"Sir, the city of Tyre is an island."

"It is?"

"And the trees aren't here. You have to go to the other side of Lebanon, then climb the Lebanon Mountains to get to them. Ha, ha, ha."

"Oh, my. I am in a predicament. What do you suggest I do? I do not know anyone in Lebanon. I do on the other side of your mountains—the King of Geshr in Bashan, but..."

"Did I hear King Talmai's name mentioned?"

The senior guard immediately rises, salutes, then bows. "Your Majesty."

The king is tall and has wavy brown hair to his shoulders and a short straight beard with some gray mingled with it. His eyes are close together, his brows heavy, and his nose long and broad.

Sett pivots on his crutches and immediately falls to the marble floor, his head all the way prostrate.

"Rise and tell me about ole King Talmai. I haven't seen him in years. Is he still alive?"

"I do not know, Your Majesty. But I have stayed with him and Queen Nura several times in his palace."

"So has young Solomon sent you to get more of my trees? You know, he ran out of money and had to pay me with five cities in Galilee. They could hardly be called cities."

"Did you see the Sea of Galilee? It is beautiful. Right on the other side of it is King Talmai's kingdom."

"I see. So, did he or didn't he?"

"Oh, King Solomon? No, he did not send me. I would never ask you to cut your beautiful cedars for me. I came to enjoy them. That is all I want to do. Spend a day roaming among them, then go home."

"I see. And home is the palace of King Saul, who was your grandfather."

"Yes, Your Majesty. Well, I do want to ask you for one thing."

"Everyone does."

"Do not cut any more of your beautiful cedars. If you do, plant more in their place. Let your forests still be there for our grandchildren to enjoy."

"Grandson of King Saul, you are a rare one. I think I would have enjoyed you as a friend. But I cannot right now. I tell you what I will do. Since I always liked King Talmai and he never asked me for anything, and you are or were his friend, I will loan you a chariot and horse to go up into the mountains to see our trees. Have it back here in three days, so I won't send my army after you."

"Yes, Your Majesty. Thank you, Your Majesty. Uh, and, uh…"

"Of course, you need a way to get to the mainland. Senior guard, etch a tile for his fare over to the mainland, and another for the chariot. Oh, and another one for a bath and clean clothes. You smell terrible."

"Yes, Your Majesty."

"Well, it was good meeting you." King Hiram begins to leave but turns back. "By the way, what happened to your feet? They look very painful."

"There was an accident on the day my grandfather and father were felled in battle. And, no, they are not painful. I long ago learned to adjust."

"Well, good luck."

The king leaves. The senior guard sits back down, and Sett waits for him. Shortly he hands Sett three clay tiles with instructions on them. They are linked together by a small rope through the holes in their tops.

Sett leaves and decides to go down to the docks since the palace is not as far from the water as he had thought.

He crosses over onto the mainland on a small boat and finds his chariot.

"Just keep going east. You cannot miss them. They stretch for over a hundred miles," he is told.

While still in the foothills, Sett spends the night in his chariot. The next morning, he climbs higher and higher into the mountains. There is still some snow on the ground, though the air is warm enough.

Sett finally stops. He ties the reins of his horse to one of the gigantic trees and slowly makes his way into the deep but not gloomy shadows. He lies on his back among the fallen branches and looks up through the tops of the trees to the blue sky far above.

*Oh, Kissara. They are so beautiful. I do not believe, in all our travels, I have seen such magnificent trees. You would have loved them.*

As he lies there on the soft carpet of the forest, the

breeze blows through his hair, the same breeze that whispers through the scented branches high above and perfumes his thoughts. Tears come to his eyes.

*Some days I can hardly stand it without you.*

He sighs, then smiles.

*Thank God you went before me. I would have hated to put you through this pain. I shall bear the pain for you.*

He sits up. He hums. He whispers a song.

*Kissara is my shining star*
*With purity of life.*

He wipes a tear. His voice trembles.

*She is never very far—*
*Kissara, my loving wife.*

Sett sits up, reaches all around him, and scoops his hands full of needles. He ties a pocket in the bottom of his robe and puts them in it. He smells them and smiles a sad smile.

*This is just for you and me. We will smell their aromatic richness together when we are alone, just you and me next time.*

Another sigh. It is time to leave. Sett stands and goes to his chariot. He looks one last time up into the towering branches, turns the chariot around, and descends the mountain.

The following morning he is again on board the *Amir* corn ship now on its way back south.

"We were ordered to wait for you," the officer says. "Just how important are you? You're definitely not a king."

Sett smiles.

The officer scratches his head and watches Sett amble away.

"Do you have a weapon on you?" he calls after him. "The pirates are out strong right now."

Sett does not reply. He returns to his spot at the foot of the captain's bridge. Once again, as the ship floats southward on the waves, he sits and watches the sailors at their work, or sings a song, or dreams. Once again sometimes—just sometimes—Sett dreams of Kissara and they are together once more.

# 36 ~ LAMENTATIONS

"Open up! Open up!"

Sett has been home two years. He has resumed sitting on his favorite pillowed bench by the reflecting pool dreaming of days gone by with his Kissara. His dreams are interrupted by a strange voice.

"Hurry. It's Micah. Open up!" the strange voice calls out through the gate.

The gatekeeper rushes to the gate and opens it.

Two strangers hurry in with Micah between them hopping on one foot.

"What happened?" Nina says, rushing down the steps from their apartment, now the king's apartment on the second floor.

By now, Sett is up from his bench.

"In here," he calls out, heading for his bedroom in the old, unused barracks.

"What happened?"

The children hear the commotion and come running.

"Stay out of the way, children," Nina exhorts as she rushes into Sett's bedroom behind the strangers and her husband.

"What happened?"

They lay Micah down on his father's bed. He groans.

"His leg has been broken," one of the strangers says. "Oh, my name is Benjamin."

"And I am Gidal. This man was just walking down the street near our booth when another man rolled a barrel out in front of him. He, of course, tripped, and when he fell— well, you see what it did."

"We hired a young man to watch our pottery shop a while, got this man on our cart, and brought him home."

Micah's eyes squint, and he involuntarily groans.

"Oh, my husband. You poor man," Nina says, pulling up Micah's long tunic far enough to see the damage. She looks over at Sett.

"No one here is strong enough to push the bone back in place. And what if we try anyway and do it wrong?"

Sett's thoughts go back to a vague distant memory. *What if we try anyway and do it wrong?* It bounces around his mind like a ball charging from wall to wall, not caring what it hits.

"Here is some money," Sett says, reaching into the pouch he always has tied to his belt. "This is for bringing him home for us. This is for you to find a physician for him. I think Prince Ithream, King Solomon's half-brother, can help you. Do you know where Prince Ithream lives?"

"Well, we know the neighborhood where the princes live. We will find him."

Micah reaches down to hold his leg near the wound as though comforting it. He breathes in between clenched teeth.

Nina turns to Pitthon, now twelve years old. "Run to the kitchen and ask the cook to bring some alangium tea. There should be some leaves in the basket on a shelf in the back corner. Hurry. Your father is in pain."

"Again, thank you for coming," Sett says.

"Melech," Nina says to her ten-year-old son, "run to the supply room behind Lechy's office and get some swaddling bands. They should be in the corner where I have baby things. Hurry now."

Micah leans back on his pillow, teeth still clenched, eyes pinched together.

The two potters leave. Nina pulls around a bench for her and Sett to sit on next to the bed.

"I'll bind it shortly, and we should have some pain tea for you, my darling. Then you can sleep until the physician arrives."

Micah turns his head so he can see his father better. "Father, while I'm awake, I need to tell you what happened."

"It can wait, Son," Sett says, putting Micah's hand in his.

"I want to tell you. I need to tell you. Father, he is at it again."

"Who? Lechy? Yassib?"

"No," Micah grunts. "Eliphelet. For over twenty-five years, he has carried his grudge at being the youngest and," he takes a quick intake of air to swallow a sharp stab of pain, "most overlooked and under-loved son of David."

"I know. We have tried to be patient."

"Too patient." Micah reaches down to grasp his leg again, then lies back. "After I tripped, he immediately said he was sorry—which he wasn't—and tried to help me up."

Micah raises himself on his elbows, cringes, and lays his head back down.

"Of course, it made matters worse—and he knew it would."

"Quit trying to talk, Son."

"Once he got me on my feet, my bone cracked in two."

"Here. The tea has arrived. Drink it," Nina says.

Micah takes a few sips, then a deep breath, and continues.

"Then, while I'm on the ground in pain, he complains his grandfather in Arabia died and willed a worthless piece of land to him in the middle of the desert."

"Why would he be telling you that right after breaking your leg?" Nina asks, brushing the hair out of his forehead and testing him for fever.

Micah grits his teeth again and fights back tears of pain. "He actually says I deserve what I got because I will inherit a palace and he a desert."

"What did he want you to do about it?" Nina asks. "Here. Drink the rest of this tea."

"Stop talking now, Son. We're going to leave you alone so you can sleep until the physician arrives," Sett says.

"Then we'll get you moved back up to our apartment," Nina says.

It is a week later.

"Hey, great one who everyone bows and scrapes to even though you could never make it as king!" they hear from the other side of the gate.

The gatekeeper looks over at Sett.

"Let him in."

The gate is opened, and Eliphelet rides in on his white mule.

"Got your attention, didn't I?" he says.

"Your son doesn't like being treated the way I have been treated, does he?" he asks Sett.

"David loved you. Your father loved you."

"How? By remembering my birthdays? No. By playing a board game with me sometimes? No. By going riding with me now and then? No. By pretending I didn't exist. Yes. You can keep that kind of love."

By now, Eliphelet is off his mule and letting it roam around the red-and-blue tiled courtyard on its own.

"Where is the ole boy, by the way? Broke his other leg, hopefully."

"Eliphelet, sit down."

"Why? So you can tell me how good my father was? So you can tell me about all the times the two of you got together to sing while I stayed hidden in my little corner of the harem's wing?"

"Father, why did you let him in?"

Micah makes his way down the steps from his apartment to the courtyard, using a crutch.

"Come to survey your inheritance?" Eliphelet says, watching Micah on the steps. "At least you got an inheritance. My father leaves everything to the youngest son of his youngest wife—Solomon. How fair is that?"

Micah joins his father on his bench. Eliphelet remains standing.

"I guess Micah told you about my inheritance—a worthless piece of sand in the middle of the desert. Even my grandfather mocks me, and from the grave."

"My father will report you to Solomon, and he will put you in your place."

"Except I have no place. I just have a piece of vacant land no one else wants." He paces, turns his back on them, then turns around.

"I guess you heard my brother finished building his palace a couple years ago. Everyone in the world is coming to see it. It is the envy of every king out there. He invites everyone to come see it. Everyone but me. He is just like our father. How I hate Solomon and my father. How I hate my grandfather for passing on to me his nothing land no one else wants. How I hate everyone."

With that, Elipelet throws a rolled-up piece of papyrus onto the tiles at Micah's feet and walks over to his mule, now drinking out of the reflecting pool.

He slides up onto his mount, the gatekeeper opens the gate, Elipelet lets out a shout, whips his mule, and gallops across the courtyard and out of Sett's palace.

"Something has to be done about him, Father," Micah says, resting his broken leg on a stool in front of the bench.

"You are right. It is time I do something about him. I have an idea that might work."

"Would you like to share your idea, Father?"

"Not yet."

Two weeks pass.

"Your son just stole ten silver coins from me!" Lechy is at the top of the stairs where the king's apartment is. The door is open, and he is shouting.

"No. You're wrong." It is Micah's voice.

"Just because you have four sons and I have none,

you think you can just turn away from knowing what your sons are up to."

"Not that again, Lechy," Micah says, leaning on a crutch and appearing in his doorway at the top of the steps.

"Not that again?" Lechy mocks. "Not that again, you say? Oh, how easy for you to forget what pains another man," Lechy declares, screaming at Micah and shaking his fist at him. "Not a day goes by I do not think of my Iptur who your father killed."

"You know I did not kill your son, Lechy," Sett calls up from the courtyard. "I have told you that a hundred times."

"Father, if this man hates us so much, it is time to get rid of him," Micah calls down to his father.

"You cannot get rid of me," Lechy interjects. "I was hired by the king."

"Why in the world would you want to stay with us since you hate us so much?"

"Because someday I am going to prove your father deliberately killed my son. And when I get my proof, not only will he be executed, but you also since you have helped him cover up his devious act."

"But why would he want to kill your son?"

"He was afraid my son would grow up and take your place."

"Take my place doing what? This is a rundown palace, and the land is playing out."

Lechy is at the bottom of the stairs now.

"You are good at deflecting the issue—that your son stole ten silver coins from me."

"He did not," Micah calls down to him.

"Then prove it by producing the ten coins."

"Okay, everyone," Sett announces from his bench. "Now we are going to help the nice Lechy find his ten lost coins. So, scatter around and find them for us."

"Children too?" Pitthon asks.

"Children too."

"Do we get a reward?" Melech asks.

"Of course not," Pitthon shoots back at his little brother. "We do good because it is the good thing to do. Isn't that right, Grandfather?"

"True. But I might let the winner try to stand up on one of my crutches."

"Wow! You've never let us do that before."

Lechy walks by. I will get the ten coins back one way or another, even if I have to steal something from you. You are so arrogant, Sett. But someday, you will be arrested for killing my son. I will prove it. Some day I will."

Lechy returns to his office in front of the storeroom.

"While you children look for the nice Lechy's missing coins, I am going for a little walk."

"Oh, Grandfather. That's silly. You don't have any feet," eight-year-old Tarea says.

"Ha, ha. You got me there. But, my crutches have feet."

Sett waits for his chariot to be pulled out, and a horse harnessed to it. He leaves out the gate and heads through the estate. He pauses at the pasture and waits.

He smiles when Dipti raises his head and gallops toward him. When the camel arrives, he snorts, chortles, whinnies, and coughs

"I'm glad to see you too, Dipti. It's been a while. Would you like to go for a little walk with me?"

Sett climbs over the stone wall. "Sit, Dipty, sit."

The camel lowers his front legs, then his back ones. Sett slides over from the wall to Dipti's back.

"That wasn't so hard. Now, up, Dipti, up."

The camel's back legs go up first.

"Whoa," sixty-seven-year-old Sett laughs. "I have forgotten how tricky you can be."

With the camel now standing straight, Sett turns the reins to the right, clicks his tongue—forgetting that's how you get mules and horses to go—Dipti translates, and starts walking.

They work their way around one parameter of the

pasture to the other end.

*I wonder if I should try this. It's been a long time.* "Run, Dipti, run."

"Whoopee," Sett cries out as the camel lets loose, whooping himself.

They reach the other end of the pasture, and Dipti stops without being told.

Sett climbs down, gives Dipti a salt treat, climbs back over the wall, gets back in his chariot, and heads for home.

"Well, have you children found Lechy's missing coins yet?"

"No, but we will," six-year-old Ahaz says.

Just as Sett gets settled, there is a knock on the outer gate.

"Sire," the gatekeeper says moments later, "a messenger left this for you."

Sett recognizes the unique type of scroll and takes it. He holds it a while on his lap. He sets it on the bench beside him and stares at it. He squints and purses his lips. "Oh, well. I may as well read what he has to say."

He breaks the Dagonic seal and is surprised when he unrolls it. The message is short and takes up the entire scroll with the large letters.

From the priest of great Dagon to the fool of the invisible God. Dagon loves me and hates you.

*Oh, my friend. You are almost blind, aren't you? You love to read. You probably cannot read at all anymore. You will not be able to write even large letters much longer. How lonely you will become without your eyes.*

Sett stands and paces around the courtyard. *I have been patient with my three arch enemies all my life. I guess patience isn't enough.*

"Micah! Nina! Come here."

He returns to his bench and waits.

"I have decided to do something about my three

adversaries."

"Good, Father. You should have done it a long time ago. I'll go with you to Jerusalem."

"No. I am going to take care of it myself."

"Take care of it how, Father?"

"I will have to take it step by step. I do not know quite yet. But it is going to involve taking a trip."

"Father, you are too old for a trip."

Sett smiles but does not reply.

The men turn their heads when they hear the shouting.

"Father! Grandfather!" the children all call out at the same time while running toward them. "We found them. We found the nice Lechy's missing coins."

"That's wonderful," Sett says.

"Did you find all ten?" Micah asks his sons.

"Yup. We found 'em all," Pitthon, the self-appointed spokesman pronounces.

He holds out his hands. "See. Five in each hand."

"And where were they?" Sett asks.

"We waited until he left his office and crawled around under things."

"And?"

"We found them behind his writing-table."

"How clever of you," Sett says.

"Well, we will have to get them back to Lechy as soon as possible, so he will quit accusing Pitthon of taking them," Micah says.

"That's fine, Son. Now it's going to take me a while to get ready for the trip. I need to write some letters. When I get my answers, I will be ready to go.

Sett now spends more time in his office. Sometimes the grandchildren hear him in there talking to himself. "Barzillai in Mahanaim is long dead, but I can write his son, Chimham. I'm sure my old friend, Machir in Lodebar is dead, but perhaps Aviva is still living. I will write to her. Garash in Ur must be dead by now, but perhaps his wife, Esheda, is still alive. Oh, I could have written to King Hiram in Tyre, but I heard he just died. So young. Only fifty-three years old. So young."

Sett continues to search his memory of long ago.

"I never stayed long enough to make friends in Assyria, Harran, or Ebla. The King of Gesher is long-ago dead, and his one daughter is dead. I've only been in Arabia twice briefly and never made any friends there. So, I guess this is it. The three letters will have to do."

Sett makes arrangements with the leaders of caravans to have his letters delivered. Then he waits.

*I think the one to Ur is the one that will be most helpful,* he often tells himself.

After six months, Sett assumes the letters have been delivered. During that time, Lechy calms back down. Sett knows his bitterness will come back sooner or later. He waits another six months.

*It is time.*

While entering the courtyard after breaking their fast, Sett makes his announcement. "I am leaving tomorrow."

"That's too quick," Micah objects.

"I've been waiting a year. I will wait no longer. I leave tomorrow."

As he speaks, the outer gate to the palace opens, and Dipty is led in.

"Father! No! You are not going to ride Dipty on your trip."

"Why?"

"For one thing, you are too old. And for another thing, he is too old."

"Neither of us is too old. I have made up my mind, and that's that."

Micah walks up to the camel. Dipty gurgles, wheezes, and sneezes at him. Micah turns back to his father.

"You're not going out into the desert, are you?"

"Well, maybe."

"Why? What is so important?"

"I cannot tell you just yet. I do not know if I will be able to accomplish what I want to accomplish."

"Father, you are going in circles."

"That may be, Son."

"At least take someone with you."

"Can't do that. I need to at least start out alone."

"But what if you never come back?"

# 37 ~ THE SEARCH

Sett and Dipti make their way down the hill on which lies the city of Gibeon. They progress down the steep, winding road to Jericho and spend their first night there. The next morning, they cross the Jordan River and head south in the direction of the Pisgah Mountain Range.

"Ah, the Forests of Moab," he tells Dipti. "Shall we take a walk up the mountain and see what Moses saw?" Dipti honks. "You don't know who Moses was?"

Sett guides Dipti to turn toward the east, and they begin their ascent through the trees, and then the brush higher up. "I suppose Nebo is the tallest peak. Still some snow there. But we are not afraid of a little snow, are we, Dipti?"

It takes Sett half a day to reach the summit. He does not dismount. Instead, he takes his tall camel over to the highest point he can find and looks west.

"Ah. So magnificent. I can see all the way to the Great Sea. This is what Moses saw that day. Kissara, you would have loved this view."

After surveying his homeland a while, Sett looks toward the other side of the peak. "I wonder where God buried the old warrior. He didn't want us to know. Maybe people would have worshiped at his grave. Whatever the reason, we shall not look for it. It is too cold to spend the night here."

Sett works his way down the south side of the

mountain, arriving just in time to stop for the night at Heshbon. "Well, this is where old King Sihon ruled Moab. Wonder where his palace was. Well, I'm not interested."

Sett finds an inn near the bazaar and rents a room for himself and a stall for Dipti. He sleeps well and dreams of Moses.

The morning is fresh. *I may as well start here.* He makes his way to the bazaar.

"Do you have any physicians in this city?"

"Most people just handle their own problems."

"I'm looking for a special kind who can perform surgery."

"Not here. Maybe down at Bozrah. It's a bigger city."

"What about a man who may go by the name of Iptur?"

"Sorry. I'm busy now."

"Thank you for your time and patience."

Sett visits several booths until he decides he has interviewed a fair representation of the city. He returns to the stable and climbs onto the back of Dipti. They ride out of the city and continue on south.

He arrives at Medeba late afternoon and sees the bazaar right away. Once again, he rents a room and a stall for Dipty.

Though he is tired, he goes right over to the bazaar.

"Do you have any physicians in this city?"

"Not that I know of."

"I'm looking for a special kind who can perform surgery."

"Check down at Bozrah. It's a bigger city."

"What about a man who may go by the name of Iptur?"

"Never heard of him. What does he look like?"

"I'm not sure."

The next morning Sett and Dipti continue on south and arrive at Dibon around noon.

"Sir, would you mind moving out of the way," an older gentleman says, looking up at Sett on his camel. "We have a funeral procession headed this way."

"Oh, I am sorry for the family. Is there anything I can do for them?"

The stranger looks up to Sett a while, then looks up the road where the funeral procession is just appearing. They both hear the wailers. "If you are serious, we need some singers. Do you sing?"

"I sang a great deal in my youth, but can still strike a melody. When do you want me?"

"Right now, if you have time."

"I would be honored to help a grieving family at such a time as this."

"You may stay on your camel. Just come out in front of them and begin to sing. They will follow you."

"I do not know where the cemetery is."

"You passcd it on the way in."

Sett turns Dipti around, heads back up the road from whence he had just come and back out the city gate.

He sings. Dipti sometimes honks, and Sett reaches around to give him a treat of salt to keep his mouth busy. *Hope he doesn't interpret this as a reward.* "Be quiet now, Dipti."

Sett resumes his dirge. This time, he spots the cemetery and guides Dipti over to one side of it. He stops singing.

*I think I'll stay in case they need me afterward. Micah sure would be mad at me for getting sidetracked like this.* Sett smiles.

An hour later, the funeral is over. The same gentleman who had stopped him upon his entrance into Dibon comes over and calls up to him.

"The family would like to invite you to take food with them now. My name, by the way, is Fahd. If you can come, just follow the procession."

Sett follows his new friend. They arrive at the house. After everyone else has entered, he has Dipti sit, climbs off, and grabs his crutches.

As he enters through the host's still-open gates, the

family and guests stare at the cripple. He pauses and begins another song. They smile.

The funeral meal takes the rest of the day. When the others learn Sett lives near Jerusalem with which they do not have good relations, he sets their minds at ease.

"Don't worry about me. I'm no threat. I descend from the usurped previous king. The new king snatched the crown from my family."

"Oh, well, that's better," Fahd says. "Well, not better because of the unfortunate circumstances of your family, but because we can remain friends."

"I have a friend down here somewhere. His name is Iptur. He doesn't, by any chance, live here, does he?"

No one knows him, and Sett returns to small talk.

Having gone through the expected time to get to know each other and to comfort the family, Fahd broaches the subject that has been on his mind.

"Uh, there is something I am curious about. What brings you down here? Our two countries are not always friendly."

"I am searching for a physician," Sett replies.

"Oh, I should not have pried," Fahd says, looking at Sett's helpless feet.

"Oh, not for me. I am looking for a special kind of physician who can perform surgery on people."

"Our family does have a physician. He has other duties in our home, but he handles our health and well being also. Would you like to meet him? I can introduce you to him after the guests leave. Our slaves do not intermingle with our guests, you understand."

"How fortunate," Sett replies with a broad grin. "Yes, indeed."

The sun turns red and slowly hides itself behind the horizon.

"Mefiboset, this is our family physician. We are tired. When you are through talking, he will show you to our guest room. Good night Mefiboset. And thank you for rescuing us with your songs."

Sett and the physician talk until it is completely dark. "Since you do not perform surgery, I guess I will have to keep looking," he tells the man.

Early the next morning, Sett mounts Dipti, and they turn south once again. During the day, he crosses three branches of the Arnon River.

Late in the afternoon, he arrives at the stronghold of Kir. It has a small bazaar and inn. The city is full of barracks. *Hmmm. Mostly soldiers. I don't think this is the place for me.*

The next morning Sett leaves without saying any more than what is necessary, and heads south.

*What am I doing? Maybe Micah was right. Maybe I am too old to be doing this. Maybe I am too late. Maybe I don't know what I am doing.*

He arrives at the Zered River and crosses it. "Well, Dipti, I think we have just crossed over into Edom." Dipti sneezes. "Don't you even care? You might have had ancestors here. This is kind of where strange animals like you came from." Dipti snorts and gurgles. "Oh, did I offend you?"

After a long day in the mountains of Moab, Sett arrives in Zalmona.

*Should I spend the night here? I feel as though I am being followed. Well, it's either stay in Zalmona or put up my tent somewhere. I do not relish putting up a tent.*

He finds an inn and dismounts from Dipti. As he does, he looks around and spots two soldiers.

"They look familiar, Dipti. I guess it is time to show them they are following the wrong man."

Sett on his crutches works his way several man-lengths in a large circle, swinging his helpless feet between the crutches more than usual. *That should do it.*

Back at his camel, he leans against the animal and looks in the direction of the two soldiers. *They are gone. I don't like it when people think I'm helpless, but it does come in handy sometimes.*

"Well, Dipti, tomorrow is Bozrah. It's going to be a big city. We may spend two days there."

Sett rises early, sees that the bazaar is nearby, and changes his mind about leaving.

"Do you have any physicians in this city?" he asks at the first booth.

"Only rich people have physicians. Try in Bozrah."

"I'm looking for a special kind who can perform surgery."

"Not here. As I said, try Bozrah. It's a bigger city."

"What about a man who may go by the name of Iptur?"

"Sorry. Try Bozrah."

After asking at a few more booths while holding the reins of Dipti around his shoulders, Sett gets back on his camel.

Three hours later, they arrive at the famed Bozrah. *So, this is the city of my ancestor Jacob's brother Esau. I guess everyone here is his descendant.*

Sett makes his way to the bazaar by the city gate.

"Do you have any physicians in this city?"

"Of course. There should be one up at the old palace. Some of the old royal family still lives there."

"Do you know if he performs surgery?"

"I have no idea."

"Well, do you happen to know a man named Iptur?"

"No. Sorry."

Sett goes to the next booth and the next. No success. Still, he tries.

"I heard there is a physician at the old palace. Do you know if he can perform surgeries?"

"All I have heard is that he is a drunk."

"Oh, my. Well, have you run across a man named Iptur?"

"Not here."

"If you do, I am going down to Eilat and Ezion Geber. Could you send word down there? Just tell them to look for a man with three-footed crutches."

Sett smiles, the man grunts, and Dipti honks.

"Let's spend the night here," he mutters, back on the street. "We'll continue on in the morning."

Morning comes, and Sett mounts Dipti.

*Lord God, help me find what I am looking for. I know it may not be possible, but could you make it possible? I am not asking for anything for myself.*

As he draws closer to Punon, Sett sees wagons and men on horses rushing by.

"What's going on?" he shouts to some of the men passing him. They do not hear.

Two panting horses gallop by with the driver of the large attached wagon thrashing the air above them with his whip. Dipti's eyes grow wide, he neighs in a high pitch and raises up on his hind legs.

Sett grabs hold of the horn of the saddle. He slides backward. He cannot hang on to the horn. He slides back farther. He grabs the hair on Dipti's neck. He continues to slide backward. Sett grabs onto Dipti's hump.

"Calm down now, Dipti," he shouts over the loud hooves of the passing horses, and the loud yells of the wagon drivers.

"Calm down," he says, still hanging on to Dipti's hump, but just barely.

Still the rushing of men and animals on the highway, daring anything in their way.

"Go over beside the road, Dipti. Over there. That's right. Over there. Now sit. Let me down. Sit."

Dipti obeys, but anxiously watches what is going on around him, his large eyes darting in every direction. Sett climbs off as fast as he can, still talking to the camel. Just as he gets close enough to the front of the frightened animal, Dipti begins to stand again.

"No, Dipti. No. Sit. Calm down. Calm down now, Dipti. You're safe. No one is going to hurt you. Calm down now."

A wagon wheel comes within a hand span of the animal.

Dipti looks around, his eyes wide, his flesh trembling. Sett sings. He lays his head down on Dipti's neck and sings.

Still, the wagons and horses rush by.

"Shhhh, Dipti. You are fine. We are fine. Something is going on down there, but we are not part of it. We are fine. Shhhh."

And Sett sings.

As the sun begins to disappear, the panic slows. "We need to find a place to spend the night. Punon isn't much farther. Let's try to make it to the city before they close the gates."

Sett slides up onto Dipti, and they head south. They reach the city just at sundown.

"I'm lucky to have made it on time," he tells a guard.

"We're not closing the gates tonight. Things are going to be happening on all night."

"What things?"

"There has been a mine cave-in. The biggest copper mine anywhere. Big explosion. Men above ground killed or injured. Men below ground probably all killed."

"Can I do anything?"

"Unless you are good at moving big stones or doctoring people, there is nothing you can do."

Sett continues the rest of the way into the city and arrives at the closest inn to the gate.

"You are lucky, sir. We have only one room left."

The next morning while breaking his fast, he watches grime-caked men gulp down their food and drink and run out.

Having seen Sett's crutches and knowing he would be useless out at the mine, the innkeeper goes over to his table and sits on the other bench.

"Too bad about the mine collapse. The owner just got a new contract with a ship-builder down in Ebion Gezer to supply enough copper to line the bottom of all their ships."

"What about the workers at the mine?" Sett asks. "How are they doing?"

"Them? They're just slaves. They can be replaced."

"Are there any physicians there?"

"Probably. Messengers were sent both north and south to bring in as many as they could find."

"I fear they won't find enough. What about food for everyone?"

"That is another problem. Someone has to pay for the food for everyone out there. It's going to take them weeks to get everything back to normal."

"I believe I can help. Tell me how to get there."

With simple enough instructions, Sett leaves the city, turns south, and then west. He follows the back trail with heavy traffic of wagons, horses, and mules.

Upon arrival at the mine site, Sett directs Dipti toward a large black goat-hair tent. He dismounts and enters it. He sees bloody injured men lying in rows on both sides and down the middle.

"You are not allowed in here," someone says. "You must leave."

"I want to help."

"We have enough cripples around here. We don't need your help."

"Farhid, let's hear this gentleman out."

Sett turns to learn who has just defended him and sees a man with blood smeared on his tunic.

"Are you a physician?" Sett asks.

"Yes, I am," he says, noticing Sett's crutches and lame feet for the first time. "But I do not have time to help you."

"Oh, I don't need any help. I understand you are going to need a lot of food. Let me buy it."

"Oh. Well, thank you, friend. Come with me."

The physician leads Sett to the far end of the large tent. "Sir, this gentleman would like to pay for the food we will be needing."

The physician turns to leave.

"Uh, sir, I am just wondering if you ever performed surgery."

"I don't like to. I do when it is an emergency to get shale rocks or arrows out of someone—things like that. But that's all. Nothing more."

The physician leaves and the mine overseer motions for Sett to sit on a narrow wooden bench. The overseer sits on a shiny copper bench.

"Now, what can you do for us?"

"Would twenty silver coins be enough to pay for your food a while?"

"Indeed, yes. That is most generous of you."

Sett hands the coins over to the overseer but remains seated.

"Well, I do appreciate what you have done, but now I am rather busy trying to save lives."

"Yes. I just have one question before I leave. Have you heard of a man named Iptur?"

"Iptur. Hmmm. He sounds familiar. I think he used to work here. Not anymore, though. I don't know what happened to him."

# 38 ~ FULFILLMENT

"**P**erhaps we did right to come here, after all," Sett tells Dipti back on the highway.

"Well, the next city is Sier. I heard it is not much of a city, though. Surrounded by cliffs on all sides. You have to go through a long narrow passageway to get to it. Pretty out of the way. Just a few farmers and a place for caravans to stop on their way from India and Babylon."

Dipti honks, blubbers, and shakes his head. "It didn't sound that interesting to me either," Sett says, laughing.

On they go down the highway, swaying back and forth. Sometimes Sett pulls both legs in, attaches a rope from his waist to the horn of the saddle, closes his eyes, nods, falls asleep, and dreams of Kissara and Esau.

Sett arrives at Sier. He is tired. He guides Dipti through the long, narrow passageway that finally opens up into a valley surrounded by tall, red cliffs. He sees a few monuments to the local gods, a few adobe buildings, a lot of caves where people seem to be living, and a black goat-hair tent, which he estimates to be eight man-lengths wide.

He stops and enters the tent. Several men are gathered at the front opening.

"Is this an inn? May I pay someone to spend the night here?"

"This is not an inn, but you can spend the night here," one of the men says. "You can pay me."

"I need food and water for my camel, also."

"Then, you pay double."

Sett spends the night in the half of the tent where the men sleep. He has a fitful night. *These men and their snoring can outdo Dipty.*

The next morning, Sett mounts Dipti, and they work their way back out to the highway. *Someone with a little skill in rock sculpting could do something with that village.*

He sees a caravan near the entrance to Sier. "Where are you traveling from?" he asks the first person who looks his way.

"We're most recently from Ur."

"Ah, yes, Ur. I used to live there."

"Then we might know some of the same people."

"No. That was fifty years ago. I doubt anyone I knew then is still alive. Or, if they are, they are much older than you. How is the city doing, by the way?"

"Growing still. We have two new temples."

"Well, I need to be going." Knowing Kissara would have been upset with remembrances of Ur and its temples, Sett hurries on.

Moving steadily down the highway, Sett notices a mountain on his right.

"That must be Mount Hor," he tells Dipti. "Moses' older brother died on that mountain. I wonder how cold it was that day with all the snow. Or maybe he died in the summer. It's sure hot down here."

They travel on.

"His name was Aaron. Can you remember Aaron? Of course, you can't. Anyway, he was our very first high priest, and he now has thousands of descendant priests. Would he ever be impressed with Solomon's new temple. I wonder what all Aaron saw from the top of the mountain before he died."

Sett arrives late that afternoon at the city of Teman. He hears music. Men and women dressed in black robes embroidered everywhere with bright colors make their way up the street, dancing as they go.

"That must be the groom headed for the bride's house. Let's have some fun." He follows them, though, at enough distance, they do not notice him.

The city is not large, and not every piece of land has a building on it. The parade ends at a large black goat-hair tent on one of those barren lots. Another group dressed in similar black and flashy colors comes out of the tent to greet them.

More music. More dancing in the street. Everyone except a veiled woman standing at the entrance to the tent. Sometimes someone goes up to the woman, says something, laughs, and returns to their dancing.

"Well, good luck to you young people," Sett mutters. "May you have as happy a marriage as I did."

He turns back toward the city gate to find an inn. There are a few booths still open at the bazaar.

"Do you have any physicians in your city?" he asks the first merchant.

"Yes, but he is getting married this week. There is no chance you can get him to treat whatever is wrong with you."

The merchant leans over his counter. "And he definitely wouldn't be able to fix your feet, even if he weren't getting married."

"Oh, I don't need him for that. I am just looking for one who can perform surgeries. I wouldn't need him for very long."

"Well, Avith is our newest capital city. You might try there. Otherwise, you might check around the ships down at Ezion Geber."

"Thank you, sir. By the way, do you happen to know a man named Iptur?"

"No, sorry. Check Eilat and Ezion Geber. Lots of people coming and going there."

It is night now. The city gates have been closed, and Sett finds an inn with a stall for Dipti.

The next morning, Sett climbs onto Dipti, and they head farther south to Avith. He arrives early afternoon.

"I understand this is your new capital city," he says to a guard as he enters.

"Well, it is new compared to Bozrah. Avith has been the capital about eighty years now."

"Who is your king now?"

"Why do you want to know?" the guard replies, stiffening and his smile gone.

"I am looking for a physician and thought I might speak to the physician of your king."

The guard looks at Sett's feet. "I doubt anyone can help you."

"Oh, it isn't for me. So, what is the king's name?"

"King Baal-Hanan."

Thank you. And where might the palace be?"

"Up on that hill. But do not expect anyone to let you in. You are obviously not Edomite. They'll never give you admittance."

"Thank you, sir," Sett says, flipping a bronze coin to the guard.

Right away, Sett can see parts of the palace towers and goes toward it. Upon his arrival, he pulls out a small clay tablet from his baggage and etches a message on it. He leans over and hands it to one of the guards by the palace gates.

"I will be at the end nearest the southern gate until tomorrow. Here is a bronze coin for your trouble, and another bronze coin for whoever delivers a reply to me."

"It is too hot to be out here right now, Dipti. Let's find some shade for you and me."

Sett has not been in his room at the inn for very long when he hears a knock on his door. Sett answers it and pays the messenger for delivering his clay tablet back to him. His reply is etched on the back.

No surgery. Check Eilat.

Sett rests the remainder of the day within the thick

shaded walls of the inn and sleeps sporadically through the night. Sometimes he hears Dipti out his window snortling and yawning.

Before dawn, he is up and eating barley bread dipped in yogurt for breaking his fast. He sees another traveler come in and calls over to him. "Do you happen to know a man named Iptur?"

"Sorry, no."

The innkeeper does not either.

As soon as Dipti is saddled and it is dawn, Sett settles on Dipti's back and rides out of the city.

"This is as far as we go, Dipti. The Red Sea is on the other side of Eilat and Ezion Geber. Will we be going home empty-handed? Will Micah have been right?"

Just before the gates are closed into Eilat, Sett enters the city and finds an inn. *I'm tired, and my bones ache. Maybe Micah was right.*

"I do not know how long I will be here," he tells the innkeeper. "This should cover a week for room and food."

After another restless night, Sett checks on Dipti then makes his way toward the city square. It borders two sides of the bazaar.

He sits in the city square a while, watching people.

"You looking for a job too?" a strange voice asks.

Sett looks in the direction of the voice.

"No, I'm just looking."

"What for?"

"Oh, nothing," Sett says. "I guess I'm resting before I get tired. Then I'll be up and about my business."

"You are not from around here," the stranger says.

"No, I am just visiting from Israel. I need to find an assayer with a little time on his hands. Maybe someone who has retired. I don't need him for long.

"You have come to the right place, friend," the stranger says. "I have done a little assaying in my life."

Sett's smile is broad. "Praise God, he actually led me right to you. My name is Mefiboset. I would like to hire you."

"I am Peduil," the stranger replies.

"This may take all day," Sett admits.

"I have all day."

"My room is not far from here," Sett explains. "I have a map, and my camel can carry both of us."

"Where are we going?" Peduil asks.

"Out into the desert."

Once they are out of the city, Sett holds up his map.

"Now, the land I am looking for should be over there. Are those the Eilat Mountains?"

"Yes."

"Where are we right now?"

"We are in the Timna Valley."

"Okay, Dipti. Head for those mountains. Let's see what we can find on the way."

Sett clicks his tongue, and Dipti translates, though he does not like to obey signals for mules. Dipti raises his muzzle, honks, shakes his head back and forth, gurgles, brays like a donkey in protest, then starts walking.

"Your camel needs to be going northwest if you are looking for what I think you are looking for."

Sett makes the adjustment, and Dipti lumbers along in the heat and sand, swaying back and forth.

"What's that over there?" Sett asks. "It's huge. Strange and huge."

"Well, it is called different things by different people," Peduil says. "The Egyptians call them giant mushrooms. I call them giant stemmed goblets."

"You said them. Are there more than one?"

"Oh, yes. They are scattered around the Timna Valley as we get closer to the mountains.

"Okay, that is what is depicted on this map. Good. Is there someplace with three of those stone goblets?"

"Yes, I know the place well," Peduil says. "Just keep going the way you are."

"I see them," Sett says after riding a little farther. "I didn't believe this old map. But I guess it is accurate after all. Now the map says we need to stand between the mountain and the stone goblet closest to the mountain at noon. The shadow it casts will fall on the land owned by my young friend.

"It will be noon soon. Why don't we climb down and wait for it under one of these goblets? There is a lot of shade under them."

"Did you think to bring along plenty of water?" Peduil asks.

"I didn't, but my innkeeper did. He also packed some fresh grapes just arrived by ship all the way from Tyre and some local cheese."

The men rest, eat, and wait for the sun.

"Uh, did you ever know a man named Iptur?"

"Hmmm. Seems like I used to hear that name in some of the mines around here. But that was a long time ago. Is it a common name where you came from?"

"Well, it is among the natives."

"Okay, let's go. I think the sun is right."

"Let's get on Dipti," Sett says. "He takes the heat better than I do."

The men mount Dipti, and he takes them slowly away from the shade of the giant goblet formation toward the mountains. Sett keeps Dipti going in line with their shadow.

They arrive at the nearest mountain.

"I need to get down and walk around. It will take me a while," Peduil says. "You may as well get a drink of water and rest again."

Peduil walks back and forth between the nearest mountain and the stone goblets while Sett alternately watches him and dreams of Kissara. Dipty voluntarily sits next to Sett and catches the growing shadow of the mountain with his bulk.

Two hours later, Peduil returns. "If you have a blank papyrus and blackener with you, I will write my findings."

Peduil writes, looks up at the land, and writes again.

"What's that noise?" Sett says.

"Oh, no," Peduil responds. "It's the wind. Look. It's carrying a bank of sand over the mountain. Duck down as close to the cliff as you can. This is going to be a bad one."

The men hunker down between Dipti and the mountain. They raise the hoods of their robes, put their heads down on their knees, and feel the grating of the first grains of sand beat down on them and scrape everything in its path.

On it comes. Sett remembers another sand storm long ago on his way to rescue his Kissara in Ur. Dipti closes both sets of long eyelashes and waits in calm.

The wind whines and pounds and roars. The sand continues its invasion on a land that needs no more sand. The mountain watches as it has done for thousands of years.

Still, the wind. Still, the sand. Still wondering if they will be buried alive.

It stops. The wind moves on eastward. The sand moves with it. The roar and disruption and devastation with it.

Quiet now. Dipti shakes his head back and forth and whinnies. Sett opens his eyes and raises his head. He feels around in the sand for his crutches. Peduil stands and helps him look. They brush Dipti's saddle off, brush themselves off, and remount Dipti.

"Well?" Sett asks as they make their way back toward Eilat.

"I hate to disappoint you, but the land looks worthless."

"Oh. That's too bad. Well, I need to go on down to Ezion Geber."

When they arrive back at the city square, Sett hands the assayer his fee. "Here is your money, and thank you."

"By the way, whose land is it?" the assayer asks.

"The son of King David of Israel. My grandfather was King Saul, who ruled before him."

The sunset reflects on the water of the Red Sea as Sett arrives in the ship-building city. *I'll bet some of these ships are Solomon's. If not all of them.*

*Let's find an inn for the night, and I'll check around for a doctor tomorrow. If I do not find one, my trip will have been a complete failure.*

Sett wakens to the sound of bells from the ships. He goes down to the harbor. He stops at each ship and calls up, "Do you have a good physician on board?" Always the answer is no.

He returns to his inn to break his fast. He sits at a corner table and is served. The inn is crowded. Every table is taken, mostly with merchants and merchant marines.

"May I sit with you?" a man asks. He is tall and wears a white linen tunic with short sleeves. He also has on his white *shendyt* down to his knees that has been wrapped around him and tucked at his waist under a wide gold-and-blue sash. With these, he wears heavy gold necklaces and bracelets.

"Of course," Sett says, smiling.

"This is a good inn, wouldn't you say? I have been to India and am on my way back to On."

"In Egypt. Of course. You are Egyptian. My name is Mefiboset."

"My name is Akar."

Eying the gold jewelry, Sett asks, "Do you own one of these ships?".

"Oh, no. My master does, but I do not."

Sett squints. "You are a slave?"

"Yes, I have been with my master all my life. He is good to me, has given me a good education, and trusts me."

"May I ask what you were doing in India so far from your master?"

"I was learning some surgical techniques," Akar explains. "My master wants me to take good care of his large family."

Sett drops his bread into his bowl of yogurt, his eyes widen, and he smiles. "Uh, when is he expecting you back?"

"I'm sure he won't begin to worry about me for another month."

"Sir, the Lord God, Creator of the world, has sent you to me."

"He has? I do not even know him."

"Well, he has, and he knows you. I would like to pay you to go back with me to Israel."

"Will it take long?"

"No, you should be back in On within the month or before. I will pay you well. Do you mind riding on a camel?"

Akar smiles. "I think I was born riding on a camel. I have my own."

"You do? Wonderful! Can you leave right now?"

"Why not? I've never been to Israel. Yes. I can leave right now."

Sett throws his coins on the table to pay for their meals. The two men rise, and Akar notices Sett on his crutches.

"How long?" he asks.

"Most of my life."

"Those are strange crutches."

"My nurse and I designed them when I was ten years old. I've been using crutches like these for sixty years.

"I believe our camels are stabled together. I need to retrieve my belongings out of my room and will be all ready to go."

Within the hour, Sett and Akar are on their respective camels headed north through the Arabah. Over the next few days, they go back through Eilat, Avith, Teman, and Sier.

"They had a mine collapse up here in Punon when I came through last week," Sett calls over to Akar.

As they near the intersection with the road veering off to the mine, they see a thin naked man running across the highway, armed men chasing after him, swords drawn.

# 39 ~ ON THE RUN

"You get the man while I go after his pursuers!" Akar shouts.

Sett urges Dipti into a run. He heads off the highway, catches up with the thin naked man, lowers his crutch, pulls in on the reins, and shouts, "Grab hold, Grab hold."

The thin man grabs the foot end of Sett's crutch, and with his strong arms, Sett lifts the man off the ground.

Now Dipti is in a full gallop, the runaway clinging to the crutch at the camel's side. Sett heads up a high sand dune and down the other side. Satisfied they can no longer be seen from the highway, Sett reins in Dipti to a stop with one hand, still holding his lowered crutch with the other.

The runaway lets go of Sett's crutch, and Sett orders Dipti to sit.

"Thank you," the man says, between gulps of air. He puts his hands on his knees to allow his racing heart and stretched lungs to ease their struggle.

Sett slides off the camel and supports himself with his crutches while leaning on Dipti. "You're welcome, sir."

Akar comes over the incline of the dune and slows his camel. "You won't have to worry about them anymore," he calls out.

Akar brings his camel to a stop. "I am very good with a sling and knocked them both out," he says with a grin. "Then I confiscated their swords. Who knows? We may need them farther up the highway. Now, who do we have here, and why were you running? Do you ever eat?"

"Please sit down, sir," Sett says to the runaway. "Here is some water. You look hungry too. I have some dried dates. Rest a moment. You do not have to talk yet. Just rest."

"How can I thank both of you?" the runaway says between gulps of water. "They were going to kill me this time."

Sett and Akar wait in silence as the man eats.

"Well, now that you are through," Akar finally says, "we need to get a robe on you and leave here. There will be more hunting parties soon. You can ride with me."

Sett takes the lead. He eases back to the highway to check for lurking pursuers. "It's safe. Let's go," he shouts to Akar.

Out on the highway, Sett puts Dipti into a full gallop, Akar following close.

Within an hour, they are on the edge of Bozrah and stop at a well outside the city. The camels drink their fill. Sett notices the runaway watching him.

Back on the highway, the camels break into a gallop once again. Their legs stretch long, their heavy bodies glide, the wind whips around their riders.

The landscape races by—sand dunes, an acacia tree, sparse bushes, patches of rock, another acacia, more bushes, more dunes. Rushing. Hurrying. Flying to freedom.

They arrive at Zalmona, and stop on the far side of the city on the Zered River. The camels drink what they need.

"On the other side of the river is Moab," Sett explains to the other two men. "I do not think they will pursue us outside their own kingdom."

Once again, Sett notices the runaway watching him.

"Let's get out of here," Sett says. "We can rest on the other side."

He leads the way across the Zered River. Sett now lets Dipti walk at his own pace.

That evening, they arrive in Kir and get a room at an inn with facilities to bathe and care for their camels.

For the first time, Sett takes the time to look at their runaway. He is of average height, has a round face, and bulbous nose. His arms and legs are muscled and strong despite how thin he is.

"Now, before the market closes completely down," Sett says, "we need to get you some more clothes besides that robe Akar gave you that drags the ground."

They make their way past the booths, though the runaway pauses at every one, gawking at everything for sale.

"Have you never been in a market?" Akar asks.

"Never."

"Well, let's get you some clothes right now," Sett says, "and you can come back tomorrow to see more."

Akar hurries on ahead of them so he can go through the rows of booths faster and find the one they need.

An hour later, they are back at the inn, and the runaway is in a vat full of water. When he climbs out, and they can see beyond the dirt of the mine, they spot the mark on his forehead, his brand.

"Hmmm," Sett says, looking at it a little closer. "It could be worse."

"Sit here so I can inspect your disfigurement better," Akar demands.

"Don't worry," Sett tells the stranger, grinning. "He is not gloating over your misery; he is a physician."

After a moment, Akar steps back. "If you would allow me to cut around that scar, I think I could bring the clean skin together with stitches, and your new scar will hardly show."

The runaway looks at Akar and back over to Sett. "Things are going too fast for me. I do not even know where I am. I do not know where I should be going. I do not know if they are following me. I do not know if I will be alive tomorrow."

He stands and walks around the room, then back to his two rescuers.

"I don't even know who you are," he continues. "Are

you going to make me your own slave? Will my future be like my past? Will my worthless life remain worthless? Will there ever be an end to this?"

"You are tired," Sett says. "Let's have some stew. I heard the innkeeper has a very good cook. Then we'll all go to bed. We can talk and try to figure things out tomorrow."

It is morning. When Sett opens his eyes, he does not see the runaway. "Oh, no."

He rushes outside and sees the man squatting beside the street in front of the inn. Sett kneels next to him.

"Enjoying your freedom?"

"Trying to comprehend it. Is it real? Am I dreaming? Will it last?"

"Friend, there are all kinds of slaveries in this world. I think everyone is enslaved to something."

"I am sorry. I forgot about your feet. How do you do it?"

"You learn to live with it, just like you did, and to look for the rare time when it is an advantage, such as something that happened to me in Assyria, and," he pats the stranger on the back, "saving you."

"Have I ever met you?" the stranger asks Sett.

"Have you ever been around the Euphrates River or Great Sea?"

"No, I haven't."

"Well, how about..."

"Are you ready to break your fast?" Akar interrupts.

The two men go back into their room and dress.

They are now outside, ready to go back to the market. "I'm going to check on the camels," Sett says.

He turns to go over to the stable when an arrow whizzes past and lands in the outer wall of the inn just above his head.

"Run!" he shouts.

The three hurry to their camels and duck behind the stalls. They look out to see if they can find their would-be attackers.

"Do you still have those swords on you?" Sett asks.

"They're on my camel. What do we do now?"

"I will run out in the street to draw attention away from you, and you can make your getaway," the stranger says.

"Oh, no, you don't," Sett objects. "Then, we'd have to rescue you all over again."

"If I let my camel loose to distract them, do you think your camel can hold three men?" Akar asks.

"That is not within the realm of possibility," Sett replies.

Another arrow whizzes over their heads, nearly finding its mark in the neck of Dipty.

"We cannot stay here."

"Everyone, come!" It is the innkeeper. He is out in the middle of the street standing in place, but turning in circles.

"Everyone, come," he repeats. He raises his arms.

"Free barley bread and yogurt for everyone. Come, my friends on the street. Do not pass up your opportunity for a free breakfast like none you have ever had in your life."

People within hearing distance wander toward the inn. Still, he beckons.

"Come, everyone, come! Free for you. Come take advantage of my good nature. Come before it is too late, and someone else eats your share."

More people come—merchants, travelers, beggars. The innkeeper looks in Sett's direction and shrugs his shoulders.

"Come, my friends," he resumes. "Whatever you are doing, stop now. You can go back to it later. If you are seated, stand, and come. If you are busy, stop, and come. If you are lying down, rise, and come. If you are on top of something, climb down and come."

Now they see them. Two men with bows climb down from a roof across the street and enter the inn. The innkeeper smiles in the direction of the stable.

"Go," he says. "Go."

Sett lays a gold coin on the lid of a basket with pieces of salt inside and climbs onto Dipty. The other two men mount their camel. The camels rise and crash through the stable out into the street. They rush toward the city gate and hope it is open.

Now out of the city and on the highway, the camels break out into a full gallop, long legs stretching, lungs struggling, every muscle straining.

Hurry. Escape once more. On the run once again.

Galloping.

Racing.

Fleeing.

Within two hours, they are at the Arnon River and the city of Dibon. They stop at the river but do not enter the city. The camels drink. The men drink.

The camels wade across the river. Back on the highway, now in a trot. Farther north and farther into the mountains. More trees. Trees everywhere. Hide in the trees. Arabs do not understand trees.

At sundown, they reach Medeba.

"Do you think it is safe here?" Akar asks.

"Let's not take any chances. I have a tent large enough for four men," Sett says. "Let's stay in it out here tonight."

"Why four?" Akar asks.

"I was hoping to bring three men back with me. Well, I got one of the three—you—so that's better than none."

Akar takes the tent off Dipti's rump to set up, and Sett stays behind to pull out supplies they will need the rest of the evening. He makes a second trip to the tent and looks around.

"Where is our runaway?" he asks Akar. They raise the flap of the tent and see him fast asleep.

"No telling how many days after the mine collapse, they made him work without eating or stopping."

"I was going to ask him to tell us about himself. We don't even know his name. Well, it will keep until tomorrow."

That night Sett dreams he and Kissara are in the

desert running from the priests of Ishtar, and Dipti has wings.

When morning comes, Sett and Akar hear a rattling noise, realize their runaway is missing, grab the two swords, and crawl out of their tent.

"Good morning. I have breakfast ready."

"How thoughtful," Akar says, laying his sword on the ground.

The three men sit in a circle, and Sett realizes the stranger is staring at him again. "I know I have never met you, sir. Or did you ever work for a miner or own one?"

"No, I never have," Sett replies.

"Well, while we are eating, we would like to know all about the naked man we found running across the desert in Arabia with two sword-wielding men after him," Sett continues. "First, why were you naked?"

"That's the way we work in the mines. At first, it is cool underground, but if you go down very far, it starts to get warm again. Then it gets as hot as the surface. If you go down far enough, it becomes even hotter than the surface. Besides, our owners do not want to waste their money clothing us any more than they have to."

"Gold was mined where my wife grew up in the area of Ur, but no one ever said anything about that."

"Maybe she didn't know."

"Have you always worked in mines?"

"Most of my life I have. At first, I was just a boy. I picked up the chunks of rock and metal the men chipped from the walls, put them in baskets, and sent them up to the surface. When I became a teenager, they put me to work chiseling the walls."

"You never get full, do you?" Akar says, smiling when the stranger wolfs down another chunk of bread.

"You must have been hungry all your life," Sett adds. "I have some cheese hidden away in a small leather pouch on my camel. Why don't you go get it? We should be home in another four days."

The runaway fetches the cheese. "I will pay you back someday for all you have done for me," he tells Sett and Akar. "I don't know how, but I will."

"How old were you when you went to work in the mines?" Akar asks.

"I don't remember. I am not sure how old I am."

"So, you haven't always been a slave?"

"I don't think so. I remember a mother and father, but I can't remember what they looked like. I remember being in a big house, but that could have been anywhere."

Akar pulls down the tent. It does not take long. "I'll load it back on your camel," he tells Sett.

"Do you remember the name of the city you lived in or your parents' names?" Sett asks the runaway.

"I don't remember the city or my father's name. But it seems my mother's name was Leeba or something like that."

"Do you remember how you became a slave?"

"Yes, that I remember clearly. I was with my father in a bazaar someplace. He was talking to someone, maybe a merchant. I don't know. Or maybe he was a scribe. He had a lot of what I now know were papyri. They were arguing. I remember pulling on his robe to go home, but he kept shooing me away.

Sett smiles. "I have a son, and when he was young, he used to do things like that to me when I was busy."

"So, what happened next?" Akar asks. "You know, in the bazaar?"

"A man in another booth held out a honey cake to me. He told me to come get it. He looked nice. I was hungry. So, I let go of my father's robe and went across the lane to get my food."

"Then what?"

"He asked me if I would like to come into his shop where he had a lot more honey cakes, and I could eat all I wanted.

"I looked over at my father, who was still arguing with the other man, so went into the nice man's shop. When I did, he locked the door, put a strip of cloth over my mouth, and tied my hands and feet. I wanted to scream. I tried to scream, but I couldn't."

"Sir, this must be hard for you to talk about. You do not need to tell us any more," Akar says.

"No, this is the first time I have ever told anyone what happened. I remember wanting to scream, but I couldn't. He kept me in his shop until long after dark. Then he put me in a large sack. I couldn't breathe in there."

He sighs but continues on.

"I thought he was going to kill me. We went somewhere. I was still in the sack. Then he dumped me out of the sack onto a floor. Two other men looked at me and made me open my mouth so they could count my teeth. I heard money exchanged and was put back in the sack. I do not know how long I was in it. I thought I was going to die in the sack. Sometimes I cried, but they would hit the sack and make me stop."

He pauses, but the other men remain silent.

"I don't remember anymore. I just remember spending the rest of my life in mines."

All three men are now silent.

Sett reaches for his crutches. "We need to get back on the highway. We will be home soon. We should be in Heshbon by tonight. Then the next day we will head west, cross the Jordan River, and spend our last night in Jericho."

"Where did you say?" the stranger asks. "What river did you say?"

"The Jordan River. Why?"

"That name sounds familiar. I wonder why. And you look so familiar. Well, would you like me to help you up onto your camel?" he asks Sett.

"No, I am fine. But what you can do for me is tell me your name. I don't think you ever told us your name. We can't keep calling you the runaway. What is it, son? What is your name?"

"My name is Iptur."

# 40 ~ REUNIONS

As predicted, the men are in Jericho two evenings later.

"I need to pick up something in the market," Sett says. "I will join you two at the inn."

"You have been to this city many times, and we never have.," Akar says. "We will stick with you."

"Besides, I never did get my chance to wander around a bazaar to see what people buy and sell," Iptur says. "Uh, if that's okay."

"All right, you can come with me. But we call it a market. Arabians, Babylonians and Assyrians call it a bazaar."

They come to the shop Sett has been looking for.

"Sir, I need three small scrolls, some blackener, and a writing instrument."

Sett pays for them and puts them in his shoulder pouch. "Now, Iptur, you choose. Go whichever way you want."

Iptur stares at the man with the papyri and then across the lane. Sett realizes what he is doing.

"No, a baker does not have a shop over there. It happened in a different city. It happened in the city of Gibeon. And it was long ago."

They wander through the shops with their camels walking behind them until the merchants begin taking their things down and closing up for the night.

Sett leads Akar and Iptur to an inn and rents a room for them. He goes out to the tavern area where the tables are and writes on his three scrolls.

"Sir," he says to the innkeeper, "I need these delivered first thing in the morning. Do you know someone who is fast and can get them delivered and back to me by tomorrow night? I will pay extra if they do. But the messages must be put in the hands of the ones they are addressed to and no one else."

"Yes, I have two sons who can do it," the innkeeper says.

"I will wait here in Jericho until I receive word they have been delivered."

The next day, Sett takes the men back to the Jordan River to sit awhile.

"You know how the Nile River is the hub of Egypt, Akar? Well, the Jordan River is the hub of Israel. It flows through our entire land."

"What is your home like? The place where you will be taking us?" Iptur asks.

"It is large. It has chipped red-and-blue tiles all over the large courtyard, high cracked columns holding up the rooms on the second and third floors, faded frescoes on the walls of my grandfather's victories..."

The day is spent resting and telling stories. While eating their evening meal, Sett receives word that his three scrolls have been delivered. He pays them the extra he had promised for accomplishing in one day what normally would have taken two.

"Get good rest tonight," Sett tells them before they go to sleep. Tomorrow some people's lives are going to change."

The next morning Sett heads for Gibeon and home on Dipti. Akar and Iptur follow behind him on the second camel.

The camels sway back and forth as they take giant steps with their long legs. Sometimes one of them honks and gurgles, and the other one replies.

*Well, Kissara, we have accomplished two of the three*

*things I wanted to do. I wish we could have done more.* He pauses in his thinking, shakes his head, and smiles.

*I can just hear you now. "Setty, you did better than most men." You did spoil me, Kissara. How I miss you. I long so to be with you again. How much longer will it be?*

They arrive at Gibeon and make their way through the center of the city. The guards at the city gate salute Sett. People gather as they pass their shops and homes, pointing at Sett and the two strange men, all on camels.

When they arrive at the palace, Sett calls out. "I am home. Let me in."

The gate opens, and he hears, "Grandfather is back. Grandfather is back!"

The two camels sit, and the men climb down.

Micah and Nina come running through the courtyard along with the four grandsons and embrace Sett.

Micah steps back. "And who do you have with you?"

"They are my honored guests. Is Lechy here? Have a seat, gentlemen, while I work some things out."

"No," Micah replies. "It was the strangest thing. He received a message yesterday about noon, then today about noon he said he had to leave and be gone four hours. Why four hours? By the way, a second courier arrived with a message for you. It is in your office."

"Well, bring it to me."

Sett waits on his favorite bench by the reflecting pool until Micah hands him the scroll. He tucks it in his belt.

"Now, Son, I want you to open up the throne room."

Micah stares at his father. "What in the world for? It just brings back painful memories. Why do you do these things, Father?"

"Obey me."

Micah stares at his father, lowers his brows, and pulls on his beard. "What are you up to now, Father?" Knowing his only answer will be a smile, he heads toward the grand staircase and calls another servant to join him.

Akar and Iptur watch as the folding doors creak and

groan, and are opened all the way back. They stare at each other, then over at Sett.

"A king? You're a king?"

"No, this is my grandfather's palace, and he was the king. But this afternoon I want to do some bequeathing. It seems appropriate to do bequeathing from a throne. Follow me."

He looks over at his family. "You can come too."

Sett leads the way up the grand staircase. When he arrives, he sits on his grandfather's copper-colored alabaster throne. "Micah, Son, you may as well sit in this other throne beside me for the crown prince. It is the one my father used to sit in. Nina, would you like to sit on the queen's throne on the other side of me? No?"

He looks back over at his guests and realizes they are prostrate on the floor. He smiles.

"Rise, my friends. You do not have to pay obeisance to me. That was in the past. Now everyone, sit on the benches along the side until our company arrives."

As they wait, Sett remembers the message Micah had handed to him and still tucked in his belt. He breaks the seal, reads it, smiles, nods his head, looks up, whispers, "Thank you," and puts it in his lap.

Shortly, they hear a knock on the gate below.

Elipelet and his white mule enter. He slides off his mount, looks up, and sees Sett on his grandfather's throne.

"Decided to usurp my brother's throne while you were gone? The older you get, the crazier you get. Now, what do you want so I can get back home and resume hating you?"

Sett smiles. "Come up here," he calls down, "and wait for the others to arrive."

"What others?"

"You shall see. It will not take long."

They wait a little longer, and there is another knock on the gate. The gatekeeper lets him in.

Yassib dismounts from his mule and stands by the gate with a staff in his hand. He taps it around on the pavement while staring into nothingness.

"Is Sett here?" he asks the servant without knowing exactly where the servant is. "Would you take me to him quickly so I can leave and go back to my nothing world?"

"Follow me, sir," the gatekeeper says.

"Follow you where? Can't you see I am blind?"

"Oh. In that case, take my arm and follow me."

The servant takes small steps toward the grand staircase. Yassib stays in step with him in silence. They arrive at the throne room.

"Where have you brought me?" he asks the servant.

"You are with me, Yassib," Sett says. "My servant will guide you to your bench. I will give you the gift I promised shortly. We have one more person to arrive, then we can begin."

They wait a while longer, and Lechy rides a chariot into the courtyard. He looks up at Sett.

"You know you cannot fire me. You are not the king. Solomon is."

"Come on up, Lechy," Sett calls down. "This won't take long. Then you can return to doing whatever you do."

"No."

"Lechy, for the sake of Leeba, come up."

"What did you say?" Lechy grits his teeth and shakes his fist at Sett. "What did you say? You are not worthy to even speak my wife's name."

Iptur stands.

"Leeba? Did you say Leeba is your wife?"

"Was my wife," Lechy corrects, running up the steps two at a time. "Stop that! Stop talking about her."

He reaches the throne room, eyes angry, face red.

"Father?"

"Huh?"

"Father?"

He looks toward the voice. "What did you say?"

Lechy stares at the man now standing before him. The man who looks so much like his wife long gone. His fist clenches and unclenches, he steps back, he breathes in and cannot seem to breathe out.

Iptur steps forward. "Father? Father? I am Iptur. I am your son."

Lechy steps back again. "No. No, it cannot be. You have been dead for thirty-eight years. Sett killed you."

"No, Father. I am alive. I am your son. Sett brought me back to you. Oh, Father."

Lechy's eyes strain. He juts his head forward. He chokes. "Son?"

"Yes, Father. I am Iptur, your son."

The two men walk toward each other and embrace. Iptur drops to his knees, still clinging to his father. Lechy reaches down, one hand on Iptur's head and the other on his shoulder.

Now both men are on their knees. They embrace. They tremble. They weep torrents for their lost years apart.

They are oblivious of everyone in the throne room watching them.

Finally, Lechy draws away enough he can look in his son's eyes. "Iptur? Iptur? My son?"

They embrace again, tremble again, and absorb the impossible.

Iptur rises and brings his father up with him. They hold each other by the shoulders. Lechy turns to Sett. "How?"

"Iptur will tell you. Now you have nearly forty years to make up. I would suggest you get right to it."

Lechy looks around at everyone in the throne room, says nothing, puts his arm over his son's shoulder, and leads him down the grand staircase.

Nina wipes her eyes. Micah blinks fast to control his own tears. The grandchildren look at their parents. "Who is that man Lechy is hugging?" they ask.

"Shhh."

Everyone looks back at Sett and waits in silence.

"Yassib, we have been neighbors a long time. You have

lamented the loss of your family at the hands of my grandfather most of your life."

"Do not waste your breath, Sett."

"I have prayed many years for a way to make up for some of your pain. I cannot, of course, make up for the loss of your family. But the only real God, Jehovah, has answered my prayers. Not Dagon. Jehovah." He looks over at his Egyptian friend.

"Akar, would you stand please?"

Akar stands.

"This is the one I told you about. Can you help him?"

Akar walks over to Yassib. "Sir, I am a physician. Would you allow me to look at your eyes?"

"Why? There is nothing left in them. I will be sightless the rest of my miserable life."

"Will you at least let me look?"

"Look away. Then leave."

Akar tips Yassib's head back. After a few moments, he steps back. He looks at Sett.

"Yes, I can bring his sight back."

Nina breathes in a loud gasp. Micah shakes his head, staring at the floor. "No, Father, no. Do not do this," he whispers.

"Explain it to Yassib, please," Sett says.

"Yassib, there is a technique practiced both in India and in my homeland of Egypt. What you have are cataracts. I can push them out of the way, and you will be able to see again."

Yassib slams the end of his staff on the floor with a bang. The sound echoes down into the courtyard below and bounces off the old walls.

"No! Do not lie to me!" Yassib looks in the direction he has concluded Sett is. "Get rid of him."

"It can be done," Akar reassures. "I have done it before. I have returned people's sight to them."

"No," Yassib says softer. "It cannot be done." He pauses. "Can it?"

"Yes, Yassib, friend. It can be done. By this time tomorrow, you should be able to see again."

"Let him do it," Sett says. "Let me—through him—return to you something you have lost and long to have again."

"I would be honored to do this for you," Akar says in a low voice.

Silence.

"Well."

"Good," Sett says. "And when you are well again, I have some of the most beautiful poems I would like you to read. They are the inspired words of King David."

"Let me help you down the steps. I will go with you to your home." Akar says.

Sett and his family, along with Eliphelet, wait for the two men to leave.

"Well, that was a nice show, Sett," Eliphelet says, rising from his seat. "I need to go now."

"No, son, it is your turn."

"There is nothing I want from you. And don't call me son. I am not your son. I had a father once and don't need any more fake fathers."

"What about your grandfather?" Sett asks.

"Hardly knew him. Then he goes and dies and mocks me by leaving me that worthless land out in the middle of the desert. Don't talk about my father or my grandfather. I'm leaving."

Eliphelet looks over at Micah. "By the way, that's a nice limp you have there. Maybe we should even you out so you can limp on both legs."

"I have seen it," Sett says.

"You've seen what? His leg?" Eliphelet says, swinging around to face Sett. "How could I have given you a chance and loved you for a while on that trip? Things were easier when I could keep hating you."

"Eliphelet, I have seen it."

"Seen what?"

"Your land. I went down to Arabia and found your land."

"So? I don't have to go all the way down there to be attacked by scorpions and sand storms on worthless land."

"Eliphelet, you are rich."

"What do you mean? I get some money every month from my father's estate, but it's running out. I will never be rich."

"But you are. At first, after I saw your land, I thought you were right—that it is worthless. I had an assayer walk the land with me, and that is what he calculated."

"I'm leaving," Eliphelet says. He starts down the grand staircase.

"Don't you want to know just how rich you are?"

"No."

"I have the proof in my hand right now, Eliphelet. Come back and see your proof."

Eliphelet stops halfway down to the courtyard below and looks back up at Sett. "You have no proof."

"Look. Here." Sett holds the scroll in his hand high above his head. "Come read it for yourself. It is from the assayer named Peduil. Come read it aloud."

Eliphelet returns to the throne room. He glares at Sett as he walks toward the throne.

"Hand it to me. Then I'm leaving."

"Read it aloud."

From Peduil of Arabia to Mefibosett of Israel. Dear Sir. After the sand storm, I returned to the land. The storm was a blessing after all. It revealed a large vein of copper. You are rich."

Eliphelet stares at the scroll, over at Sett, then back at the scroll. He reads it again. He shakes his head.

"No," he says in a low voice. "You are trying to make a fool of me."

Sett smiles. "It is signed and sealed with his official seal."

Eliphelet stares at the scroll again, and at Sett again.

"If I were you, I would find a good camel and head for Arabia tomorrow," Sett says. "But, you cannot have Dipti."

Eliphelet wrinkles his brow. He squints his eyes. He shakes his head. He stares at everyone around him. A grin forms.

"I'm rich!" he shouts. "I'm rich!"

Eliphelet runs over to Sett and gives him a bear hug. "I'm rich." He goes over to Micah and hugs him. "I'm rich." He kisses Nina's hand and hugs the children. "I'm rich."

He stands in the middle of the throne room, turns in circles, jumping as he goes and breaks into a song.

*I am rich.*
*I am rich.*

Without looking back, Eliphelet bounds down the steps, jumps onto his white mule and rides away. Even on the other side of the wall, they can hear it.

*I am rich.*
*I am rich.*

Sett rises. "It has been a good day."

Micah watches as his father expertly descends the grand staircase leading from his Great-Grandfather Saul's throne room, swinging his worthless feet between his three-footed crutches.

"Yes, it has been a very good day, and I am so blessed."

# EPILOGUE

It is Pitthon's wedding day. The ceremony is being held in the old banquet hall under the grand staircase.

Micah rises. He has a little gray at the temples now. Nina—faithful Nina, daughter of the overseer of farmhands—is next to him.

Micah looks at Pitthon's bride, pretty Yaffa, all dressed up in white and yellow and with flowers in her hair.

"On this your wedding day, we look forward to a new generation. A new generation of our family coming and going and doing. On this day, I would like to tell you about your children's—my grandchildren's—heritage. I want to tell you about the greatest man I ever knew—my father, Mefiboset."

# THANK YOU

Thanks for reading my book! I'm so honored that you chose to spend your precious time with my characters. You are appreciated. I'm an independent author who relies on my readers to help spread the word about stories you enjoy.

Would you take a few minutes to let your friends know on Facebook, Pinterest...wherever you hang out online? Also, each honest review at online retailers means a lot to me and helps other readers know if this is a book they might enjoy.

I welcome contact from readers. At my website (below), you can do so. You can also sign up for my monthly newsletter (below) for half-price paper and 99c ebooks for the whole family - novels, non-fiction, storybooks and first peek at my newest release.

# GET ALL 8 BOOKS IN THE HISTORICAL SERIES
# INTREPID MEN OF GOD

Novel 1 ~ Lazarus: The Samaritan
Novel 2 ~ Paul: The Unstoppable
Novel 3 ~ Luke: Slave & Physician
Novel 4 ~ Mefiboset: Crippled Prince
Novel 5 ~ Joseph: The Other Father
Novel 6 ~ Michel: The Fourth Wise Man
Novel 7 ~ Stephen: Unlikely Martyr
Novel 8 ~ Titus: The Aristocrat

# HISTORICAL & PHYSICAL BACKGROUND

Mephibosheth's name spelling was changed slightly (it is only an English translation anyway) to help the common person pronounce it. It also fit on the book cover better.

All characters in Saul's (Mefiboset's line) and David's families are found in the scriptures including his only surviving legal heir to the throne, Isboset, who was king two years, but did not begin his reign until five years after Saul's death. The caniving steward of King Saul's palace, Zeba, and Malchar, who took Mefiboset in, are found in the scriptures. The drought and hanging of Saul's male descendants are in scriptures.

Gibeon was founded by the Gibeonites which Joshua (who took over when Moses died) planned to destroy. They went to Joshua pretending to be from lands far away, so he vowed to let them live. When he learned they were Canaanite, he made them all slaves to be woodchoppers and water carriers.

The site of Gibeon (Gibeah) and King Saul's palace (fortress) are identified by archaeologists as *Tell el-Ful* seven miles north of Jerusalem. It was 105' x 80' with towers at each corner. However, much of the archaeological remains of Gibeon were disturbed in 1967 when King Hussein decided to build a house there. He later abandoned it.

The foot injury sustained by Mefiboset is thought to have been Neurotmesis with permanent nerve damage, complete loss of motor, sensory and autonomic function. The foot drops, the toes drag. This would be caused by breaking of a bone and severing of nerves. Also, the leg muscles are controlled by nerves from the spinal cord L1-5 in the lower back and injury to just the right place that could cause paralysis. Shoes must be worn at all times. The feet must be examined daily because of lack of feeling.

Ancient Egyptians used wooden splints to aid healing of broken bones. Ancient Hindus and Arabians stiffened bandages with seashells and egg whites.

Lodebar was a prosperous major city on an international trade route ten miles southeast of the Sea of Galilee and where the Jordan and Jardak Rivers meet.

Talmai was king of Geshur, as well as the father of Maacah, one of David's wives and therefore the grandfather of Absalom and Tamar (2 Samuel 3:3). After killing his half-brother Amnon, Absalom was exiled by his father and went to his grandfather Talmai where he stayed three years (2 Samuel 3:13-14).

Sacred prostitution was written of by Herodotus, 5th-century BC historian: "The foulest Babylonian (the area Ur was in) custom is that which compels every woman of the land to sit in the temple of Aphrodite (Greek name for Babylon Nanna) and have intercourse with some stranger at least once in her life." He went into much detail about their selection by the men.

Harran where Abraham lived after moving away from Ur is near the modern village of Altınbaşak, Turkey. The earliest record of Harran is the third millennium BC on an Ebla Tablet.

Ashur Resh Ishi II was king of Assyria from 971 to 967 BC. He was father of Tiglath-Pileser II.

Cataract surgery in ancient cultures was called couching. A wall painting in the tomb of the master-builder Ipwy at Thebes (about 1200 B.C.) reveals an oculist treating the eye of a craftsman. Because of the length of the instrument, the scene interpreted as a cataract surgery by couching of the lens into the vitreous cavity. (There is other evidence of this in ancient Egypt.)

# FORESTS IN THE BIBLE

2 Chron. 27:4 - Moreover, he built cities in the hill country **of Judah**, and he built fortresses and towers on the **wooded hills.**

1 Sam. 22:5 - The prophet Gad said to David, "Do not stay in the stronghold; depart, and go into the land of **Judah."** So David departed and went into the **forest of Hereth.**

2 Kings 19:23 - Through your messengers you have reproached the Lord, And you have said, "With my many chariots I came up to the heights of the mountains, To the **remotest parts of Lebanon**; And I cut down its tall cedars and its choice cypresses. And I entered its farthest lodging place, its **thickest forest**.

Isaiah 21:13 - The oracle about Arabia. In the **thickets of Arabia** you must spend the night, O caravans of **Dedanites**.

Zechariah 11:2 - Wail, O **oaks of Bashan,** For the impenetrable forest has come down. There is a sound of the shepherds' wail, For their glory is ruined; There is a sound of the young lions' roar, For the pride of the **Jordan** is ruined....

Nehemiah 2:7f - And I said to the king, "If it please the king, let letters be given me for the governors of the **provinces beyond the River,** that they may allow me to pass through until I come to Judah, 8and a letter to Asaph the keeper of the king's **[Persia's] forest**, that he may give me timber to make beams for the gates of the fortress which is by the temple, for the wall of the city and for the house to which I will go."

2 Kings 3:18f, 25 - 'This is but a slight thing in the sight of the LORD; He will also give the **Moabites** into your hand.'Then you shall strike every fortified

city and every choice city, and **fell every good tree** and stop all springs of water, and mar every good piece of land with stones.'".... And they overthrew the cities, and on every good piece of land every man threw a stone until it was covered. They stopped every spring of water and **felled all the good trees,** till only its stones were left in **Kir-hareseth,** and the slingers surrounded and attacked it.

Ezra 3:7 - Then they gave money to the masons and carpenters, and food, drink and oil to the Sidonians and to the Tyrians, to bring **cedar wood from Lebanon** to the sea at Joppa, according to the **permission they had from Cyrus king of Persia.**

Eccl. 2:5-6 - I made gardens and parks for myself and I **planted** in them all kinds of fruit trees; I made ponds of water for myself from which to irrigate a **forest of growing trees (In Israel)**.

Isa. 10:18 - 17And the light of Israel will become a fire and his Holy One a flame, And it will burn and devour his **[Assyria's]** thorns and his briars in a single day. 18And He will **destroy the glory of his forest** and of his fruitful garden, both soul and body, And it will be as when a sick man wastes away. 19And the rest of the **trees of his forest will be so small** in number That a child could write them down.

Ezekiel 20:46f - "Son of man, set your face toward **Teman,** and speak out against the south and prophesy against the **forest land of the Negev**, and say to the forest of the Negev, 'Hear the word of the LORD: thus says the Lord GOD, "Behold, I am about to kindle a fire in you, and it will consume every green tree in you, as well as every dry tree; the **blazing flame** will not be quenched and the whole surface from south to north will be burned by it.

———

In 1997, the World Resources Institute recorded that only 20% of the world's original forests remained in large intact tracts of undisturbed forest. [World Resources Institute, 1998. The Last Frontier Forests: Ecosystems and Economies on the Edge.]

# BUY YOUR NEXT BOOK NOW
Check out what they are about and a buy link.

## HISTORICAL NOVELS FOR ADULTS

THEY MET JESUS Series of 8
http://bit.ly/TheyMetJesus

INTREPID MEN OF GOD Series of 8
http://bit.ly/IntrepidMen

## HISTORICAL STORYBOOKS FOR CHILDREN

A CHILD'S LIFE OF CHRIST Series of 8
(Parallels Adult *They Met Jesus*)
http://bit.ly/ChildsLifeOfChristSet

A CHILD'S BIBLE HEROES Series of 10
http://bit.ly/Bible-Heroes

A CHILD'S BIBLE KIDS Series of 8
http://bit.ly/bible-kids

A CHILD'S BIBLE LADIES Series of 10
http://bit.ly/BibleLadies

# DISCUSSION QUESTIONS

CHAPTER 1:
*Everyone responds to a death in the immediate family in a little different way.  Which emotions are the most common? Which one would you most likely feel?  Why?

CHAPTER 2:
*Sometimes a family that does not get along will be united by a common thread. In what way did little Mefiboset's injury unite this family? Why?

CHAPTER 3:
*The family did not know what to do with the oldest son of the oldest son, Mefiboset. Why do you think the youngest son of Saul, who eventually became king, would not trust the boy's existence be known?  Have you ever been in a situation where you wished your competition would disappear?

CHAPTER 4:
*In this story, the queen mother made arrangements for Mefiboset to be king for a day, knowing he would never experience it in real life. In what way can you pay honor to someone who will never officially be recognized for what they did?

CHAPTER 5:
*Mefiboset was the grandson of the tallest and most handsome man in the entire nation of Israel. Wouldn't you think he would have inherited at least some of those traits? His father, Jonathan was friends with his father's arch-rival and enemy. Wouldn't you think his son would have inherited at least some of his ability to get along with his enemies.  If you were taken as someone's slave, how do you think you

would behave toward your master?

CHAPTER 6:
*Do you know of someone who no longer has a mother? What can a woman do to make that child feel a little bit of mother love?

CHAPTER 7:
*Did anyone ever tell you that you looked exactly like a relative? If so, did it make you want to know more about that relative? What would you like to know?

CHAPTER 8:
*Did you ever visit the house of a grandparent or great grandparent that you had never seen before? What did it make you feel?

CHAPTER 9:
*Have you ever heard or read that Mefiboset was doomed to be raised by a man who lived in awful Lodebar out in the middle of the wilderness with nothing?  Lodebar was ten miles south of the Sea of Galilee and near the Jordan River where there were crossroads to important world cities. In what ways do we take for granted what we are told? How can we change that?

CHAPTER 10:
*Lodebar was near the palace of the king of Bashan. Centuries earlier, the people of Bashan were giants.  The bed of their King Og was 13 feet long. Prince Absalom married a daughter of the current king. Their kingdom worshipped idols. What is your experience of observing a Christian marrying a non-Christian?

CHAPTER 11:
*David not only wrote about eating in the presence of his enemies (Psalm 23), but he invited his enemy to eat with

him. Mefiboset was next in line for the throne of Israel when David arrived in Jerusalem and set it up as his capital. Do you think you could ever show that much kindness to an enemy and still trust them?

CHAPTER 12:
*Enemies can be united if they have a common enemy or common friend. Why does it work that way?

CHAPTER 13:
*When we see a widow or widower doing things alone for a long time, we forget they were once married. The next time you visit with a widow or widower socially, ask them how they met their deceased spouse and watch their eyes sparkle.

CHAPTER 14:
*Think about a time you worked for a very long time for a certain goal, and when you should have reached your goal, everything went wrong and kept you from it? How did you feel? Did you think you could ever try again?

CHAPTER 15:
Kissara's mother and Sett had to use a lot of imagination to get her out of a heavily guarded sex slavery. If it had been you, how would you have tried to help her escape?

CHAPTER 16:
*Mefiboset had to maintain a balance of being friends of two competing families. How can that be done between competing families, companies, nationalities, etc.?

CHAPTER 17:
*How can a rape affect an entire family? Spouse, parents, children?

CHAPTER 18:

*Have you ever tried to get two former friends to like each other again? What do you think it would take for former friends to make up on their own?

CHAPTER 19:
*How can a person handle false accusations? Do you think you could be friends with someone who was falsely accusing you? Do you think it would make things better or worse?

CHAPTER 20:
*Do you know someone who is losing influence with people and may not remain their leader much longer? Or someone who has been replaced by a usurper. Maybe it happened recently or a long time ago. Get in touch with a former leader and tell them how you admired them.

CHAPTER 21:
*No matter how bad people treated Mefiboset, he loved everyone and tried to get along with them. Isn't that the way God is? We betray God by sinning every day, then expect him to forgive us every day. Do you have any enemies you need to love and pray for?

CHAPTER 22:
*During the days of the American Civil War, some brothers fought for the north and some for the south. The resentment remains in some families, What do you think the parents of these brothers would want their descendants do today?

CHAPTER 23:
*Mefiboset's step-mother did all she could to maintain the dignity of her sons. How can a family with some shame maintain their dignity?"

CHAPTER 24:
*Saul took his family on a vacation after so many tragedies. How could this help a family?

CHAPTER 25:
*How can using laughter help people get through difficult times?

CHAPTER 26:
*Sett finally handed responsibility to his son when the solution was out of his hands. Are parents sometimes slow at recognizing their children are grown?

CHAPTER 27:
*Have you had a bad experience that the sight of certain things brings back those memories? How do you handle it?

CHAPTER 28:
*Some older people might enjoy a day trip to someplace where they have good memories. Where are some places you could take them for a day?

CHAPTER 29:
*The Bible says that, while we were still sinners, Jesus died for us. How is it possible to keep trying to be nice to our enemies?

CHAPTER 30:
*If you knew you had six months to live, what do you think you would like your spouse or child or parents do with you?

CHAPTER 31:
*If anyone had a "right " to be bitter, it was Mefiboset whose feet were paralyzed at age five, never to walk with them again, and the throne of Israel was snatched from him by David. What might his life have been like if he had not forgiven David as his father had done?

CHAPTER 32:
*Does an older person in your family have a box full of old

family photos with no identifications on the back. Will you make arrangements to see that person and spend the day identifying the photos?

CHAPTER 33:
*Do you know someone who no one takes seriously? Where can you take that person where they can experience some kind of importance?

CHAPTER 34:
*How can going on a trip ease pressures at home, at least for a while?

CHAPTER 35:
If you know someone who has lost a spouse and the death anniversary is coming up, ask them if there is someplace you can take them where they and their spouse used to go? What are some places they might suggest?

CHAPTER 36:
*Have you ever done something only you knew about because you knew everyone would try to talk you out of it? Did it work out as you expected?

CHAPTER 37:
*Recall a time when you had something important to do You were sidetracked, by something important but unrelated, and it turned out to provide what you were trying to do.

CHAPTER 38:
*If you were a slave and allowed to go far away on your own, do you think you would return to your master voluntarily? Why?

CHAPTER 39:
*Have you longed for something, and it came about years later after you had given up?

CHAPTER 40:
*Who do you know or know of who is handicapped? Find out what some of their accomplishments have been. In what ways can you honor that person?

# ABOUT THE AUTHOR

Katheryn Maddox Haddad spends an average of 300 hours researching before writing a historical novel—ancient historians such as Josephus, archaeological digs so she can know the layout of cities, their language, culture, and politics.

She grew up in the northern United States and now lives in Arizona where she doesn't have to shovel sunshine. She basks in 100-degree weather, palm trees, cacti, and a computer with most of the letters worn off.

She is author of 77 books, both non-fiction and fiction. Her newspaper column appeared for several years in newspapers in Texas and North Carolina ~ *Little Known Facts About the Bible* ~ and she has written for numerous Christian publications. For over twenty years, she has been sending out every morning a daily scripture and short inspirational thought to some 30,000 people around the world.

She spends half her day writing, and the other half teaching English over the internet worldwide using the Bible as textbook. She has taught some 7000 Muslims through World English Institute. Students she has converted to Christianity are in hiding in Afghanistan, Iran, Iraq, Yemen, Uzbekistan, Somalia, Jordan, Tajikistan, Sierra Leone, Pakistan, Indonesia, and Palestine. "They are my heroes," she declares.

With a bachelor's degree in English, Bible and social science from Harding University and part of a master's degree in Bible, including Greek, from the Harding Graduate

School of Theology, she also has a master's degree in management and human relations from Abilene University. She is a member of American Christian Fiction Writers, Historical Novel Society, International Screen Writers Association, and is also an energetic public speaker who can touch the hearts of audiences.

# CONNECT WITH
# KATHERYN MADDOX HADDAD

Website: **https://inspirationsbykatheryn.com**

Facebook: **bit.ly/FacebooksKatherynMaddoxHaddad**

Linkedin: **http://bit.ly/KatherynLinkedin**

Twitter: **https://twitter.com/KatherynHaddad**

Pinterest: **https://www.pinterest.com/haddad1940/**

Goodreads: **https://www.goodreads.com/katherynmaddoxhaddad**